Raves for  **P9-COP-226**

"Set in an alternate England on the eve of World War I, the latest addition to Lackey's 'Elemental Masters' series features a strong female protagonist in search of her true calling and a sophisticated nobleman who discovers that there is more to life than magic. Verdict: historical fantasy and gothic romance combine beautifully in this fantasy adventure from the author of the popular Valdemar novels."

— Library Journal

"Lackey has delivered another fine entry to the Elemental Masters series with this tale of an abandoned child suddenly thrust into the center of a very class conscious London at the start of WWI. Readers cannot help but admire Susanne's pluck, determination, and desire to do right while building a new life and experiencing her first serious crush. The storyline and subplots are smoothly woven together and as usual, Lackey's character development is delightful. The climax offers a small surprise as assistance comes not from a magical source but from something even scarier."

— Monsters & Critics

"All in fine fairy-tale tradition. . . . It's grim fun, with some nice historical detail, and just a hint of romance to help lighten things."

— Locus

And raves for the previous Elemental Masters novel,
Reserved for the Cat:

"The Paris of Degas, turn-of-the-century Blackpool, and the desperation of young girls without family or other protection come to life in a story that should interest a broad readership."

— Booklist

"This most recent entry in Lackey's series is a nicely paced, pleasant read. Nina is a sympathetic protagonist readers will root for, and the story holds together well."

— Romantic Times

"A fantastic cat-and-mouse game among a shape-changing troll, Elemental Masters and a gifted dancer in Victorian England makes Lackey's latest Elemental Masters installment a charmer. This is Lackey at her best, mixing whimsy and magic with a fast-paced plot."

— Publishers Weekly

TITLES BY MERCEDES LACKEY
available from DAW Books:

THE NOVELS OF VALDEMAR:

THE HERALDS OF VALDEMAR
ARROWS OF THE QUEEN
ARROW'S FLIGHT
ARROW'S FALL

THE LAST HERALD-MAGE
MAGIC'S PAWN
MAGIC'S PROMISE
MAGIC'S PRICE

THE MAGE WINDS
WINDS OF FATE
WINDS OF CHANGE
WINDS OF FURY

THE MAGE STORMS
STORM WARNING
STORM RISING
STORM BREAKING

VOWS AND HONOR
THE OATHBOUND
OATHBREAKERS
OATHBLOOD

THE COLLEGIUM CHRONICLES
FOUNDATION
INTRIGUES
CHANGES
REDOUBT
BASTION

THE HERALD SPY
CLOSER TO HOME*

BY THE SWORD
BRIGHTLY BURNING
TAKE A THIEF

EXILE'S HONOR
EXILE'S VALOR

VALDEMAR ANTHOLOGIES
SWORD OF ICE
SUN IN GLORY
CROSSROADS
MOVING TARGETS
CHANGING THE WORLD
FINDING THE WAY
UNDER THE VALE

Written with **LARRY DIXON:**

THE MAGE WARS
THE BLACK GRYPHON
THE WHITE GRYPHON
THE SILVER GRYPHON

DARIAN'S TALE
OWLFLIGHT
OWLSIGHT
OWLKNIGHT

OTHER NOVELS:

GWENHWYFAR
THE BLACK SWAN

THE DRAGON JOUSTERS
JOUST
ALTA
SANCTUARY
AERIE

THE ELEMENTAL MASTERS
THE SERPENT'S SHADOW
THE GATES OF SLEEP
PHOENIX AND ASHES
THE WIZARD OF LONDON
RESERVED FOR THE CAT
UNNATURAL ISSUE
HOME FROM THE SEA
STEADFAST
BLOOD RED
Anthologies:
ELEMENTAL MAGIC
ELEMENTARY

*Coming soon from DAW Books
And don't miss THE VALDEMAR COMPANION
edited by John Helfers and Denise Little

MERCEDES LACKEY

UNNATURAL ISSUE

The Elemental Masters, Book Six

DAW BOOKS, INC.

DONALD A. WOLLHEIM, FOUNDER

375 Hudson Street, New York, NY 10014

ELIZABETH R. WOLLHEIM
SHEILA E. GILBERT
PUBLISHERS

www.dawbooks.com

Copyright © 2011 by Mercedes Lackey.

All Rights Reserved.

Cover art by Jody A. Lee.

Cover designed by G-Force Design.

DAW Book Collectors No. 1549.

DAW Books are distributed by Penguin Group (USA).

All characters and events in this book are fictitious.
All resemblance to persons living or dead is coincidental.

The scanning, uploading and distribution of this book via the Internet or any
other means without the permission of the publisher is illegal, and punishable by
law. Please purchase only authorized electronic editions, and do not participate
in or encourage the electronic piracy of copyrighted materials. Your support of
the author's rights is appreciated.

First Printing, June 2012
3 4 5 6 7 8 9

DAW TRADEMARK REGISTERED
U.S. PAT. AND TM. OFF. AND FOREIGN COUNTRIES
—MARCA REGISTRADA
HECHO EN U.S.A.

PRINTED IN THE U.S.A.

Dedicated to the Wisconsin 14, and the teachers, firefighters, and public service workers of the US.

Prologue

IT was nearly dark, and the spring air was turning cold, but Richard Whitestone did not push his horse to any great haste. The road was good, the horse knew the way, and there would be a moon up soon. He had been far too long in London; he could still taste its poisons, feel them corroding his lungs, infesting his body, and he needed to take every moment he could of this journey to purge himself of them. Most people would not have been suffering as he was; most people would escape London after one of the denser yellow fogs, breathe in the clean air of the countryside, and merely thank Providence that they were out. But of course, he would, he *had* suffered; he was an Elemental Master of Earth, one who commanded all the powers of the Earth itself and the Elemental creatures that represented those powers. Earth Masters loathed cities; Richard, who was one of the most powerful to live even somewhat close to London, had been nauseated from the moment he entered the tainted zone of the city to the moment he left it. He still felt sick, with the very real sensations of someone who had ingested a sublethal dose of, say, arsenic. Now, finally on his journey home, he was able to heal.

Earth Masters seldom left their country homes, where they tended the land and the things living on it. Nothing could have persuaded him to enter the city except the urgings of the Master of the Council, Lord Alderscroft himself. The man they called the Wizard of London was not someone you disobeyed lightly. And to be fair, Alderscroft did not call an Earth Master into London on a whim.

Even knowing that, Richard had been reluctant, but now he had to admit that Alderscroft had good reason for calling him in. While most Elementals shunned the cities, there were those creatures of the Dark that thrived on the filth and decay that was ever-present there. Normally, when such creatures lurked within a city, it was without doing much (if any) actual damage. They merely lived on what was already there. But the unscrupulous or downright evil Elemental mage could make use of such creatures, and as Alderscroft had discovered, one had set up shop in London.

Paving stones and cement were no impediment to something that could swim through earth; the mage had coerced a handful of hobgoblins to steal for him—which was bad enough—and had, quite by accident, discovered that murder was even more lucrative than theft. The Master of such creatures had to know where the valuables were, after all, in order to direct his creatures to steal them. But for a murder-for-hire? He need only give them the right scent, wait until the house was quiet and all were asleep—and turn his creatures loose. The Master had chosen his victims well and trained his hobgoblins thoroughly. The victims were all men and women, mostly elderly, with heirs impatient to gain their inheritance and not particular about how. It was easy for a gang of goblins to weight a victim down in his or her bed to be smothered. It was possible that the murders would never have been discovered at all, but the policeman who had been the first called to the scene of one of the murders by a hysterical maidservant also happened to be an Elemental mage.

Once one such murder had been brought to the attention of Alderscroft's Circle, it was not long before the others were uncovered.

Since the miscreant had been an Earth Master, it required another to track and counter him. But because he was commanding hobgoblins, it also took one who was willing and able to confront the Dark Elementals as well as converse with and persuade those of the Light.

The only one near enough to London to fit that description had been Richard, and if the blackguard in question had been engaged only in theft, he would have refused. Patience and persistence would have enabled any other Elemental Master to discover the miscreant in time. Murder, however, was another kettle of fish. Richard could not, in good conscience, allow another to take place.

Nor could he permit hobgoblins that had been taught how to murder to continue to exist. Such creatures thrived on pain and suffering, and having gotten a taste of how easy it was to create it themselves, they would not have gone back to their old ways even if their master was gone.

Tracking the wretch through the filth that was the City had been bad enough. But Richard had been forced to take the mage on nearly single-handed; his own Elementals would not (indeed, could not) come to his aid, and the Elemental Masters of the allied powers of Fire and Water had been of limited help. Of all the Elements, Earth was the most obdurate, and the hardest to subdue or destroy. Fire could be extinguished, Water diverted, but Earth ... persisted. It had not been an easy fight, and when it was over, Richard had been exhausted and sickened.

Alderscroft had urged him to remain in London to recover, and in the protected and warded confines of the Exeter Club, he would have been able to do so. But he had been away from home more than long enough.

Especially considering that his wife, Rebecca, was heavy with child. It was true that she herself had urged him to go to London, and in letters she had supported him in his decision to stay and fight. But the last thing he wanted was for her to be alone for too long when she was so near her time.

Not that he had any great fears for her. She, too, was an Earth mage, and a good one, if not a Master. Earth mages—especially those who never needed to leave their home ground—tended to be robust and healthy individuals. Earth magic was that of fertility and growth, after all. But he had missed her more with every day and longed for her company the way he longed for the good, clean earth under his feet again.

As he passed between the hedgerows, the only sounds were the clopping of his horse's hooves on the hard road and the occasional lowing of cows and baa-ing of sheep on the other side of those hedges. The homely sounds soothed him, and the presence of the beasts fortified him with their energies.

He and Rebecca belonged to the class known as "country squires." Although they did not have official titles, the very considerable property called Whitestone Hall as well as the farms Richard owned had been in his family for generations. The estate was as remote as it could possibly be in this part of England, and no substantial changes had been made to it in the last hundred years. Earth magicians were conservative in their needs and solitary in their ways. The Whitestones had been Elemental magicians for longer than they had owned the house and lands; most of them had been of Earth, although an occasional Water or Fire mage had been known to crop up in the line. The soon-to-be-newest addition to the family had already given satisfactory signs that she would follow in her mother and father's footsteps.

As he rode into the growing darkness, getting farther and farther from anything that the benighted considered "civilization," Richard felt the land healing him of the damage the goblins had done, and cleansing the poison the city had poured into him. He didn't want to approach Rebecca still tainted by the filth he had wallowed in for the last week, especially not when she was growing near her time. She was seven months along by his reckoning, and he would not take the risk of inadvertently contaminating her or their unborn child.

It was as lovely a summer evening as anyone could hope for. There was just enough of a faint chill in the air to make Richard glad of his coat, but not so much as to make him shiver. His keen sense of smell picked out the scents of wild roses, clover, and cut hay. A little farther on, he detected water—a slow-running stream by the scent of it. The slow footfalls of his horse's hooves made him vibrate in sympathy with the earth. It took careful purging to rid himself of the filth without bringing the pollution to his own ground. He had to reduce it to its component parts, be it magical energy or actual, physical poison like the soot in his lungs. Only then was it safe to deposit elsewhere. And even then there were poisons, like lead, that were impossible to break down. He would need a special session to be rid of those, one best carried out in the security of his own workroom. He could summon a dwarf to take the poisons away; dwarves were clever with such things and would make something useful of them. Even a poison could be used for something, in the right hands. It would be beneficial to both himself and the dwarf; this was how an Elemental Master should conduct his magic—without coercion, and with both summoned and summoner coming off the better for the transaction.

But these poisons could be encapsulated and isolated for this moment; cleansing and healing himself as he was doing now would give him the strength to keep such things safely contained.

Even though it was deep dusk when he crossed the invisible boundary that brought him onto his own lands, he felt it. The land recognized him and greeted him as its own.

And then he felt something else.

It struck him like a blow to the heart.

A powerful wrongness. Turmoil. And grief.

Involuntarily, he put spurs to his tired horse, startling the beast into a gallop. With a growing sense of panic, he urged the beast down the old Roman road and then past the wall that marked the lands of Whitestone Hall. His heart pounded with the throbbing of hooves on the road, and fear of a sort he had never experienced before gripped him in an icy clasp.

The horse did not need guiding; it bolted through the open gates as soon as it saw them. The lane was straight and true; they scorched toward the country house, ablaze with candle and lantern light, the doors standing open wide.

He pulled the horse to a stop to see his housekeeper, tears streaking her face, standing in the doorway, pressing messages and shillings into the hands of the stable boy and the gardener's boy. She burst into more tears at the sight of him, as he flung himself off the horse. "Master Richard! Master Richard! I swear, sir, we did what we could, but town is so far away, she started with no warning, before her time, and she tore before the midwife could get here, and the doctor was away—" She continued babbling as he pushed past her and sprinted for the room that should have been his sanctuary.

He knew, he knew what he would find as he ran up the stairs to the best bedroom. He felt it, a sudden emptiness in his heart, a wound that would never heal. He threw open the bedroom door—

He had expected to find a welter of bloody sheets, pain and chaos. He found only clean, calm death.

With a heart gone cold, he approached the ancient canopied bed in which so many generations of Whitestones had been born, loved, and died.

The curtains had been pulled aside, the sheets and coverlet stripped away and replaced. There was no sign here of the struggle that had claimed his wife, of the terrible pain she must have endured. A single candle on the stand beside the bed cast its soft light on the beloved face, the broad brow, the tender eyes, now closed, that had once been star-tlingly blue. The high, sculptured cheekbones worthy of the attention of the finest artist were pale as the marble bust of Athena in the parlor; the lips that had been full and pink as the roses she loved were now white. Someone had smoothed Rebecca's long, black hair and parted it neatly, spreading it out on the pillow. Her long, slender hands were folded over her breast. He touched one; it was already cool and growing colder.

He heard footsteps behind him: the housekeeper, wring-ing her hands, her voice hoarse with grief and weeping.

"How long has she—" he asked. He could not finish the sentence.

"Three hours, sir. She started afore her time; we tried to hold it back but something went wrong. The midwife was here, but she couldn't do anything. She tore, somehow in-side, all of a sudden. I sent the boy for the doctor, but he was out, and by the time he got here—" She broke into a fresh bout of weeping. "She was gone. All he could do was save the wee one."

"What?" He turned on the woman; what she saw in his face must have terrified her, for she shrank back as if he had threatened to strike her.

"The baby, sir. The lady was gone, but he was able to save the baby. Your daughter. She's small, but—she's alive, and he thinks like to stay so." The candle flickered, casting mov-ing shadows, like the ugly little hobgoblins he had so lately fought. "You can see her now, sir. Cook's daughter had her own wee one two months ago, and she's nursing her now—"

Rage filled him. How dared that creature, that parasite that had sucked the life out of his Rebecca, still be alive when she was not? How dared Heaven punish him by tak-ing the one person on Earth he loved more than life itself and leave behind this . . . thing, this unformed nothing, this unwelcome stranger?

His vision darkened, and he felt anger coursing through him, as if his veins were filled with burning ash instead of blood. The anger was a relief; it pushed aside his terrible guilt, the certainty that if he had been here—he could have saved her. He was an Earth Master, a healer. If he had been here—if he had just pushed his horse to get him home—if he had never gone at all—

But no. He was not the guilty one. He had gone to do his duty, and it was not his fault—no, no, none of this was his fault. No, it was this interloper that had murdered his beloved.

"I do not wish to see that—thing," he snarled. "Do what you want with it. Let it die. It killed Rebecca, and I never want to set eyes on it. Never! Do you understand me? Never!"

The housekeeper shrank back until her back was against the wall. "But, sir—she's your—" She bit back what she was going to say. "Yes, sir," she said instead, and made her escape.

Richard Whitestone sank down beside the body of the only woman he had ever, or would ever, love, and wept.

1

SUSANNE Whitestone was as full of contentment as it was possible for her to be. And how not? It was a perfect spring dawn on a day full of magic and life. The air was soft as thistledown, vibrating with birdsong, fragrant with flowers. She hummed as she walked through the dewy grass, never minding that it was soaking into the hem of her muslin frock. The dress would dry soon enough, and the dew on her bare feet felt heavenly.

An Earth magician cherished these things. The dew on one's feet, the tender grass beneath them, the scent of everything green and burgeoning, the power radiating from the soil itself on this Beltane morning . . . these things were life itself. As she walked, she unconsciously cataloged every scent, analyzing it for "rightness," looking for anything that might tell her of a problem. She was the keeper and custodian of this spot of ground, and she took her responsibilities with absolute seriousness. She had been the keeper of the Whitestone lands since she was—ten, she thought. Ever since she had met Robin—

She really didn't want to go back to the Manor, actually. Although she could make the land all around it grow and thrive, there was nothing she could do to heal the Manor. It was the bitter and blighted wound at the center of these lands, so damaged that the land itself had formed a thick protection of power about it, to keep it from poisoning the rest, exactly as a body would create a cyst around a foreign object lodged inside it.

Beltane—or as it was called among most folk here, May Day—was Susanne's favorite day of the year. Christmas was never celebrated at Whitestone Manor, at least, not within the Manor walls, and the Winter Solstice it coincided with merely marked for her another day when the earth still slumbered. Midsummer was the day when all the promise was fulfilled; it marked the moment when "growing" turned to "ripening"—joyous, to be sure, but Susanne preferred this day and all the potential of the season of promise. And while she dutifully celebrated the rites of autumn, they were still sad for her, despite the welcome of Harvest Home, because now the earth would drop back into its winter slumber, and she would be spending most of her time inside the haunted walls of her father's house.

Well, what was the harm in lingering in the meadow, anyway? For a moment, she tasted the sourness of resentment, then the bitterness of irony. After all, she wasn't a *servant,* even though she did a servant's labor. She got no wages, no "new suit of clothes" twice a year—nothing but the clothing she could make with her own two hands, the food she ate, and the little room she had to sleep in. She worked as hard as any of the others and got far less.

The resentment ebbed, and so did the bitterness. Things could be so much worse than they were now—her father could have ordered her sent to an orphanage, for instance. Not one infant in ten survived to the age of five in an orphanage. And from there, she'd have gone to a factory—

She shuddered at the thought.

Well, surely she had earned a little holiday.

She knew very well the others would not begrudge it. Although they had no idea what it was she really *did* for the Whitestone lands—or at least did not know it consciously— somewhere deep inside, their instincts surely told them. Never once, when she had been about her duties and not sharing their work, had she come back to anything other than a welcome and knowing smiles.

So instead of going back to the Manor, she made her way into the Home Wood, a tangle of wild that dated back at least as far as the Norman Conquest, and probably farther. Maybe this was no part of her duties, but a moment here left her more rested than a night of sleep.

There was a little spring-fed pond at the heart of the wood, and that was where she headed. It was the place she felt most at home, even in winter. Today, as she settled down on the grass beside the water, it felt as if the place were folding her in its arms, and the sweet power that rose all about her was like breathing, bathing in, the very soul of the land. The faint breeze left feather-touches on her skin and was like honey-water in her mouth. The birds made better music than any musician she had ever heard. The grass was softer than her bed, and all the muted colors around her, from the little mayflowers at the edge of the pool to the thousands of colors of green of grass and leaves, blended together into a harmonious whole.

This was what made it all worthwhile, all the loneliness, all the sour days spent within walls that sometimes felt as if they hated her.

She had never seen her father. She was twenty years old and had never seen her father, who spent all his time mewed up on the second floor and never came down, never allowed anyone up but Agatha, the housekeeper. From the time she could understand anything, she had been made to understand that he never wanted to see her. She would have grown up as wild and ignorant as a stray cur if it had not been for the collusion of the entire household of servants.

Cook's daughter had nursed her, along with her own little girl. Once she had been weaned, they all undertook to raise her. Old Mary, the cook, taught her how to read, with patience and great labor, out of her recipe books and old newspapers and the Bible, and then taught her to cook as well. Mathew, the stableman, taught her figures. Patience and Prudence, the housemaids, taught her to clean and mend, and Prudence taught her to sew, using the things they brought down out of the attic—everything from old gowns to old linens—as material, so that she could at least keep herself decently clothed. Nigel, the cowman, and Mathew taught her how to take care of animals as well as simple physicking. No one had to teach her how to heal; that had come as naturally as breathing.

She knew, from reading the papers that arrived with the weekly marketing, that this was not the sort of upbringing that a girl of her social status should have experienced. She should have had a proper nursemaid, then a governess to teach her things like embroidery and music and drawing— and then she should have gone to a respectable boarding school with other girls of her class. At sixteen she should have "come out" and been presented to the local version of society. Not presented at court, of course, and not the great London balls that filled the social columns of those papers, but country dances and house parties, teas and gatherings. She should have been going to all manner of entertainments and seeing young men. In fact, by this time she should have been engaged or even married.

But only the people here in the village even knew that she existed—and she existed in a very awkward social position indeed. Her own father had repudiated her, and she worked like any servant, yet she was of a higher class than any of them. It wasn't only the magic that set her apart from them.

She honestly didn't really care about missing the gowns and parties. From the time she had been able to toddle out into the meadow beyond the sad, sere Manor garden and had met Robin, she had *known* what she was meant to do, and it wasn't attend a proper school, wear fashionable clothing, and go to the appropriate parties until she found or was found by "the right man."

This was what she had been born to do. To be the caretaker of the land. To guard it, and guide it, and see that its hurts were healed. How could she have lived the life of someone who was "the squire's daughter" and still been able to do that?

And moments like this were her reward, when she could lean back and feel that all was right, sense that the May Day magics she had performed, together with the Old Religion rites furtively practiced by a small but devoted coven and the May Day country traditions openly practiced by everyone else, had done, or would do, their job. Together she and the people who lived here had bound up the land in that magic, had ensured that the power that fueled it was clean and pure. She knew bone-deep and blood-deep that what she and they had done would keep the land and the power safe and fertile for another growing and harvesting season.

How could even an extravagant London Season or the most enchanting ball ever held even begin to compare with that?

The last shadow of resentment faded, the last of the bitterness soothed by birdsong and the soft sighing of a breeze in the leaves.

Once she was settled in place, quiet as the grass, other creatures emerged, slowly, shyly. Some were perfectly "natural" creatures, of the sort that no one living in the country would be surprised to see. A doe and fawn faded out of the underbrush to drink at the pool, and a dog-fox did the same, watching her with his sly eyes to make sure she wasn't hiding a gun beneath her skirts. There had not been a hunt on Whitestone lands for decades, and as a consequence, the folk hereabouts considered foxes to be fair game in any season. The rabbits and a hare waited until he was gone before making their appearance, as did the cock-pheasant, who was no native of England but whose kind had been here so long he might as well have been.

But after them came the things that only those with her sort of sight—or Sight—could see.

The faintest of splashes warned her with its peculiar notes that the undines were poking their heads above the water to see if she was alone. Someone without the gift to see them would think they were fish, or frogs, but she tilted her head to the side and spied bright green eyes crowned with a tangle of weedy hair peeking up above the waterline.

"It's safe enough," she called softly; even though they didn't answer to her, she was an ally they knew and recognized, and they went back to the playing she had interrupted when she arrived. It was hard for them to tell one human from another at a distance unless that human was a Water mage; caution made them hide when anyone came near.

There was nothing of caution in the little fellow that came bounding into the clearing and flung himself into her lap to have his head and little nubs of horn scratched. The faun could tell where she was at any time—he was Earth, as she was—but she was around other humans so often that he rarely showed himself. "And what have you been at, naughty one?" she asked him, as she picked leaves and bits of twig out of his curly hair. Fauns were bawdy little fellows, but they knew better than to display that around her. She had ways of making her displeasure known that lasted long past the fun of shocking her.

"Stealing," he said artlessly. "Maddie at Stone Cottage be lighter of a scone!" He licked his lips, and his goat-eyes twinkled.

"Then be sure you give her luck," she admonished. "Or at least bring her a maying."

"Eh, all right," he agreed. " 'Tis no odds. Robin, he blessed her cow for it."

"Well, good. But that was Robin's doing, and none of yours. Maddie might need that scone, and if you take without giving back, she *might* stop leaving bowls of milk at the stoop." Maddie Cowel of Stone Cottage was one of those who still Believed—as well she should—and kept to the old ways. Once a week, a bowl of milk left out on her doorstep bought the loyalty of the "Pharisees" as she called the Elementals. Or at least kept their mischief to a minimum. No one hereabouts called them Fairies or Fae or Elves or anything of the sort; naming them brought you to their attention, and that might not be good. No, for the folk in cottages it was "Good Folk" or "Pharisees" or even just "Them Lot," with a sideways look out of the corner of your eye, if you were extremely cautious.

The faun pouted, but he finally nodded. "I knows a squirrel-hoard with no squirrel for it, since yon dog-fox got luck on his side this winter past."

"Half for you and half for Maddie," Susanne agreed, and with his horns nicely scratched and his shaggy head free of bits of detritus, he leaped out of her lap and bounded off to see to it.

A laugh from behind her made her turn, and she smiled brightly up at the young male who was—barring the servants at the Manor—her oldest friend in all the world. "So, you manage my subjects as well as I," said Robin, known as "Keeper," since he had never given a last name, his green eyes sparkling with good humor. "Perhaps I should have a holiday of my own and leave you to tend them!"

"Don't you dare!" she exclaimed, and patted the mossy bank next to her. "Come and tell me the news."

Now, any eyes, whether Sighted or not, could see Robin—or would see a handsome young man, chestnut-haired, green-eyed, and wearing the common rough linen smock and trousers that farm folk about here had worn for over a century, with the addition of a long leather vest and belt and boots suitable for tramping through forest and what appeared to be a shotgun slung casually over one arm. Robin was commonly supposed to be the Whitestone Manor gamekeeper. Certainly all the servants believed that he was, as did all the farmers and laborers for miles around. He never denied it, and if he looked the other way at a few rabbit snares or a bit of grouse poaching or unauthorized fishing, well, most sensible gamekeepers did that. If your gamekeeper was a stickler about enforcing poaching laws, it was an undeclared war all around. If everyone was sensible about things, everyone got along, and game was managed much better. It was well understood that since Master Richard didn't come out of his house, ever, much less take an interest in hunting or fishing his own property, there was no harm in taking what he would have, so long as hares and rabbits, grouse and pheasant, and trout in their seasons appeared occasionally at the kitchen door. And so long as when Robin came around with a warning that this or that sort of game needed some resting, you didn't set snares or drop a line in the places he warned you off of.

The fact that none of the servants had ever seen Robin himself appear at the Manor, not even to collect the yearly wages he should have been getting, never seemed to occur to any of them.

Although what certainly did persist in the minds of one and all was that Robin, known to have been Susanne's playfellow for years, had grown into as fine a young man as she was a young woman, and that one of these days they would certainly get themselves married. The Gamekeeper—like a few other servants—held the same peculiar status that Susanne did. Gamekeepers were considered not quite gentry but a good bit above a mere servant. As such, well, so far as the Whitestone servants were concerned, there was no harm in such a match.

This was useful for Susanne, as Robin was a fellow known to have a hard fist and a strong right arm and the will to use both at need. This kept anyone else from "making advances," which was exactly as Susanne preferred it. Not that she considered herself above the other young men she saw from time to time, but it would have been very difficult, if not impossible, to find someone suitable who was another mage of any sort around here. For all their unconscious connection with the land and the things in it, most of the folk hereabouts were as thick as a brick when it came to magic. And those few that weren't, well, most of them were already paired up, and the rest were too old or too young for her.

And she could not imagine marrying someone who was not a mage. It would just be too difficult to try to explain the inexplicable to him, and as for hiding what she did . . . her head swam at the very notion. Perhaps, if she married a monied fellow—but a simple country lad? "You can't keep secrets in a cottage" was the old saying, and a true one.

So it was very convenient for people to assume that she and Robin were stepping out together. Even if the notion was so absurd as to send them both into gales of laughter in private. A Daughter of Eve? Wed to a High Lord of the Fae? Hilarious.

For Robin was not Robin Keeper. He was Robin Goodfellow, the Great Puck himself, as old as Old England, and a true Force of Nature.

"The coven did good work last night," he said, dangling his arm into the water and tickling an unwary fish into a trance. "There's trouble in the Big World, though."

By this, he meant trouble outside the boundaries of England, not just outside of Whitestone Manor. She frowned. "I know very little about that . . ." she said, hesitantly. The papers that found their way to the Manor were inclined to sensationalize things like anarchist attacks and bombings, then gloat about how civilized Britain would never suffer from any such nonsense. Politics on the Continent was all a confused muddle to her, and wars and conflicts farther away than that were less real than fairy tales. At least in her world, fairy tales had some basis in reality, and the creatures in them were things she saw daily. She had never seen a Zulu or a Hindu or an Arab or even a German. There were some folk who turned up for the fairs that were alleged to be French and Italian, and there were always Gypsies coming through, but for the rest? If you told her that Russians had two heads, so long as you believed it yourself, she would be inclined to take your word for it.

"Lots of little pothers that are going to explode into something big and ugly," Robin replied, pulling his arm out of the water. "People here think they shan't be involved, but they will be; matters are too tangled up for them not to be. And the Dark Powers have their hand in it all, as well, which will make it all the worse."

"How bad? How much worse?" she asked, hesitantly.

Robin shook his head. "Can't tell. Can't say. Bad, for certain sure." He hesitated then added, "All the signs and warnings say this will be a to-do that changes everything."

She looked about her, at her serene and beautiful sanctuary, and shivered. What could be so bad that it would come to affect things *here?*

"I'll do what I can, but I've all of England to look after," Robin told her, solemnly. "And what's coming, well, the best we can all do is keep our little plots of land healthy and safe. Naught to be done about the foolishness of man in the wider world."

Then he laughed and plucked a bit of mayflower from the verge, tossing it to an undine to put in her hair. "But 'tis not here yet, and 'tis nothing to be done to keep it from coming, so let's us dance a roundelay while we can."

Sensible of course, even if she didn't much like it. But Susanne was used to not liking a great deal of her life, and she was accustomed to coping with it all.

"I suppose we'll have a better notion of what to do when it gets here," she said philosophically.

"We won't be alone," he reminded her. "There's the Sons of Adam and Daughters of Eve, and mortals have a powerful will to bend things when needs must."

"So you keep telling me!" she teased, tossing a bit of mayflower at him herself. He caught it deftly and grinned, showing his kinship to the little faun in that grin.

"Ah, well, it's naught I had to teach *you* about," he replied, sticking the flower behind his ear. "Oh, I mind you, no more than six summers old, running off out of that blighted garden and into my wood and calling me. Me! Oldest thing in Old England! Such a will you have!" He shook his head. "And a good thing for you that you do, or the power in you would have driven you mad by now."

"And a good thing for me that it was you that I called," she replied. "It could have been—well—anything."

"Hmm-hmm!" he agreed, and turned his attention to the fish again. "Except for your will, again. 'Twas a good play-mate you wanted, and with the single-minded will of a wee child behind it, it would be nothing else you got."

She wondered about that. Was it true? There was no tell-ing, with Robin. Certainly when she had felt the power coming up through her bare feet, power she had only ever tasted in little, little sips before, and she had stood there in the wood and *demanded* that a playfellow come at last, that had been all and everything she wanted in the world. Cook's daughter and the infant she'd nursed alongside of Susanne had gone back to her husband's little farm as soon as Susanne was weaned, and she hadn't seen a child of her own age at the Manor since. The maids had limited time for play, Cook had none at all, the gardener had left in disgust when nothing would thrive and had taken the boy that helped with him, leaving only the stableman and his boy, who were just as busy as the maids. Housekeeper lamented that the Manor had fallen on such sorry times, so many rooms closed up, staff reduced to next to nothing, but with Master Richard going nowhere and seeing no one, there was no reason to have more than they did. The accounting was all done by Master Richard's solicitor in the village; he turned up once a fortnight to disburse funds and paid out wages every quarter. No one came to the Manor anymore to pay their rents, and all the Manor farmland was tended by tenants who were too far away for Susanne to play with their children.

She had been lonely, she had been frustrated, and she had a very strong will. Naturally, she had taken matters into her own hands. She had gotten as far as the green space beyond the blighted gardens once and had felt a strange sensation through her feet, as if everything around her were connected to her and responding to her. She had gotten called back before she could explore that sensation, but on that special day, she knew she would not be looked for all afternoon, for it was spring cleaning. So she took an apple and bread and cheese in her pockets, waited until no one was watching her, and walked quite calmly out of the gardens to the green trees she could see. There she had demanded, wordlessly, but firmly, that someone come to keep her company. Someone nice. Someone who knew things. Someone who could explain these wonderful new sensations she was having.

She got Robin, who was quite as surprised as she was.

Suiting his form to hers, he had appeared as a child rather than an adult. She had intrigued him no end—and the Fae were always attracted to mortal children.

"I was tempted to steal you away, you know," he said, finally leaving the fish alone and rolling over on his back to stare at the sky. "You with a father that didn't want you, and all that power in you—you were exactly the sort of mortal child that most calls to us."

"I know that now; I didn't know that then." She began plaiting grass stems into a slender braid. "I'd have likely gone with you."

Robin sighed. "I couldn't. Your land needed you. I could feel it calling you. But with all that power—it was too dangerous to leave you untrained, and your fool of a father wasting his life in blaming you for what was none of your doing—you'd have been left to the first mortal Mage to see you for what you were."

"It might have been one of the Gypsies," she pointed out. "That would have been no bad thing."

"Except they'd have stolen you too, and this is the land that needs you." He sighed again. "Alas for me, there was naught for it but to train you myself. Bother responsibility!"

She pulled a face at him. "Oh, and such a burden I was too!"

"Dreadful," he agreed. She laughed.

Then they fell silent; she, considering what he had said about troubling times coming, and he—well, who knew what one of the Fae thought? It could have been nothing more important than how to pull a little mischief off, or deep sobering thoughts about keeping England safe. Or, he might not have been thinking at all.

There was no doubt that she could not have had a finer or stricter teacher. She had been given such a thorough education in the ways and means, the dos and don'ts of Earth mastery, that she very much doubted there was a mortal Master who could find fault with anything she did.

She wondered if her father even realized that the only reason why he had not attracted dangerous Elementals to the neighborhood and to himself was because she had aided the land in walling off the Manor and the gardens that he had poisoned, encysting it in the same way that an oyster or clam would cover something that irritated it in nacre. Robin himself had begun the process, and she had added to it, layer on layer, whenever she had the energy to spare.

Within the Manor boundaries, she had worked to protect every member of the household as best she could. The task was made a bit easier by the fact that her father was not actively trying to harm anything, and the blight about the house was merely the natural reflection of the blighted and embittered spirit of the Earth Master himself, not an actual curse or active poisoning.

"It's going to be war," Robin said soberly, out of the blue. "Not just a little war, neither. There's a lot of mortal nastiness afoot, beyond and above that. Wicked weapons, things that should not be allowed. It will come to touch everyone before it's over."

A chill came over her. He must have been Foreseeing, sitting there. "What must I do?" she asked at last.

"Warn the Coveners. Be vague, though, tell 'em to scry it out for themselves. They'll be more like to believe it that way. I'll do what I can to help them see true." He sighed. "And this is why so many of the Fae have cut themselves off from the mortal world. 'Tisn't just the Cold Iron, 'tis what you lot insist on doing to yourselves and the good earth."

"But you stay . . ."

"I'm the Oldest Old Thing," he replied. "So long as there is a spot of Old England where a leaf can grow, I'll bide." He quirked an eyebrow at her. "It will take more than a mortal war to drive me out."

She took comfort in that.

"As for you, missy, you'd best be off. They'll be needing you in the kitchen." He made a shooing motion with one hand without getting off the ground.

"So they will." Though the kitchen was the last place she wanted to be on a day like this, she had better get back before the servants started to think less than kindly of her. She got up reluctantly, brushed off her skirts, and made her way through the wood and back to the Manor.

From a distance, it still looked handsome. The building was made of a mellow stone, and signs of neglect were few. You couldn't tell how many windows were close-curtained or shuttered, and from here, you couldn't tell how rank and neglected the immediate grounds were, how the fountains were dry and full of leaves, the little statues covered in half-dead ivy.

She wished she could feel sorry for her father—but how could she pity a man who hated her for no good reason, who had responded to loss with bitterness, who neglected lands that had depended on the power of the Whitestones for centuries?

She shook her head and sighed. Well, no matter. If he wouldn't do his duty, then she would. At least there would be *one* Whitestone keeping faith.

As she approached the house, a movement at one of the second-story windows caught her eye. Something stirred the curtains in one of the windows.

Someone was watching her.

She felt another of those strange chills running up her spine.

Ducking her head, she decided to abandon dignity and run, picking up her skirts in both hands. She didn't stop until she was around the corner and out of sight of those windows.

Who could it have been? She wasn't sure which of those rooms her father claimed as his own; the whole of the second floor was forbidden to her. In fact, the only room she was allowed to go into above the ground floor was the attic. Even her bedroom was what had once been what Cook called a stillroom, where the lady of the house would have made her own herbal and floral concoctions. It was just big enough for her narrow bed, though a plenitude of shelves gave her more storage than she could ever possibly use.

She tried to convince herself that the chill was just another of those shivers of premonition that Robin had started with his warning, but . . .

But it had felt as if whoever had been watching her was not someone who had her best interests in mind.

So, all things considered, it probably had been her father. Not that he would know who she was, which was probably a very good thing.

He probably just thought she was one of the servants, the tenants, or a relative of one of the servants. And since he seemed to hate the entire world, well, small wonder if she felt a chill. He was still an Earth Master, and he still had command of Earth Magic. It would have been a greater surprise if she *hadn't* felt a chill.

She passed through the hedge around what would have been the kitchen garden if anything could have been induced to grow there, and entered the kitchen door. The kitchen was a very old room; from reading the papers and the occasional magazine that came into the house, Susanne was vaguely aware that there were all manner of innovations that most houses of this size and wealth had instituted long ago. Patent ranges, for instance, and plumbed water, or at least water from a roof-cistern. This kitchen was substantially unchanged from when the Manor had first been built. Water was brought in buckets from the pump in the yard. It was heated in kettles over the fireplace. Meat was roasted on a spit in the same fireplace or baked in one of the ovens on either side of the fireplace. In fact, nearly all the cooking was done at the fireplace or in the ovens. Cook often said grimly that it was a good thing that Master was this far out in the country, because here there were still people who knew that sort of cookery. "Mark my words," she would then add, "when I'm gone, he'll find nobody willing or able to! Then what will he do? I ask you!"

And everyone would look at her. Because they knew what would happen. It would have to be Susanne who took over Cook's duties if no one else could be found.

If things had been "right" at Whitestone Manor, the kitchen would have been bustling with activity right now. There would have been the master and mistress, several children, the upper servants like governesses and tutors, and perhaps some guests to be tended to. All of them would be wanting breakfast, of course, and a proper country breakfast at that, none of your tea and toast nonsense. And there would have been a full staff of house servants to be fed as well, either before or after the gentry were cared for.

The kitchen was at least big enough to handle that sort of burden, hopelessly antiquated as it was. So the handful of people in it now scarcely took up more than a corner of it.

Old Mary, the cook, looked up first, and beckoned her over with a smile. There was a plate waiting for her with that proper country breakfast on it. The rest were halfway through their own meal, which meant her father's food had already been taken up to him.

Last night Cook had baked a fine couple of egg pies, which they were all tucking into, with plenty of ham on the side. The Manor might be blighted, but the Manor farm was as right as Susanne could make it, and there was no lack of food on the Manor table. Cook had flung open all the windows and had that look about her that told Susanne she was contemplating spring cleaning. Not today, of course. There were May Day festivities down in the village, and everyone would be wanting to go.

"I'll deal with the milk," she offered, before anyone could look wistful and ask. "I've had my little holiday already."

Patience and Prudence—who did literally every chore in the house—both lit up at that. Old Mary smiled. "Well, I've ham and cold pickle and cheese, and that'll do for Master's nuncheon, and I'll just put a few trifles in the oven, and those will do for supper. I'll take Master's nuncheon up afore I go, and Agatha can take up his supper when she comes back."

Agatha, the housekeeper, nodded and added, "If you girls can tidy up the kitchen afore you go down to village, I reckon the house won't be the worse for not being dusted and swept for one day."

Agatha and Mary were as alike as sisters, of the same sort as most of the farmwives hereabouts. Mathew could have been their brother, and the two maids could have been the children of any of them. The people in this part of the world tended to be brown, round-faced, and cheerful, like a collection of sparrows. Susanne could not have stood out more among them had she been one of the Good Folk. She looked like one of those raven-haired china-dolls that little girls got for Christmas if they were very, very good: hair as black as midnight shadows, vivid blue eyes, healthy pink-and-white complexion—and she towered over all of them but Mathew by at least three inches. Maybe it was that difference that made them just accept whatever she said as being true, (like not needing a holiday) even if it probably wasn't. "Eh, that's just our Susanne," she'd heard them say more than once. So once again, when she volunteered to stay at home and work, when everyone else was having a day of fun at the village, it didn't seem to occur to any of them that she was making a sacrifice. Or she wasn't even one of the *servants!*

For one moment, she had to bite her lip to hide her resentment. But she managed to swallow it down successfully after a bit of a struggle, while the two girls, sixteen and seventeen respectively, whispered and giggled and planned what they would do, what young men they would flirt with, what amusements they would have, and whether either of them had a chance at being made May Queen.

Mathew finished his breakfast and went off to hitch the pony to the cart. The two girls, to their credit, made quick work of the breakfast things and then, in a burst of generosity, made sure that everything for the rest of the meals that could be done in advance, was. Within the hour, the Manor was all but empty, except for Nigel bringing the milk to the dairy, and once he had made his delivery, he, too was gone.

Leaving Susanne in the kitchen . . . with that dark and brooding Presence looming invisibly over her from somewhere upstairs.

With another shiver, she hurried to the dairy. Maybe the hard work of churning would drive that shadow out of her mind.

2

RICHARD Whitestone had eaten the breakfast brought to him by his housekeeper without tasting it—really, she could have fed him sawdust for all these years and he never would have noticed. In the first year after Rebecca's death he had scarcely eaten at all, and the only time he had left these rooms had been to attend her funeral. Since that time, he had taken no pleasure in anything, least of all food. He ate it if he noticed it there, and otherwise left it for the housekeeper to take away.

His life had withered, and his spirit contracted into a hard, cold thing, as infertile as a lump of stone. As he had grown bitter, twisted, and blighted, so everything he could see from his windows had grown. That gave him a grim sort of satisfaction, seeing the land itself as stark and withered as his heart.

In his soul he had hoped that this neglect of his own body would make it fail him, but his body had been too stubborn and refused to die. Two years, three? He lost count of the days as he lay for hours with his face to the wall, roused only by the housekeeper's insistence that he eat. He lost track of the seasons, noting only dully the presence or absence of a fire in his fireplace. At some point, however, it became apparent that his body was not going to oblige him. That was when he took on a semblance of living again. He ate—if not regularly, then at least once a day. He changed his clothing when the housekeeper laid out new. He even bathed now and again, hacked off his hair and beard with shears when it annoyed him, cut his nails the same way. Finally he had taken refuge in the only thing that gave him even a particle of release—not pleasure, for he still took no pleasure in anything—but the release of study and concentration.

Books were somewhat of an escape. Not fiction, though. There were enough lies in the world without adding fiction to them. He found his studies in the magical library that had been amassed by generations of Whitestones. He had scarcely looked at these books during his training; Earth Masters tended to be less than scholarly, more inclined to hands-on practicality. There had always been an Earth Master here, but the Whitestones, at least according to family tradition, had spawned all manner of other magicians, and some, like Air and Water, tended to be bookish. And, of course, once the books were in the house, the Earth tendency to "keep and hold" took over, and they were never even lent out to friends, who were perfectly welcome to come as guests to study but were not permitted to take so much as a child's book away.

It was a massive library, rivaled only by the one at Exeter House. There were books that dated all the way back to the time of Henry VII and some for which he could find no date—things written in the careful script of someone trained to copy ancient manuscripts or in the crabbed and peculiar handwriting of some unknown mage's personal grammarie.

Ah, the grammaries . . . the word was actually a corruption of "grimoire," a book of spells and incantations personally collected by an individual magician. The witches called such things both a "grammary," and a "Book of Shadows," but a true grimoire could be a perilous thing indeed, full of notes, speculation, and experimentation. Peril appealed to him now. Puzzling out the strange handwriting and odd abbreviations involved him and made him forget his pain for a little while; these books required endless hours of study, learning the peculiar quirks of the author's hand, puzzling them out word by word and transcribing them into bound notebooks to be left with the original. There were entire shelves full of such blank books, created by some past squire of Whitestone and left there for the use of successive generations. Well, he might as well use them; there would be no more Whitestones at the Manor. He was the last. And for a time, he had thought that this library would be his only legacy; Alderscroft would never permit the home of a Master who died without a proper heir to be left for strangers to paw over. He'd helped Alderscroft himself, twice, in such circumstances. A special delegation would go to the home and make sure there was nothing in it to cause trouble later. Libraries would be stripped of dangerous volumes and harmless ones left in their place, Working Rooms either sealed off completely or made to look like ordinary storerooms. Then any unique books would go to the library at Exeter House, while duplicates became the property of whoever in the party wished to take them. Some of the books here had come by that route.

So when he died, another delegation from the White Lodge would come, take the books away, and leave common things behind.

They'd take the grammaries and the transcriptions. Maybe they would find something of use in them.

None of these were the work of Elemental Masters, of course. The Masters had always had their own private printing presses from the time such things existed, and before that, they had had their own private scribes. The books for the training of new Elemental magicians and recording the results—and only the *results*—of experimentation on the part of a Master were grave and legible volumes intended to be passed down through generations. These grammaries were generally the work of one mage, who might not be altogether sane, and were never intended for any eyes but his or her own.

Rebecca had never been interested in this, so transcribing the books called up no memories of her. He had spent years transcribing these books, delving deeper and deeper into the cobwebby recesses of the shelves. They were not organized in any particular fashion, not even by date. So it was not terribly surprising when, in the middle of a shelf piled high with the maunderings of half-literate "yarb-healers" and the scratchy notes of self-styled "alchymists" that must have been three hundred years old, he found a bundle of books of a much more recent date.

Furthermore, although at first he had been certain they were just as worthless as the rest, the deeper he delved into them, the more he felt drawn, even compelled, to work with them—and the more certain he became that these books were not only of *some* worth, they were of incredible value.

Especially to him.

Because these were the private notes and detailed workings of a necromancer.

Necromancy was related to Earth Mastery, although no Earth Master associated with the White Lodge would ever study such a thing even out of the purest of motives. He had known such books existed, though he suspected that if old Alderscroft had any reason to suspect the Whitestone library held such volumes, the entire Lodge would descend on Whitestone Manor and carry them away to be burned. *Technically* it was possible to be a necromancer and practice entirely benign magic. *Technically* the Spiritualist movement was nothing but necromancers—they spoke, or at least tried to speak, with the dead, after all.

But real necromancers never stopped with merely entreating the dead to appear and listening to whatever they had to say. Real necromancers *compelled* the dead—both the spirits and the bodies too, if they were strong enough. And as such, in the eyes of most "right-minded" Elemental mages, they and their magic were absolute anathema.

But then, those same "right-minded" Elemental mages had likely never lost someone so beloved that life was not worth living without her. And the moment that he recognized the books for what they were was the moment when a seed was planted in his heart that had grown to strange proportions indeed.

These books may well have been the spoils of some former Master who had destroyed the necromancer himself and brought the books home as a kind of trophy. Although the White Lodge of London was very old indeed, not all Elemental Masters in England felt compelled to join it, and Richard was very well aware that not all the Whitestones of the Manor had been on cordial terms with the Huntmaster of the White Lodge of London. Someone who was not part of the Lodge could do whatever he wanted to with the trophies of his combat.

It had not truly occurred to him at first that he could actually use these books. He had merely allowed himself to be lost in the fantasy of bringing her spirit to speak to him, so that he could beg her forgiveness for leaving her alone, for not being there in her dark hour of suffering and need.

But then . . . then he began to think. Why *shouldn't* he bring her back? Surely she longed for him as much as he longed for her. It was the cruel will of Heaven that kept her from him. Furthermore, it was Heaven that had allowed her to die, and not any lack of devotion to him. But enough power could break the gates of Heaven itself, at least for a single soul. So why shouldn't he? Though it might be cold comfort to have only a faint ghost for company, it was better than no comfort at all.

So, in the past six months, he had begun to try.

His first effort at calling her back had been a simple one and no more hazardous than anything some simple farmer's wench would perform on All Hallows. Well . . . perhaps a *bit* more hazardous. A dairymaid would simply recite this "Spell to See the Beloved Dead" while staring into a mirror, and if it worked, she would see the person she longed to view looking over her shoulder.

But the necromantic version enchanted the mirror first, so that not only would the spirit summoned be compelled to answer, but once present, it would be caught and held in the mirror itself. When you looked in the mirror, you would not see your own reflection. You would see the spirit caught in the mirror.

He worked on that mirror for three days.

To no avail.

He performed the incantation perfectly. Everything was correct. He had not left out a single step.

But nothing whatsoever happened. There was not even a shadow in the mirror, a suspicion of a figure.

In a rage, he dashed the wretched thing to the floor and shattered it, grinding it to powder beneath his boot heels, then flung himself into his unmade bed for a torrent of furious weeping. He had been so sure, so *sure* it would work! He had put all the force of his formidable will behind it!

And yet . . . nothing.

His fury collapsed as his strength and energy ran out, and his choking sobs turned from angry to heartbroken.

It must have been his own fault. He was not single-minded enough. He must have allowed his concentration to slip at a crucial moment. Perhaps one of the components had not been sufficiently pure.

Then, from a state of heartbreak, he slipped, as always, into a state of despair. How could he ever have thought this would work? He should have known better. He didn't deserve Rebecca in life, and why should that have changed?

He lay in bed without changing his clothing or even getting up to eat for three days, alternating between despair and anger.

Anger won.

At the end of three days he rose, more than ever determined to restore Rebecca to his side.

He tried incantation after incantation, spell after spell. All were utterly unsuccessful, and he was going nearly mad with frustration. He *knew* necromancy worked! He had *fought* necromancers before! So why did these spells keep failing? What was it that they did that he was not doing?

And then, finally, he came across a passage that he must have skimmed over a hundred times—

These are but Trifles, and apt to Fail, unless the Spirit is willing to Come, and the Veil between Life and Death is thin. The farther from the Time of its Death the Spirit is, the less it can feel the Compulsion of the Living Mage, and the harder it is to find its Way to the Living World. Only if the Mage is willing to Pay the Highest of Prices can the Veil be thinned enough by Magical means to allow the Reluctant Spirit, or that held Fast by the Other World, to be pulled Back.

Now . . . now he began to understand just what that passage was (rather coyly) saying. "The Highest of Prices" could only mean Blood Magic.

It had been nearly twenty years since Rebecca had been taken from him. That was a very long time indeed. Even spirits that *wanted* to remain faded over time, and for all of his trying he had not seen a single sign to tell him that Rebecca remained on this side of the Veil.

Of course not. She had always been the most docile, sweet-natured, and biddable of women, which was something of a disadvantage when what he wanted was for her to rebel against those who would insist that she pass through the Great Door and into the Light. She had, in fact, probably done exactly that the moment that her body gave up the uneven struggle against blood loss and pain. She had been on the Other Side hours before he had arrived at her bedside. And while he had no doubt whatsoever that he could persuade her to remain if he forced her back, until he actually had her standing in some form before him, her current guardians would see to it that no voice reached her ethereal ears but theirs.

It was a moment of great epiphany for him—and while on the one hand it meant that in order to get her back he would have to engage in the very sort of magic he had always fought against, on the other, well . . . he knew that this would be easier than anything he had tried until now. Blood Magic always was. There would be no need to spend his own strength; the power of the magic came from the life force he would take. The younger the sacrifice, the greater the life force, as all the years the creature *would* have lived translated directly into greater power.

This was why those who sought magic and had no power of their own went straight to Blood Magic. If you had the tools, the sacrifice, and the will, you didn't need your own power.

He did not for a moment hesitate when he realized what it was that he would have to do. He opened the third volume of the set, the one he had set aside when he realized it was a treatise on Blood Magic, and began to study it.

The words fairly leaped off the page and into his mind, where they burned themselves into his brain. For months now, he had lived, breathed, eaten, and slept his studies. When the house was asleep, he would slip down into the yard and find some animal that no one would miss—kittens and puppies (that were going to be drowned anyway, no doubt), the odd hen or rabbit. These were his instruments of practice, learning how to shape the spells, how to eke the most power out of the sacrifice. It was easily done; the remains went into the privy-hole, the rest was trivial to clean up. The more he practiced, the more he began to realize that he actually was going to be able to do more, much more, than bring Rebecca's spirit back. If he was bold enough. He was intelligent, he had a strong, trained will, and he had a considerable amount of personal power.

One thing he would not do. He would not reanimate what was left of her beautiful body with the spirit he would capture. That might do for a necromantic servant, but not for his beloved. No, Rebecca's spirit would have a new home. She would live again!

He could do that. He would need to disinter her, of course, for he would need her bones. But on that framework, he could create a body for her. The spells were there. He could actually restore her body. Not reanimation but restoration, building her from power and blood, if he could just find the right sacrifice—or sacrifices. It might take more than one. They would have to be human, of course.

And that led him to the first problem. Where would he find them? He couldn't sacrifice his own servants; they would be missed. He himself might be isolated from the rest of the community, but the servants were very much part of it.

Perhaps the common itinerant laborers that came at harvest time . . . or perhaps the Gypsies. If he took Gypsies, though, he would have to make sure he got the entire group. And he was just one man . . . no, that was out of the question. He could wait until harvest. The traveling laborers were often lone creatures, or at best traveled in pairs. He could dress like one, say he'd found work at Whitestone, lure his victim to one of the outbuildings no longer used, ply the sacrifice with liquor. It would be easy . . .

But what if someone saw him? What if one of the servants grew suspicious? Worse still, what if he somehow picked someone who was expected, who was supposed to meet with a larger group?

For the first time, he wished he lived near a city. The cities were full of people who would never be missed if they vanished. Could he go there? Could he make forays, like a big game hunter, into the city to stalk his prey?

But how? Once, perhaps, but over and over again?

How would he even get there? He didn't have a motorcar, and he wouldn't know how to drive one. If he took the pony and cart or the lone riding horse, it would be missed, and he'd probably be caught up as a thief.

Then when he got there—how would he ever find his way about?

The problems seemed insurmountable, but he kept studying, kept trying to find a way around the problem. Surely he was not the only necromancer to confront such difficulties!

Then, as he delved deeper still, he realized that he did not need to find several sacrifices, he only needed to find one, a single perfect one.

Because he did not need to create a new shell. That was doing things the hard way. There was a much, much easier way.

If he dared—and if he could find everything he needed, which included an even more exactingly perfect victim than simple sacrifice—he could oust one soul from the vessel he needed and give the shell to his Rebecca.

It would shock her, of course. At first, it might well appall her. She had been taught the same things he had, after all. She had been raised to believe that necromancy was utter anathema. But he could persuade her . . . he had always been able to persuade her.

She would live again, and not within a fragile creation that had been restored by magic—a shell that could just as easily be sundered by magic. No, she would live as a soul, in a perfectly ordinary body, as firmly bound to it as if she had been born into it.

There was the matter of finding the correct vessel, however. It would have to be someone who would not be missed. It would have to be someone either fourteen or twenty-one—multiples of the powerful number seven. Twenty-eight would be too old, because most women who would not be missed were dead before then—or if not dead, were certainly disease-ridden and gin-raddled, if not worse. Perhaps he could find a suitable widow or spinster, but not without more searching than he was prepared to undertake. And seven was much too young; he wouldn't have the patience to wait for a child to grow up.

It would have to be someone who looked as much like Rebecca had as possible, to lessen the shock of the spirit being bound into a new body. The closer the vessel looked to her original form, the more likely she was to settle into it quickly and with few objections.

Another reason why using a child as a vessel would be inadvisable. Even a fourteen-year-old would be risky. Ideally — twenty-one.

He brooded over this for many days, trying to formulate a good plan. The largest numbers of young women who would not be missed were among the poor of the cities, and cities . . .

His initial thoughts on gathering victims had born *some* fruit.

Well, cities were not as much anathema to him as they had been. His forays into Blood Magic had skewed his powers rather drastically. No longer were the fauns and Brownies in the least attracted to him, but he could summon kobolds and redcaps, goblins and other unsavory Earth creatures. They thrived on the filth and decay of cities. He had realized that he did not need to hunt, physically, himself. They could search for him, although they were of limited intelligence. Still, even creatures of limited intelligence could recognize a picture.

Once they had found a suitable vessel, he could . . .

And that was where he found himself stuck on the same rock again. He had not left the house in so long that he was not sure where to start. It wasn't as if he could simply help himself to a horse and cart and drive off to the city, then return with a bag full of girl. People would notice. And there was a very good chance he would be caught by the law. He certainly couldn't entrust such a task to a troll or a kobold, they weren't bright enough.

What to do?

He paced the floor for days, alternating his pacing with fevered forays into the books. Slowly, painfully, he developed a plan. Night and day passed, and he did not pay a great deal of attention, except that at night he had to light candles to read, and by day that irritating old housekeeper kept bringing up food she insisted he eat.

He came to realize that he was going to have to control some very dangerous creatures if he was going to succeed at this. The redcaps.

If he could control them, if he could command them *not* to slaughter his prize, they were capable of abducting someone for him. Unlike trolls and kobolds, abducting victims even from the heart of a city was something they did all the time. Strong, wicked and intelligent, powerful out of all proportion to their small size, and vicious, they got their name from the caps they wore that they kept red with the blood of their victims. Murder was literally meat and drink to them.

And although scrying did not come easily for an Earth Master, he could do so if he bent all of his will to the task.

So, if he could get control of some redcaps, he could send out the kobolds and goblins to hunt for him, and when they found someone, he could scry to see how suitable she was. Once he found the right vessel, he could send the redcaps to take her.

Once they brought her here, he would have to keep her bound in magical sleep in one of the unused rooms on this floor until he was ready. And that opened up another series of problems: There was a time limit to how long he could do that before his victim died of dehydration or became too weak to withstand the shock of being un-souled. So he would have to have everything prepared the moment she entered the house. He would get only one chance once he finally summoned Rebecca.

He groaned with sudden realization; that opened up yet *another* series of problems. Once Rebecca was bound into the vessel, how would he explain the presence of a strange woman here, one that just *appeared* in the upstairs rooms?

Problems piled on problems . . .

I shall not give in to such petty obstacles! he swore to himself. *I will find a way! I—*

The crowing of a rooster interrupted his thoughts, and he swung his head angrily in the direction of the sound. The window was open. The housekeeper must have done it, under some vague notion of "healthy fresh air." Through it came not only the "fresh air" but also the infernal clamoring of roosters and birds. Furious at the interruption, he shuffled to the window and made to close it, when movement at the edge of the forest that bordered the dead lawns caught his attention.

A woman emerged from the forest, and for one moment he was paralyzed with shock.

Rebecca?

Had her spirit at last answered his entreaty and returned?

His gaze flew to the calendar on the wall—he had lost track of time—but yes, it was Beltane, when the veil between the material and spirit worlds thinned and spirits could pass over. Could it—could it be, at last?

His hands clenched the windowsill so hard that his nails bit into the wood. He leaned forward, peering at that distant figure. But his impulse to shout a greeting was stilled by the realization that this was no spirit, but a very material and very mortal young woman.

Who? Who could this be? Who was the image of his beloved? Surely none of the little mudball farmers around here could have given birth to this dazzling beauty!

She headed in the direction of the Manor as if she had every right to be there, walking slowly but deliberately toward him. Instinctively he pulled back from the window, so that he could watch without being seen. The nearer she got, the more bewildered he became. She was so like—yet so unlike. This was not the Rebecca that had died in that bed in a room he never allowed anyone to open. This was the Rebecca he had first married, the young woman whose innocent body had not yet been awakened. Who *was* she?

Whoever she was, he *had* to get his hands on her without

drawing attention or suspicion down on himself! This girl was the answer to every difficulty! She was *here,* she was the image of Rebecca, she was surely the right age, and from the threadbare condition of her gown, she was not someone anyone would miss. At least, not outside of this household, since from the way she acted, she belonged here.

Then she looked up, as if she sensed his stares. And it was then, when he saw eyes that were the color of his own and not Rebecca's, that he realized there was only one person she could be.

This was his daughter. His despised, wretched daughter.

And that was when all the fragments of his plans tumbled into place.

This—was—perfect. Perfect in every possible way.

She was the right age, or soon would be. She was such a twin to her mother that Rebecca would awaken in the new shell and never realize what he had done. He would not have to kill his sacrifice, and thus, there would be no messy blood rites to alert the Elementals or Alderscroft's wretched White Lodge.

And given the blood link between mother and daughter, he would be able to easily displace the girl's soul and replace it with Rebecca's.

Well, certainly, *technically* he would be killing his daughter, but who was she, anyway?

Nobody. Uneducated, no better than one of those lumps of servants. No one would miss her—or rather, it would be trivially easy to manipulate all this. All he need do would be to take a sudden interest in this girl. The housekeeper had been at him for decades to do just that. He wouldn't need any messing about with sleeping spells or kidnapping, just a repentant father finally taking an interest in his daughter. Then, once the transformation was accomplished, he could—yes, he could take her away on a holiday. He would direct his solicitor to replace all the servants. When he returned, it would be not with a daughter but with a wife. There would be no one here who would know that the wife had been the daughter, and he rather doubted that anyone outside these grounds had ever seen her.

And this would be justice. The girl murdered her mother. It was only right that she be sacrificed to bring her mother back to life.

He closed the window, then, unable to restrain himself, broke into a shuffling little dance of joy.

3

THE Exeter Club was thought by the "smart set" and the Bright Young Things to be the stodgiest of gentlemen's clubs in all of London—probably all of England—and perhaps even all of the Empire. Nothing about it had changed in a hundred years—except first the laying-on of gas and then electrification.

The doorman, Cedric, was a fixture himself; he'd been a steady daytime presence for as long as Peter had been a member, and Peter suspected that *his* father had been in place when Peter's father first joined the club. With a respectful nod, Cedric held open the door for him; Peter gave him a little two-fingered salute and a half smile.

The paneled entryway gave out into the main Club Room, and it was here that the atmosphere of stodginess was most apparent. No hand had changed the interior in decades. The wallpaper remained the same—something Japonesque that Whistler, had he ever seen it, would surely have approved of. The furniture remained the same—prickly horsehair settees and spindly-limbed little chairs in the Visitor's Dining Room (until recently, the only place in which females were permitted to set foot) and overstuffed leather monstrosities everywhere else. Though gas fires had replaced the coal-burning fireplaces in the Members' rooms, the Club Room stubbornly retained its cheerful grate and firedogs, its carved mantle, and its coal and wood. Even the carpets were the same, brought back from Turkey by some globe-trotting member when Victoria was merely a princess. The menu in the Member's Dining Room had not changed in decades either. And anyone looking into the Club Room and the Member's Lounge could be pardoned if he got the impression that the old gentlemen in their dark suits drowsing behind their newspapers had been installed there as part and parcel of the furnishings.

In fact, as Lord Peter Almsley was well aware, all this was a façade. Most of the members seldom set foot in the public areas of the Club except to dine. And those old gentlemen drowsing away were nothing more than camouflage for what really went on in the Exeter Club.

The club was the home of Lord Alderscroft—the actual home, since he had long since given up his London residence, and his country estate was managed *in absentia* by the "tenants" who ran the school for very extraordinary little girls and boys that was quartered there. These days Alderscroft never went there except for the occasional hunt and hunt ball, and now and again, when the heat in London became unbearable.

But this was his true home, the headquarters, as it were, of most of the most powerful Elemental Masters in Britain. And Lord Alderscroft was the Head of one of the oldest and most powerful White Lodges of Elemental Masters in all of the Empire.

Of course, that's partly because trying to organize Masters is like trying to herd sheep with a cat, Peter thought to himself, wryly. *It's probably only tradition that keeps our lot muddling along as well as we do.*

He had passed rapidly through the public rooms and

into the Dining Room today; the Old Lion had summoned
him for a consultation, and he badly wanted a bite to eat
before he braved the old fellow in his den. He had hoped
for a quiet table to himself, but as soon as his beaky nose
cleared the door of the room, he found himself hailed by a
group that had uncharacteristically gotten the servants to
shove several small tables together to form one long one.

"Peter, old man!" said Nigel Harcourt, making an impe-
rious gesture in his direction. "Come join us, we were just
mentioning you." As ever, Nigel was impeccably clad in the
work of a tailor so exclusive that even half the Royal Enclo-
sure couldn't get fittings with him. Then again, Nigel was so
perfect a specimen of British Manhood that he made the
ideal body upon which to drape such an exquisite suit. And
besides that, Nigel was the one who had discovered the
man.

"Oh, I very much doubt that," he replied, genially, putting a good face on it. "Really, old fellow, I'm just down
from the family barn. I've been quite out of touch, and I
don't know what I could possibly add to any sort of earnest
conversation." But he joined them anyway. It was partly out
of politeness and partly out of curiosity. Curiosity was an
Almsley byword. The family arms, after all, featured a domestic cat about to investigate an open chest, with the
motto, translated from the Latin, *No fortune without risk*.

"What d'ye think about all this saber-rattling on the
Continent?" Nigel asked, both fair eyebrows furrowed,
flourishing a folded newspaper in the air as if he supposed
Peter could read what was on it remotely. "You spend half
your time over there, chasing French ballerinas and Italian
opera singers—it's all nonsense isn't it? It'll all blow over by
Christmas."

"Oh, I very much fear it won't," rumbled General
Smythe-Hastings. The general looked just like any of the
old fellows out in the Club Room at first glance, but at second, aside from the keen intelligence in his eyes and the
vigor in his movements, there was no mistaking his military

background. It was there in the set of his shoulders and the posture of his neck. "This is too like the run-up to the Boer War for my liking. You mark my words. The Continent is seething, especially the Balkans. Good gad, it's always the Balkans! But they're itching for a dust-up, and the Germans and Austrians are itching for an excuse to stop prancing about in fancy uniforms and shoot something. Preferably something French."

"But that's the *point*, old man!" Nigel cried. "How on earth does tossing a few Balkan anarchists into gaol turn into shooting Frenchmen? It doesn't make sense!"

"Whoever said war was logical?" sighed the Hon. James Minton, who had lost the better part of his youth in Egypt. James looked as old as the general, though he couldn't be a day over forty. What he had seen there would have turned anyone's hair white.

The conversation circled around and around this subject while Peter grimly tucked into his saddle of mutton. He had just come from Heartwood Hall, the family estate, and plunging into this conversation was rather like plunging into ice water. He had gone from what could only be described as a pastoral atmosphere of benign and provincial ignorance to—this.

"Our German and Austrian colleagues have completely withdrawn all contact with the rest of Europe," James pointed out. "And I mean completely. There's nothing coming from behind those borders now."

And if anyone should know, it would be James, since he's the Magic Liaison to the Foreign Office..

"But that just might be a precaution," Nigel objected. "You know that lot. The least little thing happens, and they pull in their necks like so many turtles."

"Which is how they avoid having their heads chopped off," the general said.

If I dared, I would finish this excellent roast, bid them all a fond farewell and go trotting on back home, Peter thought wistfully; he was altogether too sure now that what the Old

Lion wanted him for was—precisely this. He had an overt reputation as a Continent-hopping, genteel rake, and no one took him seriously but those of his fellow Masters who had actually worked with him. This could be very useful when you were fishing for information. The Old Lion found him *very* useful in this capacity indeed, in fact. Most, if not all of the Masters of Austria, Hungary, and Germany were under the impression that Peter had much more hair than wit, and one could discuss virtually anything under his nose without him taking any more interest in it than a greyhound in grand opera.

He thought wistfully of the atmosphere he had just left at the Almsley estate. Sometimes ignorance *was* bliss. The people back home were sailing into summer full of serene plans about tennis parties and picnics, of ways to entertain the youngsters during the Long Vac, and thinking about the hunts in the fall and the inevitable Season once winter set in. His brother was entirely wrapped up in managing the minutia of the Home Farm and all the tenants and their farms—not to mention his pet cattle-breeding project, which was finally proving to be a great success. When Hall and Village looked at the foreign events in the papers, it was with a sense of detachment, for certainly nothing a lot of unwashed anarchists could do would ever affect *them*.

Unfortunately for his peace of mind, Peter had far too much imagination and intelligence to believe that.

"We're sailing into dangerous waters, young Harcourt. Dangerous." The general shook his head sadly, his face looking altogether like that of a sad hound. "Things are unstable. It's not just the Masters of Germany and Austria that are withdrawing contact. They've closed off the borders to any sort of traffic, including the Elementals. For the last two weeks, not even a sylph has crossed over."

"The Kaiser wants a war, and he's going to get it," James added, glumly. "The Masters are making sure we get no information whatsoever, and that has to be on direct orders from Kaiser Wilhelm himself."

If that was true ... well, then it was bad. Kaiser Wilhelm was no magician, but like the king, he was well aware of, and made use of, the mages of his own country. Normally this was for very minor things; far more than Britain, Europe was the home ground of some very unpleasant Elemental creatures indeed, and too much meddling could make them take an unhealthy interest in the affairs of mortals. Unhealthy for both sides, ultimately, but it was generally innocent bystanders that suffered the most. So generally, no head of state who was aware of magic actually asked his country's magicians to do much.

This might change all that, however.

War had a way of changing everything.

"I'm afraid the general is right, Nige," Peter said apologetically. "I was hoping the rumblings in the thickets I was hearing this spring were going to turn out to be things that could be smoothed over, but it sounds as though the situation is growing pear-shaped. I think we had best prepare for trouble. Our brethren on the Continent don't engage in business likely to rouse up the Old Things without a damn good reason, and closing the borders is likely to do that."

Nigel swore, and the atmosphere around the table took on a funereal color. No one here, not even the general, was under the illusion that Britain would be able to stay out of a Continental conflict. And no one was under the illusion that once Britain *did* enter it, things would be wrapped up in time for Tommy to come home for Boxing Day.

"We'd better go consult the mirrors and oracles, then," Nigel said with a frown. "If the avalanche has started, it's time for the pebbles to try to reckon how bad it's going to be and make preparations."

"It will be bad," the general replied. "Very bad. Those idiots in the War Office think we can face down machine guns and gas with cavalry and sabers."

"Oh, it's not that bad surely—" Nigel began, then swallowed at the look on the general's face. "Oh."

"Ugly," the general said, nodding. "I haven't been snoozing

in a chair at the fireside. Almsley here—and more important, young Hawkstell—have been keeping me informed. The Austrians have enough torpedo-firing submarines to run a pretty effective interdiction force on our merchant fleet. They have big guns with incredible range, they have those infernal machine guns, and they have and will use poison gas. They have armored vehicles with guns mounted inside them. They have highly trained and organized troops, a superb rail system to transport all of that, and a great deal of their army is motorized—nothing to get tired or frightened or need care and feeding. And *we* have the army of the last century."

At that point, Peter decided to forgo the sweet course. He wouldn't have the appetite for it anyway. He pushed away from the table. "Sorry, chaps, but I *was* summoned, and it doesn't do to keep Alderscroft waiting."

"Quite right," the general replied. "Off with you, lad. Speak with me later, if you like."

"I shall, sir," Peter said respectfully, and withdrew to the stairs and lift for the Members' Rooms.

"M'lord is expecting you, Lord Peter," said the lift operator. Peter immediately got a flutter in his stomach.

"Thank you, Collin," was all he said, however. Were things worse than even the pessimistic projections of the general?

But when he was ushered into Lord Alderscroft's sitting room, it was clear that whatever the Huntmaster had summoned him for, it had not been *urgent.* Alderscroft waved him to a chair and had his valet present Peter with brandy (accepted) and cigars (declined) before getting down to business.

The Old Lion was well-named. He had a great mane of unruly silver-gilt hair, a moustache and beard to match, and the powerful build of a born fighter that he had not permitted to run to fat in the least.

"D'you need me to run to the Continent, m'lord?" Peter asked diffidently, once the valet had gone and they had both had a sip of Alderscroft's excellent liquor.

"I've got Hawkstell out there now, and if I send another of you, it might put the wind up them," Alderscroft rumbled, surprising Peter. "No, I have something domestic in mind for you. There's a scent of necromancy up in Yorkshire; I want you to look into it. The only Earth Master in that part of the world is—or rather, *was*—Richard Whitestone. There's no point in even trying to contact him. He mewed himself up after his wife died twenty years ago, and no one's gotten so much as a glimpse of him since. Necromancy's an Earth business, but you're Water, so you'll have to do."

Peter could not have been more surprised had Alderscroft asked him to don rags and join a Gypsy band—incognito, of course.

"I say," he objected. "M'lord, Yorkshire? Anyone performing necromancy is pretty blamed secretive, and I'll stand out there like a pig in a cathedral! I'm not bad at disguises and all that, but Yorkshire—no native will be fooled for a minute by me, and whoever your necromancer is will know I'm there for only one reason!"

He has no idea how insular the average Yorkshire man is, nor how impossible it is for an outsider to get anything useful out of one, he thought somewhat desperately. Even among the gentry, he wouldn't have the right accent!

"You'll manage, my boy, you always do," Alderscroft said serenely. Peter wanted to bang his head on the back of his chair in frustration.

"You've got leave to make as much 'noise' magically as you please," Alderscroft continued. "Provided you don't frighten our game, of course. With the way our Teutonic neighbors are acting, with any luck at all they'll assume that you are doing something that they should be interested in, and you might also distract them."

Peter bit his lip. "My lord, if a distraction is all you want, I can provide it from London, or better still, from Paris or Milan."

The old man snorted. "I have plenty of people to provide

distractions. What I need is someone who can reliably find a beginning necromancer. Don't play the silly ass with me, Almsley. I know you too well. You can chase your opera singers in whatever time we have left after you find him."

Peter sighed. "Yes, my lord," he said with resignation.

After some idle pleasantry, an inquiry after his mother and grandmother, and another after Peter and Maya Scott, Alderscroft suggested he might want to be on his way. Taking that as the dismissal that it was, Peter finished his brandy. The valet appeared as if summoned and showed him out.

Frustrating. It was very frustrating. Alderscroft seemed to think that he was some sort of arcane Sherlock Holmes, able to chameleon himself into any shape. *I appear to have done my job a little too well,* he thought ruefully, as the doorman summoned a taxi for him. Yes, he certainly could find entry into many places on the Continent, but that was because he could fling money about and be the silly English ass that everyone found amusing, use his knowledge of antiques and literature to fit in among the Ancient Aristocrats, and use his knowledge of art, socialism, and American ragtime to find a place among the Bohemian crowd. And of course, the Bohemian crowd gave him access to the criminal element.

But he would no more be able to pass as—say—a Basque shepherd than fly. He could—just—manage to get about the London underworld, but it was dodgy, and he'd rather do it under the wing of someone like Peter Scott's reformed burglar. He could never, not even with someone guiding him every step of the way, pass as an ordinary Yorkshireman.

He brooded about this tricky problem while he set his valet and general indispensable partner, Garrick, to packing a trunk and a valise. What he needed was someone from Yorkshire to give him houseroom. He might, just might, be able to pass himself off as a harmless and not-too-bright visitor. So long as he had a good reason for visiting, that is.

Who could he inflict himself on? *Do I know any artists*

out painting the moors? He wondered. Although . . . that was a thought, what about setting himself up as an artist? He wouldn't have to be a good one, just be able to say he was an Impressionist and put sky colored daubs at the top of the canvas and moor-colored daubs at the bottom.

He posed this notion to Garrick, and Garrick considered it. "Your artistic friends tend to have very little money and are living in very little space. I fear you would be sleeping in an armchair in a one-room cottage and eating out of tins. Perhaps an old school chum would be a better notion, m'lud," he said diffidently. "Had you rung up Charles Kerridge yet?"

Peter blinked. "Garrick, I could kiss you!" he exclaimed. "Just the thing!"

"Thank you, m'lud," Garrick replied with a little smirk. "Shall I take the liberty of sending a telegram to Branwell Hall? Although, for the purposes of wandering about the moor, posing as an artist would do very nicely indeed. If I might suggest that you ring up one of your artist friends for a kit suggestion while I make arrangements?"

"Oh, most estimable Garrick! I shall do exactly that," Peter replied, feeling much relieved.

The first artist friend that was actually in and willing to answer her telephone was that *rara avis* indeed, a member of his own set who was a damn fine artist and was actually making a good living at it. This had enabled her to politely tell her family—who had wanted her to marry this or that moneyed fellow for some time—to go hang themselves. It had caused quite the dust-up at the time, though they had settled themselves down to it when she showed no signs of wanting to marry an anarchist or worse, Take Lovers. When Clarissa heard what he was up to, she invited him over for tea.

"Get out of Garrick's way and let him make arrangements," she chided. "Tell him where you're going, and have him get you from here."

Garrick highly approved of this and wanted to know only one thing: "Train or motor, m'lud?"

"Motor, of course. That way I can bumble about the moors free and lonely as a cloud," he said on his way out the door.

One curiously satisfying tea of thick cheese-and-pickle sandwiches and gunpowder black, and a quick lesson in how to fake being a bad painter who is certain he is good, and Peter was on his way to Yorkshire, with Garrick in the passenger's seat, the boot stuffed with luggage and Clarissa's own portable painting kit.

"You won't fool anyone if everything looks new," she had chided, bundling up a couple of stained smocks to go with the paint box and portable easel and stacks of stretched canvas and primed Bristol board. "And remember, light to dark when you are working wet. Once it's dry, you can layer on all the nonsense you like."

"Well, Garrick, I didn't get the chance to tell you, but Alderscroft has me hunting a necromancer on the moors," he said, over the Bentley's rumble.

"A necromancer on the moors, m'lud? Sounds quite like a Sherlock Holmes tale," Garrick observed. "And is Lord Kerridge to be informed of this?"

"I think it advisable. Alderscroft won't believe it, of course, but to my way of thinking a mage on his own ground is the equal of any Master who is a stranger to the place." He concentrated for a moment on a tricky bit of curve. "What's more, he's Earth. He'll be more attuned to the place than I am from the beginning."

Garrick, who was a minor Water power himself, nodded. "Ah, if I might be so bold again, m'lud . . . does Lord Kerridge have the same family complications as you do?"

Once again, Peter blinked at his man's acuity. "By Jove . . . that could be a problem. Could be tricky to find a time and place I can explain this."

"Might I suggest, since we have gotten a late start, a slight detour to Heartwood House? You can use your Working Room, overnight there, and continue in the morning." Garrick coughed. "I am given to understand that there is quite a bit of fauna wandering loose on the moors, and a collision with something weighty at night would be unfortunate." There was the faintest of disapproval in Garrick's voice. Peter's valet was a city man, and he disapproved of unconstrained wildlife on principle. Peter suppressed a smile.

"I don't suppose this suggestion would have anything to do with a chambermaid named Daisy, would it?" he suggested slyly, and was rewarded by the reddening of Garrick's ears. "Don't worry, your secret is safe with me."

"I have no idea what you are talking about, m'lud," Garrick replied in a slightly strangled voice.

The rest of the journey proceeded uneventfully, interrupted only by a stop at a familiar pub for a quick bite, and Peter pulled the Bentley into the packed gravel drive of Heartwood House just as the sun was setting. He was not at all surprised to find some of the staff waiting for him. That would be his grandmother's doing of course. She would have known he was coming almost as soon as he had decided it. He suspected she had one or more sylphs watching him at all times.

He waved off the servants who went to the boot. "No unpacking, we're just staying the night," he said. "Has my grandmother retired for the evening?" He was safe enough from his mother; she was in London.

On learning the dowager duchess had gone to her own rooms, he trotted inside and bounded up the stairs. As he expected, she was in her private parlor, waiting for him with a pot of tea and two cups. "You wicked boy, what *are* you up to?" she asked, as he bent to kiss her cheek. "Or rather, what has that wretched man Alderscroft got you haring after?"

He took the tea she handed to him, and explained it all to her while she sipped and listened attentively. "Well, as usual, Garrick is right," she said when he had done. "You'd better contact him now and explain it all to him. It is a great pity you can't dragoon that charming Maya Scott into helping you with this."

"It's a greater pity the resident Earth Master has turned into a hermit," he grumbled. "Alderscroft doesn't seem to have noticed that there is a great deal of Yorkshire to search. All right, I'll pop up into our workroom; Water to Earth at least should not take too long."

He and his grandmother shared a workroom, a former "priest hole" concealed in the back of her maid's room. It was slightly inconvenient for him, but the inconvenience was more than compensated for by the guarantee of privacy. Two of the family ghosts were waiting there when he slipped the catch on the paneling and stepped inside. One of them obligingly glowed enough that he could see to light the lamp just inside the door.

His grandmother had anticipated his needs; a pitcher of fresh water and his scrying basin were already on the marble table that served them both as an "altar." Not that either of them ever performed anything vaguely like a religious ceremony here, but the nomenclature for a table in the center of a Working Circle was an "altar." The protective Circle in this room was permanently inlaid in the floor except for a tiny bridging piece that fitted into the circle of bronze like a puzzle piece. He fitted that piece in, and the Circle was sealed.

Once it was, the permanent protections sprang up into life. When a mage had a personal, secure Working Room like this one, it was a matter of great convenience to have magic protections permanently in place. This room had served generations of Almsley mages and, God willing, would serve generations more.

Peter's brother Charles knew all about the room, of course, but he would no more have set foot in it than make himself up as a pantomime cow and cavort for the edification of the villagers. Charles took after his mother, the only difference being that Charles knew magic existed, and she didn't. He had learned about it just as Peter had; he knew that their father had been a powerful mage and that Peter had stepped into their father's shoes, and he even knew that their grandmother was just as powerful. He just refused to acknowledge anything having to do with magic, as if by doing so he could make it go away. He even ignored the family ghosts to the extent of deliberately walking right through them, which caused no end of ruffled feelings that Peter and the dowager duchess ended up having to soothe.

So, there was less chance that Charles would barge in here than there was that His Majesty would loom in the door.

The energy of Air was generally dominant in this room, since it was his grandmother that did the lion's share of the Work here. Peter rested his palms on the little table and set about investing it with his own Element. Energies of every color of green there was, from the deep near-black of a storm-tossed ocean to the thin tint of aquamarine of a tiny freshet, condensed out of the air like fog. Tender threads, tiny tendrils of power, coalesced seemingly out of nowhere, each one a different shade of green; they sprang up and flowed toward him, joining thread to thread to make cords, streams, all of them flowing to him and into him, and he began to glow with the growing power he had gathered into himself.

Now he took a carved quartz "singing bowl" from under the table and a pitcher of pure water. He filled the former and cupped his hands around it. Something stirred in the bowl, like a trail of bubbles in the clear water, a momentary fog passing over the surface. The water in the bowl rippled. And then—there, perfect in miniature, was an undine. The two ghosts—too wispy for him to tell which two they were—nodded approvingly.

"Would you go to the creatures of the Earth Mage Charles Kerridge and ask them to tell him I need to speak to him, please?" he said politely. The undine laughed up at him, in a voice that was as much inside his head as in his ears.

"The Earth Mage already wishes to speak with you, Water Master!" she said gaily. *"You have but to clear the bowl."*

Of course, he should have expected that. With a chuckle, he bade farewell to the undine, who vanished in a flurry of bubbles, and waited for the water to clear and steady. As he looked down into it, drawing on his memory of his old chum and muttering the incantation that would link his bowl with Charles' scrying plate, the water took on a mirror-like finish. But it was not his reflection that looked up at him.

"Well, old man," Charles said, peering up at him with a quizzical expression. *"I can't imagine that you've suddenly got a pash for the moors, so why the abrupt need for an invitation? Your man couldn't be too specific with my man."*

"That, old fellow, is because it's magic, as you probably guessed," Peter replied. "Alderscroft has me stalking the wild necromancer in your parts. Haven't nosed anything out, have you?"

Charles shook his head. *"Not a hint nor a whiff, but there's a lot of moor."*

Peter sighed. "Exactly what I told the Old Lion. Ah, well, I have my marching orders. I reckon to impersonate a gentleman artist. No one expects an artist to act sensibly, and it gives me the excuse to ask all manner of things under the guise of finding scenery and subjects."

"You're welcome to stay as long as you like. We can swap lies about our Oxford days like a pair of old codgers." Charles grinned. *"Actually, you can tell me what's going on with the blasted Germans. My Elemental friends are not happy."*

Interesting. Charles, out in the wilds of Yorkshire, had Elementals that were more aware of the Kaiser's threat than the fellows in London had . . .

"Your Elementals are right to be unhappy," he replied with a shake of his head. "Grim times coming, old man. All right, I'll catch you up on all that when I arrive tomorrow night. Garrick is coming with me."

"Top hole. Good night!"

And with that, the water cleared. Charles was a "mere" magician, not a Master; holding communication open for

that long had probably taxed him. Peter dismissed the energies, unmade the spell, took the loose piece out of the circle
on the floor, and carried the now inert bowl of water to the
window and poured it out. It was just a good idea to be in
the habit of clearing everything but the permanent protections on a Working Room when you were done with magic.
Some people preferred to leave things that they used often
half-enchanted, but Grandmama and Peter's father had
taught him better than that. There was always the chance
that someone could break into your Working Room and
take something, and if it was half-enchanted, then they had
a direct line into the heart of your magic.

He rubbed his eyes and yawned. It had been a very long
day, and there was another long day of driving ahead of
him. Fortunately, he could count on Garrick to have his bed
turned down, his nightclothes waiting, and the window wide
open when he stumbled up to his room.

"Good night, chaps," he said to the waiting spirits, who
nodded affably and faded into the walls. He closed the door
of the Working Room behind him and tottered out to where
his grandmother was waiting. She'd want to hear all of it
and tender her own opinion on the subject.

Which, given that she had been a Master more than
twice as long as Peter had been alive, would be a very good
thing to hear.

4

FOR once, the weather decided to cooperate with this journey. Peter had been keeping track, and it was a fact: Four times out of every five that he had to take a long trip by auto, it would bucket down rain. He never had dared to trust his luck in winter; he was afraid that if he did, he and Garrick would not be found until spring at the bottom of a melting snowdrift. In winter, he took the train, or he managed to keep far enough out of Alderscroft's reach that he couldn't be sent off on journeys like this one.

The drive was astonishingly pleasant; Garrick was something of a minor wizard at knowing just where to stop, and luncheon at a crossroads pub in the middle of nowhere turned out to be an absolute delight. Garrick was also very good at interpreting maddeningly indecipherable signs at crossroads; Peter suspected that this was some odd aspect of his minor Air talents, because he couldn't imagine any other way that his valet could have gotten sense out of signs so faded scarcely a ghost of the lettering remained.

It was well after dark when they pulled into the drive of

the pleasantly situated country house that Charles Kerridge and his family had lived in since the time of George the First. Charles' family was by no means as exalted as Peter's— Peter's brother was, after all, the Duke of Westbury—but their country house, Branwell Hall, was one of the most impressive Tudor manors he had ever seen, and Peter knew of several palaces that were smaller. Add to that, Branwell Hall was surrounded by an estate of over two thousand acres . . . it wasn't exactly a cozy little cottage.

The estate had passed into the hands of the Kerridges as a result of "an unfortunate gambling habit" combined with a complete lack of interest on the part of the previous owner in marrying and begetting an heir. A distant connection had made the transfer of ownership a bit more palatable to the locals, and after two hundred years, the Kerridges were now firmly ensconced in the squirearchy.

Of course, having Earth magic run in the family had certainly helped that along. Charles, like every Earth magician Peter knew, was a good and careful steward of his land, his tenants, and "his" village. That was abundantly clear in the vibrant health of everything that could be considered within his reach. Even though it was dark when they passed Branwell Village, Peter could *feel* the rightness of the place.

As Charles had promised, they were watched for. A light was burning at the gatehouse as they entered the open cast-iron gates, and he stopped the car as the gatehouse door opened, and a figure approached Garrick's side of the car.

"Lord Peter?" inquired the surprisingly young man who peered inside, looking at Garrick.

"Indeed, but I am not Lord Peter," Garrick said patiently. He was used to this. "Lord Peter prefers to handle this temperamental creature himself. I am Garrick."

"Beggin' yur pardon, m'lard," the young man said, tipping an invisible hat to Peter and looking embarrassed. Peter suspected that he was more embarrassed *for* Peter, who was—horrors!—handling the wheel of the auto himself, than he was at his own mistake.

"I know, I am a disgrace, but she won't *go* for Garrick, don't you know," he said apologetically. "We're expected up at the house?"

"Aye, m'lard," the young man said. "Yur t' go straight oop."

"Thank you kindly," Peter replied. The young man touched the invisible hat again and backed away from the car. Garrick waited until they were out of earshot.

"I will be sure to let the staff know that you are the *younger* son, m'lord," he said, with a hint of amusement.

"Ah, yes, of course, all manner of ramshackle behavior is to be expected from a *younger* son," Peter replied, and chuckled. "Then, of course, when I start gadding about as an artist, I'll stop shocking the poor folk, and they can commence to gossip about my eccentricity in comfort."

"Quite so," Garrick agreed.

It was a very *long* drive, but the Manor was visible for the entire distance. There were lights in most of the windows on this side—the soft glow, however, told Peter that this was probably candlelight as opposed to oil, gas, or even electricity. Not that he expected electricity. Unless there was a fast-flowing stream somewhere very nearby so that Charles could run a dynamo from that. He couldn't imagine any Earth magician allowing a filthy generator running within his purview.

The lamps on either side of the great door were, however, electric. And waiting on the top of the steps was (probably to the horror of his staff) Charles, himself.

If Peter was—at least in looks—a stereotypical example of the "all nerves and nose" scion of British nobility, Charles was just as much an example of the best the squierarchy could produce. Where Peter was thin and moved with the nervous grace of an antelope and was the sort of fair-haired chap that looked faintly washed out, Charles was tall and brown and looked as if he ought to be leaping from crag to crag on a mountaintop somewhere. Under his voluminous driving duster, hat, and goggles, Peter's suit nearly screamed

"Savile Row." Charles was all tweed and leather elbow patches, and he'd probably been walking the bounds with the gamekeeper. The only person on the face of it that Peter was less likely to have as a friend was a Cockney thief.

Which, of course, was another sort of odd duck he was friends with.

Peter was in no condition after so long a drive to leap from his auto, but he did manage a "dignified exit with haste." "Charles!" he saluted his friend, as he mounted the stairs, hand outstretched. "Bless you for giving me house-room! It has been *far* too long."

"Oh, it was an effort, but we managed to find you a closet to stow your tackle in," Charles replied with heavy irony, clapping him on the back. "And it *has* been far too long. Are you entirely fagged out?"

"Not a bit of it," Peter replied cheerfully, as Garrick directed a small army of servants on the disposition of the various pieces of kit in the boot of the car and the back seat. "I'd be honored to meet your sire and dam."

"Well, then, come along, because they are rather interested in meeting *you,*" Charles, and the way he emphasized that last word made Peter suddenly wary. What was Charles up to?

His friend led the way through a great entry hall that Good Queen Bess probably would have recognized, and from there, through a warren of passageways and rooms until they arrived at a very pleasant chamber at the rear of the house. It had been furnished very comfortably, with windows open to the night breeze, overlooking the garden. And that was when Peter finally got the joke—when Charles' father and mother both had the same aura of Earth magic about them that Charles had.

And when the introductions were over, and they were all settled, Peter acknowledged that he'd been rather less clever than he'd thought he was.

"Well, I feel about as thick as two short planks," he said, with a sigh. "Here I should have been talking to you about why I've been sent up here, and not just to Charles. I apologize most profoundly."

Michael Kerridge, who looked like an older, slightly more dignified version of his son, waved the apology off. "Quite all right," he said, looking at Peter over the top of his wire-rimmed spectacles in a kindly fashion. "Charles told us about your mother and brother. Deuced thing, when you have to keep half your life a secret from half your family."

Elizabeth Kerridge, as tweedy as her husband and son, and the slender sort Peter expected made a fine showing at hunt weekends, nodded. "I should also add that we have a most unlikely situation here. Virtually everyone on the staff is a minor magician of one sort or another. You needn't worry about hiding your powers from any of them. So, perhaps you can make up for this faux pas by telling us why in heaven's name Alderscroft thinks there's a necromancer somewhere about."

Peter blinked. "The entire staff?" he said incredulously, ignoring, for the moment, the question of the putative necromancer.

Charles nodded. "It's been that way for donkey's years," he said proudly. "I can't think of any other place that can say as much. Makes things deuced convenient, I can tell you that."

"Charles, you have a positive genius for understatement," Peter said fervently. "You just might find me here so often that you'll regret making my acquaintance. By Jove, this is practically paradise!"

"Don't be a silly ass, Lord Peter," Elizabeth chided. "This place is a barn, and we rattle about in it. You're welcome to take up a little corner of it as often as you like. Now tell us about this necromancer." The last was clearly an order and Peter took it as such.

"That's the problem, y'see," he said apologetically. "The Old Lion hasn't got any direct evidence. Only indirect. A few Elementals telling him 'things aren't right' here. More nasty Elemental customers round about here than there should be. There's been nothing overt, certainly no walking dead or bound spirits that we know of, only a sort of 'Things are not right' sense. Whoever this fellow is, he's clever, and he knows how to cover his tracks and shield what he's doing."

"Assuming he exists at all," Charles said, skeptically. "You seem to be describing what I can only call a hunch on the part of the Huntmaster. And if I didn't know better, I'd say Alderscroft had some ulterior motive for sending you on what might be a wild goose chase."

Peter pulled a face. "There is a great deal of nastiness brewing on the Continent. And he doesn't want me there. I'm sure that plays a part in it. But I cannot imagine the Old Lion sending any Master out after something that doesn't exist."

"I can," Elizabeth grumbled. Her husband chuckled.

"My dear," he said fondly, "You do not merely hold grudges, you cherish them. Seriously, I agree with Lord Peter; I cannot imagine Alderscroft wasting the talents of any Master, given the current dark clouds on the horizon." He turned to Peter. "I have had word passed up to me by some of the local hedge practitioners that at least one of the Great Powers has warned that this business overseas is going to be more than merely nasty. It's possible Alderscroft wants to keep you here in case he needs you for some worse situation." Michael shrugged. "In any event, we've not seen any sign of a necromancer, but that doesn't mean there isn't one slinking about here. There is a great deal of Yorkshire, much of it sparsely populated. People and animals go missing all the time. The Elementals here are as shy as moor ponies. A clever necromancer would be very difficult to detect." His brows furrowed. "The last time I heard of one . . . well, that was something old Whitestone dealt with. The vile creature had been very clever indeed, no one had any notion he existed until he was extremely powerful. Whitestone was one of the strongest Earth Masters I ever knew, and even he was caught off guard."

"Yes, Whitestone." Peter pinched the bridge of his nose a moment, then looked up as a bit of movement in the door caught his eye. "Ah, Garrick, please, join us."

As Peter's valet moved diffidently into the room, Peter grinned. "No standing on ceremony, Garrick, we're all just magicians here. Garrick, this is my old chum, Charles, and his mother and father. Michael, Charles, Elizabeth, this is my right-hand man, Garrick, without whom I would be utterly lost."

"Sirs, milady," Garrick said with a little bow.

"Elizabeth, Charles, and Michael," Elizabeth insisted. "Garrick, our entire staff is talented or gifted in magic, though we have no Masters here. They all know about us, so you needn't waste energy and effort trying to hide anything."

Garrick looked visibly relieved. "That will simplify matters a great deal mila—Elizabeth," he said. "I trust Lord Peter has given you the reason we have imposed ourselves on your hospitality?"

"So he has, and in full," Michael told him. "Not that this helps us a great deal, since we have seen nothing."

"To be honest, I'd have no idea where to look or what to look for," Charles admitted.

"Is there any chance of winkling this Whitestone fellow out of his hole?" Peter asked hopefully. "He'd be deuced handy."

"Even if we could . . ." Michael shook his head. "The likelihood of him doing anything to help once he learned Alderscroft sent you is roughly the same as the likelihood of the Kaiser inviting some of those Balkan anarchists to tea."

Peter was startled. "Good heavens, I had no idea . . . Alderscroft said nothing about that."

"Alderscroft probably isn't aware," Elizabeth said tartly. "Whitestone's wife Rebecca was with child when Alderscroft dragged him off to London to help with a rogue Earth Master. Whitestone was on his way back when she miscarried and died of it; he arrived mere hours after she was dead. He blames himself for not being there, and he blames Alderscroft for taking him away. I think he would as soon see Alderscroft at the bottom of the Thames as help him with anything, no matter how dire it was."

Michael nodded. "He hasn't been seen outside his house since he buried her, and he has cut off all contact with every mage he ever knew. I think the only people who set eyes on him these days are his estate manager and his housekeeper. There will be no help coming from that quarter."

"Alas," Peter sighed. "Well, Alderscroft graced me with this thing, so like the patient donkey, I shall bear my burden. I'd very much appreciate it if I could impose a bit more on you. Could you, would you, nose about and ask about? See if anyone has gotten a hint of the more subtle forms of the black arts? I suspect that even with your backing, they'll be more reticent with me than they are with you."

Michael laughed. "You don't know your Yorkshire lads and lasses very well. They're more apt to tell you bluntly to your face 'Eh, you-ur th' worst young nowt as ever was! Now get thee gone an' use you-ur eyen!'"

Peter laughed. "Well, then, look at it this way. You're the squire, and it's your duty to tend to their troubles. If someone *has* gotten himself into dark magic, they are more likely to tell you, once they know you know about it, than they are a stranger. You'll try to put it right. I'd just haul up the miscreant before the Law—in this case, the White Lodge."

"A very good point." Michael nodded. "We can certainly start making concerned noises and see who responds."

"For that, I am in your debt," Peter replied. "Now, for pure investigative purposes, Garrick and I are going to haul artistic kit all over the moor. It's a wonder how much you can do when you're pretendin' to paint. Especially when you are pretendin' to paint bad Impressionist work. You can slap up anything at all, and as long as you're sufficiently enthusiastic, people will shake their heads and tell each other that it's a good thing you've money, for you surely don't have talent, and they'll look no further than that."

"Oh, very clever, Lord Peter," Elizabeth exclaimed in admiration. "And every good, practical Yorkshireman knows artists are mad. It won't matter what you do out there; they'll put it down to harmless insanity."

"I'm counting on that," Peter replied solemnly. "Now, I take it that no one will mind if I set up my own Work Room somewhere about?"

"I put you in the Green Suite," Elizabeth told him, with a hint of pardonable smugness. "It already has a little Work Room specifically for Water mages. Branwell Hall has been playing host to mages and Masters for two hundred years, Lord Peter. We're quite prepared to have the entire White Lodge housed here, should the need arise."

"May it never arise," Peter replied fervently. "First of all, the only thing I can think of that would need the entire Lodge would be an arcane invasion of England. And secondly, Owlswick would send you mad in white linen within a week. *I* wouldn't wish Owlswick on the Kaiser himself."

"On that note, m'lord, I came to advise you that all is in readiness," Garrick put in diffidently.

"We keep country hours, Lord Peter," Elizabeth advised, before he got a chance to respond. "Mind, if you choose to loll in bed until the sinful hour of ten, you certainly can, but breakfast will be but a memory by that time."

Peter laughed. "My dear lady, I had scarcely a day in London before being sent off here. Before that, I was at the tender mercies of my grandmother, the dowager duchess, who keeps country hours and does not believe in bed-lolling. This is probably why my mother escapes to the city as much as possible."

"Or your grandmother keeps country hours to keep your mother *in* the city," Elizabeth observed shrewdly. "Well, good. I should also point out that to preserve your character of an artist, you naturally will want to take advantage of all the light." She paused and looked puzzled. "I'm not sure what that means, exactly. When I've had occasion to talk with Sebastian Tarrant, he raved about light for at least an hour, and on the few occasions I have been to a gallery, there was quite a lot of talk about light . . ."

"I've had a thorough groundin' in artistic palaver," Peter assured her. "I can babble about light with the best of them. And you are correct, it would look deuced irregular if I didn't wander about at dawn a few times, at least. And if I recall my fakery instructions correctly, a 'dawn' paintin' would be a vague pinkish blur with some gold-colored streaks runnin' across it, above a vaguely purplish blur. That'd be dawn coming up over the heather, don't you know."

"I'll take your word for it," chuckled Michael.

"Well, with your kindly permission, Garrick and I will take our leave and take full advantage of your hospitality," Peter said, rising.

Goodnights were said, and with an inclination of his head, Garrick conducted Peter to his suite.

For suite it was. Most country houses afforded their guests a bedroom, with perhaps a shared bath. Peter was now the inhabitant of a five room suite: a sitting room, a bedroom, a bath, a Work Room, and a room for Garrick. And it was clearly decorated to soothe a Water Master's mood; everything was in greens with a touch of blue, with watery motifs and decorations everywhere. Peter stopped dead in the middle of the sitting room just to stare and admire.

"Well!" he said, finally, "They certainly do the thing handsomely, don't they?"

"They do indeed, m'lord," Garrick replied, making no attempt to conceal his admiration. "Oh, I took the liberty of gaining you a brief repast. You will find it waiting in the bedroom. Is there anything else I can arrange for you, m'lord?"

"Most estimable Garrick! No, not a bit. Toddle off to your own well-deserved rest."

"Very good, m'lord." With a faint smile, Garrick withdrew to his little room, and Peter passed on into the bedroom.

He was immediately struck with envy. And then struck

with the determination that, no matter what he had to put up with back at the familial estate, his own rooms in his town house were going, by god, to be modeled after these. He had never felt so relaxed on entering a room in his life. The level of sensitivity to a Water Master's comfort was extraordinary.

"You know, Garrick!" he called.

"Yes, m'lord?" Garrick immediately came to the door.

"Make sure we introduce the Scotts. It'd do Maya good to come out here now and again, and it would do our hosts good to have a Master who is also a physician about once in a while."

"Very good, m'lord. I quite agree."

Garrick knew his master very well after all this time. There was a little toast, a little smoked salmon, tea. The decanter of Peter's own single-malt had been unpacked but the box remained unopened; Peter would not touch anything strong until after he had discovered whether or not the tale he'd been sent to investigate had any truth to it. And the food was such that it would keep until after he had conducted a little preliminary Work.

As he expected, the Work Room was on the other side of the bedroom, beside the bath. It had probably once been an enormous closet; now a brace of handsome wardrobes served to house the clothing of any guests in this room. He passed through the chamber and into the Work Room with scarcely a glance at the waiting food or the comfortable bed; to linger for even a moment would be to invite temptation. The Work Room was all ready; Garrick had brought his valise of Tools in and left a lamp burning.

In short order he had cleansed the room, sealed it (temporarily) to himself, and set up his shields and wards. Now, should the need arise, he and Garrick could take shelter here from the worst arcane attacks. Although he did not for a moment suspect his old friend, it did not do to be too complacent. There were too many times when treachery came from the source least suspected.

Only when that was done did he return to the bedroom.

While he had been busying himself, a bat had flown in through the open window and was chasing moths around the ceiling. He smiled, finding that quite reassuring. Bats were very sensitive to the arcane and avoided places that had been contaminated with evil.

"And unlike me," he told the little creature, who had managed to catch all but one of the moths in the time he'd been watching it, "you work for a living."

Well, at least he didn't require his manservant to undress him, as if he were a powdered and periwigged seventeenth-century dandy, like some of his acquaintances. And while he missed the electric lighting of his flat, the oil lamp on his bedside table was quite good enough to allow for a little bedtime reading.

The bat flew out of the window again as he picked up his book, having skillfully cleared the ceiling of anything it could eat. With his tea beside the lamp and the plate balanced on the coverlet beside him, Peter turned his attention to his reading.

It was not something for those inclined to nightmare; he had decided to take Alderscroft's task at face value and assume that there was a necromancer in these parts. So this volume was a handwritten account, taken from his father's personal arcane library, of the tracking and defeat of a particularly crafty necromancer roughly a century before. Like this one, the necromancer had practiced his art out in the country. Like this one, he had been very difficult to find.

Peter made a number of notes as he read; the necromancer in question had not been an Elemental magician, which had made finding him problematic from that standpoint. He had learned his art during a stint in Jamaica, where he had managed to save the life of one of the local lads that did that sort of thing. The author of the book speculated that this had been cunning on the then would-be necromancer's part, that the man had himself been responsible for putting the Jamaican in danger in the first place in order to gain access to his knowledge. If so, that was both clever and unscrupulous.

Once he had mastered his craft, if such horror could be called that, the newly minted necromancer had returned to England and settled in Cornwall, as far from anyone who might trouble him as possible. Clearly he had been aware that *someone* in magical circles would take an interest in him and his work.

He had been the black sheep of a family of wealth and means, who gladly gave him a generous allowance to stay quiet and far away from them. Hence, the jaunt to Jamaica and the ability to settle anywhere he cared to. Once installed on the coast he had done something more clever still. He bought children from orphanages and the indigent from workhouses; oh, it wasn't called slavery, but it was the same thing. The highly respectable citizens who ran such institutions did not much care what happened to those in their charge so long as they were gotten off the poor rolls — and they themselves were "rewarded" for their cooperation.

He murdered them, of course; he used both their spirits and their bodies. Some of the spirits he bound to serve him as immaterial servants, the others, he bound back into their bodies to serve as his very material slaves. This got him a houseful of silent, obedient servants who never made any trouble. He had to replenish them from time to time, of course, as their bodies wore out and fell apart, but there were always more in the workhouses.

Eventually he got the bright idea to reopen a mine on his property and created yet more dead-alive creatures to work it. Remote as he was, it took some time before his activities came to the notice of the Lodge, and it took longer still before they could actually *find* him. He had layers and layers of protections and shields, and many years to build them up.

Peter's tea was down to dregs by the time he got through the litany of all the things the Masters of the Lodge had

tried in order to ferret the fellow out. The details encom-
passed several chapters, and Peter wisely decided that he
didn't want to read the actual confrontation just before
sleeping.

He set the book aside and turned the lamp down, extin-
guishing the flame. "Sufficient unto the day are the evils
thereof, old boy," he said to himself. After all, first he had to
find out if this particular wild hare even existed.

There was one good thing at least. These days, it wasn't
possible to just walk up to an orphanage or a workhouse
and purchase a wholesale lot of orphans or the indigent.
Oh, you could certainly still buy a child, or even an adult, in
the larger cities—you could probably buy as many as you
liked, women especially. But you couldn't get them in job
lots anymore. It would take time, a great deal of time, and a
great deal of money. So this fellow would not have the
means to produce the sort of army that the Cornish necromancer had built up. He could, possibly, have amassed a
houseful of servants, but—

But someone would have noticed. Country people knew
everything about their neighbors, and someone with a big
house but no one coming to church or chapel, the village or
fairs, would certainly be noticed, and someone would have
told Charles and his family by now.

So *if* he existed, he was probably a lone recluse, off in
some little cottage on the moors.

So it wasn't likely that Peter would find himself confronted by several hundred walking dead.

"For these blessings, thanks," he muttered ironically to
himself, and then sent himself to sleep.

5

THE best way to approach this is obliquely, Richard thought. He had to be careful about this. He had to be convincing.

He heard Agatha tap on the door, heard the door open and close again. He was standing at the window, as he always did when she turned up. "I saw a strange young woman on the property," Richard said peevishly to his housekeeper, without turning away from the window. "You know I don't like strangers here. If you've hired a new girl, you should have consulted me first. And if she is a visitor, you know I don't allow visitors."

The woman put down the tray with his lunch on it. The crockery rattled as she did so. He must have annoyed her. Good. He wanted her to be the one that brought up the girl. "That, sir, is no stranger. 'Tis tha' own daughter." Her voice rose; it sounded as if he had provoked her. Even better. "And I know tha' said never to speak of her, sir, and I know tha' can dismiss me for it, but 'tisn't right, the daughter of the house brought up no better than tha' meanest servant!

And now she's a young 'oman, and what's to become of her? She's not fit for her own class and not right for ourn!" She must have been very angry; her Yorkshire accent thickened considerably when she was angry. This was the first time in twenty years that she had shown her temper with him. He could hear the trembling in her voice. She was probably sure that he was about to give her the sack.

Ah, perfect. And now for the fairy-tale turnabout that she was probably praying for, but scarcely expecting. This could not possibly have been better for his purposes. He composed his face into a look of astonishment before he turned to her. "My . . . daughter? That is what my daughter has become? A young woman grown?" He allowed his voice to falter. "Has it been that long?"

That worked, as he had known it would. The sentimental old fool immediately softened her tone. "Aye, sir, it has been. Near twenty-one years. Tha' has missed all that growing up. But she's growed t' be th' image of her mother."

It was astonishing how easy it was to manipulate the woman.

He sat down in his chair with a thud, as if astonished, shocked. He turned his look of surprise into one of pleading. This, of course, was exactly what the suddenly repentant father in a sentimental novel would do. At last, she would think, he had come to his senses. He had finally awakened from his long sleep of grief. It took no prompting at all to get her to describe how Susanne had grown up. How she had been essentially raised by the servants, sketchily educated, serving alongside them, as one of them, except, of course, that she got no wages. The more he heard, the more satisfied he became, though he took pains to feign guilt and distress. The more sorrowful he looked, the more Agatha waxed eloquent.

Meanwhile, it was all that he could do to restrain his gloating. This would be ridiculously easy. Agatha was ready to throw the girl at him at the first hint of interest in improving her lot. The girl was so very uneducated, so very naïve, she would be overwhelmed when he took notice of her. Any improvement in her life would astonish her and probably bewilder her.

And he would immediately launch a lightning campaign to keep her bewildered. New quarters, new wardrobe—females were obsessed with wardrobe—new status. Agatha indicated that she could at least read and write, so he would bombard her with "lessons" in the form of etiquette books from his library, ostensibly to prepare her for her new status.

And all of this would serve to isolate her from anyone who might possibly continue to have an interest in her welfare. The servants would all draw back from any intimacy with her—she would now be "gentry," above their station, and not to be treated as a casual comrade. He would keep her so busy she would have no time for them, anyway.

Then, when all was in readiness, he would "send her away to school," and they would think nothing of it or assume that he was belatedly rectifying her neglected education.

And, of course, the last thing that they would expect would be to hear from her. The gentry didn't write chatty letters to their servants.

Of course, she would never actually leave the property. He'd have her secured and execute the spell to bind Rebecca to the body immediately. Then he would leave, taking her with him, and direct his solicitor to dismiss all the servants and close the house. It would be best to pension them off, of course. Certainly they were mostly old enough to be pensioned off, and that would stifle any ill will.

He didn't need to be here, after all. His lands would continue to produce income in his absence, and he and Rebecca could live elsewhere for a year or two, or more. Italy perhaps. She had always wanted to visit Italy, and the rents for a remote little villa of the rustic sort were dirt cheap.

In fact, that would be ideal. He wouldn't care about hiring local servants, not when he could easily create much more satisfactory ones. Getting the reputation of being a magician would do him much more good than harm there; there was no equivalent to Alderscroft's White Lodge in Italy, and so long as he did no harm to anyone within the parish of the local priest, the clergy would leave him alone. *Animate criminals and no one will care.*

As for Rebecca, he simply had to look sorrowful and hint that *signora* was not in her right mind, and he had brought her here for her health, and it wouldn't matter what she said or did. Being in a country where she didn't speak the language would keep her isolated, particularly if he took a house in some remote area, far from where one would expect Englishmen to wander.

So if she had an attack of conscience . . . he would exert control over her to get her to Italy—or perhaps Spain. Then once there, he would release that control and begin persuasion. Rebecca had always been biddable, easy to bring around to his way of thinking. He would convince her of the rightness of what he had done, reconcile her to it, and, yes, use magic to help that along if he needed to.

Then the two of them would return to a house staffed entirely by people who had never met Susanne. She would be the woman he had met and befriended in Italy. They'd concoct some story about how they had met and fallen in love and married. He wouldn't need to concern himself about Alderscroft at that point, because there would be nothing for Alderscroft to find. Once Rebecca was one with him in this, he would never need to practice necromancy again.

But first—time to become the repentant father.

"Send her to me," he directed, doing his best to sound as if he was moments away from tears, when the woman finally ran out of things to say. "I have been a wretched fool, and no kind of father to my own child. It is time to make up for my neglect."

The woman went off, babbling. He paid no attention to her. He was much too busy planning the opening gambit in the campaign.

Susanne had gone out to the clearing in the wood as soon
as morning chores were done—and since she'd given everyone else such a good holiday, there were fewer of those than
usual. She wasn't disposed to argue. She'd had an uneasy
feeling all morning, as if someone was watching her, and not
in a good way.

Someone? Oh, she knew who it was. Her father, of
course, although she had no idea why he would be watching
her. He was the only person who could possibly evoke such
unease in her.

She had hoped that Robin would turn up and give her
some advice. She didn't like this, not one bit. Why would her
father be watching her? Why, after all these years, had he
suddenly noticed her?

A dreadful thought occurred to her. Maybe he had assumed that Agatha had gotten rid of her somehow as an
infant—as, in fact, he had demanded. Was he getting ready
to order that she leave?

The mere thought made her sick with uncertainty. Unconsciously, she clutched at the moss she was sitting on as
she stared at the still surface of the little pond. Leaving?
That was impossible! This was her home, the only one she
had ever known!

Where would I go? What would I do?

As she sat beside the pond, the uncertainty escalated to
a state of near panic, and she fought to retain her composure. She'd never been farther away from home than the
village. She knew nothing of the outside world except what
she read in the newspapers! She'd never had to fend for
herself—never had to do without a roof, a place, meals,
clothing—

Think, Susanne, she chided herself, clasping her hands
tightly together and evoking the self-discipline she used
when she worked magic. She forced herself to breathe
slowly. What advice would she have given someone else?

Say, if her father had dismissed one of the girls? Slowly, as she calmed herself, she realized that she was not without resources. Actually, she was better off than if she had been "properly" educated! At least she had skills that people were willing to pay for!

It won't be the end of the world if I am turned out, she told herself. *It won't even be much hardship. I have a great many skills now. I could be a kitchenmaid or a maid of all work nearly anywhere. I could work at the pub or the inn, or even Branwell Hall.* Not that she had ever been next or nigh Branwell Hall, but she knew vaguely where it was, and such a big place was bound to need a great many servants. *I know all the work of the dairy, I can do plain cooking, and anything a cook directs me to do. I can clean and mend, I could be a housemaid. Agatha and Mary would give me references.* In fact, now that she thought about it, such a situation would actually be an improvement over the one she was in now, so irregular as it was. She would be doing essentially the same work, only she would be paid for it. The more she thought about it, the more she wondered if she just ought to pack up and leave, and not wait for her father to drive her off. Granted, she would not be able to run off to tend to her land-magic when she wanted to—she would have to wait until her working hours were over—but there would be no great difference between working her magic by moonlight and working it by sunlight. The Coveners did almost all of their magic at night.

And if she got a place at Branwell Hall, she might even end up working less rather than more. There were dozens of servants at the Hall; not that she had ever been there to see, of course, but people talked. The more she thought about the idea, the better and calmer she felt. She pictured herself in a really good, big dairy; she loved making butter and cheese, she found milking to be a soothing occupation, and she was good at it. *I would make a good dairymaid. And, of course, cows always behave for me.* It might be hard to get one of the well-paid and prestigious places as an upstairs maid, or even a ladies' maid, but why would she want that? Dairymaid would suit her much better.

But . . . no. The others more or less depended on her now. And they would be terribly hurt if she told them she was leaving. It would not be in the least fair to them. Things were melancholy enough at the Manor without her leaving hurt feelings in her wake.

She sighed a little. *I will just wait and see what happens. And no point in thinking too hard about going to Branwell Hall—who's to say if I really could get a place there? The grass is always greener, and all that.*

She had come here longing for Robin to turn up and tell her what to do, but now she realized she didn't need Robin—and that realization made her spirits rise a little more.

In fact, Robin probably wouldn't have been of much use. He was brilliant at magic, of course, being mostly made of it. He knew everything there was to know about the Elementals and the lesser and greater magical creatures of the land. And he was equally brilliant at knowing all there was to know about nature—telling you what plants were good for what, and where the larks were nesting. But his solution probably would have been to tell her to come live in the woods like a Gypsy, which would be fine in summer, but not so pleasant once the weather turned. Not to mention the fact that all the land hereabouts belonged to someone or other, and there would be some interesting explaining to do if she were found camped on it.

She chuckled a little and stood up, feeling like herself again. She brushed off her skirts and made her way back to the manor. Her father could do whatever he chose; she hoped it would not be to drive her away, but if it was, well, she would find somewhere else to go.

As she approached the kitchen, however, she saw Agatha waiting for her anxiously by the door, straining her old eyes as she peered toward the wood. Agatha had to be waiting for her and no one else; there was no one else likely to go off at this time of day but her, everyone else had duties to perform.

And as soon as she came within sight, Agatha lost some of that anxious look and bustled toward her.

"Where has tha' been?" the housekeeper asked anxiously, brushing at little bits of grass and twig on her skirt. "Has tha' got a clean gown?"

"The woods," she replied, taken aback, since Agatha knew very well—or should have—where she was going. What on earth was the housekeeper going on about? She knew very well down to the last stitch what clothing Susanne had and what state it was in. "And yes, yesterday was laundry day, and everything I own but what I have on is clean—but—"

"Nay, no time for talk! Thy father's asking for ye!" Agatha's Yorkshire was as thick and broad as a slab of her best butter now, and her agitation was back. Her round face was creased with anxiety. "Hurry! Wash and brush and clean gown! He won't like to be kept awaitin'!"

Before she knew what she was about, Agatha had hustled her into the house like a hen shooing a single chick, and from there into the tiny closet she called her room. Before Susanne even had a chance to protest, off came the gown she was wearing, and Agatha chivvied her into a wash-up at the cracked basin she had on the dresser, standing there in the shift that was what plain country-folk used for undergarment and nightgown alike. As soon as Susanne was clean enough, Agatha whisked the newly laundered gown over the top of her head, clucking the whole time in disapproval because although it was clean, it was nothing like "fine" or even "best."

Then again, Susanne didn't have a "best" gown. Her "best" skirt, a good five years old, had gotten irretrievably stained this winter after a fall into mud. There might be some old gowns still in the attic that could be cut up and made into a new one, but what with the spring cleaning and all, no one had gotten a chance to look. And it wasn't as if she needed good clothing all that badly; the only time she wore it was when she went to church on Sunday, and by her reckoning, if God didn't care that she was more than half pagan, He wasn't going to care that she didn't have a "good" skirt and waist to wear to His house.

So all she had were the things she worked in, the most presentable of which was a severely simple thing that probably made her look as shapeless as a tree trunk. There was only so much they could do, piecing together whatever fabric they could out of things that had been stored in the attic for decades.

Before Susanne could say anything, Agatha took the worn old brush from her, and brushed her hair and bound it into a twisted knot at the nape of her neck so tight it almost made Susanne's eyes water. "Haven't even got a bit of ribbon," Agatha fretted. "Well! At least he'll be seeing what a pretty pass he's put his own daughter to, and Prudence with better gowns than tha' has!"

Susanne tried to put on an apron as well; Agatha snatched the garment out of her hand. "Nay! Tha' bain't a servant! Tha'rt th' daughter of the house!" And flinging the apron aside, Agatha herded her out of her room, out of the kitchen, past the servants' sitting room, into the best parlor, then up the stairs to the forbidden floor, fussing and clucking the entire time. Her father's rooms were down the hall on the right, but all the rest of the rooms on this floor were closed up too, so that the gloomy hall presented a vista of closed doors all the way to the end.

But once they reached the door that Susanne had never seen open, Agatha stopped and stepped back, nervously.

"Aren't you coming with me?" Susanne whispered.

"Nay! 'Tis not my place!" Agatha replied, aghast. "Go! Tha'rt wanted, asked for!"

The hallway was *very* gloomy, the stairs behind them more so. The only light came from a single window at the end of the hall, and the entirety was floored and paneled in dark wood. Nervously, Susanne put her hand on the door handle; the door moved at her touch.

She *wanted* to hesitate, delay—but she had the feeling that if she didn't move, and soon, Agatha was going to shove her from behind. So she pushed the door open completely and walked slowly into the room beyond.

It was almost as gloomy as the hall; all the windows were heavily curtained: velvet outer curtains, gauzy inner ones. The velvet curtains were pulled slightly aside. The man who lived in these rooms was nothing more than a man-shaped silhouette against the white of the inner curtains. Susanne swallowed hard.

She expected the room to smell musty. It didn't, though it did have a peculiar scent to it. Heavy perfume with more than a hint of smoke; it wasn't exactly unpleasant, but it wasn't particularly pleasing, either.

The door closed behind her, leaving her alone in the room with this strange man. Her father. A father she had never even seen and who could only have seen her from these windows. A father she *still* couldn't see.

Slowly the shadow-shape turned away from the windows and toward her. "Susanne," her father said. His voice sounded as if he hadn't used it much; a little hoarse and rough. But it wasn't the thin, querulous, peevish sound she had expected; it wasn't an old man's voice. This was a strong, low tenor, with the inflection of a man who expects to be obeyed and has every means he cared to use to assert his authority. She shivered a little. "You would be . . . my daughter, then."

"Yes, sir," she replied, forcing herself to speak in normal tones and not in a whisper.

"My daughter, Susanne."

"Yes, sir," she repeated.

"And I have left you all these years to be treated as a servant. How you must hate me." He paused, gauging her reaction.

"I don't know you to love *or* hate you, sir," she replied, with blunt Yorkshire honesty.

"Well, that would fairly well sum it up, wouldn't it?" he replied. "Come. Sit down. At least we can begin to rectify that."

Nervously she moved farther into the room and took a seat, sitting bolt upright, feet and knees pressed together, hands folded in her lap.

She still couldn't see him. He kept his back to the window, with her facing it and him. All she could see was a shape. Despite the promise of his first words, he spent the next hour or so questioning her. Not that she would have had the temerity to put questions to him, but he gave her no chance to. The questions seemed to come at random, too. First he quizzed her like a schoolmaster on the subject of her education. Who had taught her? What books had she read? She could do sums, but did she know geometry? She burned with humiliation as she unveiled her ignorance. If only he'd questioned her about magic! She could hold her own, there. But he didn't. In fact, if he even realized that she was an Earth Master, he gave no sign of it.

What about geography? He questioned her ruthlessly on that subject; she was only able to vaguely indentify other countries as being off to the east, somewhere, or the west, and then only because she'd read stories about them in the papers or had occasionally seen a map.

What about history, then? There she was on slightly firmer ground as long as it was nothing to do with anything outside the shores of England. And books, she knew, so long as they were in the part of the library that she and the servants had access to.

"Can you embroider?" he asked. She shook her head dumbly. "Sing? Play the piano or the harp? Play tennis? Ride? Any skill at archery?" Again, she shook her head, wondering at him. When would she ever have had the time or the teachers for such things? But these were all the accomplishments of young women of her class—she knew this, because of what she read in the papers.

"Well. What *do* you do?" he asked, finally.

"Plain sewing, sir," she replied promptly. "Plain cooking. Washing, ironing, mending. Cleaning up. Milking, making butter and cheese. Laundry—"

She was about to say "and work the Earth Magic for this land" when he interrupted her. "Enough," he ordered, holding up his hand. "There will be no more of that. You are my daughter, and the daughter of the house does not scrub pots. You will be a lady now. I sent my solicitor a note; there will be a new wardrobe arriving for you as soon as he can procure it in York. There will be a better one coming later, when you can be fitted for it."

She looked down at her lap to hide her frown. A new wardrobe? Well, that would be fine, and in her heart of hearts she had often wished she had a pretty gown or two— not the sort of thing she saw in the newspapers, of course, but something that hadn't been cobbled together out of whatever she and Agatha could find in the attic. Something of new fabric, something made by someone whose idea of style was somewhere in *this* century. And perhaps . . . a hat. She had never owned a hat that wasn't made of straw she braided herself. A real hat of felt, with a ribbon and some feathers. And a pretty white gown with lace. Even Prudence had one of those for summer. But surely Mrs. Pennyfair down in the village was perfectly capable of—

"—and then in a school for young ladies," he was saying, as she realized he was still speaking. "You'll learn French, music, dancing, all the things a girl of your station should know. That should take about two years. That will give me time to reopen acquaintance with the rest of the neighborhood and shake off the habits of a hermit. Then we can introduce you to those you should have known all these years."

She forced herself not to look up in shock. *Sent away to*

*a school for young ladies? But—if I am off elsewhere, how
can I possibly tend the land?*

Then, with a start, she realized that she wouldn't have to.
Her father would see to it. He had been an Earth Master
for longer than she had been alive. And if he was going to
do all these other things, then—

Then it followed that he was going to take up his duties
again.

This should all have been very good news indeed. Her
father was going to come out of his self-imposed isolation,
and, after all, this was exactly what he *should* have been
doing. The blight on the Manor would be lifted at long last.
She wouldn't have to keep the rest of the land walled off
from what *he* was doing, and that was more than half the
work she was put to. She was going to experience a complete reversal of fortune. New clothing, new lessons—no
more servants' work—lying abed to eight of a morning if
she chose. An entire new life.

A father; something she had never known ...

And she still had not seen his face.

With his next words, he confirmed that this had been
deliberate.

"It will take me some time to accustom myself to this,"
he said from the window, where he still stood. "So I will beg
your indulgence, but this probably will be the last time you
are in these rooms for some time. I am not used to the company of my fellow humans, and less accustomed to the idea
of having a daughter. I know what I should do in abstract,
of course, but ... truly, the mere sight of you fills me with
trepidation. It will take me a goodly while before I can face
strangers with equanimity, and we are both strangers to one
another. So, you may go now. I will see to it that your every
need is taken care of, as I should have been doing. The
housekeeper has been opening up the suite of rooms that
should have been yours."

The shadow reached out and tugged on something. A
bell rang, muffled by walls and distance; she recognized it as

the one hanging in the kitchen that he rarely used to summon Agatha.

"My solicitor will be arriving with Miss Susanne's new wardrobe this afternoon," he said without preamble when Agatha appeared at the door. "Take her to the rooms I had you open for her. Assign one of the maids to act as her lady's maid for now. Susanne, in an hour or so, Agatha will bring you your first assignments; I think I can remember enough from my own school days to set you lessons for a while." He chuckled dryly. "You have a great deal of catching up to do, and the sooner you start, the better."

"Yes, sir," she replied, since that seemed to be a dismissal. She got up and followed Agatha out; the moment that the door closed, she turned to her old protector and mentor, with an attempt at a joke hovering at her lips.

But before she could say anything, Agatha spoke. "Come right this way, Miss," she said, quite as if she had never nursed Susanne through scraped knees and burned hands and taught her everything from letters to laundry. "I've got your new rooms all aired out and lovely. I hope you'll like them."

The formality of it knocked the breath right out of her, and with the feeling that the bottom had dropped right out of the world, she followed Agatha to the end of the hall, to commence what was beginning to feel like an exile.

6

THERE was a white dress with lace—in fact, there were several. These seemed to be the sort of thing that the solicitor thought a young lady should wear in the summer. There were three summer skirts and three winter skirts and boxes of shirtwaists and all manner of undergarments that bewildered both her and Agatha, never mind Prudence, who couldn't imagine wearing all that clothing at once. For that matter, neither could Susanne, and in the end she did without most of them.

She wished she could have done without the corsets, but none of the skirts and only half of the shirtwaists would fit until she had her middle squeezed in one. For some reason, the white dresses had been cut on more generous lines, so those were what she was wearing until she could alter some of the other things. The solicitor had been uncertain of her size, so two of the skirts were too long. That meant she could alter from the top and enlarge the waistband. She had never worn a corset before this. And at the moment, she was in total sympathy with the Rational Dress movement.

She was working on one of the skirts now, while puzzling her way through a child's French lesson book. Despite not having anything she would have called "real" work to do—though certainly altering her clothing was work—her last two days had been very, very full.

It had begun shortly after she'd been shown her new rooms—two rooms and a closet as large as the place she was using as a bedroom now. The windows had been wide open, the room dusted, and the bed stripped and remade with fresh linen. She had stared around, dumbfounded and feeling very much as if she should have had a dustpan and a broom in her hand. These couldn't be hers . . .

The very first thing that Agatha had insisted on was that she take a bath—a bath in a huge cast-iron tub that Agatha and the others had laboriously filled with hot water lugged up from the kitchen, not a bath in a basin or under the yard pump while all the men were shooed away and the females took it in turns to bathe or guard. Her hair had been washed, and she was glad that she took scissors to it on a regular basis, for at least it hadn't taken all day to dry. The new clothing turned up while she was bathing, and when she emerged, pink and tingling, it was to find a bewildering choice laid out in the bedroom.

It was only today, with the aid of advertisements in the newspapers and occasional magazine that found its way here, that Susanne had managed to puzzle out everything that she was expected to wear. And clearly, the solicitor had just gone into a shop and told a clerk to completely outfit a young lady.

The first layer was a chemise. This was something even the poorest wore, and most of the poor used it as a night-gown too. Then came an article to which the stockings were clipped. Silk stockings, not limp cotton or heavy wool. Susanne wasn't quite certain what other girls and women wore, but she never wore stockings in the summer, and in the winter, she wore wool ones she had knitted herself and she tied them up to a band of fabric around her waist. Nothing like this elegant thing.

Then came the wretched corset, which fitted under the breast, then hip pads, to make the waist look even smaller, objects which had given her no end of confusion. She hadn't been certain if they were to go on the bum, like a bustle, or be stuffed into the front of the chemise to augment her bosom!

Then came a pair of drawers and then a corset cover, which made the instrument of torture look pretty and dainty. Then one or more petticoats. Then, finally, the outer garments. Small wonder that Prudence, who knew only of a chemise and a pair of drawers, had been confused by them all. "Town women," except for very poor ones, wore corsets, but Susanne suspected that Prudence and Patience had never seen one. She certainly had not until now, except in advertisements.

And certainly Prudence had had no idea you were supposed to wear all that, and Susanne had decided that she simply wasn't going to do so. If she got sent to this school, well, she could do it then, but not now. There was no reason to; who would see her and know? She certainly didn't need to impress anyone here at the Manor.

That first day, with Agatha and Prudence both puzzled by all of the clothing, she had adopted that measure, much to their relief. Agatha knew what the corset was all about, of course—in fact, she probably wore one herself, since she was several cuts above a plain little Yorkshire farm lass who ordinarily wouldn't have gotten a place at the Manor years ago, much less been pressed into service as a lady's maid. But Agatha was extremely reluctant to lace Susanne into the thing, and poor Prudence hadn't the least notion *how*.

They tried, of course, but the results were unsatisfactory at best and excruciating at worst, and Susanne asserted her rank for the first time, ever, and said she wasn't wearing the wretched thing. And that was that. The other two gave up with visible relief.

By then, it was suppertime, and before she could even get out of the door of her rooms to go down to the kitchen and join the others, Patience appeared with a tray, which she put down on a little table in the sitting-room. The others vanished, leaving her staring at it glumly.

She ate her supper of course, every last crumb. She couldn't possibly be annoyed with them; after all, it wasn't *their* fault that there were rules about how the gentry were to be treated, and it wasn't *their* fault that her father would probably fly into a rage and dismiss anyone he suspected of treating her with anything less than servile respect. So she couldn't be annoyed and she couldn't blame them, and even though this was enough to make her spirits sink very low indeed, she wasn't going to insult Cook by not eating it all.

She was just grateful that it didn't occur to anyone that Prudence should come up here and help her get undressed. Since she hadn't been corseted to immobility, she was perfectly capable of doing that for herself.

Her first morning as "the daughter of the house" had begun strangely. She'd slept long, but not well, with uneasy dreams she couldn't remember. She woke when Prudence arrived with yet another tray. It seemed that since her father wasn't going to take meals with her, and she couldn't take them with mere servants, she was going to be fed in isolation.

She had begun picking out the first of the too-small garments to alter when Patience appeared, laden down with books and a handful of notepaper covered in careful script. Her father hadn't forgotten those promised lessons. . . .

She felt more than a little appalled when she looked the books and notes over. Grammar, penmanship, French, and perspective drawing in the morning; geography, history, literature, and arithmetic in the afternoon. *It is probably too late for you to learn to play the harp or piano,* he had written, *so you might as well master some smattering of plays and poetry so you may hold your own in conversation.*

There were exercises, which she was expected to send back to him via Agatha. She could only stare at it all in disbelief.

But there was nothing for it; her father expected her to learn all this. So learn it she would. He would just have to be patient with her.

So she spent the entire second day bending her mind around all the lessons. The arithmetic, to her relief, proved to be nothing more arduous than what she had already been taught. And the literature was lovely. Agatha hadn't had the temerity to borrow books from the Manor library, and by the time Susanne herself was old enough to consider doing so, she had never had any time. Between the magic and the kitchen and dairy chores, she was just generally too weary by the end of the day to read for pleasure.

So now she finally was reading something besides the simple children's books Agatha had found in the nursery, or the hymns and Bible verses and responses at church. And despite having to puzzle through some unfamiliar words, she found herself utterly enthralled by the play he had set her to read. She could see it all in her mind, and the fact that it had Robin in it was just the sugar on the cake. She hated to set it aside to go on to the arithmetic exercises.

When Prudence appeared with her tray, she felt as if her brain had been stuffed full. And when she went to sleep that night, it was to toss and turn as bits of the lessons went round and round in her head.

By the end of this, the third day, however, she was beginning to feel rebellious.

She hadn't been out of these rooms in three days. There was all that glorious sun and spring out there, and all she got of it was what came in through the window. The view from her window only showed the distant border of green outside the area of blight; it was not a vista that pleased. She ate her dinner with a faint feeling of being stifled, watching the sun set over the dead gardens. And just as the light dimmed to twilight, she made up her mind. She stood up and decided that she was going out.

What matter that it was late? She had never had any fear of being out after sunset, and there were times when magic had to be done by moonlight. There was not an animal on these lands that would harm an Earth Master, she was more than able to protect herself against any magical creature, and as for humans . . . well, she could summon just about anything to help her—perfectly natural animals that would have no difficulty attacking a human that threatened her. A goat or a dog would probably be the best, but any attacker could find himself beset by a swarm of bees, charged by an angry bull or cow, attacked by geese or a fox—

Oh, woe betide the man that tried to meddle with her! At the very least he'd spend the week afterward wondering if his nether bits were going to just fall off or rot first—and wishing they would make up their mind to do one or the other.

She took off her shoes so as to make no noise as she slipped down the hallway. There was no sign of life in her father's rooms, not even a light under the door. He seemed to keep no hours at all, much less regular ones; according to Agatha, she had just given up on providing him "appropriate" meals, because he was as likely to be eating breakfast before going to bed as he was to be eating it after he got up.

There was no one in the parlor, nor any of the other rooms that would have been used by the family had her father been leading a normal life. All of the furniture was swathed in sheets and remained that way except for the spring cleaning. There was no reason to take the sheets off; no one ever came here anyway.

For the first time in her entire life, she went out through the front door of the Manor. Servants did not do that; they were expected to use their own entrance, and until now, she had done the same. She almost expected the door to howl in protest as she set her plebian hand on the latch, but nothing happened. She had expected the hinges to shriek in protest as she opened the door, but whoever was in charge of such things had kept the hinges nicely oiled. The door swung open quietly, and she closed it behind her just as quietly.

And finally, for the first time in three days, she drew a breath of free air.

Then she undid her stockings, tucked them in her shoes, left both on the doorstep, and ran for the wood.

Once out of the blight, the air was alive with scent, and she realized how much she had missed that, stuck inside the house. Beneath her feet, the grass and earth hadn't quite lost the heat of the sun. All around her she heard the hundreds of little sounds of things going to sleep, things waking up. The silence in the Manor was so thick it was oppressive; she had missed this, too.

She wanted to dance with the heady wine of freedom bubbling inside her. But the moment she entered her special clearing, she was swarmed by Elementals.

Fauns leaped around her, driven, as near as she could tell, by joy and anxiety in equal portions. Brownies clung to her skirts. Things she had always called "tree-girls" peered down at her from the canopy or from behind trunks. Other grotesque yet charming creatures, clothed in what looked like old leaves or dresses of feathers, with bodies round or spindly, tiny or as large as a child, scuttled around her. All of them seemed overjoyed to see her. All of them seemed fraught with anxiety. And all of them, with the exception of the tree-girls, chattered at her in a thousand voices, so that she lost any sense of what they were saying.

There was nothing for it but to sit down among them and murmur soothing things at them, dispensing a comforting aura of energy. Gradually, as she managed to get them to calm down, they settled.

But they settled around her. This was—well, this was very odd indeed. The first time, in fact, that she could ever remember something like this happening. They clung to her as if they expected her to vanish at any moment, as if she had been away for years rather than days.

"What on earth is troubling you?" she asked one of the fauns, who had cuddled into her skirt like a puppy.

As she scratched the nubs of his horns, she sensed he

peered up at her. It was now dark enough under the trees that he was nothing more than a shadow against her white dress.

"You were with your father. Don't like your father," the little creature said laconically. "He's dark, and he drives our kind away."

"He brings dark things," piped up something else from out of the shadows. "Things that hurt. Things that like to hurt us."

"What sort of things?" she asked, but couldn't get any kind of answer from them. They just repeated, "Dark things," and they couldn't or wouldn't say more than that. It was a little frustrating, but if she was going to calm them down and keep them calm, she had to keep herself from feeling that frustration. She kept her mind centered on the tranquility of this place, the soft, warm shadows, the scent of water and crushed grass, the sleepy murmur of birds above her.

"Well, why were you so worried about me?" she asked. Subtle stirrings around her told her that the Elemental creatures, now reassured, were moving away from her, and off on business of their own. Which was a good thing because, after all, she couldn't sit here forever. The faun was staying, however, nearly glued to her side.

"Your father . . . I remember when he was Master of the land," the little fellow said, slowly. "He was a good Master but . . . hard. An Earth Master should not be hard. And now . . . now he is dark, and he brings dark things, and he does not care that they can hurt us."

"But dark things happened to him," she reminded the faun gently. "His wife, my mother, died." The fauns didn't really understand death; they lived entirely in the moment so far as she could tell. That was the case with a great many Elementals, actually. They could be killed, although so far as she could tell, they didn't age or die of old age, but they didn't seem to think about death until it happened, and then it came as an incomprehensible shock. "No wonder his thoughts are dark, and sad things haunt him."

"Not like this," the faun insisted. But he couldn't be any clearer than that, and talking about it seemed to frighten him, so eventually she stopped pressing him. Slowly he relaxed.

"You will not go away from us?" he asked finally. His warm little shaggy body pressed up against her leg. "When you were in that house, it felt as if you had gone away from us. Will you stay with us always?"

"You know I cannot promise that," she told him. "I'm just one mortal Daughter of Eve. I can't make promises like that."

He sighed. "Dark times are coming. Robin said. We want you here, with us, when they come."

"But I cannot make that promise," she repeated. "I can only promise to try."

It seemed that was enough. He pried himself away from her and stood up.

"Be wary," he said. "Take care."

And then he was gone.

Alone at last, she allowed herself to sit and do nothing, think nothing at all, until she felt the smothering weight had lifted from her. Only then did she rise and make her way back to the Manor and her bed.

Knowing now that the Elementals could not sense her inside the Manor, Susanne decided that she was not going to stay inside. After all, why should she? The next morning when Prudence came up with her breakfast, she asked for two baskets, one empty and one with a lunch in it. Prudence went away looking baffled, and it was Agatha that returned.

"And just what will you be wanting with baskets? Miss . . ." Agatha began, then belatedly remembered that Susanne was gentry now. Evidently she had forgotten that when Prudence appeared with the request! It made Susanne laugh, which flustered Agatha further.

"I'm going to do my lessons outside," she explained. Then added shrewdly, "The light is bad in here. I'm going to get a squint."

That idea must have alarmed Agatha even further; perhaps she thought she would get the blame for it. In any event, the poor woman mumbled "Yes, Miss," and took herself back downstairs. Moments later, Prudence returned with the requested baskets. Susanne peeked in the smaller and saw a couple nice thick sandwiches—much more satisfactory than the ridiculous tea-and-toast and cress-and-butter sandwiches she *had* been getting—and a corked stoneware bottle. It was probably cider. It looked just like the lunches that they'd all made up for field workers during the harvest—the overseers got the good ones, in baskets. She hoped that if it was cider, it wasn't as strong as the stuff the field workers got, because they had heads as thick as planks, but half a bottle would probably make her terribly tipsy.

In any event, this was much more to her liking! She had found a small tea tray and a small old rug bundled into a corner of the closet; the tray would do as a desk and the rug to sit on. These pretty white dresses had the distinct disadvantage that they got grass stained and dirty rather too easily.

With her ink bottle wedged into the empty basket by the books, the rolled-up rug on top and the tea-tray under her arm, she set off for her clearing. She half expected to be swarmed again, but the Elemental creatures were nowhere to be seen. After last night, she was more relieved than otherwise.

She quickly discovered that it was much easier to study in these familiar—and unstifling—surroundings. She was able to relax, which she was not able to do in those stuffy rooms. She could kick off her shoes and stockings. She got so absorbed in her work that only the growling of her stomach told her it was midday.

"And I don't suppose you'd be sharing any of that?" she heard Robin say from behind her as she unpacked the basket.

"I don't know why not," she replied. "I cannot fathom Agatha. When I am brought luncheon in the house, she gives me three tiny butter-and-cress sandwiches with the crusts cut off and a pot of tea. But when I come out here she gives me enough to feed a ploughman and his boy." She straightened, with a sandwich made up as a packet in brown paper in her hand, and turned slightly to hand it to him as he came to sit in the grass beside her.

"Hmm." Robin bit into the sandwich approvingly. "I am constantly reminded of why our kind tries to steal food from yours."

She peeked under the top slice of country loaf to find pickle-and-tongue. She took a bite of hers, happily. "At least I get a decent tea," she continued. "Robin, when I came out here last night, all the magic things were practically in a panic. It was as if they thought I had deserted them."

"You can't be sensed inside that house," Robin told her, frowning over his food. "Even I can't—or rather, I *could,* but your father would know I was prying and peering. I don't want him knowing I'm about."

She blinked in surprise and put her half-eaten sandwich down. "But—why?"

"He's meddling in dark things," Robin said, his frown deepening. "And I may be strong, but there are things as strong as I am, or stronger, unless I call on things I had rather save for some dire time."

He snapped his mouth shut, as if he had said more than he intended to.

"But . . . the others said that, too, and wouldn't explain," she ventured plaintively. "I know that he's blighted things just by his extreme unhappiness, but I've never noticed anything else." She paused a moment. "Will he hurt me? Harm them? What does all this mean?"

Robin shook his head with irritation. "I bain't a mind reader," he snapped, his accent turning odd and thick. "This be mortal magic, and none o' mine. Happen ye should be the one lookin' out for it, bein' mortal an' all. If 'e harms the *land,* that's my business. If 'e meddles with the Sons of Adam and Daughters of Eve, 'tis yours."

Startled, she looked into his eyes at that moment and found her breath caught in her throat. Those eyes . . . those were not the eyes of Robin, her playfellow, nor Puck the prankster, nor even Robin Goodfellow, her mentor and teacher. Those were the eyes of something old, old as the moors, old as the stones beneath them. Those were eyes that had seen Queen Elizabeth alighting from her barge on some Great Progress, had seen the Wars of the Roses. He had watched the Saxons overrun what was left of the Romans, watched the Romans slaughter Boudica and her daughters, had borne witness as the Druids made their sacrifices to the Three-Faced Goddess and the Horned God. Those eyes had watched all of that, and he had done nothing—because these were all mortal affairs, and Robin's care and concern was for something much larger than human lives.

She once again was conscious of how *other* and *different* he was. And how much like a mayfly she must seem to him—short-lived, due to die in a day.

She had seen glimpses of this, the true Robin, before. It didn't frighten her, but it did remind her very sharply that Robin was not, had never been, and would never be "safe."

"I beg your pardon," she said, casting her eyes down. "You're right, of course. Unless he does something unthinkably vile to the land, this *is* my responsibility. I won't forget that again."

"Eh, lass," Robin replied, his tone softening. He put a finger under her chin and tilted her head up so she could look in his eyes again. They had gone back to being—just eyes, without that terrible sense of age to them. "Forget the fellow's your father. It may be he's come to his senses again. But perhaps not. What he meddles in—" Robin shrugged. "It's nothing that answers to me; he's got his protections up and about him, and I can't get past them without him knowing that I have. It may be that his protections are nothing more than to keep the meddlesome Masters from disturbing his gloom, but there is something going on behind them that casts a shadow on the land. Take care. Be wary."

And then, as abruptly as it always did, Robin's mood changed. "Is that a treacle tart I see in there?"

7

PETER held his thumb up at arm's length and peered at it. He had no idea what this was supposed to have to do with painting, but he had been assured that all painters did this. Something to do with perspective, though what his thumb had to do with it, he was dashed if he knew.

Just another reason why all painters were balmy.

Another reason was probably in the paints themselves. As a Master he was well acquainted with poisons, because all too often the hand of man was dumping them in his precious waters. He knew their effects, he knew how to get rid of them, and he certainly knew how to recognize them, and the tubes he was lugging around and plastering indiscriminately on his canvas were full of deadly things. Lead, cadmium, arsenic, mercury, cobalt . . . he knew plenty of artists who absent-mindedly held brushes in their teeth or even licked a brush to get a pointed end. He had never quite realized until now how dangerous that was.

He was being as careful with these things as if they were explosive. Each brush was cleaned carefully, and the resulting contaminated turpentine was properly dealt with. He badly wanted to deliver a stern lecture to each and every artist he knew, now, but . . . well, most of them wouldn't even listen, and the ones who would, already knew of the dangers. Small wonder so many artists died young.

"Are we still bein' observed?" he asked Garrick in a low voice. Garrick, who had a pair of binoculars to his eyes, chuckled.

"No m'lord, and we haven't been for the last ten minutes or so. I beg your pardon, but my attention was caught by that kite." Garrick's disguise was that he was an avid bird-watcher and was taking advantage of his master's mania for painting to indulge his own predilection. It made for an excellent reason for Garrick to peer around with a pair of binoculars. And that permitted him to be on lookout duty.

"Well, good, because I am dashed if I can make anything better out of this nasty daub." With relief, Peter put down his palette. "I'll be only too happy to chuck it in a fire when we get back. And here I thought you were getting a bit too caught up in your own disguise."

"I know enough about birds, m'lord, to be quite interested in them. Though it is largely an interest driven by what, m'lord, they can tell me about what is going on below them." Garrick had the binoculars up to his face again. "For instance, that kite has been following the two children that were watching us. I suspect they are frightening things up ahead of them."

"Acting as the beaters, eh?" Almsley chuckled. "Deuced clever of the bird. So?"

"So it is steadily moving away from us, so although I cannot see the children, I assume they are doing the same, m'lord." He set the optics down. "Now, m'lord, the usual?"

"The usual, Garrick. Time to earn our keep." Peter put the palette down and capped the paints, then moved away from the easel to a spot he had selected earlier.

It was a good thing that no one was watching them now, for they would have been certain the two of them were insane. Garrick handed Peter a small basket; Peter sat down right on the grass, and Garrick took a knife and cut a circle in the turf around him, then went four times around the circle again, each time laying down a line of colored string, blue, red, green, and yellow. He tied each line of string with a neat, tight knot before going on to the next. Meanwhile, Peter took a shallow bowl and a stoppered bottle from the basket, and poured pure water into the bowl from the bottle.

What no one but another Elemental magician would have recognized, of course, was that Garrick had just created a shielded space, a magic circle, with Peter in the center of it. Each of those strings represented a great deal of spellcasting on the part of Masters in the White Lodge; each string, when knotted, created an Elemental shield. Red for Fire, yellow for Earth, blue for Air, and green for Water. Most Elemental magicians without such kit with them had to rely on their own personal shields, which left them vulnerable to three other Elements. If there *was* a necromancer about, he wouldn't detect Peter's snooping now.

Peter was conducting his searches outside of the well-appointed Work Room in Branwell Hall because the Hall was too well-protected and the things for which he was looking were too subtle. And this sort of magic had limits — distance limits. Peter could effectively search an area not much more than five miles in diameter. A stronger mage, or several working together, could have ranged farther; someone like Garrick could have gone no more than a mile.

He sat with his legs crossed like a mediating fakir and stared down at his bowl, holding his hand directly over the middle. That hand held another, smaller bottle of the same prepared water, and he dripped a single drop of it into the bowl, in time with his own pulse.

The drop struck the surface, and a circular ripple spread out from it. It was these ripples that he watched. The Old Lion was right about one thing; although an Earth mage would have been better for this, since an Earth mage would more easily detect the kind of *wrongness* in the Earth that a necromancer produced, but a Water mage was a good second choice. Water went *everywhere*, and if there was some contamination by necromancy, Water would pick it up and show it.

The drawbacks were twofold. First, that Water purified, so it lost the traces of contamination that Earth would hold. Second, that Water moved; Earth didn't. Contamination could get picked up and moved for miles.

Nevertheless, this was a good way to start.

Like rocks just below the surface of a lake, this necromantic contamination would make interruptions in the ripple. That was what he was watching for. He'd need to do this for at least a quarter of an hour, because the traces of shadow-magic left by a necromancer might not show up every time a ripple passed over the surface of the water. And because he needed to see whether it stayed put or was moving. If the latter, he'd have to figure out the source.

When the fifteen minutes were up, Peter sighed, and lowered his hand. He put down the bottle, and shook his hand vigorously to loosen it up.

"Nothing, m'lord?" Garrick asked politely.

"Not a blessed thing," Peter replied. "No more than there has been all morning. I am more than ever convinced this was all a plot on the part of Alderscroft to keep me out of Europe. And to think! I could be sharing coffee and biscotti on the veranda of my hotel room at Monte Carlo at this very moment with the most ravishing soprano ever to rattle the rafters of La Scala."

Garrick coughed politely. "I venture to say that our stay in this salubrious climate is doing your health a world of good, m'lord."

"That soprano can do more for my health than a hundred moors," Peter said wistfully, and sighed again. "Ah, well, can't be helped. Unwind me, old thing, and let's be off. The sooner I can burn this disgusting imitation of a painting, the better I'll feel."

* * *

Garrick took the car around to the carriage house, which still contained vehicles meant to be drawn by horses as well as a couple of motor-cars, and Peter was bowed into the house by one of the footmen. He met Charles just inside the door, coming in from another direction. "Still nothing, Peter?" asked Charles, who wore his tweeds with the air of a man who rarely wore anything else.

"Not a blamed thing. I tell you, Charles, I am beginning to think this was all made up by Alderscroft to satisfy his puritanical nature," Peter replied crossly, as they crossed the Great Hall—echoingly empty—and passed two card rooms and the billiard room. "He thinks I'm nothing but a ne'er-do-well playboy. He envies me my divas and dancers, I swear it."

"Poppycock." Charles grinned, as they passed the music room and the library, then sobered. "Actually, I've just gotten a brace of letters from a couple of friends in the know, as it were. I haven't totally rusticated; what happens across the water has repercussions on prices here. The rumblings from across the water are getting worse. I think he wants you within easy reach in case things explode."

"Hmm. And much as I hate to admit it, if that is his motive, he has a point." Peter grimaced. "I'm fittest of the lot to go anywhere at a moment's notice. Money's not a problem, which means transportation's not a problem. I can fit in almost anywhere, and where I can't, my contacts can. I'm good at improvising. And I'm probably the best choice for sending off posthaste into deadly danger."

Charles raised an eyebrow, which looked rather comical on his long, horsey face. "That's coming a bit strong, isn't it? Boasting a bit?"

Peter aimed a cuff at his ear. "Don't be the village idiot, Charles. I'm the second son. The spare. If something fatal happened to me, I wouldn't be missed. The family could toddle along very nicely without me. The worst that could happen would be that Mater immediately find my brother a suitable mate and fling him into a church and then into the poor gel's bed posthaste."

"I wouldn't be so sure of *that,* old man," Charles retorted, looking a bit flustered and uneasy. "You do have friends that would miss you, you know! I know what's wrong with you; you've been out breathing healthy air and seeing sunlight for a change, and your body doesn't know what to do with either of those things. Come along and have a spot of luncheon, that'll put you right."

For a moment, Peter reacted with irritation. *Isn't that just like an Earth mage! All healthy and hearty and "have a spot of food, that'll put you right!"* But then he had to laugh at himself, because it *was* just like an Earth mage, and it *was* good advice. He'd been tramping about the moors all morning, when he was used to town hours. Good lord, at this hour, he'd still be perusing the morning mail and papers. He'd been exerting himself magically too, setting up his scrying bowl three times; that was using his own energies three times, when he wasn't used to Working any sort of magic more than once a day at most. And like most Masters, he disciplined himself to ignore the needs of his body when he was Working, but that didn't mean those needs went away.

"Hang it, Charles, you wretched man—" he began.

"Why am I right?" Charles laughed. "You aren't the first Master we've had stay with us, and except for the Earth Masters, you're all alike. Even when you aren't out Working all morning, you're keeping country hours, hunting or fishing or tramping about, and you aren't used to it. Come along, let's get some grub into you. I'm not too proud to admit I'm famished. I've been out all morning myself, making some polite inquiries among the cottages. I've drunk a lake of weak tea, but I haven't had a bite since brekkie."

Charles led the way to the dining room. Luncheon things, like breakfast, had already been laid out on the buffet. Peter approved. If this was how things always were here, it would be very convenient for him.

"We're informal except when we're actually entertaining," Charles said, as he took a plate and helped himself to cold roast, bread, and pickle.

"And I don't count as entertaining?" Peter chuckled.

"Of course not. You're Working. You can't interrupt a Work just because it happens to be lunch time." Charles moved on to cold asparagus, which Peter eyed greedily. City asparagus left something to be desired. "This way, provided you have the sense God gave a goose and actually feed yourself when you're burning up energy, grub is ready for you when you're ready for it. And try those bread rolls, Cook's particularly proud of her bread."

They sat down together at the long dining table; only one end of it had been set up with snowy linens laid over the shining expanse of wood. Charles dug in immediately, and Peter paused only to butter one of the rolls. "Garrick always says that anyone with patience can bake bread, but it takes a genius to—my *word!*"

He had just bitten into the roll he had buttered, and the sheer perfection of it took his breath away. Hearty, buttery, slightly sweet, a hint of salt, an aroma that filled his head. He'd eaten it in three bites before he even realized it.

"You see?" Charles said. "When I was a nipper, there were times I lived on them. Earth magic, of course. Cook's a kitchen-witch. The closer a thing is to its own basic self, the more magic ends up in it. We've got her a helper to do the sauces and French stuff when we entertain—it's not that what she does when she tries her hand at it is *bad,* but it doesn't compare to her plain cooking, and it frustrates her. She doesn't like following recipes, she doesn't like doing the fancy, and we don't see any reason why she should."

Peter put his second roll down. "When you said that everyone here had at least a bit of magic—"

"I was not exaggerating, no." A lock of Charles' straw-colored hair fell over one mild blue eye, and absently he brushed it away. "The Kerridges have been in these parts forever, long before we bought Branwell Hall." He waggled his eyebrows roguishly at Peter. "You *do* know what they say about Earth mages and women—or men, if the mage is a woman—right?"

Peter rolled his eyes. "Really, Charles . . ."

"All those old pagan fertility doings . . ."

"Charles!" Peter was laughing now. "I'd pay a fiver to see you dancin' about, painted blue."

"Still, it can't be denied, this spot is absolutely teeming with those with magic in their blood, and if informal family history is to be believed, a good many of my ancestors were strongly in favor of sowing their wild oats in as many fields as possible." Charles chuckled and grinned. "Now, I will admit that once we got our hands on the Hall, we went out of our way to hire those who had at least a touch of magic in them. As Mother and Father said, it makes things ever so much easier when you don't have to try to hide what you're doing from the servants. And even more so when the servants are actively helping you. Speaking of which, do you want to borrow anyone for your doings? They wouldn't at all mind. When I say 'borrow,' of course, I don't mean I'd just lend them out like a dressing gown, you'd have to ask for volunteers. But I can tell you that you would get more of them than you asked for."

Peter considered that for a moment. "Let me say, I'll definitely ask for help if I need it, and thank you, but they aren't used to the way I work, nor am I used to them."

"That's fair." Charles applied himself to his food, and so did Peter, finding it to be a most satisfactory meal. But it was not the sort of luncheon that Peter was used to having.

Peter's mother had very firm ideas about what servants should and should not do—mostly, servants should not inconvenience their masters in any way. But it seemed that Charles' servants had no compunction about coming to him with things to be settled even in the middle of lunch, and he was not in the least perturbed that they did so.

Since that was basically how Peter treated Garrick, this didn't perturb him, either—though he had to admit that

Garrick ruled his own small bachelor establishment with a firm hand, and no other servant was allowed to disturb his lordship unless his lordship asked to be disturbed.

On the other hand, Garrick was a mage, and the other servants weren't. Here, if a servant didn't have a touch of magic, he or she still knew all about it. It occurred to Peter that this was probably the root of the unique relationship the Kerridge family had with those who served them.

It also became apparent rather quickly that the Kerridges were very forward-thinking in how they treated their tenants, their servants, and their neighbors above and beyond giving them the respect of fellow magicians. To their tenants, they were senior partners, rather as if the estate was a huge business firm; if things were bad, adjustments were made. If things were good, everyone got a share. To their servants, they were employers to be sure, but also the elders of a great family, who took the well-being of everyone in the household seriously. To their neighbors, they were never overbearing, holding alliances of interest rather than acting as competitors.

Well, except perhaps in the livestock shows . . . Peter reflected, hiding a grin, as one of the livestock managers had a brisk conversation with Charles about the quality of the cattle one of the neighbors was likely to send to the next show. Clearly a great deal of pride was riding on the outcome.

Very many of the people in Peter's set—those who *weren't* Elemental mages for the most part but, sadly, even some that were and should have known better—still treated those on and in their estates in a decidedly feudal manner, and not in the traditional sense. Servants should be invisible and have no lives of their own, tenants should do as they were told and pay their rents regardless of what conditions were like, and neighbors—well, it depended on whether there was an outstanding feud or not. But certainly if the neighbors were not of one's own social class, then they were regarded as inconvenient and beneath one's notice. Peter's mother was a lot like that, and although his brother had gotten most of it schooled out of him, he still treated servants as if they were nonentities. He called all the maids by the same name, "Sally." And most of the manservants by "You, there."

It's the Earth-magic, of course; you can't have that flowing in your veins and not be acutely aware of the comfort of those around you, he thought, watching as Charles' father and the steward came in, discussing the accounts. *Unless you turned to the dark and you're thriving on misery, you're pretty much forced to do something about making sure everyone does well.*

The place was not bursting with abundance, but it was thriving, and clearly no one here suffered at all.

Peter had noticed that there seemed to be more servants here than normal; that would be because they were not worked half to death the way they were in some establishments he had visited for weekend parties and hunts. They were treated like human beings too, and not like furniture or automatons.

This . . . this was a fine thing, actually. Servants *wanted* to do things for you. They hurried to answer a bell, instead of loitering on the way.

Granted, everything here was just a little worn; not shabby, but not bang up-to-the-minute either. He thought he knew the reason. Why waste money on show when you could put it back into what made *people* comfortable and happy?

Well, there was one danger here, and it was that this was all very seductive. It tempted one to relax, and right now relaxing was not something he should do. He had a job in front of him, one that required concentration.

"How is the Work coming, Lord Peter?" Michael Kerridge asked, looking up at last from the accounts, which he and his steward had spread between them.

"'Tisn't," he replied with a grimace. "And that's the plain fact."

"Be patient, you've only been at it a day, and there is a great deal of moor," advised Elizabeth, coming in at that moment. Peter noted she was wearing exactly the same gown she'd worn at breakfast, and he approved. It was fashionable—it was clear she was not the sort of lady who was perfectly happy to muck about in a pair of old boots and a skirt with a draggled hem. Not that Peter had any objection to that, either—there were a good many female Earth Masters who were cut of exactly that sort of cloth, and very good they were to have at your side. But Elizabeth was, again, very like Peter's grandmother: practical, but a lady.

Elizabeth's gown was well-made, it was suited to the country, and it was fairly clear that Elizabeth did not see the need to change her clothing five and six times a day.

Unlike his mother . . .

And very like his grandmother.

"I feel very inclined to pray with Saint Francis, 'Dear Lord, give me patience and give it to me now,'" he replied with a wry smile.

"Did Saint Francis really say that?" Elizabeth asked, looking skeptical.

"Well, if he didn't, he should have," Peter replied firmly. "At any rate, you will be pleased to know that the immediate environs of Branwell are utterly free of any hint of Darkness."

"I would have been very surprised if they were not." Michael turned to the steward, and at that moment, Peter was struck with the notion that perhaps Charles was right, and a long-ago Kerridge bestowing his favors *was* responsible for the number of mages here. Because there was a distinct resemblance between Michael and the steward—and now, Peter realized, between Michael and virtually every servant he'd seen. They were all what he thought of as "horsey Saxons:" tall, lanky, blond, very nearly homely when their faces were in repose, but their animated expressions made them handsome. The noses were the same, and the chins. It was remarkable to see; he reckoned now that he had noticed, he'd be aware of it constantly.

"Hudson, have you heard anything from the tenants that might have a bearing?" Michael was asking.

Peter had expected an outright denial, but instead, Hudson looked slightly uncertain. "*Not* anything about anyone on estate lands," he said slowly. "And really, not anything about anyone specific. But a couple of the lads have ventured, when I put it to them, that they've been feeling a bit uneasy for some months now, and the unease seems to be to the west of us. The trouble is, they can't put their finger on it, if you take my meaning, so they're not anxious to name names or make accusations." The steward drummed his fingers on the table for a moment. "How to put this . . . 'tis like there's a bad smell, but no one in the village can tell where it's coming from. So no one wants to start a quarrel about drains."

Peter was astonished. He'd expected nothing, and instead he had three of the four directions eliminated. "My good sir, *west of here* is a hundred times better direction than I had before this. I am in your debt!"

The man actually blushed. "Na, I'd have brought anything real up before this, but the squire has enough on his plate without bits of rumor."

"Well this was the perfect time and place to say something," Michael said firmly. "Here we have Lord Peter who has the nose of a ferret and the tenacity of a terrier and, moreover, the mandate from the White Lodge to get to the bottom of this. *I* don't have it on my plate, he has it on his. I'd take it kindly if you could spread that bit of news about. Anyone who can give him any signs or portents at all, should. After all, he's a citified lord who's fair lost out here where there's no street signs and no Harrod's." He winked as he said that last.

"Oi!" Peter cried with mock-indignation. "Who's citified?"

"The man who had to have his tweeds aged for him,"

Michael grinned. "You are caught, m'lord. Your clever work will pass muster at a distance, but not beneath the eyes of servants who handle them."

Peter flung up his hands. "I am crushed. And not appreciated. I shall take my maligned carcass elsewhere."

"So long as it's west of Branwell Hall, Lord Peter!" Michael called after him, as he made an exit as full of drama as anything done for a panto. "As long as it's west of the Hall!"

Despite the frustration—and the fact that he was not looking forward to spending the afternoon staring at his water bowl without results—he found himself grinning. It was such a relief to not have to watch every word and to speak in a kind of cryptic code about anything magical. It was even more of a relief to know that he had help for the asking. The number of times when he and Garrick had been in sticky situations with no help at all did not bear thinking about.

Not that he really expected this to turn into a sticky situation. If they did need help, it was far more likely to be something that would require many hands doing something terribly tedious. But many hands would divide the tedious task into manageable portions.

Right now, however, there was only one set of hands that could do what he was doing, and those were on the ends of his arms. "Once more into the breech, dear friends," he murmured to himself, and headed for the Work Room to prepare more purified and energized water.

There were some things it was better not to entrust to any hands but your own.

Peter had set himself up right at the southwest corner of the estate lands. Away from the Hall, of course, he had to resume his ruse of painting, since the tenants and villagers were mostly not magicians.

"If I were you, m'lord . . ." Garrick said, his solemn expression not varying in the least as he looked at the mess Peter had made on the canvas.

There was no point in Garrick pretending to look at

birds. They were within walking distance of the village of Stype, the nearest to Branwell Hall, and every child in the village and every adult with nothing better to do was walking out to have a look at what the "painterin' lord" was doing. Peter would get no peace to Work until they had all satisfied themselves.

Now, he knew he was no kind of painter. And it wasn't as if anyone was ever going to want to look at his daubs. But it was getting downright annoying that all he could manage to produce were canvases covered in varied colors of mud.

"Well?" Peter snapped, after a long silence. Then he felt guilty about snapping. "Beg your pardon, Garrick. Didn't mean to take your head off."

"No offense taken, m'lord," Garrick replied. "The thing is . . . I believe you are not giving the paint time to dry, m'lord."

"But . . ." He stabbed at the canvas with the palette knife in frustration. "Hang it all, she *said* to lay on the paint thick with the knife or the brush and—"

"But m'lord, all you are doing is to muddle up the colors. You're doing the same thing on the canvas that you do to mix colors on the palette, scrubbing them all together. If I may be so bold."

Peter blinked. "Dash it all, you're right. So, what do you think I should do?"

"If it were me, m'lord, I would lay in my basic colors in big swaths, as your friend told you to do, but set the canvas aside when you have done and let it dry. Then come back to it to slice the new colors on with the knife. No mixing on the canvas."

"Hrrm. Well, it can't come out any worse than it already has done." He discarded the ruined canvas with a grimace. Another one for the fire. Then he chose the basic colors for the grass, the drift of heather across one hill, and the sky. And then he stopped. Setting the canvas aside, he started on a second and was astonished to find that the colors had already changed as the light changed.

He finished the second and started a third. "How is my audience?" he asked, not looking up. He was feeling much more cheerful now. Thanks to Garrick's advice he thought he was making some progress on this.

"Growing bored, m'lord," said Garrick. "There are only a couple of children. I should try the thumb now, if I were you."

"Right-oh."

After a great deal of holding the thumb out, walking about, squinting, peering at the canvas, then repeating the procedure, Garrick finally indicated that the last of the children had gone. He settled himself in the grass and began scrying.

He still didn't really expect to see anything. The "general unease" could have been anything at all, from a premonition of bad weather coming to ruin the harvest to some repercussions from what was going on over the Channel. And the first three drops he let fall into the bowl showed him nothing at all.

But the fourth . . . the fifth . . . the sixth . . .

Something was definitely disturbing the waters to the north and west—only a little, but the traces were there, and they didn't disappear no matter how many more drops fell into the bowl.

Since he had set his water and his scrying spell to look for one thing and one thing only, it was clear that Alderscroft had been right. It was not a wild goose chase.

There really was a necromancer, after all.

"Bloody hell," he said, looking up and seeing Garrick's expression of mingled shock and alarm.

"Well said, m'lord," Garrick replied, taking out a very white handkerchief and mopping his brow with it, in an uncharacteristic display of rattled nerves. "I could not have put it better myself."

8

HER father was watching her.

Even though Susanne hadn't seen him since that single interview, she *knew* he was watching her. She practically felt his eyes on her. There was always a shadow at his window when she went out, and when she was inside . . . well, he *was* an Earth Master. Robin hadn't yet taught her scrying, but she knew that all the Masters had the means of looking elsewhere—and sometimes looking into the past as well. He could be scrying her. He could also have some Elemental servant watching her. And if he had ordered that servant not to be seen, well, *she* wouldn't see it.

The feeling of being watched was so intense indoors that she had taken all her lessons outside. At least there, the sensation was diminished. Maybe he couldn't scry her as well when she was outside the shields she had placed around the Manor to contain the blight. Maybe her own Elemental friends warned off whatever creature he had spying on her. Whatever the reason, the relief was profound. What she would do when cold weather came . . . well, she was not sure. Perhaps by then she would have satisfied his requirements, and he would have sent her away to school. She certainly hoped so.

It had gotten bad enough after the first four days of the change in her status that she had begun to suspect he came into her room at night when she was asleep. She knew very well that just seemed insane. What possible reason could he have to do that?

Unless it was the same impulse that made parents look in on sleeping children, just to be sure they were safe. That was possible. It could be, now that he had awakened to his responsibilities as a parent, he was doing now what he should have been doing when she was small.

Or she was just imagining things. That was possible too. How could he possibly come into her room without waking her? She slept very lightly; she always had. That was one reason why she hadn't shared a room with Prudence and Patience. She didn't think it was possible for anyone to slip into her room without waking her.

Unless he wasn't doing so physically . . .

Nevertheless, it was . . . well, very uncomfortable, in a way she didn't quite understand. Time and time again, she wondered if it was just her imagination, yet time after time she could not shake the feeling that he was brooding over her all during his waking hours.

During the times when she was absolutely certain he had his eyes on her, it felt somehow unhealthy, obsessively wrong. Yet there was so much about her father that was wrong already that she tried to persuade herself that this was nothing more than another symptom of the terrible damage his heartbreak had done to him. After all, he had been a virtual hermit for two decades, seeing no one but Agatha, never leaving his rooms. She tried to persuade herself that he was trying to mend and heal, and, eventually, though he would have scars, it would come around right.

The problem was, it just didn't feel that way; it felt as if there were a huge part of this puzzle that she could not even guess at, as if she were one of the blind men trying to say what an elephant was like when all she could feel was the trunk.

In fact, it felt as though this was something that would never get better. Something fundamentally and deeply *wrong*.

It felt so very wrong, in fact, that she just didn't want him to know about her clearing. There was no way to prevent him from using magic to spy on her, but she didn't have to encourage it either. So instead of going to her clearing after that first day she went outside, she took her lessons to the orchard just outside the blighted area, outside those shields she had set up to contain the blight. He would still be able to see her physically, and that should keep him from using magic to keep track of her.

Without a telescope or binocular lenses he would not see her very well, but those white dresses stood out very well against the green grass. So he would know exactly where she was, if not exactly what she was doing—and that should keep him from going to more extreme measures.

The first day she did this, she still felt as if his eyes were on her the whole time, but it seemed they were his actual, physical eyes, not some proxy. She did her best to ignore it; after all, she wasn't doing anything that she was worried about him seeing, and if hc chose to spend his entire day peering at her from behind his curtains, well, she couldn't stop him.

Since then she had gone out every day as soon as she had breakfasted. There was no reason to go back to the house until suppertime, and she was very glad of that. Agatha put up good luncheons for her, and it was actually easier for her to concentrate out here. Even without the pressure of her father's regard, she found being stuck indoors to be stifling.

She leafed through a new book he had sent her, one on manners and deportment. And she made a little face over it. He assumed she didn't know any of this, and of course he was wrong. Servants had to know these things. Servants had to be even more polite than their masters.

From here she could see the girls hanging the laundry out to dry, and she felt a stab of guilt for not being there to help. But of course, that was impossible. After the first two days, she'd actually tried to lend a hand when Prudence came up to clean her room, and Prudence had been so horrified she'd stopped immediately.

Poor Prudence. It had to be her father's orders, of course, that Susanne be treated "properly." The poor thing was probably afraid that if he found out that his daughter had been cleaning grates, Prudence would find herself dismissed. And Prudence's family needed the wages. She was the eldest of eight and the only one in service.

She tried very hard not to hate her father for that. Suddenly, she was all alone; the new divide between her and the people who used to be her friends was extremely uncomfortable.

I understand why this is. I don't like it, and I don't agree with the reasons, but I understand. We aren't the same class. Of course, class is ridiculous, I am the same person I was before all this, and so are they. But Father is the master here in the Manor, and it is his rules we all must live by.

After three days of being out in the orchard, she had noticed something. There were times when she felt those unseen eyes on her fade away, sometimes for hours at a time. And the curious thing was, when that happened, the birds and animals that had kept their distance from her would then move in closer, the way she was used to having them act.

She kept a sharper watch, and finally she had the proof that it wasn't just her imagination; the animals were reacting to *something*. And if the animals felt it too, then this wasn't nerves or an active imagination; it meant that her father was not merely watching her, he was concentrating on her in a way that even a rabbit knew wasn't healthy.

She began to get angry at that point. There had been that lingering doubt, that perhaps she had been feeling unease about the change in her situation and ascribing that to her father, since after all, he had caused it. But . . . no. And this morning over breakfast she decided that she'd had enough. If he was going to spy on her, well, she was going to turn the tables on him.

"I'm going to trick him," she said to the robin that had come to sit on the edge of her rug and stare meaningfully at the basket that held her luncheon. "And serve him right, too. All these years, it has been *me* that has had the care of these lands, kept the earth healthy and sound. I'm the one that has taken care of all of the magic things that needed doing. And did he notice that someone else had stepped in after he ran away from his responsibilities and hid in his rooms to brood? No. Did he think to find out if anyone would? No. And now, oh, *now,* he uses his magic, and for what? To spy on me? He hasn't made one bit of effort to take up his duties again! And with all this spying, has he even noticed that it's *me* that is caring for everything? Has he noticed that I am an Earth magician *at all?*"

Giving voice to this raised her ire rather than cooling it. Saying these things out loud made her examine the injustice of it all, and she was so angry now, she would have given her father a right tongue-lashing if he'd been in front of her. After all, she wasn't just his daughter, she was his peer, his equal in magic, and he should have given her that much respect, instead of acting as if she were somehow feeble-minded because thanks to *his* neglect she didn't have the education proper to a girl of her station!

"Well, we'll show *him,"* she said to the bird. "And if he doesn't realize what I've done, well, the more fool he."

She assembled what she needed swiftly: a clean white handkerchief, a scrap of the dress she was wearing, snipped from an inside seam, a little earth moistened with her own blood, a single hair, an appleseed. She tied it all up tightly in the handkerchief, set it down in front of her, and concentrated. She built up in her own mind the image she had studied this morning in the mirror, all the while calling the Earth's slow power to her. She fed that power into the little packet, drop by drop, as she imposed her will and her image on it. She was a child of Earth, a Daughter of Eve. And she was going to create a reflection of herself.

She closed her eyes to concentrate better; she'd actually done this several times in the past, when she was much younger, and she had wanted to run off to the woods to play with Robin but didn't want to frighten Agatha. Robin had taught her how to make an image of herself, something that would repeat a single action over and over so that there was some movement and life although it wouldn't hold up to close scrutiny. She had loved to swing, so that was what she had the image do; and every time Agatha looked out, she would see what she thought was Susanne, swinging in the orchard, and be content, when Susanne was actually far, far from the Manor.

But that only had to fool ordinary folk. This would have to fool an Earth Master, at least at a distance. It not only had to look like her, it had to *feel* like her. It still wouldn't pass muster from up close, but he would never come out to look, and the others wouldn't come disturb Miss Susanne without direct orders from her father.

Finally she opened her eyes.

And looked into her own eyes.

The simulacrum stared at her, blankly. It was obvious the moment you got close and looked into those eyes; there was no intelligence there, no warmth, no real life. But no one was going to get close. Her father had put up a wall between herself and those who had been her friends, and *he* was not going to leave his rooms.

"Read," she told the thing, and it took one of the books and cast its eyes down, occasionally turning a page. She stared at it for several moments, and finally she was satisfied that it passed muster.

Before that *watched* feeling could return, she ran off deeper into the orchard, pausing only long enough to scatter some breadcrumbs for the robin, who accepted them as his due.

Once she was far enough under the trees that she was sure she couldn't be seen from the windows, she doubled back, this time using every bit of the stealth she had learned as a child, creeping and hiding from those who would demand she return to some tedious chore, like shelling peas.

She knew a dozen ways in and out of the Manor that did not require the use of doors, but there were only a few that could be negotiated when wearing a white dress. That was enough for now, and so she came around to the front of the Manor and all the disused rooms there, with furniture shrouded in sheets. The windows themselves were curtained heavily, and Agatha only went into them a few times a year to make sure that moths and mice were not getting into things.

She studied the front of the house, finding the window she wanted, one on the ground floor. This wasn't the first time she had wanted to come or go without anyone knowing. There, in the room that had probably, in days when the squire entertained, been used by the men to gather after dinner, was her best access: a window with a broken catch, a window that she kept meticulously lubricated and spotlessly clean. She should be able to get in and over the sill without snagging or dirtying her dress.

She scurried up to the side of the building and ducked in behind shrubbery that was rank and overgrown, leaves yellow and blighted. A piece of log she'd propped against the side of the building served as a stepping-stool; she slid the window up and climbed over the sill. She swung her legs over, dropped to the floor, and closed it again.

She paused in the gloom of the smoking room for a moment, stilling her own breath, and cast another simple spell. This one gave her hearing as keen as a rabbit—or a robin, who could hear an insect burrowing under the earth—or an owl, who knew exactly where the mouse scuttling through the grass was. As the magic settled in place, she heard the sounds of pots and pans, of cutlery, and laconic conversation. She identified Agatha, the cook, Patience, and Prudence. At this moment, all the house servants would be in the kitchen, preparing supper. This hadn't been true when she'd been one of them, but now, they were at least one pair of hands short, and other things that didn't matter so much—such as cleaning unused rooms—would just have to go undone. The men wouldn't come any farther into the house than the kitchen, and then only to be fed. No one would find her prowling about.

So there was only one person left to guard against ... one person and, just possibly, something that wasn't human. She had left her shoes and stockings in the orchard; her feet were so calloused and so unused to shoes, at least in the summer, that the soles were as hard as leather. Now she closed her eyes and invoked the power of the Earth again. This time she wrapped herself in another sort of magic, the kind that worked on the minds of those around her. Again, this was something that Robin had taught her, so that she could slip up unseen on the shyer of the forest creatures and spy on young hawks and owls in their nests without ending up with a face full of talons.

I'm not here, the magic whispered into those minds around her. *You see only what you expect to see.*

It wouldn't work if she made a noise; it also wouldn't work if someone expected to see her, or if she touched them. But for anything else, yes, it worked beautifully.

This spell, this magic, had a *feel* to it; it felt as if she had wrapped herself in a veil or a cloak. Sometimes she wondered if this was how the fairy stories of cloaks that granted invisibility had started.

When she felt herself shrouded in the magic, she moved, keeping close to the wall and taking step by slow, soundless step up to the second floor, and the part of the house where her father's rooms were.

Let's see how he likes being spied on. . . .

She listened closely at the door, pressing her ear against it, and heard ... nothing. Not even the sound of breathing. So unless her father was dead, and the eyes that had been upon her all this time were those of a ghost, there was no one in that first room.

Slowly, she turned the knob; slowly, she eased the door open. First, just a crack, which she put her eye to. Then, she opened it just enough so that she could slip inside. It was well oiled; she remembered once how Agatha grumbled about the master insisting that every hinge of every door, used or not, be kept oiled so that creaking wouldn't disturb him.

She closed the door behind her, kept her back tightly to the wall just inside, and looked around.

By now her eyes had adjusted to the gloom in this part of the house; the window was curtained so she wasn't staring into glare from darkness, and she was able to actually see the room she had been brought to by Agatha. This was obviously the study. There were books lining the walls, floor to ceiling. If there had ever been any objects on those bookshelves other than books, they were gone now. The only place where there were no bookshelves was above and to either side of the massive wooden mantel around the fireplace. Above the mantle, there was a place where a painting might have hung once, but now the wall was blank. There wasn't much in the way of furniture—a couch, two chairs, a desk in front of the window with a third chair behind it. The carpet, like the one in her room, was old and worn. She eased around to the doorway she saw on the other side of the room and peeked in.

A bedroom, This was like her own set of rooms, then: the study or sitting room and a bedroom. The bed was made, and the room was empty.

So where was her father?

Just as she wondered that, she heard the sound of creaking wood from what she had thought was a wall full of bookshelves on the right of the fireplace. Even as she watched, her mouth falling open with surprise, the bookshelves moved—

No! It was a false wall, and the bookshelves were actually mounted on a *door!*

She held her breath and ducked around the frame of the doorway into the bedroom, sure she was about to be discovered.

But instead, her father strode impatiently into the room, looked about, muttered something, and seized a book from the desk and went back into the opening behind the shelves. The door swung closed, and she heard a latch click.

She hurried out, scarcely knowing what to think.

Except—there was a secret room. What that could mean she couldn't imagine. All that she knew for certain was that she needed to get back to the orchard and dismiss the simulacrum. Or rather, dispel the image. She was going to keep that little bundle because she was going to need it again.

There was a great deal more going on here than she had thought. No one among the servants knew about this room. Now, perhaps her father was using it for the practice of magic. It certainly had been a secret for a lot longer than she had been alive, because Agatha had been here for forty years at least, and she would have known all about a newly built "secret" room.

But if he was practicing magic, it certainly wasn't in the course of his responsibility as the local Earth Master, because there had been no stir in the Earth magic hereabouts, no rumors among the Elementals, and no shift in her own protections and spells.

So what was he doing in there? And why?

So father is keeping secrets? Whatever they were . . . she was going to uncover them. She had a right to know. And if they had to do with magic—she had a responsibility to find out what they were.

There was more than enough moonlight to see well in her clearing. She had slipped out of the Manor again, once everyone was asleep, and come straight here. She knew how to call Robin when the need was urgent, and she had done that tonight; she pinned an oak and an ash leaf together with a thorn, impressed her need on them, and called one of the fauns and asked him to find Robin as quickly as he could.

Robin had come. And she had made her request.

"Why do you want to know true invisibility?" Robin asked, looking at her oddly. "It's not easy magic. Humans take years, decades, to master it."

She frowned. "I don't have years." She had never been less than scrupulously honest with him and now was not the time to change that. "I discovered something. My father has a secret room in that house and he was in it today . . . Robin, I don't know *why*. I only know that I have to find out how to get in there. I have to know what he's hiding. I think it's important. And the only way I can do that is to become invisible, because I can't let him catch me doing it."

Robin scratched his head. There were Gypsies passing through, and today he looked like one of them: curly black hair, big dark eyes, skin as brown as if he'd stained it with walnut hulls. "Well," he said, finally, "I think you're right. And I have no power inside houses, so I can't tell you what's in that place. Wanting to be invisible though, that's quite a different matter from learning the magic. And that, I can help you with, better invisibility than any mortal can manage." He felt around in his belt pouch. "Here," he said, finally, pulling out a ring made of finely woven horsehair. "That will give you invisibility five times." He handed it to her. "Put it on; that's all you need do. Take it off to be seen again. After the fifth time, it will fall to dust, and you'll have to come back to me for another."

She took the ring and impulsively kissed his cheek. "Robin, *thank* you!"

"Eh," he said, with a shrug and a grin, "Those are things I keep about to give to folks as want to do a bit of mischief. Made some for my Gypsy friends so they can snare some coneys, maybe take a hen or two. They know who I'll let them rob and who to leave be. And they know they had best not confuse one with the other." He sobered. "I think you are right, though. There's something very wrong about the man that is your father, and the keys to it must be in that secret place. Be more careful than you ever have in your life when you do this, though. Something warns me that you do not dare be caught."

🍂

Four times, Susanne had put on the horsehair ring. Four times she had left her image in the orchard—an image now strengthened by Robin himself—and slipped into her father's rooms to watch him.

The first three times, she had caught only part of the trick to getting behind that bookcase. But today she had been close enough to him to watch as he pulled out three books one after the other; they were false ones, nothing more than empty fronts. He had reached over the top and pulled a lever behind those false fronts. She'd heard a *click,* then watched him put his fingers behind a particular place in the side of the bookcase and pull. This time there had been no creaking of wood; he must have oiled or tightened something.

Tonight she had waited until the house was quiet before putting on the ring for the fifth and final time and slipping up the stairs. The best time to get into that room was going to be when her father was asleep. Turnabout, again. If he was going to spy on her sleeping, well, she could prowl his secret room while *he* slept.

But she knew how quiet he could be; she was going to make certain he was asleep before she tried.

To her utter shock and relief, she discovered something else about that ring that Robin hadn't told her about. The moment she slipped it on, she could *see,* see as well as a cat in the dark! Everything was in tones of dim gray, like twilight without any blue in it. This was going to make things much, much easier.

She opened her own door and closed it behind her. She had left the image working at her desk, under a single lamp, as if she couldn't sleep. With movements that were beginning to feel like routine, she moved soundlessly down the hall and listened at his door.

Not a sound.

She eased the door open; the study was empty. She entered and hurried across to the bedroom door, which was closed. She listened intently with the help of her spell, and heard slow, deep breathing.

Well, she would have *preferred* snores, but . . . it sounded as if he was asleep. And she was not going to take the chance of waking him to crack the door and find out.

She hurried back across the room; she found the three books and pulled them out in the right order; this time she heard a very faint sound as she pulled out the third one, not quite a *click,* more as if a bolt had been slid back. When she reached in behind them, she felt a lever; she pulled it down, and felt no resistance. Now she heard that *click,* and she put her hands on the place where she had seen her father put his. Beneath the molding, she felt something like a latch. She squeezed, and pulled, and slowly the hidden door swung open.

Suppressing a grin of triumph, she examined the other side; she was going to have to shut this thing, and the last thing she wanted to find out was that she had accidentally locked herself in!

But no, the opening mechanism on the other side was simple enough, a latch and a door handle. She pulled the bookcase closed behind herself, turned, and surveyed the room.

It was full of bookcases and the dusty smell of old paper. *A library?* Why would there be a secret library here?

What could be the need to keep books hidden away like this?

There were a few books piled on a little table right by the door; probably books her father had been reading. She picked one up, and carried it to the window, hoping there was enough light to read it by.

It was handwritten, and touching it gave her an odd,

queasy feeling. She peered at it but was completely unable to decipher the peculiar, and very small, writing.

She put it back and picked up another, which made her feel even stranger when she touched it. It, too, was hand-written, but this was a different handwriting, a bit larger, a bit clearer, but still impossible to decipher in the uncertain light. She was going to pick up a third, when she heard the latch at the door starting to move.

Quickly she backed into the shadowed corner next to the window. There weren't any books here, so it was un-likely her father was going to come in this direction. She was consumed with both fear and excitement—now she just might find out what he was up to, but he *was* a Master, and she just might get caught.

She had no idea what he would do if he *did* catch her, but she doubted it would be pleasant. Punish her in some way, probably—

But the door swung open, leaving her no more time to speculate.

Her father looked as if he had been sleeping in his cloth-ing; he wore a rumpled jacket and trousers, and his hair was unkempt. He ignored the table beside the door, instead moving farther into the room, his steps slow but steady.

He hadn't seen her; hadn't noticed her. Marvelous.

Cautiously, moving without so much as a whisper of sound, she followed him.

On the other side of the bookshelves, there was a kind of alcove built into the wall, with a curtain over it. This was where he was standing, lighting candles on either side of it. Then he parted the curtain, and the light from the candles revealed that the curtain had hidden a portrait, a painting.

A painting—of *her*?

It certainly looked like her!

She stared, mouth agape with shock. It was a portrait of the head and shoulders, the background dark draperies. The young woman in the painting was wearing a white summer dress and gazing slightly off to one side. Her hair was knotted low on the back of her neck, exactly the way Susanne wore hers. It didn't look anything like any of the other young women hereabouts . . . and if it *wasn't* her, then who could it possibly be?

How had he gotten a painting of her?

All she could think, in a somewhat dazed fashion, was that he had gotten it made magically . . .

"It won't be long now, my lovely," her father murmured aloud, touching the painted face. "Not long at all. Days, no more. I'm nearly ready; at moon-dark all will be prepared. And once I'm done, I'll take you to Italy. I have already gotten an agent to rent us a villa; he swears to me that the staff is old and incurious but hard working. It will be just the two of us. We'll make love until you can't think of anything but me—"

As Susanne listened in horror, her father continued on in this vein, describing what he had planned, which were *certainly* things no father should even dream of doing to his daughter, not even in the depths of delirium! Her entire insides knotted up as she listened to him, and for what seemed to be an eternity, she was frozen where she stood. Her stomach cramped, she began to tremble, knees shaking. She nearly threw up then and there, listening to him describe what he was going to do.

He's going to take me to Italy? And . . . oh dear Lord in Heaven!

Finally, as his fingers traced the painted bosom, she managed to shake off some of her shock; her revulsion overcame her paralysis, and she was able to retreat, step by careful step, to the door that was still open.

Once out in the sitting room, it was all she could do to keep herself from tearing open the door to the hallway and bolting. With shaking hands, she eased the door open, slipped out, and eased it closed again. She was hot and cold by turns, and she fought dizziness. She stole a precious moment to steel herself; this was no time to give way to the vapors. It took tremendous willpower, but she managed to slow her hammering pulse, banish the urge to sit down. Then she tiptoed as quickly as she could to her own room. Because she wasn't going to spend one more minute under this roof! She had to get away, and get away quickly; once he knew she was gone, her father would start a hunt for her, and she would need every yard of distance she could put between them.

Quickly she went through the wardrobe and found her old clothing, frugally stored in the back as she had asked—Agatha had finally seen the wisdom of keeping it, in case she might have to do something that would ruin her pretty new things. Now . . . those pretty things made her skin crawl, and she couldn't be rid of them fast enough. She stripped herself to the skin and redressed in minutes—the lack of corsets and fancy undergarments made things so much faster. She glanced around the room; other than her old clothing, there was nothing else here she wanted. It was all from *him,* and the idea of having any of it touch her now made her want to vomit.

The ring was still on her hand—she was still invisible. Good!

She paused for a moment. Should she leave her image? It might delay pursuit . . .

No, she dared not leave anything so personal in her father's hands. She stuck the packet into the middle of the bundle, resolving to burn it at the first opportunity, and instead, made a rough dummy in the bed with pillows and clothing. That would have to do. And she thanked God and his angels that nothing, nothing that she would leave behind had enough of "her" on it to allow him to cast magic from a distance on her.

She bundled her remaining clothing, her old shoes and stockings, and the comb and brush she had been using into her old shawl, then tied the sleeves of her winter coat around her waist, and slipped out into the hall and down the stairs. She could drink stream water, but until she could get far enough away to feel safe from pursuit, she would have to carry what she needed to eat. Which meant, much as she hated to, she would have to steal.

The night-vision that came with the ring made it possible to get things without fumbling or lighting a candle. After working in the kitchen for so many years, she knew exactly where everything was. Within a few minutes, she had half a loaf of bread, some sausage and cheese, a couple of meat pasties, a knife, an old cup with a chipped rim, a box of matches, and a little tin pot. Those went into her bundle as well. Then she slipped the latch and went outside.

Then the horror really took hold of her, and she ran.

Somewhere deep inside, she knew the wisdom of following the actual road. Even though it was the obvious way to go, she also would not leave any trace of her passing on the hard-packed dirt, and thanks to the ring she could see where she was going in the moonlight as if it were broadest day. And on the road, her skirt wouldn't hamper her. So she ran, ran until she reached the little village, then paused for a moment on the edge of it, bent over with her hands on her knees, panting.

It was late; there wasn't a single light showing. She couldn't stop here though—no, everyone here knew her, and no one would believe such a wild story if she dared to tell them. They'd just return her to her father—

So after she paused to tie her bundle on her back instead of carrying it, she ran through the village, past the well in the middle of the square, past the church she attended every Sunday, past the Nonconformist Chapel, and out again. Not even a dog barked at her. Now she was as far from home as she had ever gone, and she continued to run, heading eastward on blind instinct.

The road stretched out ahead of her, bordered on either side by a hedge as high as her head. It felt like a nightmare, actually, the sort where something unseen was behind and ahead was a road that never ended. She ran until she couldn't run anymore, slowed to a walk (but didn't stop) until she caught her breath, and ran again.

A break in the hedges opened out onto the moor, and she took it. The moor was open, and the grass was easier on her bare feet than the road. She paused only long enough to tie her skirt up above her knees, then started running again.

It seemed she had been running forever; she had an ache in her side and was panting like a racehorse. And even then she kept moving. Once, she disturbed a flock of sheep, which were alarmed by scenting a human they couldn't see and bumbled away from her in the darkness, making little *baas* of distress. Once, she ran into a small family of wild moor ponies, which outright bolted when they smelled her.

Finally, just as the first gray light of dawn lightened the sky, she stumbled down into a grove of trees at the bottom of a hill; that was when she heard the sound of running water, and suddenly aware of how parched she was, she followed it until she discovered a tiny trickle of a stream.

That was exactly what she needed. Shelter, water, a place to hide. And this place should be far enough from the Manor that no one would expect a mere female to have gotten this far. Especially not since she had been running most of the way.

She filled her cup and drank until she couldn't hold any more, then found a good spot under some low-growing bushes to get some rest. She padded it out with grass and bracken and spread her other skirt over it. She tied her food up in the bush just over her head to keep the insects out of it, made a pillow of the rest of her clothing, and finally laid herself down, curled into a tight little ball.

Still, there was one thing that she could not leave to chance. The ring might or might not last much longer—but she needed more concealment than simple invisibility would provide now.

She cast a spell of protection and distraction over herself, extending it into the Unseen as well as the Seen world. Granted, this would also hide her from her Elemental allies, even Robin, but—

Well, Robin could easily withstand her father, but the lesser Elementals? Many of them could not. And when he knew she was gone, it would be natural to send them hunting. She had to keep herself hidden from them as well, at least until she could get past his reach. The clothing she had left behind had not gotten enough of her energy imprinted on it to do him any good, so he would have to rely on the Elementals to find her now that she was off Manor lands. The farther she was from the Manor, the harder it would be for him to control and direct them—so what she could muster now would probably be enough to shield her. And tomorrow, well, she would be farther away still.

When she was sure that her concealing magic was as strong and sound as she could make it, then she let herself go and fell into the sleep of utter exhaustion that had been waiting for her, just as a distant rooster heralded the first rays of the sun on the horizon.

9

SUSANNE had always had a knack for waking completely aware and alert, and that knack did not fail her now. It certainly helped that she usually slept very lightly. She went from sleeping to waking in less than a minute, with perfect recollection of where she was, how she had gotten here, and everything that had transpired last night, all before she actually opened her eyes.

When she did, she moved very slowly, observing as much as she could from her hiding place under the bush first, and listening as hard as she could.

It seemed quiet enough. There were birds and perhaps a small animal or two nearby; she could hear soft chirps and twitters and the faint noises of something moving through the dead leaves. So, unless her father had learned how to stop frightening the wildlife with his magic, he hadn't found her yet.

She dared to let out her breath in a sigh and uncurl herself enough to get a better look around.

She was alone in this little stand of trees and bushes; if

there were any animals about, they couldn't be much bigger than mice.

She untied her food and crawled out from beneath the bushes, taking her things with her. Her mouth tasted . . . nasty. There were twigs in her hair. And her skirt and shirt-waist were very much the worse for all that running last night.

But she spotted a patch of wild mint and picked some leaves to scrub her teeth with; more leaves went into the little pot along with water from the stream. Mint would help settle the nausea she still felt every time she thought about the things her father had been saying. It was probably safe to stay here long enough to make some mint tea and eat something—and, not incidentally, burn that image-bundle.

Less than an hour later, she emerged from the grove as tidy as she could make herself and looked around.

There was nothing to be seen but the rolling moors and the sky, dotted with white clouds not unlike flocks of sheep. The moors stretched on all sides, patchy greens and browns and swaths of purple where the heather was in bloom, and cut across by distant lines and patches of deeper green that marked where there were trees. She had put out her fire and scattered the ashes to the winds; now it was time to move on. She had run eastward last night, so eastward it would be from now on. The most important thing she could do right now was to put distance between herself and her father.

There were farms and even villages out there, and some might be not too distant, but like the Manor and her home village they could be hidden in a fold of land, and she'd not see them until she was right atop them.

She set out resolutely—though now she wore her shoes and stockings instead of carrying them. She'd been incredibly lucky last night not to have cut her feet on a flint. She wouldn't press that luck any further. Her winter coat was now part of the bundle on her back as well.

About the time she had finished scattering the ashes of her fire—and her image-bundle—she had felt the horsehair ring on her finger start to unravel. In moments, it had gone to dust. She tried not to regret losing it too much; it had gotten her this far, and that was more than she'd had any right to expect. For that matter, there was no telling if it had disintegrated because it had been protecting her from her father's magic while she slept.

She wished she dared call Robin, but that would probably expose her to her father. Other Elementals would certainly "hear" that call, and at this point she had no doubt that some would be under her father's coercion to report any trace of her.

So, the best thing she could do would be to hold that "I am not here" spell tightly about herself and hope for the best.

Last night the road had been her best route away; now, however, it was to be avoided. It was midmorning by the sun, and at this point everyone in the Manor would know she had run away, even if they had no idea why. With all the best intentions in the world, her friends would collude with her father to find her and bring her back. They would all assume, because she was just a female, that she would stick to the road—or at least, that was what she expected of them. Since anyone coming from the Manor or the village would be *looking* for her, her spell wouldn't work on them.

So for at least today and possibly tomorrow, travel would be the hard way, cutting across country.

This was going to be difficult.

It was all very well for the papers and magazines to talk blithely about hiking on the moors for pleasure—pleasure walkers had maps and haversacks full of provisions and tools, and they expected to spend each night warmly tucked up in a bed in an inn or even a hotel. And they had proper boots for such walks. She had a little food, no money, and a pair of worn old shoes meant for wearing indoors, and she dared not stop at inns or even farmhouses.

"'Tis what 'tis," she said aloud, and resolutely headed east.

By midafternoon, she was tired, hot, and had been forced to make long detours to avoid the road three times. Unfortunately, those detours had taken her miles out of her way—if she could be said to have a "way"—and, more importantly, had taken her away from watercourses she could only stare longingly at. Then, just as she was beginning to think she would have to dare the road, she had struck upon another tiny stream and had finally stopped to have a rest and some food.

Once sitting down, she took an inventory of that food, and she grimaced. She'd been fair starving when she stopped, but it was clear that her provisions were meager indeed. *Two more days, three at the most.* She didn't have the skill to snare rabbits or even catch fish. If she didn't want to starve, at the end of that time she would have to hope that she was far enough away from her father that no one would be hunting her, and she could safely try to find someone who would hire her. Another thing to worry about.

Worry about it when you get that far. What is important now is distance, she reminded herself. And with a faint groan, she got to her feet and resumed her walk.

Roads took the easy route; roads had bridges, and roads were relatively smooth and even. She had to trudge through grass and weeds that were knee-high, stumbling over unseen stones, and while heather was very lovely at a distance, it was scratchy and dense and hard to force your way through. Down and up slopes whose grasses and heather hid more rocks for you to turn your ankles on, and roots to trip you, this was hard work made all the harder by sun beating down on you and clouds of midges to plague you.

When her path intersected another watercourse near sunset, she gratefully took shelter in the trees that lined it. This time she had a chance to pick a good spot for her bed and to make a kind of crude mattress of springy gorse with a cushion of grasses over the top of that; then she made another batch of unsweetened mint tea. And despite being quite used to hard work, she found that she was quite unused to walking all day over rough ground; as she settled down on her bed to eat, the aches began. And not a willow tree in sight, either.

At least she was fairly certain she'd be undisturbed. The only predators to fear out here were the human ones, and she hadn't seen a single soul all day. In fact, she hadn't even seen a flock of sheep all day. And if her legs and back ached, at least she was entirely without that feeling of constantly being watched!

There was, as everyone was fond of saying, a lot of moor . . . and she was one very small creature upon it, moreover, a creature that was trying very hard not to be seen. An Air Master would have had a much better chance of finding her; sylphs moved quickly, and she could never have completely hidden her presence as she crossed the open expanses. But Earth Elementals did not move quickly, and . . . well, she just might have gotten beyond his reach, today.

If he still had not found her by the end of tomorrow, then she would be certain that, at last, she was safe.

By sunset the next day, she was certain enough she had gotten beyond pursuit to dare the roads and weary enough that she needed to. Once again she had spent an unrestful night, compounded by her aching back and legs. Storms had been blowing up all day, and although she had managed to avoid most of them, she sensed her luck was running out. She was completely exhausted from outrunning the rain; she knew she didn't dare get caught by the storms, because she didn't dare get sick, and she'd actually had to run nearly as much to avoid storm clouds blowing up behind her as she had to get away the night of her escape.

And then, just as the sun began to crawl below the horizon, barely a blot of red behind thick cloud cover that spread out as far as she could see, covering a good third of the sky, her luck came back in again. Because there was a wall ahead of her, and a wall meant buildings and people.

Moreover, there were gates in that wall, and they weren't locked, as she proved by pushing open the first one she came to.

But there was more to it than that; the moment she crossed the boundary, she sensed—

Magic. *Her* sort of magic. It was a little like stepping out into a warm meadow with the earth comforting under her feet and the scent of wildflowers in the air. Someone here was an Earth mage, and that someone was using his—or her—magic for the good of the land, just as she did. It felt clean, wholesome; for a moment she clung to the wall as her entire self responded to that magic as if she had been parched and been offered cool, sweet water.

Whoever this was—no one like this would ever turn her over to her father. Nor could her father hide his darkness from them. No matter what happened, even if she was not welcomed here, she would not be betrayed.

She used the dregs of her fading energy to enforce the magic of not-being-seen as she finally approached the largest building she had ever seen in her life—and all the associated outbuildings. This *had* to be someone important's great country estate . . .

And maybe, if she could manage to get herself cleaned up in the morning, she could get herself hired here.

Oh . . . please. It was a prayer of sorts. If only—she could be happy here, whatever menial capacity she was in! This was *so* unlike the blight that had hung over the Manor, and whatever ugly, tainted stuff her father was meddling in, that it felt like a glimpse of paradise. *Please . . . please let me stay.*

But a warning rumble of thunder told her that if she didn't want to look like a half-drowned vagabond or, worse, come down with pneumonia, she was going to have to get under a roof. Now.

She chose the building that looked the least occupied and stole toward it, eyes darting everywhere, on the watch for anyone who might catch her. Since there was a magician—or more than one—there was that much more danger that her ever-eroding spell would run up against someone who could see through it. She didn't want to present herself as the ragged fugitive who had been sleeping rough on the moor for the past three days—and looked it. She wanted to present herself as a neat and tidy, clean and capable potential worker.

Her luck held. The threat of a storm must have driven everyone inside, and she slipped into the building without encountering a soul. In the last of the light, she saw that this was not a stable, as she had thought, but a carriage house. There were still two carriages here, but most of it was empty except for three motorcars at the far end.

The carriages, and the motorcars, tempted her almost past bearing. There would be padded seats inside them, the closest thing to a bed she had seen in three days. But inside a motorcar, she would be trapped if someone came in. Better to find a dark corner, perhaps one of the stalls.

But then she saw something even better. A pile of lap rugs heaped up on a storage chest, right next to some packing crates full of straw. In the last of the light, she made herself a bed using both; then, as the storm broke and thunder shook the walls, she ate the last of her food and wrapped the warm rugs around herself with every intention of concentrating on making herself as close to invisible as she could.

But a full stomach and a truly soft and warm place to lie in—and the comforting aura of nurturing Earth magic about her—all conspired to ambush her. She had not even begun her spell-spinning when her eyes closed of their own accord, and she fell deeply, dreamlessly asleep.

Only to awaken abruptly and with a start, to find the building full of sunlight and four sets of eyes staring down at her—two equine, with indifference, and two human, with bemusement.

One of the grooms-turned-mechanic had come to fetch Charles and Peter just as they were about to go out for a canter by way of a change from Peter's impersonation of an artist.

"Eh, Marster Charles, tha's got a sleeper in auto barn," he said, without any sort of preamble. "'Tis a wench."

"Young wench or old? Cleanly or slattern?" Charles asked, immediately turning his horse's head toward the part of the carriage house where the autos were kept.

"Cleanly, an' middlin'," the groom said immediately. Charles nodded.

"Come along, old chap," he said to Peter. "We'll have a look at her."

So they found themselves looking down on a young woman bundled into lap rugs meant for winter journeys. She looked worn and a little disheveled, but as the groom had suggested, clean. Her clothing suggested she had seen better days, or at least more prosperous ones. The fabric was very good, suggesting that she'd remade some hand-me-down from someone well off. She had a good face in repose: dark, nearly black hair, aristocratic nose, good cheekbones, and a firm chin. He wondered what color her eyes were—then got an immediate answer when they flew open.

Blue.

"Don't be alarmed," Charles said immediately. "We've no intention of driving you off. This is Branwell Hall. I'm Charles Kerridge. And I assume you are looking for work?"

The young woman sat up slowly, then got to her feet and gave a little deferential •curtsy. "Begging your pardon, m'lord," she said, instantly. "Aye, m'lord, come looking for work. Didn't mean to trespass here, but I been crossing moor, 'twere dark when I got here, and yon storm—"

"Oh, nonsense," Charles replied, waving his hand. "The gates are unlocked and that *was* a wicked storm last night. Since you aren't from Branwell Village, you couldn't have known that you could present yourself at the kitchen any time if you're looking for work."

"I *am,* m'lord!" she said eagerly, looking up at both of

them, directly in their eyes. "Been working for an old man, he died, here I be, no job and no one to give me a character. I'm a plain housekeeper, plain cook, kitchen maid, good in yon dairy—"

"Jill of all simple trades eh?" Charles interrupted her. "Excellent. Just run off to the kitchen, we can use another dairymaid, Cook told me that weeks ago. Tell Cook I said to take you on trial." Charles smiled at her, and she looked dazzled for a moment. "You'll find the kitchen that way," he continued, pointing, by way of a hint.

She shook herself out of her daze, bent, and picked up a bundle from among the rugs, then curtsied again. "Aye, m'lord," she said hastily. "Thank you, m'lord."

Charles didn't wait for her to withdraw, although she scampered off like a puppy after a stick; instead, he urged his horse back toward the door. Peter followed.

"Do you always do that?" Peter asked curiously, once they were out of the building. "Offer strays a job?"

Charles nodded absently, as if there were something else occupying him. "Usually. If they're up to no good, the offer of work generally makes them do a bunk, and if they're honest, they're grateful. But in this case, Peter, it would have been a crime to turn her away! Didn't you *feel* it?"

"Feel what?" Peter asked, reflecting that at the moment the one thing he was feeing was *thick*.

"Magic! Earth magic! The girl is an Earth mage!" Charles exclaimed. "She's heavily shielded, but there's no doubt in my mind. As soon as she realizes what she's stepped into, she'll fit in here in no time." Charles looked to Peter as if he were going to start rubbing his hands together in glee at any moment.

"Oh," Peter said, blankly. Then, "Oho! That was what I was—"

But Charles snorted. "Don't pretend you were sensing Earth magic, Peter, old man. I saw you. The girl is a hand— some thing, I'll admit to you, and I don't blame you for looking, but she's not to be meddled with. We might have a wild past, but this is the twentieth century. You can't trifle with her, and you certainly can't marry her, so it's best not to think about her at all."

For one moment, Peter was taken aback. In the next moment, it was a good thing that Charles had ridden on ahead, because he was consumed with outrage. How *dare* Charles suggest that he would—

And then the outrage was replaced by a more impersonal indignation. Just what kind of arrogant blighter was Charles Kerridge, saying "You certainly can't marry her"? Not that Peter was interested in marrying anyone at all but, since when was Charles Kerridge so much loftier than this girl? For all Charles knew, she was a better magician than he was! And what was wrong with—

Then the indignation ran out too. *Everything is wrong with the idea,* he thought bitterly. It was that old double standard of "gentry" and everyone else, and never mind that attitude should have died with a stake in its heart ages ago. The fact was it was alive and well.

Take Peter himself, for instance. Oh, it was all very well for people like him to run about the Continent and toy with opera singers and ballet dancers and professional courtesans, but the arrangements were always perfectly understood by both parties, and the boundaries were established from the beginning. There were generous presents, generous living arrangements, and generosity when the time came for the arrangement to end. But there was no talk of marriage.

Despite certain aging peers making a habit of marrying actresses, these were *aging* peers, with no other family, and these days people were amused rather than scandalized. But if someone Peter's age and rank even hinted at an interest that was anything other than irregular, there would be hell to pay.

And to show a similar interest in servants? His mother's outrage would last until Everest melted. There would be more trouble than he could sort out in a year. All very well for the squire to marry the Poor But Honest Country Lass in some romantic bit of fluff, but the plain truth was, it was impossible. She'd never fit in. She'd be snubbed by the other women in Charles' circle; country society was even more backward in that regard than London society. Her former peers would be insufferably jealous and hateful. Her life would be confined to Branwell Hall.

So incredibly unfair. Because if she was strong enough to have shielded her magic from *him,* she'd have made a perfect partner for Charles—

Oh, good lord, now I'm matchmaking, he realized with chagrin.

"Well, if we can tame this one down quickly enough, she might be able to provide me with the information I need," he said, urging his horse up beside Charles.

"She's certainly stronger than I am," he agreed. "It will be a matter of winning her trust, though, and seeing just how trained she is. *I* don't recognize her, I doubt Alderscroft knows of her, so she might be entirely self-taught, which could be less than useful."

"And she might run off when she realizes she won't be able to steal the butter," Peter added glumly. "Just because she's pretty and an Earth mage, it doesn't signify that she's honest."

Charles grinned. "Do I detect a sadder-but-wiser tale behind your words?"

Peter snorted. "*Moi? Mais non!* I was as wise in the wicked ways of the world when you were still in your cradle, my lad. Just reflecting on the failings of mankind." He rubbed the side of his nose as their horses ambled off down a shaded lane. "Mankind, be it noted, not womankind. No, her tale has the sad ring of truth to it. I can certainly imagine someone hired out to an irascible old skinflint who dies without making any provision for her. I just hope she really does have the skills she claims, for her sake as well as yours."

Susanne wasn't sure where that story about an old man dying and leaving her without a place came from; it just popped into her head, and she recited it with (she hoped) the conviction of the honest. The story certainly explained away everything that needed to be explained, and in a reasonable fashion. The moors were dotted with reclusive old men with just enough money to hire a single girl to "do" for them, and girls like Patience and Prudence were often desperate enough to take any work at all, never thinking ahead to what would happen when their employer died. By the time Susanne got to the kitchen door, she had her story firmly in her head.

The door was open, and inside was all abustle with preparations — not for breakfast, for that was long over, and the cleaning up for that meal was half done — but for luncheon. She opened her mouth to say something, when someone who wasn't the cook spotted her.

"Tha must be Mary's eldest, Jane, and thee's come not a moment too early!" the woman exclaimed, and the next thing that Susanne knew, she was enveloped in a bleached, clean apron and elbow-deep in bread dough, doing the kneading before the second rising. No sooner had she finished that than she was presented with a mammoth bowl of potatoes to be peeled for boiling, and when those were done, with another mammoth bowl of turnips to be mashed for the "downstairs" meal. She set to all of these tasks with rising cheer; she knew she was good at them, and she was going to make a good impression by helping without complaint and even without being officially taken on!

It was only when the gentry's food was sent upstairs and the "downstairs" meal laid out on the now-clean kitchen table that anyone actually took a good look at her.

"Mercy me, thee's not Jane!" exclaimed someone at Cook's end of the table.

For a moment she, and they, stared at one another. She cleared her throat and put on her broadest accent. "Eh!" she said. "I come across moor, when Marster died an' left me nowt, not even a character. I come lookin' for work. Marster Charles said I was to let Cook know to try me in dairy."

The Cook looked her up and down, then smiled. "Well, 'tis true tha' didn't sneak away from a mort of hard work. Thee's not the first Marster Charles sent here. Thee's a good hand in kitchen. We'll try thee in dairy. But first, thee's earned tha nuncheon."

The kitchen maids on the bench nearest her grinned at her and scooted over, making room for her. Someone found her a plate, a cup, and some cutlery, and then the cheerful chatter, like a tree full of starlings, began.

The ones nearest her plied her with questions about where she had come from and what she had done until they were satisfied and turned back to their own gossip. Susanne was quite sure that Cook's sharp ears caught every word of her answers, and she was pleased to find that the others made sure to include her in the gossip by explaining who they were talking about as they twittered. Susanne was careful to keep her story as simple as possible; she had been taking care of an old man who never saw anyone and lived in a lone farmhouse out on the moor to the east. Her mother had hired her off; Susanne borrowed Prudence's family shamelessly for that part of the tale. Yes, she had done something of everything for the old man. A cousin had turned up when he died and turned her out. No, she couldn't go back home, there were too many mouths to feed as it was. Everyone nodded at that. So she had come across the moor to find another place.

From there, her story swerved right into the path of pure truth. She talked about making her way across the moor with her meager belongings, sleeping rough. She spoke of outracing the storms, elaborating on it as the eyes of the other maids widened. She talked of finding the unlocked gate and hoping this was a sign she could find a place.

She deviated from truth a little, then, claiming she had stumbled into the carriage house when the deluge began;

no one begrudged her taking shelter without leave when a storm like *that* one was raging.

In return she heard all about who was courting, who was marrying, who was "no better than she should be"—the latter seemed to be confined to a couple of girls in the village of Branwell—that the vicar was well-liked but his wife "had a tongue in her head," and that there was a most intriguing visitor here.

"Oh, Quality! A lord!" exclaimed one of the girls. "Lord Peter Almsley, Master Charles' old friend from Oxford! And a nicer gemmun you could never ask for! His man, too, polite as polite!"

"Aye, Garrick's a favorite here," the cook murmured, her eyes twinkling. "Were I twenty years younger—" she sighed theatrically, and the girls giggled.

But there was another undercurrent here, one she sensed by what they were *not* saying. Every time the subject of conversation got around to anything that might lead to hints of magic, there was a quick veer into something else altogether. Susanne was too used to dancing that dance herself not to see them doing it.

Which either meant they were *all* geased against talking about the subject, or they were keeping her from getting any hints of it. She rather doubted the former, but the latter?

With narrowed eyes, she assessed her fellow diners. One by one, she looked for signs of magic on them.

It was with considerable shock that she realized that at least part of the strength of the magic hereabouts was in these unassuming people!

Oh, they weren't very strong, but there were a great many of them, and a bucket could as easily be filled drop-by-drop as by a barrel. All it took was time—

Just as she wondered if she should show her own colors, Cook clapped her hands to get their attention.

"All right now, I've given thee a bit extra time because we have a new girl. But the work needs doing." She stated it as a fact, rather than as an order, but the reaction she got would have done justice to the troops of a great general. Everyone got up off the benches, took their plates to the sink, and went straight to work.

One of the girls—Susanne was pretty sure her name was Polly—came and tugged on her hand. "Cook wants thee in dairy, 'tis what I do too," she said.

"We will be milking?" she asked.

Polly laughed. "Lord love thee, nay," she said. "The herdsmen do that. Just dairy."

Susanne was a bit relieved that there was to be no milking; there were always cows that seemed to take it into their heads to be the very devil whenever they were milked.

As she knew, when it wasn't a small place with only a couple of milk-cows, the chief business of a dairymaid was to *clean,* not just ordinary surface cleaning. Every bit of the dairy was scrubbed twice daily at a minimum, because the least little bit of foulness could, and probably would, contaminate milk, cream, butter and all, and spoil it. Polly would have taken care of the morning scrub, but it was afternoon now, and it was all to do over again to get ready for the evening milking. So first they scrubbed with ash and water, floors and walls. Then they changed to a different set of brushes and scalded and scrubbed the milk-pans from the stack—they were already clean, but you skipped this step at your peril. They scalded all the tools, scrubbed and scalded the churns, scalded the very brushes they had been using to scrub with. Then they scrubbed their hands and arms, put on enormous clean aprons, so big they were practically dresses, and went to the rising-room where the milk from the previous day and this morning waited in its flat pans. The cream had risen satisfactorily on the former; she and Polly loosened it from the edge of the pan by running a clean finger around the inside, then, as Polly watched critically, Susanne took a skimmer and began to take the cream off the top of the milk. When Polly was satisfied that Susanne knew what she was doing, she tackled her own set of pans.

"Will we be churning?" Susanne asked, as she transferred the cream into her cream pot.

"Aye, we make all the butter for the Hall," Polly said with pride. "'Twill be fresh today, tomorrow 'twill be salted for winter. An' once a week, 'tis cheese."

Susanne blinked. "I've never made cheese," she faltered. She had, of course, but it was plain white cheese, not the sort the gentry ate.

Polly laughed. "'Twould be a wonder if tha had," she chuckled. "Nay, no worries. I'll teach thee, 'tis no harder than butter."

A little of the cream went into a pitcher that one of the kitchen maids came to get, along with cans of the skimmed milk for cooking. The rest of the skimmed milk was collected by someone else and carried off. Polly and Susanne turned to their churns.

At the end of the day, they carried cakes of fresh butter up to the Hall, along with a can of fresh milk for Cook, and left the rest of the afternoon's milk standing in the clean and scalded pans. "Eh, tha' can see why I need help!" Polly laughed, as the two of them entered the kitchen and handed over their goods. "I was havin' to make more cheese an' less butter, for I couldn't get to the cream before it began to turn."

Now, Susanne absolutely did not believe that, for she had sensed Polly using very gentle Earth magic to keep the cream from spoiling. And she had augmented that, since it was exactly the same sort of thing that she herself had done. There was Earth magic in use all over that dairy—to keep the milk from turning, the cream from spoiling, the butter from going rancid, the cheese from acquiring molds that were not desirable. All very minor magics, but the impact was not so minor, not on a place that had as many people to feed as Branwell Hall did.

Supper was a relatively light meal for the servants; the gentry might eat heavily, but the servants' main meals were breakfast and luncheon. The day was nearly over for Polly and Susanne; they would get up at dawn or before to clean the dairy and clean and scald all their implements and pans and pots. It was clear to Susanne that this was a much larger dairy than anything she was used to; it was very likely that Branwell Hall provided not only for its own needs, but sold a substantial surplus. As a consequence, a lot of the duties that a dairymaid had in smaller households were given to other servants.

"Where will I be sleeping?" Susanne asked diffidently, as both of them spread the fruits of their labor over fresh, hot rolls that tasted utterly heavenly.

"Oh, with me. Housekeeper'll have got tha' uniforms already, like mine." Polly smoothed down her light blue dress with pride. "And she'll have got tha' bundle to our room. Put tha' gown with mine, they'll be taken off for washing, I'll show thee where."

"You can't be too clean in a dairy," Susanne said sagely, and she was rewarded with Polly's nod of approval.

"Aye, it's clean uniforms every day for us." Polly helped herself to a big bowl of soup as the communal pot came by, and so did Susanne. Both did the same with the stewed turnip tops, which had a satisfying amount of bacon added. The food was all plain and good. They finished off their meal before the rest, who were still sending up grander food to the gentry's table. Polly stood up and bade a cheerful good night to the others; Susanne took the hint and followed her.

The room she would share with Polly from now on was just under the attics; from the look of things, the floor they were on was where all the servants slept. Sure enough, Susanne's bundle was on her bed, and there were three clean blue dresses and six bleached white aprons and matching caps hanging on a hook on the wall.

"Change apron after nuncheon," Polly said by way of explanation. "Cap too." She showed Susanne the basket just outside their door where they were to leave clothing to be taken away for cleaning. Susanne donned her somewhat threadbare nightshift with a little embarrassment and sensed that Polly was eyeing it with curiosity, but the girl only said, "Old man tha' was with wasn't half the skinflint, eh?"

"He'd pinch a farthing until it squeaked," Susanne replied.

"Well, 'tis different here. 'Do not bind the mouths of the kine that tread the grain.'" Polly said piously, and climbed into her bed.

Clearly it *was* different here. The two of them had their own little beds. Back at the Manor, Prudence and Patience had to share a bed not much bigger than these were.

Outside, it was just dusk; dim blue light filtered in their window, which Polly left open to the breeze. The pretty muslin curtains fluttered as Susanne turned on her side to watch. Polly was asleep in moments, but Susanne still had too much to think about to get to sleep just yet.

This place—it was unbelievable. How could she ever have fallen into a situation so perfect? She would have been suspicious of some sort of trap, except that the magic didn't lie, and this place was—good.

But above and beyond all that . . . was Charles Kerridge. He was the handsomest man she had ever seen in her life. The way he had immediately sensed her panic and moved to calm it when she first woke to find him looking down on her—

I've never met anyone so handsome or *so kind,* she thought dreamily. She hadn't had much time to think about him until now . . . but now that she did, the memory of those mild gray eyes looking down on her was enough to give her shivers. And she knew that she would have taken a far worse position than dairymaid in order to be near him.

And with that, and vague daydreams of how she could—somehow—gain his attention, she at last fell asleep.

10

"So, the new dairymaid is an Earth magician?" Michael Kerridge asked, buttering his toast as he lifted an eyebrow at Peter and Charles.

The windows on the garden were wide open, and birds of every description were singing their hearts out. Peter could not help but reflect that this was one of the things that made him—briefly—regret living in London. The part of town where he lived might be genteel, but it could never give him birdsong with toast.

"It would seem so, O Pater Familias," Charles replied. "And very closemouthed she is about it, and herself. She hasn't come out and declared herself even to young Polly, and Polly hasn't done anything to hide what witchery she is doing in the dairy."

The servants were all being their willing spies on the new girl; it was Polly who had first seen that the girl was helping her own magic along, told Cook, and Cook who had set the others to find out what they could. Peter thought this was an estimable system, one that could be put together only in a place like this, where literally everyone had magic, or something as compelling, in common. Common good, and commonality.

Alas, it seemed that most people were more interested in conflict than commonality. Especially—

He wrenched his thoughts away from the increasing tension across the Channel and back to the subject at hand.

Elizabeth came in on that last. "I can only tell you that Polly told Cook, who told me, that the new girl is helping her, strengthening her spells but not in any way that Polly has actually caught. Under other circumstances I would admire her circumspection, but at the moment it is rather aggravating." She joined them at the table. "She's been just as silent on the subject of where she came from before this. I've no notion who could have trained her in the first place, although it is entirely possible it could be someone we never encountered, some irascible old hermit who has no use for other people. Earth mages do tend to bury themselves in the countryside. It might even be the old man she claims she was the servant to. But on that subject, she has given no details at all, which makes me begin to doubt this old skinflint hermit ever existed. I don't doubt that she is a decent young woman," Elizabeth added hastily. "I merely am concerned that she might be running from something."

"Something that might follow her here and cause trouble?" Richard replied with a frown.

"I'd suggest an abusive husband," Peter said slowly, "Except that I didn't catch anything like that about her, and— well, let's just say I've seen girls who've been running from that sort of thing before. They tend to be skittish 'round the lads, and this one ain't. It's a trust sort of thing. When the fellow you thought you loved turns out to betray you, you rather lose trust in all fellows."

Elizabeth nodded. "It could be anything from a debt she can't pay, being turned out of her home by her parents, losing her parents and having nowhere to go, or running from an unwanted suitor to, well, running from someone really dangerous. And ..." she hesitated a moment. "It is just barely possible it could be that she encountered the necromancer you are looking for, at least recognized that he was dangerous, and fled. I know that if I were all alone and knew no other magicians, that is what I would do. I would run as fast and as far as my legs would take me."

The breeze coming in from the garden seemed, for a moment, to grow colder.

Peter pursed his lips. "You know, that could be the answer. The necromancer must be working far from others to avoid being uncovered. You don't have any guesses as to where this girl is from, so she, too, would have to be from some isolated place. As circumspect as she is, she would probably uncover him before he uncovered her. Getting the young woman to confide in us could solve my problem and hers in one go. If we can get her to tell us who and where he is, we can deal with him and protect her at the same time." He considered this while eating thoughtful bites of buttered toast. "The question is, how to get her to talk."

"Polly has tried, according to Cook," Elizabeth offered. "Cook herself tried. The young lady is remarkably self-contained. Another reason why it is unlikely she has fled from an abusive spouse. Also, Polly says that she has no sign of injuries to her body."

"Hmm. That is telling. Of course, a country girl like Polly would have no squeamishness about examining her fellow worker, now would she? And being in the same room, and washing together, it would be difficult to hide such things. Well, it'll be no use calling her in and questioning her like a Scotland Yard detective," Peter observed. "That would only ensure she won't talk. And we can't befriend her and try to get her to speak in that way."

"Certainly not," Michael agreed. "We're egalitarian here, but only to a point. Say what you will, Peter, but our sort and hers just do not mix. In the ordinary course of things, we wouldn't even be aware she exists. She'd just be one of the girls in the dairymaid uniform at the end of the line when we hand out Christmas treats."

Peter restrained his wince. But he also wondered . . . he considered Garrick perhaps his best friend. But how did Garrick feel about it? Was there that great a gap between master and servant?

Well, this was all not to the point. The question was whether or not the young lady herself felt that gap, and as near as he could tell, she did.

So they would have to deal with this according to her sensibilities. "I wonder . . ." Peter sipped his tea and breathed in the steam. "It could be we're approachin' the wrong end of this horse. I wonder if she isn't the sort of young woman that simply wouldn't confide in another woman. We've decided she ain't afraid of men. Well, what if a man came along and acted like a friend?"

They all turned to look at him, in varying degrees of surprise. He shrugged. "I'm the sort that women like to confide it. They think my unprepossessing face and mild manners mean I'm 'safe,' and my monocle and Oxford manner mean I'm intelligent."

"Well, you can't befriend her, either," Charles pointed out. "Your rank is even higher than ours."

"Not as myself," Peter agreed. "But I have a knack for disguise and a positive genius for mimicry." He cleared his throat, and tried out the accent and idiom he had secretly been practicing ever since he arrived. He had been less than honest with Alderscroft; drop him into any situation where he knew the basic language, and within three weeks he would have the accent and the local vernacular. "How d'ye do. I'm Peter. I know tha'rt Missus Elizabeth, and Marster Michael, and Marster Charles. I come lookin' for work. An' I can keep secrets. I'm keepin' secrets all th' time. Eh! How could I not?"

Their eyes got wider and wider with every word in broad Yorkshire he spoke.

"Good lord," Charles said at last. "You're better than a

parrot. That'll do, lad, that'll do. What did you think you'd impersonate?"

He'd already thought this out, in case he needed to get even closer to folk than Garrick could. "I noticed you haven't a gamekeeper—"

"That's because we wouldn't want to put that kind of onerous duty on anyone from among our own people, and there's no one we trust enough from outside," Michael told him. "Any of our folks would be getting tremendous pressure to allow them to poach more than we'll stand for from his friends, and anyone from outside wouldn't understand the game management system I use where we look the other way a certain amount of the time."

He was delighted to hear that. He had no compunction about laying down the law in that manner and was perfectly prepared to handle the inevitable fool that had some notion that the "understandings" would not apply to him. "So, gamekeeper it is. Garrick and I shall hie away, and I'll return as your new gamekeeper. I very much doubt she'll remember my phiz from when we found her; I'm eminently forgettable. I assume there's a gamekeeper's cottage somewhere about?" At Michael's nod, he beamed at them. "I believe I shall have Garrick impersonate one of those desperate scholars that goes about collecting every single version of every folk song ever sung. We can make a bachelor nest of your cottage, and he can see to it that we're snug."

"Oh, poor Garrick!" Charles laughed. "You are pitiless, Peter."

That sense of rightness he always got when he'd found the correct plan to follow settled in. "Yes, well, it won't be the first time he's used that ruse, he's used to it." Peter smiled. Garrick was tone-deaf, and it didn't matter how badly someone sang, Garrick couldn't tell. The worst part was probably the tedium of getting through the four hundred or so verses of the local version of "Matty Groves."

"Well, since the last gamekeeper was married with a swarm of children, it is a very nice cottage," Elizabeth observed. "One bedroom down, one up. We've made sure it was kept up, kept relatively up to date, and kept clean. One never knows when one will need a retreat for a visitor. Quite cozy for the two of you. I'll send a couple of the maids and one of the boys out to clean it and air it out."

"And I shall tell Garrick to make preparations for our immediate departure," Peter said with satisfaction. "Shall we say, three days time?"

"Three days will be plenty to ensure that we've got the place fit to live in. Should I stock the larder?" Elizabeth asked.

"Please do. Garrick will remember the luxuries, but I'm not sure he knows the makin's for soup." Peter felt a great wave of pleasure coming over him. This was the sort of thing he was best at. This, more than playing at being a painter and running the same spell over and over again, was what he was the best at. Real investigative magic, real detective work, real combat magic.

"And you do?" Charles laughed. "You? Cook? Keep house?" Peter fixed him with an admonishing glare.

"I will have you to know that I once lived entirely on my own in a Tuscan goatherd's hut for an entire month," he replied with just a touch of acidity. "These fair hands are good for more than just a handshake, limp or vigorous as the occasion calls for. I do not need Garrick to make my toast, thank you very much. Am I allowed to poach?" he added, turning to Michael.

The elder Kerridge spread his hands wide. "You will be the gamekeeper, who will there be to stop you?"

"Glorious! There's some variations on snares I've been itching to try." He couldn't keep the glee out of his voice, so he didn't try.

Elizabeth rolled her eyes, but smiled at him fondly. Evidently she found the fact that he could make soup to be charming. "Honestly, Lord Peter, if I didn't know better, I would think you were eager to get away from us."

"Fortunately, you do know better," he chided. "I'm just as

pleased as a schoolboy at the start of the Long Vac because we've finally got something to work with and because getting a nice young lady to talk to me is more in my line than making hideous messes with paint." He didn't trouble to hide his self-disgust at the last.

"Oh, they weren't that bad," Charles replied, grinning. "Not that I know anything about art, but they weren't that bad."

Peter shuddered. He was quite the connoisseur of fine art, and what he had been producing had grated on his soul. "They were not that good, either," he replied. "Thank you, my dear friends, for your generous and varied hospitality. When the Old Lion assigned me to this task, I was at my wits' end. If it had not been for you, I do not know what I would have done."

Michael just waved the thanks away, and Charles laughed. "Thank us when it's over," Charles advised. "The girl might prove more stubborn than you think. You might find yourself still living in that cottage at Christmas."

The dairy was cool—not too cool, but enough that working hard wasn't making her sticky. Susanne plunged away at her churn, well into the rhythm of the job, waiting for the changes that would tell her that the butter was starting to come together. She was happily oblivious to anything else around her. It was strange, but for the first time in her life she was comfortable. She was in a place where people took magic in their stride. She knew her place among the servants, rather than being not enough of a servant and not enough of gentry to fit in; she was among people who, if they had their frictions and quarrels among themselves (as who didn't?), considered themselves to be something of a family and seemed to be prepared to accept her into that family. She was working hard, but she was not overworked.

Maybe some other girl would have been unhappy here, but until her father had singled her out, she had never really felt like gentry, so she really didn't feel as if she had come down in the world. If anything, it felt as if she had finally found a place where she belonged.

Even this, the rhythm of the work under her hands that connected her to the land, to the animals that had given the milk, to her fellows, to the magic that they all worked at — this was completely *right*.

So she took in great lungfuls of lovely, fresh air that wasn't tainted by that faint aura of blight and sorrow, listened to the birds (who wouldn't come anywhere near the blighted area), and felt whole.

There was a twinge of guilt — that she was no longer able to "do" for the land around Whitestone Hall. But perhaps faced with her flight, her father would come to his senses and resume his duties. Or perhaps Robin would find someone to take her place. But it was as clear as anything that it simply would not have been possible to remain in that place, not a moment longer, and she was certain had she told Robin what her father's plans were, he would have been furious.

But the guilt was easily submerged in the rosy haze that enveloped her whenever she thought about Charles Kerridge.

If there was one thing that was not utterly perfect, it was that Charles Kerridge was not a fellow servant. Or that she was not anyone he would ever notice, barring a miracle. The fact that he had probably forgotten her right after he sent her to Cook to be given a place did not for one moment keep her from dreaming about him as she fell asleep, or thinking about him whenever she had an idle moment, or trying to get a glimpse of him, wishing that the miracle might occur, that he would turn and look into her eyes and realize —

She sighed.

Oh, it was foolish, something right out of a silly romantic story, the kind that was serialized in the papers, and she knew that. She also knew that nothing had ever made her quite so happy as just catching a glimpse of him. Her logical side knew without a doubt he had probably forgotten her the moment he sent her off to Cook; that didn't matter to the part of her that kept on dreaming. She still went off into a happy daze if she saw him; she could nurse that feeling for hours.

She'd gone off into a slough of despondence for almost a whole day when she learned he was the only son, and thus the heir to this entire estate. Branwell was . . . just so enormous. You could easily have fit four Whitestone Halls into it and still had room, and that didn't even begin to cover all the outbuildings, the Home Farm, and the estate lands. She had been absolutely certain that he must be engaged to some daughter of rank and privilege by now. Had things been normal at Whitestone, she certainly would have been married at his age, and Whitestone wasn't even a fraction of the size of this place!

Then, when she discovered he was neither married nor engaged, she had gone off into such transports of joy that she'd had to exert every bit of her self-control not to go dancing around the dairy, which surely would have puzzled poor Polly no end.

It was foolish of course. Utterly, completely, ridiculously foolish. She was just a squire's daughter, and, as her father had taken pains to point out, she was utterly uneducated even in the things she *should* have known, and never mind the things that the girls that Charles was used to being around knew. She had no notion of clothing, or manners, or any of the things that her father seemed to think were important for a properly brought up girl. And when you added in all the sorts of things that she read about in the society news in the London papers—

Balls? She couldn't dance. Card parties? She didn't even know how to play Patience. Tennis, archery, croquet, riding, shuttlecock? Complete mysteries to her. Visiting for high tea? What did you talk about? Politics? Fashion? Gossip about other people in your circles? She was utterly ignorant. She didn't know how to manage a household of this size, how to address people by their correct titles, how to—

Well, the list of what she didn't know how to do was endless.

She didn't think that having magic would make up for that ignorance, assuming that the Kerridges themselves actually knew what was going on here. It could all be a gigantic conspiracy on the part of the servants, to keep the knowledge from their masters. Even at Whitestone, the servants had had their conspiracies. Cook gave the skimmed milk and some of the food out the back door to some poor relatives of hers. Martha helped herself to the furnishings and linens in the closed-up rooms to use in her own quarters. Whitestone didn't have nearly the lands that Branwell did, but everyone poached them. Old John, who took care of the two horses and four cows, ran a little carting trade with the horses and farm cart on the side. So it was not out of the question that the Kerridges had no idea that there was magic going on right under their noses.

The magic itself here was all very minor stuff, by her standards. Spells to soothe beasts and keep water fresh and food from spoiling. Cook had little spells she used on her cooking. The gardeners all had their own to keep the plants flourishing, blight from the roses, insects at bay. It was not so much a matter of making the place into an Eden of plenty as it was to keep things from going wrong.

This was, of course, the right way to use magic if you weren't a Master, and often if you were. *"Take care,"* Robin used to say. *"Suppose you were to make it rain here, and over in Devon you made a drought?"* So, when you used magic, you used it in little ways, to keep things healthy, not to change them, to cleanse, but not to stimulate.

"Think about growing things," Robin had said. *"Growing is good, but not if it makes one thing choke out another. Stick to healing, keeping the land healthy and the poisons out of it, and you can't go far wrong."*

Of course, there was another factor. An Elemental Master

could get the help of the Elementals, which meant he didn't depend on his own strength for his spells. But people who worked smaller magics took all of that strength out of themselves. That tended to make you husband your power for when you needed it or to find ways to make a little do a lot.

"Well, tha's fair pleased 'bout somethin'," Polly observed, interrupting her thoughts.

"I'm happy here," she said, giving Polly part of the truth.

"Eh! There's a good deal t'be happy about!" Polly agreed. "With two o' us doin' the dairy, there's nowt too much work, nowt too little. Good victuals, fair wages an' all. Body could do worse'n serve at Branwell Hall."

"A lot worse," she agreed. Polly regarded her thoughtfully, but she said nothing. Perhaps she was trying to read something into her brief answer.

A history of bad treatment at the hands of Susanne's imaginary employer, perhaps?

Well, Polly was going to have to be disappointed. One lie about her origin was actually one lie too many; the problem with lying was that the more elaborate a lie became, the harder it was to keep track of and keep straight. Susanne was not going to compound trouble by telling too many lies. The less she told, the less she would have to remember.

Today had been a cheese-making day, so there was some extra work. The milk had been made into curds, the whey drained, the curds cheddared, then cut into pea-sized pieces, salted and packed into their molds for pressing. Tomorrow afternoon the cheeses would be turned out of the molds, wrapped loosely in cheesecloth, and stacked on their racks to dry. The cheeses from the last cheese making, which had developed their rind, were wrapped in bandages and moved to the ripening racks. These were carefully marked with the date. The longer the cheese aged, the sharper it would be. A cheese aged for a year was very sharp indeed, and a great favorite on the gentry's table.

Ah, there it was—the change in "feel" that meant the

butter had finally started to come together. Polly cocked her head and nodded. "Soon," she said.

Susanne nodded agreement. "'Tis been a good day's work," she said happily, glad to take her mind off the pleasant, but vexing, subject of Charles Kerridge.

An hour later, the two of them were washing and scalding the steel milk-pans used for cooking the curds as their last chore before supper.

"Missus Elizabeth is wantin' cheese for gamekeeper's cottage," Polly said. "Two, she said. Three month an' six month. Seems Marster Michael hired gamekeeper."

For a fleeting moment, Susanne wondered if this could be Robin Goodfellow, taking on the same role he had back at Whitestone. But—surely not. Not even Robin would be bold enough to present himself to a human and try to deceive the man into hiring him on. *Especially* not in a household where there were so very many Earth magicians! If it were Robin, most of the people here would know what he was within two days of his turning up in person.

"Gamekeeper has half-brother," Polly continued, smiling, as she read Susanne's expression as astonishment. "Scholar, 'tis said. They be stayin' i' cottage. Reckon nowt much call for scholarin', so 'tis his brother what puts victuals on table." She chuckled. "Anyway, 'tis a fair lovely walk, tha'll take one, I'll take t'other, then we can get our supper."

Since Susanne hadn't seen much of the estate since she arrived, she readily agreed. The cheeses each weighed a good ten pounds, heavy enough to justify two girls for the single errand. They finished their washing, put everything back in its proper place, and went to select the cheeses. Polly had some way of telling which were the best that Susanne hadn't yet deciphered. The very best were kept for the gentry, of course, so Polly spent a good several minutes muttering to herself, tapping and sniffing, until she found two that met her criteria of "good enough for the gamekeeper and his daft brother," but not of such inferior quality that it would shame her and her skill to give them to the new hirelings. Polly always kept back what she considered "failed" cheeses to give to Cook to use in the cooking, rather than the serving or to be sent off to the poor.

With the cheeses wrapped in cloth in their arms, they made their way through the parkland that surrounded the Hall. The path they followed soon brought them into real forest, left to tend to itself, although the path was well tended and groomed. Susanne breathed in the forest air with sensual joy, and Polly showed no sign of nerves, simply looking around with pleasure. Which was lovely; Susanne didn't have much use for a girl who was looking for apocryphal wolves and bears behind each bush and jumping with fear every time a branch broke. "Eh! There'll be wild strawberries soon," Polly said. "We should come of a Sunday t'pick 'em. They be ever so much better than tame."

Susanne's mouth watered at the thought. There were no "tame" strawberries at Whitestone, unless they came from one of the tenant farms, so all the strawberries she'd had either came from the market or were ones she had picked herself in the woods. And she agreed with Polly; the wild ones might be much smaller, but they were much better. "Strawberries and cream," she sighed. "Eh, 'tis a fine part of summer! Better still with a scone or cake . . ." She hadn't had them with cake more than once or twice, but the memory was sheer bliss.

"Better nor plain cream. I know th' way of makin' Devon cream." Polly licked her lips and her eyes sparkled. "Tha's never tasted th' like. Like cream, but thick as butter, only softer."

Devon cream? Susanne had read of such a delight, but only in papers, when stories were written about the fabulous tables that the wealthy set. "Is there anything in a dairy you don't know how to do?" Susanne asked, her eyes going round.

"Nowt much," Polly replied, and laughed. "But I canna milk a cow. Cheeky beggars kick over pail, *every* time!"

At that point, they arrived at their goal. The gamekeeper's cottage was a tidy little place, and although according to Polly, it had been empty as long as she had been keeping the dairy, it hadn't been permitted to fall into disrepair. It was partly of stone, partly of whitewashed plaster and black beams, with a thatched roof. The thatch was in very good condition and was home to several bird nests. When they pushed open the door, it was obvious that others had been here already.

There were three rooms: one main room that served as kitchen, dining room, and sitting room—and probably workroom, too—and two bedrooms. One of the bedrooms was much smaller than the other and might have served some other purpose before the bed had been—barely!—fitted into it. A narrow wooden staircase went up to a low second story that could probably serve for more sleeping space or for storage. It had its own well, as evidenced by a sink in the kitchen with a hand-pump, which was as good as the one at the Hall. An enormous stone fireplace took up most of one of the end walls, with a settle next to it, but a modern iron stove had been installed inside the fireplace for cooking and heating. That was just as well; the fireplace was surely big enough to roast an entire pig in, and you would be either too hot or too cold, or the chimney wouldn't draft right. The place had been opened up and aired out, the shutters flung back, and the glass windows opened to let in air.

As for furnishing the place, well, whoever had directed just what was to be done here had not scrimped. The table was covered with a clean linen tablecloth, and from what Susanne could see of one of the bedrooms, the beds were as nice as the ones in the room her father had assigned to her. There were even bits of carpet on the stone floor. The whitewashed walls must have just been refreshed; it was much brighter inside than you would have guessed from the exterior, for all that the ceiling was so low a tall man would need to be careful he didn't knock his head on the beams.

"Eh! I'd be glad to live here, that I would!" Polly said

with surprise. "Marster must set great store by this game-keeper. Well, let's put cheese up."

She marched straight to the big cupboard that must serve as a larder and found space in it for their cheeses. She examined the doors before shutting them and nodded with satisfaction. "No mouse be gettin' in there," she pronounced, as she set the latch in place.

They both looked around a little more, and Polly sighed. "On'y one thing for it. Gamekeeper's brother, he be scholar. Likely from Oxford. So gamekeeper's brother mus' be friend of Marster Charles from school," she said.

Susanne nodded. "That would explain—all this." She waved her hand at the careful preparations and the high degree of comfort. "And 'twould explain hiring a game-keeper when there wasn't need."

"Aye." Polly nodded sagely. "Could be they fell on hard times. Or maybe Marster foun' out that they was doin' poorly an' felt he had to do for 'em."

Susanne was thinking very hard now. If that was the case, then the "daft" and scholarly brother might be a way to get closer to Charles . . .

"Well, nowt more to see, an' supper'll be over if we don' run," Polly said, breaking into her thoughts. "We'll find out when gamekeeper gets here."

"Eh, true," Susanne replied, as they left the cottage and shut the door firmly behind them; her stomach growled to emphasize that, and she grinned. "Last one there forfeits extra tart!" she added, and dashed up the path.

"Oh, tha' do think!" Polly squealed in outrage, and sprinted after her.

Susanne let her win at the last minute. Friendship was worth so much more than a second helping of treacle tart.

"And what have we learned, Garrick?" asked Peter, as they settled the last of the gear that the farm cart had hauled out to the cottage for them.

He was ridiculously pleased with the cozy little cottage. He had certainly lived in much worse surroundings. He and Garrick could take it in turns to cook on that little stove, which was infinitely superior to the many fires and fire pits he had been forced to use in the past.

I wouldn't mind being the gamekeeper here in truth, actually. Then he had to laugh at himself. Of course he would mind, after a while. He was at heart a London man. He'd miss it eventually. More than miss it; he'd come to pine for it. Not to mention that there were many other things he would miss. *Be honest my lad. You love your luxuries. One week without your Harrods hamper and you'd be whimperin' with deprivation.* Still . . . it didn't take being an Earth Master to want desperately to be away when the choking peasoup fogs of winter descended. When that happened . . . well the wild winter winds of Yorkshire would be a blessed relief. It wouldn't matter if they "wuthered" so long as they were "wuthering" about walls as stout as these.

Perhaps I will take Garrick and escape here for a bit in the winter. The shooting should be grand, too.

"We have learned, m'lord, that I am presumed to be Charles Kerridge's friend from school and that you and I are either the sons of an impoverished vicar upon whom Master Charles took pity or have fallen on hard times." Garrick stowed the bounty of the hamper from Harrods in the cupboard with great care; Elizabeth's generosity had not left him much room.

"I like the 'sons of an impoverished vicar.' It has a nice soundness to it, and vicar's sons are presumed to be either impractical scholars or relative black sheep." Peter sighted along the rifle he was holding, then stowed it in the rack they had brought with them. "If we take on those personas, I shall retain a touch of the Yorkshire dialect, but I needn't try to pass myself off as a deep native. It will be presumed that our joint father either beat or prayed the greater part of the accent out of me."

"Very good, m'lord." Garrick tucked in the last jar of

marmalade and shut the larder door. "Might I suggest, m'lord, an air of thoughtful silence for the most part? And perhaps not a black sheep as such. Rakes are often found to be attractive by young ladies. Some are attracted to the danger and some to the possibility of 'saving' them. That could be very inconvenient, not to say distracting."

Peter blinked. "Good Lord, you're right. All right, not a black sheep. Well then, we had better work out our mutual history."

"Very good, m'lord," Garrick replied, his head half inside the mammoth fireplace as he lit the cast iron stove. "I suggest you are the elder, the product of an impetuous marriage that resulted in early widowhood, and I am the offspring of the second marriage. The impoverished vicar would be an excellent choice. And in that way we can have different surnames. Said parent being an excessively stern father, determined that we follow in his footsteps, even though you were not of his blood. You, being of a more rebellious nature, occupied your youth with woodland studies to the detriment of your books and departed at the age of sixteen to take up a position as under-gamekeeper for Lord Alderscroft, who will be certain to corroborate this ruse. I, on the other hand, took to my books but refused to study anything resembling divinity—but dissembled so that our father was unaware I was not obedient to his wishes. He died, leaving me completely unable to support myself in any way, including tutoring; my friend Charles, however, came to the rescue with this position for you on learning of my desperate plight. You, of course, were glad of the opportunity, since you were unlikely to rise to full gamekeeper for at least ten years, and were completely unable in your current position to support me."

The sound of applause from the door made them both turn. "My word, Garrick, you should be a writer! That's both a satisfactory story and one that will be easy enough to bring off."

Peter had come instantly to his feet, and now made a stiff

little bow. "It'll do, Marster Charles," he said, already in his gamekeeper persona.

"I should think. It's quite solid." Charles turned to Garrick. "So how woolly-headed and timid were you, Garrick?"

"Quite, sir," Garrick replied without losing his composure a bit.

"Good. Then you were my fag your first year and were more or less under my protection for the two years I had remaining. I had a reputation for protecting the easily overwhelmed by appropriating them before anyone with a cruel streak could." Charles grinned a little.

"So you did, Charles, so you did." Peter put the servile manner aside and sprawled in one of the three chairs. "And no one here will know the names of your fags; the only reason I still recall them is because my memory seldom lets go of anything, however trivial. I must say, your mother has done the deed proper here. I expected to be camping rough, and here I find the rustic equivalent of a luxurious hotel!"

"It's occurred to both of us that this might prove to be a good retreat for a mage with rattled nerves, or one who wouldn't feel comfortable as a guest up at the Hall but would be at home in a cottage," Charles replied, taking another chair. "How do you intend to approach the girl?"

"Strawberry season, Master Charles," Garrick replied, still fiddling with the stove. "And please tell your good mother that her choice of stoves was excellent. I don't expect to have any trouble with this one at all."

"I'll tell her. What the deuce do you mean by strawberry season?" Charles demanded, looking at Garrick's back as if he thought that the man had gone mad.

"For that, I must defer to Lord Peter," Garrick said with great dignity. "Regardless of my familiarity with stoves, I am a man of the city at bottom."

Peter laughed. "And for that, old fellow, I am indebted to my first nanny, who was a bright little country lass and a protégé of my grandmother. She taught me that wild strawberries are infinitely tastier than the ones from the garden, and, furthermore, there are no gardeners guarding them like Cerberus at the gates of Hades. M'mater would have been horrified to know that we would go rompin' through the fields in the season, and I'd stuff myself until I was sticky. You can lay money on it that every one of your servants who doesn't think it beneath him—or her—is going to be huntin' berries in the next few days. I've got some choice patches spotted, thanks to some cross-Elemental gossip, and I'll be waiting for our quarry to either find them herself or be led to them. Or at need, I'll lead her to them myself."

"And thus," said Garrick, straightening up from the stove, "the deed is done."

Charles shook his head. "It's clever, but deuced if I can see how you come up with these schemes. I'll leave you to your supper. I suppose it's poached," he added, with cheerful resignation. "Oh, what *are* your names, anyway?"

"Clive Garrick and Peter Devlin," Peter said instantly. "Devlin is my middle name, and Clive is Garrick's."

"Good, easy to remember. Well, on that note, I bid you good night, O Feeder on the bounty of my land." He stood up and let himself out. Peter chuckled.

"Charles knows me altogether too well," he said.

Garrick made a slight face. "And is it your fault that fish bit on an empty hook?" he demanded.

"I cannot tell a lie, of course it is," Peter responded cheerfully. "I'm a Water Master."

Although the girl did not make an appearance in the first two days, Peter didn't consider the time a loss. He was busy making himself familiar with the woods; although Water Elementals were not as useful as Earth or Air would have been in helping him find the spots where people set their snares, they were perfectly happy to tell him what those other Elementals were gossiping about. The Earth and Air Elementals had no problem with divulging where snares and traps were and where men lay in wait to take animals and birds with guns. And the Water Elementals were second to none at finding the weir nets and fish traps. Charles had given Peter a rough count of how much poaching was going to be allowed; Peter monitored the snares and traps for a couple of days, estimated the populations of fish and game, and removed about a third of the traps. He didn't break them or throw them up into a tree as some gamekeepers might. Instead, he piled them all neatly beside one he had *not* removed, as an object lesson. "See, you know better than that," was the unspoken message. "Don't be greedy."

The poachers took the hint, and the number of traps dropped by exactly a third.

Meanwhile, Peter was making discreet inquiries among the Elementals about the girl as well. And the first thing he discovered was that the Earth Elementals were utterly besotted with her.

It was partly the fact of sheer novelty. She was the first person they had encountered in decades who was not from the Branwell lands or the Kerridge bloodline. Earth Elementals were highly territorial and rarely left their patches of ground unless they were driven out by something unpleasant or dangerous. So it was only natural that they wouldn't have encountered this girl before. And it was natural for them to be very welcoming to an Earth mage new to them. Fire Elementals were arrogant and needed to be wooed, Water were retiring and shy and needed to be reassured, Air flighty and absentminded and needed to be charmed with something interesting, but Earth Elementals could always be counted on to welcome a new magician of their stamp in their lands. The stronger the mage—so long as he or she was of the cooperative and not the coercing kind—the greater the welcome. While Earth Elementals were happy to contribute to the welfare and health of the land, they didn't have the ability to apply power the way a mortal magician did. The bond of mage and Elemental was always a cooperative one when the magic was used properly.

What was not usual was the degree of warmth with

which they responded to her. That could only mean that she, in her turn, was a warmhearted, considerate, and thoughtful steward of her power.

The wild things in particular were entirely enchanted with her. A small gang of fauns even came stomping aggressively up to him as he was patrolling the forest to demand that he not "be a-troubling of her." For a wild Earth Elemental to approach a Water Master with such a demand was almost unheard of. He was both taken aback and utterly charmed. What a remarkable young woman she must be to have earned such loyalty in such a short time!

Evidently they had gotten wind of the questions he was asking about her. He was able to reassure them that he meant no harm, and they vanished back into the undergrowth apparently satisfied. But he had to wonder—why would they be so perturbed that someone had been asking questions about her?

And—besides his—just what questions were being asked, and by whom? That part—that was potentially very troubling.

Susanne was alone in the dairy and would be for the next several days. Polly had leave to go tend her sister, who had just had a baby a day ago. "If I'd thought tha' couldn't manage—" she had begun, before Susanne waved her off.

"Tha's got leave, and tha'rt takin' one of tha' holidays for it. I can manage, and Cook's promised me little Caro for help," Susanne had replied. Now, she knew, and she suspected that Polly knew, that Caro hadn't a bit of magic in her. And for one moment, Polly had looked concerned.

But then her expression cleared, as if she had suddenly thought of something. "Oh, aye, tha'll have no trouble with Caro, she's a sturdy bit of a thing. Take care she doesn't gorge herself on cream, though. She'll make herself sick."

"I won't—I mean, I will," Susanne had laughed.

Everything had gone well. And she had kept an eye on

Caro, who learned very quickly that the new dairymaid was even harder to gull than the old. Now Caro was scrubbing out the milk-pans, while Susanne cleaned the churns—a task that required magic, so far as Susanne was concerned, because the least little bit of old milk or cream or butter in them could easily spoil and turn the entire churn sour the next time you used it.

So Polly—and now Susanne—used a little spell that allowed them to "lift" the offending dribs and drabs to the surface of the water and keep them there. She was concentrating so hard on the task that she didn't hear the footsteps behind her.

"Aha," said a satisfied voice behind her. "Caught thee out, then, didn' I?"

She whirled. It was Cook, who planted her feet wide and nodded, crossing her arms over her chest.

"I don't know what—" Susanne began, trying to suppress her spell and failing entirely.

"Oh, don't come all coy with me. That there's magic," Cook said, pointing to the churn. "Earth magic. I knowed tha' could see farther into a millstone than most!" She beamed at Susanne, stilling any fears that she might have somehow broken an unwritten rule. "So, learned a bit did thee?"

Susanne nodded. She was not about to let on just how much she knew.

"'Tis the same with a good three or four of us, an' the rest know all about us," Cook told her. "Don't go hidin' that light 'neath a bushel. This be a place where we use ev'ry gift the Good Lord give us. We know that there Bible verse ain't 'tha' shalt not suffer a witch t'live,' it's 'tha' shalt not suffer a *poisoner* t' live.' We know what we know, and we knowed it for—well, goin' back to far beyond when King Alfred burned them cakes."

Susanne sighed with relief. This sounded just like the things Robin used to tell her, and the Coveners, about the Old Ways and the Old Days.

"There's things as need more than just one, an' when that happens, we huddle t'gether an' fix 'em," the Cook finished. "I'll be expectin' thee t' join now, eh?"

She swallowed, and nodded. "Yes, Cook," she said

"Thee needn't think this's somethin' hidden, leastwise not from anyone within the walls. Marsters an' the Missus all knows, an' more than knows, they has the power too an' uses it." Cook smiled at her little start, but how was Cook to know that this fact hadn't startled her so much as given her a little shock of happiness? The Kerridges themselves had the magic? So Charles was an Earth mage, too! Oh, that was good! Maybe having magic *would* make a difference in her stature! It meant she just *might* be able to convince him and his parents that she was a very valuable asset indeed. Maybe more than just a "valuable asset."

Which would mean she might have a chance with Charles.

"Now, then, let's see what tha' can do," Cook continued. "I know what Polly can, so let's see if tha' can better her."

Susanne swiftly finished the rest of the scrubbing-up, with Caro's help. Then she went into the butter room and cast a spell of her own over the waiting pats. It was a very good spell, sound, economical, and with no holes in it. She was rather proud of it, actually. This butter would stay sweet and would remain edible and wholesome indefinitely. Polly's could only hold it sweet for about a fortnight.

Cook nodded at that as well. "'Tis clear there be no one here that can teach thee," Cook said thoughtfully. "Eh! That's not so bad. And now I've drug thee into the light, thee can use tha' magic whenever tha' chooses. I'll be makin' sure the rest all know what tha' can do and that tha' can be trusted to do it without interference or overlookin'."

She nodded with relief. Cook was right. One less thing to be worried about.

"Is it all right if I leave out a saucer of cream and a bit o' bread at night?" she asked, tentatively. "Not that I'd leave a mess for a brownie t' be cleanin' out of on purpose! That'd drive 'em away, sure as sure, bein' lazy! But just to know if I miss something, they'll be findin' it, and catchin' it afore it makes a deal of trouble, would be a great ease of my mind."

Cook laughed. "Lor' love tha', what dost tha' think I do, last thing? 'Tis a great ease of the mind, goin' up to bed knowin' that it'll all be perfect in the morn even if we're nearly done to death by one of the big to-dos. 'Tis clear thee knows what'll happen if brownie thinks tha'rt shirkin'."

Susanne made a face. "Oh, aye. Not just drive 'em away. They might let in somethin' that'd make mischief, faun or the like. An' 'twould serve me right."

"Well, then, we're all of a mind. Aye, Caro?" Cook asked.

Caro nodded, her eyes big and round. "Wish't I had th' magic," she whispered wistfully.

"Eh, 'tis as much work as usin' hands, honey," Cook told her. "Harder, belike. Nothin' comes without strivin', just because tha' don't see hands workin', doesn't mean hard work ain't bein' done."

Susanne nodded. "Eh!" she told the girl. "Think on't. Ain't it hard, when tha'rt puzzlin' out a problem! Don't it make tha' weary?"

Caro's brows furrowed, and finally she nodded.

"'Tis the same," Susanne told her firmly. "Bigger the magic, wearier it makes tha'."

"True, that. Now, I tell thee, tha'rt not due for a half-day afore harvest, but tha'rt a good child," Cook continued, "and Polly's another, and she'll come back fagged near to death by that sistern of hers, an' it won't be no holiday for her. So. When Polly comes back, here's what. I'll give thee both a half-holiday together. I'll get leave for it from Missus easy enough. There's butter and cheese enough put by, Missus Elizabeth is fair fond of givin' milk t'poor mothers, an' we can do that for the day if tha' cannot find a way to keep it back. I hear there might be strawberries in yon woods," she finished, with a twinkle in her eye. "And a bit of cream might be saved back to go with 'em."

Susanne smiled with her whole face. This was altogether

unexpected, but completely welcome. This would give her a chance to become more familiar with the Branwell lands and all the creatures in them—and she wouldn't have to hide that from Polly, either!

But more than that . . . with a half day off, she just might be able to get more than a glimpse of Charles Kerridge.

11

"**A** HALF-DAY!" Polly exclaimed again, with delight, as she and Susanne pulled on their uniforms. "Eh, who could've thought it! Missus Elizabeth, she be an angel! An' Cook's another!"

Susanne laughed at that, but she actually felt somewhat in agreement. "Well, *I* think we ought to be working twice as hard this morning as ever was."

"Oh, aye," Polly agreed, her eyes sparkling. "Now that thee be usin' tha' magic open-like." She sighed a little wistfully. "Tha'rt so much better nor me."

Susanne just shrugged as she buttoned up the rear of Polly's apron for her, then turned so Polly could do hers. "An' I'll never make as good a cheese as thee," she pointed out. "Nor be able to tell how ripe 'tis without tasting. But we can leave naught for Caro to do but pour the pans for rising cream."

"Even th' tweenie canna ruin that," Polly agreed. "There! All done!"

They dashed out of their room, scampered to the kitchen

for breakfast, ate quickly, and headed for the dairy. And they had the satisfaction of leaving it at lunchtime with every container that was not actively holding something scrubbed and scalded, the milk-pans for the afternoon laid out, and a little spell on the pans with rising cream to hold them until morning. It would mean more work—but not that much more. Certainly about the same as weaning time when the calves were no longer allowed to suckle.

When they arrived at the kitchen, they found another wonderful surprise waiting for them. A luncheon basket packed for the both of them, with the rare treat of two bottles of lemonade, and two empty baskets.

"Think I don't know what two girls will be doin' in woods of a June afternoon?" Cook said, her eyes twinkling. "Just be bringin' back lunch basket more full than empty. I'm partial to a wild berry, but eh! My days of scramblin' about on hands and knees are gone."

Susanne shared the burden of the laden lunch basket with Polly and felt absurdly as if she were just a happy child again as they strolled out of the warm sun and into the park and then the untamed woodlands. "Have you got a thought of where to go?" she asked. The air was rich with forest scents, and the birds seemed to be everywhere. More than birds, too, unless she was very much mistaken.

"I know one patch. Never had a whole half-day t' pick afore," Polly replied. "Might be we'll pick that patch clean."

"Then let's go there, pick enough to have with nuncheon, an' be huntin' after," Susanne suggested. She thought a moment. This would be the first time since she had arrived at Branwell Hall that she would be outside, in wild lands, with food . . . and that combination usually conjured a bit of an infestation of fauns. "Ah . . . we might get . . . creatures. Wantin' to share."

"What? Birds?" Polly glanced at her oddly. "Eh-h-h. Tha' means sommat else." Her eyes got round. "I been wantin' t' see th' like for ever so long! Oh, will we? Tha' think? I bain't ever seen such with me own eyes, but I know they be about. Can feel 'em, sometimes."

"We'll see," Susanne temporized. But—she could feel them too, watching her from the woods, knowing what she was. Eyeing that heavy basket and feeling sure that she should, properly, be sharing. Wondering if they could hood-wink her and thieve some of it away, then eyeing her again and thinking it might be too risky even for one of them.

She felt other eyes too, not fauns, something greater, re-garding her thoughtfully. It wasn't something she recog-nized. But it wasn't dark like a boggart or inimical like a redcap. Elementals of another element entirely? Was that even possible? Would they take notice of her?

And just as they came to Polly's berry patch, she thought she sensed another presence, familiar as her old shoe, and welcome. Would he come out with a stranger there?

Oh, how she hoped so! She longed to see him so much!

There was no telling. Robin would do what Robin would do, but it made her blissfully happy to know her oldest friend had found her at last.

Knowing the ways of fauns, she kept the luncheon bas-ket right by her side while she and Polly gathered the tiny, honey-sweet berries from under their leaves. They were no larger than the tip of her littlest finger, but as she popped a few into her mouth, they burst on her tongue with such in-tense flavor that there was no comparison with garden ber-ries.

They found a sunny bit of meadow nearby, spread out the old blanket that had been folded on top of the luncheon basket, and laid out the feast. And a feast it was! There had been chicken on the gentry's table last night, and here it was, cold, reappearing for their lunch. And there were cress-and-butter sandwiches, simple jam sandwiches, and some of their own cheese, and lovely tart pickles that made your eyes water. There was a bottle each of fizzy lemonade, something neither of them ever saw outside of a Fair Day, though Master Charles was partial to it and there were stocks of it sent from the grocer regularly in summer. Susanne knew about this partiality, as she had obsessively learned everything she could about Charles Kerridge, and the notion she might be drinking one of *his* lemonades made her simultaneously giddy and guilty. She didn't want to deprive him of his treat—but he had as much as ever he could want. Surely he couldn't possibly miss one. Surely Cook would not have given them the bottles if Master would be deprived in the least.

There were scones too, and a pot of their own cream, ready for the berries, and thick slices of plain cake. And as she had expected, the moment the food came out, there was a circle of eyes on them.

The first to appear, though, were the birds; they were bold enough to come right to the edge of the blanket and stare, waiting for crumbs. Since there was more than enough for four girls to have feasted on, the birds got their crumbs without needing to beg for long.

But soon after the birds were pecking at their own feast, Susanne heard the rustlings in the grass that meant *something* was creeping up on them, and she raised her head from her chicken wing, to announce to the air "Tha' might as well stop skulking. We know tha'rt there."

A little horned head popped up from behind a bush. Big round eyes stared at her. Beside her, Polly gasped, but she didn't move. When Susanne looked at her out of the corner of her eye—because with a sticky-fingered lot of fauns around, you didn't take your eyes off them—her expression was a mix of delight and disbelief.

"Us'll share," she told the faun. "But tha' must be patient an' good, an' if tha' steals, there'll be no sharin'." She knew what it wanted above all things—the buttered bread, cake, and scones. The Elementals that actually *ate* rarely got to taste baked things; as a consequence they craved the taste.

Well, by her reckoning they had a full loaf of buttered bread in that basket and they were never going to eat it. She held out one of the sandwiches. The faun edged nearer, until his little goat-legs and hooves and tail were clearly visible. Polly looked as if she were about to burst, but she managed to stay quiet.

The faun edged closer still, nostrils quivering, then stopped, eyes going even wider, if that was possible. "Eh!" it squeaked. "Tha'st scent of Old Thing abaht tha!" It spoke an even broader Yorkshire than the people at the Hall.

"'Twould be curiouser had she *not,*" said Robin from behind Susanne's right shoulder. "Take thy victuals, and tell the others there'll be sharing when thy Master has had her fill."

With an alarmed squeak, the faun snatched the sandwich and vanished, leaving nothing behind but waving meadow grass.

"Robin!" Susanne exclaimed happily, turning to greet him. He was clothed in the seeming he wore most often around Whitestone, that of the young gamekeeper.

"Well met, damozel," Robin replied with a mock bow. "And pleased I am tha's found a safer bower, though it took me fair long to track tha' to it." He had a broad Yorkshire accent himself today. Perhaps to throw Polly off a bit.

"I'm sorry for that," she replied, shamefaced. "But I left in rather a hurry."

Polly's eyes were going from Susanne to Robin and back again, as if she were watching a game of tennis. Finally she could sit silent no more. "Is tha' th' new gamekeeper?" she blurted.

Robin laughed. "Oh, gamekeeper of a sort, Polly Dobbins, but not of Branwell," he replied, silencing her by knowing her name in full. "Nay, I be a friend of Susanne, come to see if she be settled well. And she be, so I'll be off again." He turned back to Susanne. "I've much to do, now tha's gone, and tha' th' only Earth mage about." His eyes warned her not to ask more. "But tha's better gone than stayed. I warned thee that there was badness in those parts. Best tha'rt gone. But there be worse to come, not just for our parts, but for all England and beyond. Bad times are comin', and I think we will not see each other for many seasons. Now I know tha's safe, I can do what I can. Merry met, powers be thanked, and merry part."

"And merry meet again," Susanne said faintly, as she understood that Robin was saying good-bye, perhaps for years.

"Powers willing." He gave her a little nod and turned and somehow vanished as completely as the faun had.

Polly stared at Susanne as if she wanted to ask a thousand questions but understood she would be given no answers. Finally, she took a bite of the chicken leg left neglected in her hand and, instead, began chattering about her sister, the new baby, and what her visit had been like.

Susanne recovered quickly. Robin had warned her from the very beginning that once he considered her trained enough, he could disappear for days, months, or even years. That if she desperately needed him, he would come if he could—but that there was no telling if he would be wrapped up in some greater trouble.

She'd understood that. And indeed, he did vanish for months at a time. But this was the first time he had actually said something like "good-bye."

It sounded as if the things he had been predicting were getting much, much worse—and it sounded as if no other Earth magician had stepped forward to take over her care of the Whitestone lands. Which just made her want to take her father by the shoulders and shake him until his teeth rattled for his carelessness.

And pigs will fly before I would dare, she thought wryly, but also with a touch of fear. The more she thought about her father, the more dangerous he seemed to be. On the one hand, she wished she knew more. On the other . . . she was glad that she did not, and gladder she had not found out the hard way—by remaining at Whitestone.

She put all that aside, firmly. There was nothing she could do about any of this—not the nebulous prophecies of bad times to come, not her father, and certainly not that Whitestone was without an Earth magician. She schooled her face to show Polly a more genuine smile and settled determinedly to enjoy her lunch and Polly's company.

They had gotten to the cake and scones and strawberries and cream when someone else—someone that Susanne thought for a moment was Robin come back—stepped out of the trees and waved at them.

But as the man neared, Susanne saw that he was carrying an actual gun, not the illusion of one, over one arm. And that pale wheatstraw-colored hair was nothing like Robin's curly brown mop.

So *this* must be the new gamekeeper! Polly waved back at him; a moment later, Susanne did the same.

"Hullo!" he called. "Tha'rt from the Hall?"

"Aye," Polly replied for both of them as he neared. "An' thee must be new gamekeeper. Eh! Y'needn't look us over for snare wire or fishing gear. I wouldn't know what t'do with a hare or a fish if I caught one."

"Nor I," Susanne asserted, and then blinked, because she could see the green-gold of Water magic hanging about this man so thickly that if she looked at him with the kind of Sight that showed her such things, his features were entirely obscured by the shields made of it. "But—tha—" she gasped, and remembered that it was safe to talk about magic here. And surely, if Master Charles had hired him, Master Charles knew—knew what he was— "Tha hast—the Water magic! An' so much!"

He smiled sheepishly. "Water Master, aye," he said. "An' a fair famished an' foolish one, for I forgot to bring victuals out an' 'tis a long walk t'cottage. I saw thee havin' thy nuncheon, an' came in hope!"

"We've plenty!" said Polly, and patted the edge of the blanket where the birds had been devouring their crumbs. "But we've naught t'drink."

"That, at least, I have." He had a game bag at his side, and he pulled a leather bottle out of it. "'Tis usually my brother that's the woolly-minded one. Might've been the thought of strawberries that made me so careless."

"Tha' canna live on berries," Polly said sternly, and she pressed a bit of chicken, two bread-and-butter sandwiches, and a slab of cheese on him. "I'm Polly, this is Susanne."

"Peter," the young man said, giving them a little two-fingered salute. "Peter Devlin. Kitchen or parlor?"

"Neither," Polly laughed. "Dairy."

"Then I'll compliment tha' on most excellent cheese," he replied immediately, bringing a bit of color into her cheeks. "And butter. Magic tha' has, and sure-eh-ly. Kitchen magic! The usefulest kind!"

Susanne studied him and liked what she saw. Though he was slight of build and mild of feature, though his pale hair and light green eyes made him look a little washed out, there was strength in those slender limbs, and a look in those deceptively guileless eyes that made her think he was not one to be trifled with.

Well, was any Master?

Me, maybe, she thought, remembering ruefully how she had run from her father without even trying to fight him.

Then again, what else was she to have done? Even Robin thought she had been wise to escape. *I must learn more about magic,* she decided, slowly. *It isn't enough to be the caretaker of the land. I have to learn how to protect myself and others. I have to learn how to recognize dangers that aren't obvious. If bad times are coming, what if they unleash things I don't know anything about?*

This man, she sensed, *did* know all about such things. As she passed him strawberries and cream and cake, and Polly extracted from him the location of more choice beds of berries, she wondered if he would be willing to teach her.

And there was another incentive, too, and one that was, perhaps, more immediate. This was, after all, a household that recognized and valued magicians. And if she really became an Elemental *Master* in every possible way, Charles might take notice of her.

Maybe more than take notice of her. And maybe his parents might think it no bad thing to have a Master about the Hall.

Maybe—maybe there might be a chance.

A check on the dairy had shown that all was in order, which meant that she and Polly were still free to do what they wished until suppertime. She and Polly handed over their basket, but she hung about the kitchen a moment longer, and Polly stayed with her.

Cook had been very pleased to see that they had filled all three baskets and had brought her two. More than pleased enough to offer a little gossip.

"Oh, aye," Cook said, when Susanne made what she *thought* was a discreet inquiry about the new gamekeeper. "That one sees fair *through* the millstone, he does. Tha' should see the undines about him. Besotted! Altogether besotted!" Cook chuckled as she carefully and deftly removed the berries from the two baskets Susanne and Polly had brought her—the third being in their room, where they could have themselves a bit of a treat. Each layer of berries had been carefully cushioned with watercress leaves to keep the berries cool and from crushing each other, and Cook was thriftily setting those aside for cress soup. "We was a-wonderin' what Master Michael was thinkin', hirin' on this fellow Peter Devlin, even allowin' that Master Charles was his brother's friend, but seems he was thinkin' clear. There now! These will be a rare treat, an' thanks to the two of thee." Polly helped herself to a handful of the last berries in the basket, and Cook simply wagged a finger at her. She put the berries away to reappear in some other form, probably for the kitchen meal, and turned back to Susanne. "Now, might not be my place to say, but if I was in tha' shoes, I'd be thinkin' I could do worse nor take magic studies with that one. An' if tha' was t'ask for leave t'do so once work at dairy is done, well, I'd be givin' it."

Susanne blinked. Had she been that obvious?

"'Tis plain as tha' nose that tha' has a fair bit o' power, more nor anyone here, plain that tha' knows how t'use it, an' plain that tha' does not know *all* the ways tha' can'st," Cook continued. "'Tis plainer that he does. Undines would not be makin' thesselves fools over anybody not a Elemental Master. Maybe he ain't thy Power, but Master can teach Master, or so I allus heard. Asides, Marster Charles says that the man what doesn't keep learnin' is a man who'll fair grow into a fool. Since I don't take tha' for a fool, tha' should be learnin' more."

Susanne took a deep breath. "Well, then," she said carefully. "Have I leave t'ask new gamekeeper for lessonin'?"

Cook nodded. "Go after supper. If he says aye, then tha' has leave t' venture there long as need be. I'll be askin' Missus if there be workroom tha' an' he can use when weather turns, come fall. An' as tha' be here, might as well have tha' victuals now, afore the rest."

She set their food down in front of them both, and it seemed a little strange to be so alone at the big table. For once, Susanne was in a great hurry to finish her meal.

Polly sat next to her and watched her inhale her food, with great curiosity. "What's this lessonin'?" Polly asked. "Why's Cook givin' tha' leave for it into winter?" When she explained to Polly in detail what she was going to do, Polly looked a little envious.

"'Twill be more than a little time with him, then. Here I thought tha'd just go, get a lesson or twain, and no more. Eh! An' he's a fine man," she said wistfully. "Tha'll be spendin' some time with him, no doubt, an' likely for a long time. That might lead t'courtin'. Were a person t'be courted by such a man, a person might be sayin' 'aye' before long."

Susanne shook her head, which was, to be sure, too full of Charles to see anything other than "pleasant man, possibly good teacher" in Peter Devlin's features. "Don't be seein' more than there is t' see. Cook thinks strong I be needin' more lessonin' in magic, an' I'm thinkin' strong she's right," she explained. "But no more than that. 'Tis only teachin' I want, naught else."

Polly sighed again. "I'll save thee berries," she promised. Then she brightened. It didn't take magic to divine what she was thinking. If *Susanne* wasn't interested in the handsome young gamekeeper, that meant the field was clear for Polly to campaign.

Susanne laughed. "Tha'd best!" she said warningly, and leaving Polly to amuse herself until bed, she set off for the gamekeeper's cottage, taking the path to the woods once again.

Peter was pleased, but not at all surprised, when the girl turned up at "his" cottage mere hours after he had left her and her fellow dairymaid. If he'd let fall any more hints and indications that he was a Master and was willing to teach, the poor thing would have been buried in them.

He was sitting on a stool by the door, cleaning his gun, when she turned up just after supper. He had purchased wild mushrooms from one of the locals who knew what he was about in that regard, and Garrick had made a fine omelet with them. Of course, the undines here would have warned them both, long before the mushrooms hit the pan, if the fungi were poisonous. The local undines were charmingly attentive; they tended to get short shrift at Branwell since most of the magicians on the estate seemed to be Earth-oriented. They adored Peter and Garrick and took every opportunity to flirt with them.

It had been a most satisfactory supper, and Peter would have been perfectly happy to lounge about in bucolic idleness, waiting to see if the girl turned up. The gun, however, had been fired today, and consequently wanted cleaning. It had unfortunately been necessary to make it clear to one of the few unsavory local poachers that he knew what he was doing and that he knew how to use the rifle he was carrying.

It was possible, he acknowledged, that he had been a bit

more aggressive than was strictly warranted. On the other hand, the man had been setting leg traps for hawks and owls.

Now, first of all, you couldn't eat an owl or a hawk. Second, if you were trying to catch one for falconry, a leg trap was *not* what you would use. Third, there was no reason other than sheer spite or evil to trap and kill a hawk or an owl, and especially not on someone else's land, where you couldn't even make the claim that you were protecting your chickens. And finally, of all the ways to trap and kill a bird of prey, the leg trap was the most cruel.

Fortunately the trap hadn't actually caught anything yet, or Peter would have lost his temper entirely. As it was, when he told the man to be off and never be found on estate lands again, he'd used some language.

It might have provoked the poacher, but on reflection, Peter thought—not. The man rushed him with the attitude of someone who uses his fists to get what he wants and has no idea that the word "no" applies to him. The man was very large, clearly a bully, and probably accustomed to getting his way with just about everyone.

Think I'll pop by the pub and verify that. And with luck, he'll come at me again, and I can humiliate him, Peter thought vindictively.

Attacking had been a very grave mistake; he might have thought he could intimidate someone like Peter, relatively small and not anywhere near as heavily muscled as he was. Peter had stopped the rush by shooting—very accurately— right between the man's legs. The poacher had certainly felt the sting of the bullet's passing. "There is another shell in this gun," he'd said, calmly and clearly, with no trace of Yorkshire accent. "Keep coming and I'll aim higher."

The bully had turned several interesting colors, growled that Peter wouldn't be so brave without a gun in his hands, and reluctantly lumbered off, leaving the traps behind. Peter took them with him, and once he got back to the Hall, he handed them over to one of Charles' people that had a bit of a forge. "Do what tha' want with 'em so long as no body can ever be usin' 'em again," he'd told the man. "An' make right sure the folks hereabouts know I brought 'em to thee. I won't have no leg traps for hawks an' owls on this land. Ever. I'll have every one of 'em that I find destroyed, an' I *will* find every one of 'em."

At least now the local bully knew he meant business. But he was all too well aware that this was only the first stage in what would be an escalation of conflict until he trounced the blackguard in a way that discredited him completely or got him sent to gaol.

He was reflecting on this when he spotted a girl in a white apron and blue gown coming up the path toward him, and it didn't take being a Master to make a shrewd guess at who it was. He finished with his business as she approached and put the cleaned and lubricated gun just inside the door as she got to within a few feet of the cottage.

"Good evening, Miss Susanne," he said, genially. "Bit late for huntin' strawberries, isn't it?"

"Strawberries aren't what I came hunting, Mister Devlin," the girl said politely. "'Tis the instruction that tha' made known tha' could be givin'."

Ah, Yorkshire! he thought fondly. *Blunt and straight to the point.* In other places—like London!—the girl would have danced around the subject for hours before getting down to her request. But in Yorkshire everyone spoke his or her mind, straight out. It saved a tremendous amount of time.

"And ready I am to do so," he said. "Would tha' be comin' inside, or would tha' prefer to speak out here?" He had dropped some of his accent. She didn't seem to have noticed, perhaps because she was a bit nervous already. As she hesitated, he added, "My scholarly brother Garrick is inside also."

"Inside, then," she said, as the tacit offer of a chaperone decided her.

He waved her inside. Garrick was tidying the last of the

supper things away, but he immediately offered their visitor a cup of tea.

"Not now, thank thee," she replied politely. "I'm Susanne, from Hall. I work in dairy."

Interesting. Most of her accent is gone as well. She's not entirely what she seems, either.

"And I am Garrick, and I collect songs," Garrick replied just as politely. "It might not seem very important, but the songs are disappearing as old people die and young people only listen to the gramophone. And if I go on any longer on the subject, my brother will be cross with me."

"Eh, haven't I heard it every time tha' meets some'un?" Peter said good-naturedly. "Have a seat, Miss Susanne, an' we shall see what we shall see. Now, first thing, us must find out what tha' knows, Miss Susanne from Hall."

He began to question her closely, starting with the simplest things that her mentor had taught her and ending with the most complicated. Could she *see* the power? Could she see other peoples'? Did she know what Elemental Magic was?

It took quite some time, and before too long she was glad to accept that cup of tea after all. He watched as she came to realize that she knew much more than she had thought she did; however she had gotten her teaching, it had been quite thorough, though it had been much more on the order of the practical rather than the theoretical. Garrick placed an oil lamp on the table between them, and the soft light gilded her features. He wondered, inconsequentially, if she had any idea how pretty she was.

Peter sat back in his chair when he came to the end of his questions. "Well!" he exclaimed. "That be a no-nonsense course of learnin' if ever I saw one, if a bit bare, and lackin' here an' there. Who taught thee?"

She pondered the question for quite some time. Long enough that he wondered if she was going to tell him it had been the apocryphal old man she had supposedly served. Peter hoped she wouldn't. She had been taught by a Master, and the Master magicians all knew each other, or at least knew *of* each other. It simply was not possible that this unknown Master had been carrying on his work without so much as causing a ripple in Alderscroft's network. And he really did not want to start all of this with proving she was a liar. The truth was best.

"Robin," she replied.

"Robin?" he repeated, and rubbed the back of his head, feeling puzzled. "I never heard o' any Robin Earth Master hereabouts."

"Robin Goodfellow," she elaborated. "The Land Ward."

It took him a moment to catch on, but when he did, his eyes widened. *Good Lord. Robin Goodfellow? The Puck? He's more than an Elemental, he's a godlet!* "Eh-h-h!" he exclaimed. "An' why?"

"Why did *he* teach me?" she hazarded. "Because I was strong an' a child, and that is a bad mortal thing in magic. Because I hadn't anybody to teach me. Because our land needed an Earth Master. And because it amused him?"

"That last be more likely," Peter muttered. But then he smiled at her. "Eh, he made good teachin' of tha', that's plain to see. But now it's late, time you were getting' back. Come ev'ry night after supper, or at least, ev'ry night thee can. First thing I teach thee, 'twill be how to defend tha'self. Robin never did teach thee that, and is more than time tha' learned it."

When she was gone, Garrick brought out stronger stuff than tea, a glass of single malt, neat. "I fancy you might need this, m'lord," he said.

"You fancy correctly, estimable one," Peter replied, and downed his drink with indecent haste. "So, Robin Goodfellow, aka the Puck, aka the oldest Earth Spirit to walk our fair fields that *I* know of, undertook to train this girl."

Garrick pursed his lips. "That is on a par with the Chancellor of the Exchequer deciding he needed to train some shopgirl how to keep her books, if you don't mind my saying so. Extraordinary!"

"Not if the shopgirl in question was a mathematical genius, my lad," Peter replied absently. "But there are great gaping holes in that education. Nothing offensive, very little defensive, all geared toward land service. Well at least I know how to fill *those* gaps."

"I should think so, m'lord," Garrick replied with no irony at all.

"And speaking of which, get your skulking gear. I'm going down to the local pub, where I anticipate I am gong to find the laddy I chased off today." Peter stood up and jammed his hat down onto his head. "I fully expect him to try to beat me into pulp, and I intend to put him in his place."

Garrick's eyes lit up. He didn't often get to see this more aggressive side of his master, and Peter was well aware his normally pacific man got great pleasure from such demonstrations. "Very good, m'lord," was all he said, however. "I'll get the car. We can park it outside the village, and walk in."

❧

It was an unusual night at the *Stag and Crown*. To begin with, Harry Dobbs, the barkeeper, had gotten an earful from old Dan Bennet, on the subject of the one man everyone in Branwell Village treated with extreme caution.

That was Rod Cooper, a fellow who'd been big and strong and a bully as a lad and had grown up to be big and strong and a bully of a man. He'd always gotten his way by shoving others about, his father had encouraged that sort of behavior, and he'd never grown out of it. He was a ne'er-do-well and lazy too. He lived in his dad's little tumbledown cottage, subsisting on poaching and doing as little work as possible. If you had asked Harry, he would have said stoutly that a stint in the army would do Rod Cooper a world of good. But there were enough people willing to pay Rod to move this, or haul that, no matter what sort of a man he was, more was the pity. That, and what he got for what he poached over and above what he ate, gave him the cash money he needed for what he couldn't snare or trap. Which was mostly drink, so far as Harry could tell; he wore the same clothing year in, year out, and the same patched boots. He didn't smell bad enough to make Harry throw him out of the bar, but that was probably because he smelled so strongly of woodsmoke that nothing else registered. The chimney at that cottage hadn't been swept — except by the crude expedient of discharging a shotgun up it once a year — since Rod's father died. How the man breathed in all the smoke that must ensue was a mystery.

According to old Dan, the new gamekeeper up at the Hall had given Rod his comeuppance, destroyed his traps, and sent him packing. Now that was worth a round in any man's estimation, but Harry did worry a bit what would happen when Rod screwed up his courage and went after the gamekeeper prepared, or caught him off the estate and unarmed.

But then, even as he was polishing glasses and pondering this question, two strangers came in and introduced themselves, and Harry found himself looking into the mild blue eyes of the very fellow old Dan had been talking about.

As the fellow got his pint and made idle talk, introducing himself to the regulars and endearing himself to them in the proper manner by buying the house a round, Harry found himself worrying about the chap. Because he was a little rabbity fellow who looked as if he'd break in two in a storm.

And his manner was completely inoffensive. He quickly laid down hints about the acceptable amount and kind of poaching he would accept — he called it "wastage" and "culling" and went on about how a certain amount had to be done to keep the park, fields, and forests healthy. And everyone nodded sagely and agreed. The more Harry listened, the less he wondered why the fellow had been hired in the first place. He knew his business.

"An', of course, us don't cull out of season," the man continued, "No one could object to takin' fish now, for instance, but shootin' a rabbit that might be nursin' or a pheasant that might have chicks or eggs?" He shook his head. "That's bad, an' no good gamekeeper'll stand for that. I be as partial to a jugged hare as next man, but not till the kits are on their own. Now as for fox—"

Harry braced himself. Foxes were a sore point with farmers, because the gentry liked their fox hunts and didn't want anyone else to ruin their game.

"Marster Michael don't ride to hunt, no more do Marster Charles. Tha' got fox comin' for hens, and it happens tha' canna get he, come be tellin' me. We'll lay a cunnin' trap for he that won't trap dog nor child."

Everyone perked up at that.

So there it was, laid out nice and proper. It appeared this fellow was the right sort of gamekeeper for these parts. Everything was settled and the good-fellowship spreading, when the door was shoved open, and Rod Cooper loomed up in the doorway.

Harry went cold. This could not be good.

The talking stopped. Rod strode deliberately to the bar and just as deliberately shoved the gamekeeper aside so roughly that he spilled the man's pint clean over. There was no doubt at all what would follow.

"Pint," said Rod, his glare challenging Harry to say anything, anything at all. He shoved his money across the bar. Harry filled a glass and shoved it back at him, while the gamekeeper reached over and helped himself to Harry's towel to mop up the spilled lager.

Absolute silence fell. All eyes were on Rod and the gamekeeper. Harry braced himself and thought about the stout cricket bat he had behind the bar. Would he dare to use it on Rod?

"Think tha' owes me a pint, laddie," said the gamekeeper calmly and fearlessly.

There was a collective intake of breath. Rod whirled on the gamekeeper.

"I warned thee!" he growled. "I warned thee! Now tha' hasn't thy gun, and what're tha' t' do about it, wee man?"

"Put my pint on tha' account," the gamekeeper replied, not shrinking back a bit. "An' waitin' for tha' apology. Tha'rt in the wrong now, an' tha were in the wrong then. Be a man, an' step up like one."

Rod swung a fist that had laid out many a man before this. Rod might be big, but he was also fast, something that had caused men before this to underestimate him. But the fist swung through empty air, the gamekeeper wasn't where he should have been. Rod was off-balance for a moment, spun halfway around, and the gamekeeper landed a hard blow to the back of his head that sent him reeling half across the bar.

Those anywhere near them cleared off and away, but to his relief, Harry saw that a few of them were carefully putting their pints somewhere safe, cracking their knuckles, and looking determined. There would be no beating of the gamekeeper at least; if he couldn't hold his own against Rod, the others would pull the local off.

Then again, the gamekeeper was beginning to look as if he could hold his own.

Rod caught his balance and turned, looking all around for the gamekeeper. He spotted the man and, more cautious now, moved in on him.

Afraid for his tavern, Harry was about to put a stop to this himself when he saw the man's brother standing at the door. The brother put his finger to his lips and motioned him back. Before Harry could react, Rod charged.

"Tha's not very polite," the gamekeeper chided. "Tha'rt actin' like a wee spoilt boy." He ducked out of the way at the last moment, then spun about like a top as Rod passed him off-balance again, and planted a foot in Rod's backside, sending him flying out the door that the brother was now holding open.

That was a deep relief, and Harry began to feel more optimistic. There would be no breakage in the bar from whatever fighting ensued, and it looked as though the gamekeeper knew exactly what he was doing.

He followed. So did Harry and the rest of the regulars.

And there, in the light of the lamps outside the tavern door, Harry and the rest were treated to as neat an exhibition of scientific boxing as he had ever seen. For all that the man was little, he must have been whipcord tough. He was cool, collected, knew exactly where to land his blows, and exactly how hard they should be. Within five minutes, Harry knew that he could have ended it at any time, but he was not going to. He was going to beat Rod so completely that no one in this village would ever be afraid of Rod again. He had to give Rod this much—he always came straight at a man he was going to beat up. There was no sneaking about and lying in wait and no filthy tricks. Possibly that was because Rod was too dim to think up any filthy tricks or plan an ambush, but at least this meant the gamekeeper wouldn't have to keep watching his back.

No one cheered, and no one laid any bets. They simply watched, bearing witness to something each and every one of them had hoped for and never expected to see.

And no one went for the constable.

Rod was unbelievably stubborn—or stupid. Perhaps both. Long after both his eyes were blacked, his face was a pulpy ruin, and both ears were swollen to the size of small apples, he was still fighting. Long after he was gasping for breath following yet another crippling body blow, he was still fighting.

Finally even the gamekeeper grew tired of it. Or perhaps his hands were getting sore. He landed a gut punch that had Rod bending over and ended it with a clasped-hand blow to the back of Rod's neck.

The bully went down and did not rise again.

The gamekeeper stood there for a moment, shaking his head sorrowfully.

"Pride goeth afore a fall," the brother said from the doorway.

"Aye." The gamekeeper shook both his hands vigorously. "I could use that pint now." He glanced down at Rod. "Reckon 'e needs a doctor?"

"Doctor won' touch he," old Dan offered. "Not 'less he be dyin.' Said so."

"Well, 'e won't die." The man chuckled. "Only wisht 'e might. So us'll have that pint."

A dozen men scrambled to be the first to buy it for him. They all streamed into the pub, leaving Rod lying alone, to drag himself home and disguise his bruises as best he could.

12

THE atmosphere at Whitestone Hall seethed with emotion. The servants were all keeping out of the Master's sight, even his housekeeper, who would slip in with a tray, place it on a table, and slip out again when he wasn't in the room. Richard Whitestone was not merely angry, he was furious. He hadn't known his daughter was missing until well into the afternoon of the day she vanished; he was ready to murder the housekeeper and the maid who had found her room empty that morning and had not seen fit to inform him. Instead, they had engaged in a futile search of the house and grounds themselves, with an inquiry at the village.

Not until past teatime did the housekeeper come, reluctantly, to inform him. And of course by that point the trail wasn't just cold, it had been obliterated. Too many people had passed over the roads she might have taken; too many animals and people had trodden any path she might have used to cross the fields. Not that he expected her to cross fields, she was only a female; women didn't go tramping cross country, it took too much effort, and they were too ill-prepared. A man might decide to cross the moors, but Susanne? She'd have not the first idea of how to go about such a journey. She was used to regular meals and to sleeping in a bed at night. She would never know how to camp rough; she probably wouldn't even think about provisions other than to pack a little buttered bread and think she had done enough. No, she would keep to the roads, and think herself sleeping rough when she slipped into a stable or barn to bed down on straw.

That said, she had to eat, but a woman wouldn't know how to forage, certainly would not know how to fish or hunt, and definitely would not know how to cook over a fire. Women expected things to be "civilized." She must have hidden some money away somewhere; perhaps by taking things from the house and selling them. How would he have known if she did? He didn't go prowling through the place, taking inventory! It could not have been a great deal of money, but she was used to eating the same simple meals as the servants, so a little would take her a long way.

He paced up and down in his rooms, refraining from smashing things only by an effort of will. He could only assume that she had decided to try her hand at working as a servant elsewhere. It was the only logical course she could take. He supposed that since she had been working unpaid as a servant all this time, the idea of doing so for wages was rather attractive, despite that she was technically gentry.

And so, he seethed. First, over the simple fact that she had escaped him. The ignorant little chit had the unmitigated gall to *run away!* It didn't seem to have occurred to her that she was *his*, his possession, body and soul, to do what he liked with. It even said as much in the Bible, and the vicar preached regularly on the subject; since she went to church along with the housekeeper nearly every Sunday, she should have had that drummed into her by this time!

And what was wrong with her? He had finally taken notice of her, elevated her to her proper stature, given her luxuries she hadn't even dreamed of. And she repaid him by *running away!* Wasn't this exactly the sort of thing that those maudlin serialized stories in *Punch* and other papers were all about? Wasn't this the sort of Cinderella tale that servant girls were supposed to wish for?

Why had she run from him? It made no sense.

He paused in his pacing to pass a hand over his face, trying to find a motive. If he had the reason, he could surely find the girl.

Was it rebellion? Was she simply so contrary that whatever he wanted for her, she would do the opposite?

No. There is nothing to suggest that. He'd watched her closely. If anything, she had given him the impression of someone in the habit of obeying orders.

Was she angry because he had neglected her all these years? Was this her way of getting her own back?

But I saw no signs of anger, either. And surely she would have shown them when she was away from me. There was nothing in her previous behavior all these years to suggest she was resentful; if anything, she was too accepting, taking the country attitude of "it is what it is" and dealing with what she had been given.

Was it something more complicated than that? He knew she was uncomfortable in her new role; had she run because she felt out of place as the daughter of the house? He'd counted on that to keep her off-balance and preoccupied, but maybe she was more sensitive in that regard than he had thought.

Oh, surely not. He snorted with impatience. She'd been a servant, for pity's sake. Servants were dull creatures of leaden sensibilities, just barely human.

But there is one way in which she could have completely fooled me. A man. It was more likely that she had a loutish lover somewhere. Had she fled to him? Stupid, romantical female ... she would have known he couldn't approve of a marriage to anyone from the village or the farms. Had she thought that if she just ran off to him, her father would be forced to agree to the misalliance?

If so, that was extremely vexing. He thought he'd checked thoroughly for that possibility immediately on discovering she was the perfect vessel for his purposes, and had found nothing. How could she have been so cunning that she'd hidden a secret alliance?

But females who fancy themselves in love are cunning. Look at how even the most stupid of them can fool those around them until it is too late! And I did not spend nearly as much time on such an investigation as I should have.

But if that was what she had done, where was she? She could not possibly have met a man who lived too very far away.

His first thought on considering *that* had been that she and her lover had elected to run off together. That was certainly foolish and romantical enough to appeal to a callow girl. He'd sent the stableman around to see what he could learn, but the results had been disappointing. No young man was missing from the village or surrounding lands, so whatever she'd done, it hadn't been to "run away together" with anyone at all.

He resumed his pacing. On further consideration, romance seemed unlikely. She just did not have any opportunities. Oh, there *had* been some gossipy nonsense about a gamekeeper, but he didn't employ a gamekeeper, nor did anyone hereabouts. In the end, he had to put the rumor down to the tendency of silly females to make things up when there was nothing to talk about.

Suddenly another thought occurred to him. Had she gotten some sort of fright?

His blood ran cold for a moment at the idea she might, against all odds and precautions, have found him out. That she might have learned what he planned for her.

What if she did? Where would she go? Would she know enough to find another Elemental mage and reveal his true nature? He paused again and reached blindly for the back of a chair to support himself. To be exposed . . . to be hunted by that wretched Alderscroft and his Lodge as he himself had hunted others . . .

They would show him no mercy.

But then, sound good sense took over. She couldn't possibly have discovered what he planned. He'd never told anyone, not even the redcaps. The only way for her to have learned such a thing would be from some preternatural source, some occult source such as a vision or a dream, or —

—Or reading his books.

Again, he froze for a moment of absolute terror. Those books were explicit. There was no doubt what they were about. And Alderscroft would know exactly where he had gotten them.

No, that was impossible. Even if she had been able to read them, all his books were safely hidden away in the secret Work Room. No one in the house knew he had such a room, much less where it was, except for him and the creatures he bound to serve him.

And even if the human servants had known the room existed, no one else in the house knew how to get into it. He kept it locked at all times, except when he was in it.

The boggarts and redcaps wouldn't have told her. And if she had seen the boggarts and redcaps, she wouldn't have stopped to chat with them, foul little beasts that they were. She'd have run screaming at the sight of them. Any sane person would. And they did have the ability to make themselves visible to perfectly ordinary human beings without a touch of magic in them.

Could that have been it? Could she have gotten a glimpse of one of his bound servants and fled the place in horror?

No, that made no sense. A female, confronted with one of the little terrors, would turn to the nearest strong man for protection. She would have come running *to* him, not away from him!

As for occult means, such as visions and clairvoyance—

that was just nonsense. Being able to do such things without a complicated and costly spell? Impossible. Besides, she'd shown no more occult powers than a paving stone.

He resumed his pacing. There had to be a reason. Nothing ever happened without a reason.

Perhaps she *had* gotten a fright, but it was not of the obvious sort. Perhaps it was merely that she was frightened of the education he "planned" for her. He had set her to a lot of difficult lessons, and with her mind dulled by years of servant work, they might have proven so hard that she was coming to hate the idea of more.

Women are intellectually lazy. They only exert their minds if they are forced to. Even Rebecca had shown that unfortunate trait, perfectly content to settle into a placid round of household tasks and feminine handiwork. If he hadn't kept encouraging her to exert herself, she never would have taken herself out of the domestic round.

That seemed the likeliest of all; either because Susanne felt she was incapable or because she was lazy, further quickening and filling her mind could have seemed a nightmare to her. Simply put, she might have run off rather than be sent to university. Perhaps she feared the snubs of those with better educations. Perhaps she was certain she would fail. Perhaps she was simply afraid of so much work. Stupid chit! It was all the more vexing because, of course, he'd never intended to send her to university. And if she'd felt intimidated, all she had to do was express her concerns. He would have had another chance to appear to be the regretful father eager to make amends. Instead . . . she bolted. Like a little boy afraid of the tutor. And she was more than old enough to know better.

He paced angrily in his room. Neither boggarts, nor goblins, nor redcaps had found her, either, and he'd spread them all out to a day's run in every direction. Using trolls was out of the question of course, and simply finding a misplaced girl was exactly the sort of thing that the smaller creatures were good at.

Except they had found nothing. She had vanished right out of their ken. And the other Earth Elementals would no longer obey him. He couldn't even force them to; the moment he had spilled blood in Blood Magic, he had broken the Compact, and they were not obliged to answer him to *be* forced.

That left using a Hound, but she hadn't left a thing behind he could use to trace her—not a hair, not a nail paring, not a stocking. A Hound needed the scent, for it worked by the Law of Contamination. The wretched housekeeper had confirmed that she had taken all her old things, and *only* her old things. "All them pretty dresses, she left, Master Richard," the old hag had quavered. "Reckon she didn't want t' be beholden to you, sir."

The notion that she didn't want to be "beholden to him" would have been amusing had the situation not been so dire.

Not that necromantic magic was very effective for the tracing of people who didn't want to be found. A Hound was a great deal like a real bloodhound, and it could easily lose the trail if enough other people crossed it. He was only this moment realizing how much he crippled himself by devoting himself to necromancy only, and alienating the other Elementals. Short of having something he knew was hers—hair, blood, skin, nails—he had no way to find her. The new clothing he had given to her was too new to have anything but the faintest association with her, easily muddled, and he couldn't even use his blood tie with her as her father because he had effectively—and magically—renounced that very tie when she was born.

Words in the mouth of a magician have power. He knew that, and it wasn't the first time he'd inadvertently created a spell with his words either. Here he was, ironically, the cause of his own undoing. But how could he have known, twenty-one years ago, that she would turn out to be exactly what he needed?

He more than half suspected that someone in the household had colluded with her on this escape, even though they all seemed as bewildered by it as he was. He didn't know them well enough to be certain the surprise was genuine.

How else could she have slipped away in the dead of night so easily and completely?

Well, before too long, they were going to get what was coming to them. And finally he would have completely obedient servants.

But not yet. He was not ready to take that step just yet.

What else can I use to hunt for her? If not the Hound, what about something that can work by sight? Something patient and slow?

That was when it came to him, and he smiled a little.

One of the many, many advantages of having a property like Whitestone Hall was that the Hall had its very own cemetery. Many of the great houses and stately homes had one; it was much more convenient than going to all the trouble of a burial at the village church. Oh, none of the family were buried there, although in the truly great manors and palaces the opposite was almost always true. Such places had their own chapels, and the family were often buried in crypts beneath the chapel. Not so here; this had been a little plot for the servants, where they could tend to the graves of their own without the inconvenience of walking all the way out to the village and the church and back. It hadn't been used since Rebecca had died, and most of the graves were of children or servants with no family. That was why he hadn't had Rebecca buried there. For his purposes, this could not be better.

He waited until the house was quiet, and everyone was asleep. Then he slipped into his Work Room. He needed to call up one of his bound slaves. For this, although a redcap might seem the obvious choice, a boggart was actually better. He wanted something that would try to be unobtrusive. Boggarts were small and weak, and except when they could swarm a victim or knew they were more powerful, they tried to keep hidden.

Once in his workroom, he got out his tools, made his preparations, and began the magic. He cast his controlling circles with great care. It would not do for the thing to get loose until he released it with his coercions upon it. The books all called for this to be done somewhere that had been polluted with dark and dire things—a battleground, a murder site, or some other cursed place. It was not practical for him to do this in the open, on appropriately tainted ground, so instead he had a broad, shallow box filled with earth mixed with blood that he used for such purposes. The physical components of his circles were hemp rope steeped in more blood and other noxious substances. The curious thing about Elementals was that although they conformed to some physical laws, they seemed completely immune to others. Boggarts, for instance, had real bodies; they were not spirits, and they could accomplish tasks like the one he was about to set this one on, things that needed physical bodies that could act in the physical world. They could do things for him, you could touch them—and yet he could call one right up out of a box of dirt sitting on the floor of a room on the second story of his home. He didn't know where the creature was going to come from, or how it would get to the box. When he dismissed it at last, it would vanish without a trace back into the earth. He supposed such things would drive a scientist mad.

He felt the dark power of the blood-soaked earth as he prepared his spells, potent and heady. It had a scent; part putrefaction of the sort that was sickly-sweet, and partly bitter, like poison. To his eyes, it had a color—that of dried blood overlaid with a sullen orange. And it left a faint residue on the skin, sticky rather than slimy. If the power of the Earth that he had mastered before was like wine, *this* was stronger stuff, raw whiskey, straight from the still. It took a man with a lot of willpower to handle it. It was like holding a tiger; you were safe as long as you didn't let go, but if you did—

Well, it could use you. It could open you up to the very things you were trying to control, and you would be the one that became the slave. Dangerous. Intoxicating. Very personal in a way that Earth magic was not. *He* had created this power, with the deaths he had made with his own two hands. No one else could use it but him.

He forced it into the shape he wanted; the channel through which a boggart would manifest. As he imposed his will on the power, it shaped itself in the physical world in a way that ordinary eyes could see. Rusty-red tendrils oozed upward from the ropes around the box, weaving together until they formed a transparent, half-dome cage over it. Earth power glowed; this did not. This was more like smoke; it moved to currents he couldn't quite sense, thickening and thinning. Another half-dome of the same power extended below the floor, not visible from here.

When you made such protections with Earth magic, you got the same dome, but that one would glow with a golden radiance like ripe grain in the sun. He'd once in his early days as a Master been curious enough to find out if the power passed through the floor and was visible in the ceiling of the room below a Work Room, and he had gone to look. It did; it was a bit uncanny to see the half-dome glowing away, exactly like some lighting apparatus from a Jules Verne tale of the future. He'd been very careful to set up his spell-casting area above a place where such a phenomenon was not likely to be seen—the linen closet. Unlikely that anyone would be rummaging for fresh sheets in the middle of the night, and even if they did, his dark power would not be visible in the shadows of the ceiling.

It was so much easier to use this type of power than the Earth magic he had been taught to wield. There was no coaxing, no cajoling, and no insidious leaching of his own strength. It was astonishing how much latent power there was in something as simple as a chicken—and, of course, the power available increased to an astonishing degree the more intelligent the sacrifice was.

Now that he had dared to think of using human beings as his sacrifices, the potential power made his mouth water.

The amount of power a sacrifice yielded also depended on its age. The younger, the more potent. All those years yet to be lived lay coiled inside under tension, like a spring.

He wrenched his concentration back to the conjuration; at this stage he could not afford a lapse. He bent all of his will on the box of earth. He needed a boggart. He *would* have a boggart!

With his mind alone, he traced the sigils of conjuration on the earth in that box rather than cross the barrier. The earth glowed dully where his thoughts branded the signs in place. Eight sigils, placed at equal distances around a circle, and then the final, most important one of all, right in the center.

And with a faint groan, the earth split, and the boggart crawled out of it.

The earth closed back again, snapping shut like an ill-tempered mouth.

The boggart glared at him across the barriers that kept them apart. It was a hideous thing, about the size of a child just beginning to toddle, but with a wizened body that looked made of knotted roots. Sometimes Richard wondered if the artist Arthur Rackham had actually *seen* Elementals, Earth Elementals in particular, since the withered, wrinkled, long-nosed face certainly had its counterpart in the fairy-tale drawings that fellow had done. But with one difference. Had Rackham ever portrayed the hate and anger visible on this creature's face, children would have run screaming at the sight of his drawings, not been charmed by them. The skin was a putty gray, the hair looked like dead grass, the ragged clothing had no color at all.

It did not speak. It did not have to, because it was here to obey him, not have a conversation with him. And it knew this. This was part of the reason for the anger. It simply looked at him, full of impotent rage, and waited for instructions.

"Go to the graveyard to the east of this house," he told it. "The one that I have marked with my sign. Find any revenants and discover their graves. Then bring me a finger-bone from each grave that hosts a revenant. Bring them here. Then I will release you."

All such graveyards were haunted, to a greater or lesser degree. He was grateful that, years ago, he had not gone to the considerable trouble of sending those revenants to their respective "rewards." At the time he had just had too much to do; the revenants were not harming anything and were so unobtrusive that the worst anyone had ever reported from the cemetery was a vague feeling of unease and sadness. Not surprising; no one buried in that earth had suffered a violent death, none had any great passions at all, really. They were just too bewildered, too apprehensive, or too ignorant to move on. Such spirits often needed help if they lingered past the moment of their deaths. The Door only stood open for so long, and once it closed, the spirit had to find its own way across by desiring a new Door to open. Most of the time, eventually, the spirits got so tired of living a shadow life that they reached for the Door in desperation.

It was an ironic thing that many were so convinced that their tiny little sins were so enormous they would be going straight to Hell that this fear alone stranded them on the metaphorical shore. That was the fault of the chapel preachers, of course, with their fire and brimstone threats and their utter condemnation of anything but the straightest and narrowest way. The child-ghosts, if they had been dragged regularly to chapel by a parent, were the most likely to suffer from this delusion. Of course, to a child, everything seemed enormous, from sin to blessing. And from time to time, in the past, that had bothered him a little. Eventually he had assumed that either he would help this sort of revenant, which was what the little cemetery abounded in, or they would learn to see and not fear the Door themselves—but he never had gotten around to it, and it took some creatures a very long time to realize that lingering in a gray half-life was a kind of Hell in itself.

But now, of course, since they were still there, he could use them.

This was one of the first pieces of business that a necromancer learned: how to find and bind revenants to do his will. There were more of them about than most people had any notion. Aside from those who lingered out of irrational fear, there were others who refused to cross. Some simply were not aware they were dead, though these were in the minority. Some were bound by emotion or tragedy to the place they had died or were buried. Some desperately wanted to live again. Some remained because of other bonds, of debt, or hate—and some because they actually *were* destined for an unpleasant afterlife and were in no hurry to speed to it.

The one thing they all had in common was that it was possible for the necromancer to use them, willing or unwilling. All he needed was something that had been intimately theirs. Once bound, they made the perfect spies. They could go anywhere; you closed your door in vain against them unless you were a mage yourself.

The problem with using revenants was a matter of energy. Since they were no longer living, they no longer produced any of their own. That was why ghosts faded over time; the very act of manifesting consumed some of their substance, and very few ever learned how to feed on other things to replace that substance. That was why a ghost seldom went far from the place (or object) it was tethered to—moving away took energy, and that was something a ghost could not spare.

Once a necromancer found a revenant that was particularly useful, it was generally possible to go beyond coercion into—well, something like indentured servitude. The next stage of the necromancer's acquisition of power was to learn ways in which to feed revenants and strengthen them without making them too strong to control. Revenants being fed were not in a hurry to lose that source. Revenants being fed *enough* could act in the physical world to a limited extent. This made them ever so much more useful as servants.

But still not as useful as cooperative Elementals. . . .

Curse it, he was half-crippled by the fact that his Elementals would no longer respond to him.

Bosh. There are better things. I just need to find them.

A movement in the earth of the box alerted him to the fact that the boggart was back. It crawled its way out of the dirt, brushed off its leather garments, and dropped a dirty bag at its feet. "Got bones," the boggart said, in a strange voice that sounded like an unoiled hinge.

He merely nodded. It wasn't an outstanding performance, so did not warrant a great reward. He flung it a bit of power; it sucked the stuff down greedily and eyed him for more. When more wasn't forthcoming, it looked disgruntled for a moment, then its face assumed its habitual sneer.

Richard restrained an impulse to punish the wretched thing. That would be counterproductive. Instead, he merely collapsed the magic about the boggart, forcing it back to where it had come from, rather than dismissing it. It was a peculiar effect; the sphere of sullen, ruddy smoke shrank, like a child's balloon deflating, growing more opaque as it shrank, until there was nothing but a pea-sized sphere of darkness lying atop the earth. Then that, too, vanished.

There was no sign that the boggart had ever been here but the bag of bones. Richard examined the bag carefully, looking for some sign that the boggart had left an unpleasant surprise for him among them. But no, it was just a bag, containing around twenty index-finger bones.

He took those to his workbench and looked them over too, to make sure the boggart hadn't cheated him by gathering the bones from only one or two individuals. Despite his suspicion, it had given him exactly what he asked for.

He extracted one for each of the servants, picking the smallest, which would likely be children. Children were the easiest to manipulate.

This time he did away with the circles and protections

altogether. He didn't want to frighten these revenants, after all. Instead, one by one, he forged a tie between bone and spirit, as a more powerful extension of the tie between revenant and its full body. Then, one by one, he reeled them in.

When he had them, he fed them—not much, just enough to waken them a little more. As it was, they were wispy little things, so weak that they didn't even really have faces anymore, just suggestions of faces. When he thought they were sufficiently alert, he gave them their orders.

"I want you to haunt my servants," he told them. "I want you to walk through their dreams, speak to them there, and ask them a question." He paused. "And that question is this: *Where is Susanne?* They will know what that means. All you have to do is get an answer from them. Do you understand?"

The little things nodded awkwardly.

"Good. Now go." He had everything he needed, of course, from the servants themselves. It was child's play for his boggarts to nip into their rooms at night, cut a lock of hair, and bring it back to him. He tied a strand of hair to each of the fingerbones so the revenants would know whom they were to haunt.

"Go now," he told them. "Return when you have my answers."

He heard the results of his work almost immediately, moans and groans coming faintly from the bedrooms below. Having a spirit walk through one's dreams always caused nightmares.

He smiled with satisfaction. The wretches were going to pass an uneasy night, which they roundly deserved for allowing Susanne to escape.

He sat himself in his most comfortable chair and waited for the revenants to return.

One by one, they did so, but each time it was with the same result.

No one knew where Susanne was, and, amazingly, no one had helped her escape. The servants were all genuinely be-

wildered that she would run away. They could not imagine
how she could give up the favored position he had granted
her. The two youngest had been absolutely pathetic in their
dreams, from what he learned from the two ghost-children
he had sent to them. They had desired those gowns and
furbelows with a passion he would never have suspected
they were capable of.

And with Susanne gone, they secretly hoped the gowns
would be given to them. They had, in fact, been dreaming
that very thing when the spirits came walking through their
minds. In their waking state, of course, they knew this was
utterly impossible, which made their dreams all the more
pathetic.

He did not unbind the ghosts when they had finished;
instead, he commanded them to linger nearby, removed the
strands of hair, and put the bones in a very safe place. He
might well need them again, and soon.

He wanted to rage, break things, kick the box of earth
over and trample it. He did none of these things. He was
disciplined. He had to be.

So he put everything away in its proper place, exited the
Work Room, and made sure the lock caught behind him.

Then he went to his favorite chair and flung himself
down into it, his emotions seething all over again.

He simply had to get Susanne back. There was no better
vessel. He could not bear the thought of trying to find another. His stomach knotted, his teeth hurt from clenching
his jaw, and he had a furious headache centered right between his eyebrows. He closed his eyes and tried to will it
away, concentrating so hard that when the housekeeper
spoke up from the middle of the room, he actually jumped.
He opened his eyes to see her squinting to make him out
against the draped window, twisting her hands together in
her apron.

"Master Richard, sir?" she said timidly. It sounded as if
she were afraid he was going to blame her for this. He
couldn't, of course,

But she doesn't know that. He decided he liked having that sort of hold on her.

"Yes, what do you want?" he asked gruffly.

"It's about Mistress Susanne, sir." She in her turn was concentrating very hard as well, trying to keep the "Yorkshire" out of her words. "I wonder, had you taken thought to hiring one of them detective persons to find her?"

The words sounded as if they were being spoken in a foreign language for a moment, and they took him completely by surprise. "Eh—what?" he said, startled. "What do you mean?"

"There are these detective persons, sir. You read about them in stories in the papers all the time," she replied, sounding both apprehensive and eager. "You hire them. They can find things for you. Like heirs, and runaway children, and servants. Sometimes they can find stolen things, too. I can bring you the papers. They put advertisements in them."

Hire someone? Hire a person to hunt down Susanne? *Not* rely on magic?

The sheer novelty of the idea made him feel disconnected for a moment.

"You'd need a picture of her, of course. So he would know who he was looking for," she continued. "I don't suppose you have a picture?" Doubt had crept into her voice now.

No, I don't suppose—he thought savagely, angry that hope had been held out in one hand to him and snatched away by the other.

And then, suddenly, it was given to him all over again.

"Wait," he commanded, and went to a locked cupboard that he hadn't unlocked for . . . years. Decades. He took the key from his waistcoat pocket on a ring with several others and put it in the lock. The key resisted, then turned stiffly.

He opened the double doors, and there, on the shelf where he had left it, was the thing that had been such a

novelty, such a delight, to Rebecca in the year of their engagement and the first year of their marriage.

It was a fat, leather-bound volume with thick pasteboard pages. He took it down, blew the dust off of it, and
opened it.

And there they were, the photographic portraits of Rebecca and himself, separately and together. He had ob-
tained a box camera and had undertaken to document their
engagement, teaching her to use it as well. He had also
hoped to document the Earth Elementals, but that was not
a success; they would see the camera and flee, no matter
how carefully he moved in on them or tried to ambush
them with it. Still, here was Rebecca, looking even more
like Susanne, in all seasons, in portraits posed and natural,
at the fairs, at the races, at picnics, any place he could take
the camera. In the middle of the book were the professional
photographs of their wedding, and then came the ones he
had taken afterward for about a year. But then they had
both grown tired of the toy, and he had put it away, intend-
ing to take it out again to document the growth of their
children.

He had no idea where the camera was now. Perhaps he
had even smashed it in those first weeks of unrelenting
grief.

But the pictures were here. And they were perfect for his
purposes.

He paused for a moment. There was a problem with this.
If he hired an outsider, someone outside this household
would know he had a daughter and that she had run away.
This could prove inconvenient when he invested Rebecca's
spirit into Susanne's body.

Or not. Because he had already decided, had he not, on
certain matters.

He extracted several photographs from their pasteboard
frames and put the book back in the cupboard. Then he
went to his desk and wrote out a substantial check. He gave

both to the housekeeper. Her eyes widened at the size of the check, and widened still further at the photographs.

"When did you—how did you—"

He was pleased. Clearly she did not realize that she was holding pictures of Rebecca, not his daughter.

"I leave this in your hands," he said brusquely, in tones that conveyed he would answer no questions. "Hire this man. Hire more than one if need be. Just bring my daughter back. But do not tell him she is my daughter." He paused. "I don't want her shamed; I do not want her name in the papers."

After a moment the woman nodded. "What shall I say, sir?" she asked timidly.

He thought a moment. "Tell him—tell him that she is the daughter of a distant relation who left her in my care."

"Aye, sir." She nodded. "Perhaps, I could hint she might not be thinking too clear?"

Well, showing some initiative! Evidently guilt had a stimulating effect on the mind. "That is a good suggestion," he replied. "Or, well, you could say she is a servant that took something unspecified."

That made her look uneasy, but again she nodded.

"I leave this in your hands," he said finally.

And with that, he turned his back on her, giving her the clear message that the interview was over. She hesitated, then said, "Immediately, sir," and went away, closing the door behind her.

He closed his eyes. The headache was gone. It had been replaced by a feeling of rampant satisfaction.

13

"Now," said Peter genially. "Let's try this again. Why is it that to call up a faun you'd use the same sigils you'd use to call up a gnome?"

He and Susanne sat at the tiny table in his cottage, across from each other with a candle between them. A little of her dark hair had escaped from her severe chignon, and her expression was serious indeed. There was a book on the table as well, a book of magic theory. She had expressed shock on seeing it; evidently, she had never realized there was such a thing.

Susanne thought about that, very hard. "You'd only do that if you wanted a forest gnome. Then you'd use the same sigils because the sigils describe the place where you find what you are looking for, so forest creatures are called up using the same set of sigils. You'd make the difference in whether it was a gnome or a pixie or a dryad by what you put inside the circle."

Neither of them was speaking with much of a Yorkshire accent. Peter wondered if she realized this. He certainly did.

It told him something else about her; it was hard to get rid of that accent if you had been accustomed to it from the time you were an infant, and it was comparatively easier to pick it up and drop it again if it was something you had heard all the time but not, so to speak, your "native tongue."

Someone had gone to considerable effort when she was a child to be sure that the first things she learned to say were not in broad Yorkshire.

"I do believe you are getting the sense of this," he said, approvingly. "You're doing very well. Not that Robin taught you poorly, of course!"

"Oh, aye, but he taught me to go on what I felt." she replied. She shut the book he had lent her and looked at him earnestly across the little table. "That's good, when all that's to do is take care of the land."

"Feelings and instincts," Peter nodded. "And the care of the land is, of course, the Puck's first concern. But once you go beyond merely tending to the land, you need fundamentals and logic. You need to know *why* you use things as well as *how.* Now, if you were to have to defend yourself against a boggart, what would you do first?"

"Get into the open," she said immediately. "And then . . . well, he's earth, so he's my element. Any protective circles that I can cast should hold him out. He's a house creature, so he won't like the forest, so I should enlist the forest Elementals to help me against him."

"Good." They had been working together for some time now. Susanne had a good mind, and a quick one, and he thought she had come to trust him. "Susanne, would you say I am your friend?"

She blinked at him, then laughed. "Of course, tha' great loon!" she replied, slipping into broad Yorkshire again. "If tha' weren't my friend, tha'd not be spending hours and hours setting me aright!"

"Then at this point, I think I have the right to know," he said, letting a little steel creep into his voice. "Just who *are* you, Susanne-the-dairymaid? Where do you come from, who are your people, and what in heaven's name were you running from when we found you in the stable?"

She stared at him for a very long time, her face still and without expression. Then she sighed, and it was almost as if she were putting a tremendous burden aside. "Tha — You're right, Peter. You do have a right to know." She clasped her hands together on top of the book. Before she did so, he could see they were trembling a little. "My name is Susanne Whitestone. I come from across the moor from the house of the same name; it was about three days afoot."

Whitestone? That sounded familiar. Very familiar. He pummeled his brain. Trying to think where he had heard that name.

"My family is prosperous and my father is the local squire, but I spent most of my life doing the work of a servant. My mother died when I was born, and my father did not even want to see me until a few weeks ago," she was continuing. "Housekeeper and Cook raised me. I spent my life with the servants and did what they did, and when I came early into my power, Robin taught me the magic. My father never left his rooms. I never even saw him until just after May Eve. Then suddenly, as if he had just discovered that I existed, he wanted to make it all up to me . . ." She faltered and grew a little pale.

Peter leaned forward over the table and patted her hand, all the while thinking, *Whitestone . . . where do I know that name? And the story sounds familiar.* "I take it that there was something more going on than just an old man's remorse," he said quietly.

"It just didn't feel right," she whispered. "I didn't know why, but it all just didn't feel right. He set me to lessons, all sorts of lessons, and kept telling me that I had to learn all these things to be fit for my place, that I had to remember I wasn't just a servant. He knew I hadn't been properly educated, and I didn't know all the things that girls of my age and class should. He said when I was ready that he was going to send me off to school, even University. He bought me all new clothing, and he corrected my lessons himself. But he didn't seem to realize that I had magic at all."

"Wait—he knows about magic?" Peter interrupted.

She nodded. "He is an Earth Master. He was the one who should have been tending to the land, not me."

Earth Master . . . Earth Master. I should know this.

She had grown very pale, and her obvious distress distracted him from what he was trying to remember. "I cannot explain what was so wrong. It was as if he wasn't ever really looking at me, just at something he wanted to be there, something he . . . owned. As if I were a *thing* and not a person." She took a deep, shaking breath. "And he was *watching* me. All the time. Even when I slept. Even when I did things that couldn't possibly interest him, he was watching me. I didn't understand why. But then I found out he had a secret room, and I got into it and that—"

She gulped, and her face went red and white by turns. "The first time, he had books and things in there, and the books were . . . they felt *wrong.* I couldn't read them properly, but in my hand, they felt wrong. The second time, he was there already, and I heard him, saw him. He had a picture of me in there, and he was talking to it, and he was saying—he was saying things, horrid things. Things no one should ever say to a *daughter.*"

Peter blinked, puzzled. "I'm afraid I'm being a bit thick," he apologized. "What sort of things now?"

She hung her head. "Things . . . things you should only say to a wife. Things you plan to do to her . . . with her . . . when you're alone together. It was horrid, horrid. I mean, that's all right and good and proper if it's your wife, but . . . Why would he want to do those things with his *daughter?*"

"Eh?" said Peter, then "Oh!" as it dawned on him. He flushed with anger. "By Jove, did he?" *If I ever find him, I'll thrash him within an inch of his life.* He patted Susanne's hands. "And so you ran. Sensible girl. Well you're safe enough here, now." He tried to keep his tone light to avoid frightening her further. She looked up at him and managed a tremulous smile.

"I don't understand how he could be like this," she continued. "He used to be the Earth Master for thereabouts, I mean, really, truly, the Earth Master. Robin said so, that he not only tended the land, but he did things for the Chief Master in London—"

"He what?" Peter interrupted. *Whitestone! That's where I remember the name! Richard Whitestone, the one Alderscroft was telling me about, the recluse!*

"He used to be the Earth Master, and it was his duty to see to the land all about Whitestone Hall," Susanne said, and a touch of irritation came into her voice. "The land needed him! But when my mother died, he just threw it all away, he completely neglected his duty to the land. He closed himself into his rooms and never left, and the area all around the Hall just *died*. It's worse than neglected, it's blighted. I had to enclose it to keep the blight from spreading farther. And you would think, wouldn't you, that a Master would notice that someone had taken over his duties? Would notice someone had shielded the area around the Hall? And you would think it might come to him that the person might be his own daughter ..."

Isolation ... blight ... could it be ...

It was beginning to sound as if Susanne did indeed know who the necromancer was, and it was her own father! But perhaps—no, she'd said nothing about the sort of magic he was doing, or even if he was doing anything at all.

"Did you ever see anything—" he groped for words. "—nasty about? Elementals that were not something you'd care to run across?"

"What, boggarts and kobolds and all?" she asked, and before he could reply, shook her head. "Never. All I got were those feelings of being watched. The only thing that was ... nasty ... were the books."

"Books?" Peter repeated sharply. "What sort of books?"

"Well, I don't know precisely. They just made me feel a little sick when I touched them, and he was keeping them all in that secret room." Now besides her pallor, she was looking a bit green.

Peter made up his mind. "Come," he said, closing his hand around hers, standing up, and tugging her upright. "We need to go straight to Charles about this."

He could see the puzzlement in her eyes. Not surprising, considering he was referring to the son of the house by his first name. "But—"

"Now," he insisted.

She let him draw her to her feet and lead her out of the cottage and down the path to the Great House.

While having Charles Kerridge notice her was very high on Susanne's list of desires, she was not sure that having him notice her in this way was going to get her the sort of attention that she wanted.

Nevertheless, when Peter's way of speaking changed to something very much posher, and he insisted that she come with him, she was so taken aback that she found herself following him as faithfully as any chick following a hen. It was still light out, which was a good thing, as otherwise she was so dazed that she would have stumbled along like a little fool and probably tripped over something and gotten her gown all dirty. She hoped her hair was tidy. Oh, how she wished that she had something better to wear than this uniform! Right now she would have given a great deal for one of those pretty gowns she had left behind! She didn't want him to look at her and see just a faceless dairymaid, she wanted him to look at her the way Peter did, seeing *her* and not the uniform.

She fretted so much during the long walk that she hardly noticed they were at the Great House until they were literally at the door. And not the servants' entrance either, but the door closest to the path to the gamekeeper's cottage, which was one of the family entrances, used only by the estate manager and the Kerridges. She was shocked into silence at that point and just let Peter lead her. He stopped once to send one of the housemaids after Charles Kerridge; the girl obeyed him with no question. Another shock.

In no time at all she found herself in Charles Kerridge's office. There, the gamekeeper addressed him familiarly and by his given name, and Master Charles reciprocated. In fact, they sounded like old friends. Clearly, this man was not just a gamekeeper, anymore than Robin had been. She stood there with her hands clasped under her apron and listened, flushing with embarrassment, as Peter—*could it be* Lord *Peter?*—summed up everything she had told him.

Finally the two of them turned to her. "Sit down, Susanne," Charles said, with the same understanding smile he'd worn when she first saw him. Gingerly, she took a seat on the very edge of the chair he offered and clasped her hands tight in her lap. Peter took another chair, and the two of them began a gentle but very firm interrogation.

From time to time they paused in their questioning to confer, but then they came right back to her, asking more details. She understood then that she knew far more about her father than she had thought she did.

And all those little details meant a very great deal to *them.* Especially the part about the books.

"Were you there?" Charles asked Peter. "No, wait, we were both too young. But Father might have been. He told me about the Exeter necromancer, the library he had. I had always thought the books were destroyed. What was Alderscroft thinking?"

"That this was an Earth Master who could be trusted and that we might one day need what was in those books," Peter countered. "No, I can understand that, and far safer those volumes were in the hands of someone as sound as Whitestone was then." He pinched the bridge of his nose between two long fingers. "It's obvious the death of his wife unhinged him."

"More than unhinged him," Charles replied grimly,

looking a bit sick. "I can think of a damn good reason for that obscene behavior Susanne described—once you add 'necromancer' into the sum. Think about it, Peter."

"You can—oh, lord." Now Peter looked sick. Susanne looked from one to the other as if she were at a tennis game. "Oh, so can I, now." He looked at Susanne with an expression of horror. "He wouldn't—"

"He would," Charles said, and stood up. "I'd better go consult with Pater and Mater. They knew him after all."

"Master Charles, wait!" Susanne exclaimed urgently. "He wouldn't *what?*"

"Don't worry your little head about it," Charles said, and rushed off.

Peter rolled his eyes. "That is just about the worst bit of idiocy Charles has ever spoken. I'm sorry, Susanne. Being told not to worry about something is only likely to give you nightmares." He paused. "Although, I can't imagine you could have a worse nightmare than what we think Whitestone has in mind."

"Tell me!" she demanded, sounding shrill even in her own ears. Charles might still intimidate her, but Peter did not.

"Well . . . let me start at the beginning." He leaned forward a bit, looking at her earnestly, and she wondered then how she could ever have thought he was "just" a gamekeeper. It was obvious, when you looked at him, that competent as he was at the job, he was right out of the peerage.

Then again, he seemed to be something of a chameleon, able to take on the color of wherever he was.

"There is an organization of Elemental Masters out of the Exeter Club in London; it's led by Lord Alderscroft. We call him the Old Lion, and he has his finger on the pulse of most of what goes on in England, magically speaking. He got wind of something in this part of the world that he didn't much like and sent for me. The long and the short of it is, I was sent here to find a necromancer, and with what I've done and what you've told me, Charles and I are both pretty sure that your father is that necromancer. Now, do you know what I'm talking about?"

Susanne shook her head.

"Necromancers aren't the sort of thing you run into very often, thank goodness. They're a kind of perverted Earth Master, and everything they do has to do with the dead. They can talk to the dead, but mostly they don't just talk to ghosts, they force spirits to come to them and then tether the spirits to something in the real world and keep them here. They can animate dead bodies and even bones, which is sickening enough, but they can also drag unwilling spirits back by using bits of those bodies, an' they can imprison those spirits in a body to make it self-controlling, so the necromancer doesn't have to act like a puppet master all the time."

Peter spoke very calmly, but Susanne was feeling sick at the mere thought of all of this. It completely revolted her to the core, it was so very wrong. "But how can you *do* that if—if the person has gone to heaven?" she asked, unable to think of how God could be so thwarted.

"You can't. But if they're lingerin', and a lot do, then you can. And there's always deception." He drummed his fingers on the desk. "See, if a spirit wants a body again, and they're clever enough, they can make the necromancer think they're the right one."

"So if the person has gone to heaven, it won't matter if the necromancer has . . . bits," she said, and Peter nodded. "And if a clever spirit comes and says that she's the right one, the necromancer might not know."

"The thing is, old girl," Peter continued, "We're both pretty sure that unhinged as he is, he's been trying to do something about bringin' his wife back, and she might be the sort that lingers, makin' sure that you are all right, for instance. Except, of course, at this point she wouldn't be very pretty, eh what? But if he can drag her spirit back, there's one thing he *can* do that will give him a livin' body rather than a sack of bones. He can shove your spirit out of your body and put hers in it. Which is what, we think, he was goin' on about when you overheard him."

For a moment Susanne was quite sure she hadn't heard him right.

But then she remembered those horrible moments when she'd listened to her father talking to that painting . . . and of course he couldn't possibly have a painting of *her,* now, could he? He hadn't even really known she existed until a few weeks ago. Paintings required that you sit for them, and they required an artist to paint them. There'd been no artists about Whitestone Hall, and she certainly hadn't sat for a painting.

So the picture had to be of her mother.

Which meant that Peter was right.

"I think I'm going to be sick." she said, faintly. She fought down both a wave of nausea and one of absolute terror.

"I'm not going to say it's going to be all right," Peter told her with candor that was as good as a glass of cold water to the face. "But of all the places you could have come, this is the best and safest. It's absolutely stiff with Earth mages, and I'm a Water Master. "To get to you, he'll have to get through us, and I don't think he can do that. I'll be letting Lord Alderscroft know all about this immediately. And you are an Earth Master, so you are not exactly defenseless. You might not know the sort of combative magic that I do, but you have many allies among the Earth Elementals, and their sort don't much like necromancy. You've been keeping your side of the Compact all this time, doing the land-work. They'll honor their side."

She nodded, slowly. Not that this made her feel any better . . . but he was right. She *could* fight back.

"Now I think you could use a good lie-down," Peter continued, kindly. "Can you get to your room by yourself?"

She nodded again, and he helped her to her feet. "Don't worry too much, if you can help it," he urged, as he opened the office door for her and let her out. "And even if Charles thinks you 'needn't worry your little head about it,' I will make sure you know everything we are doing."

"Thank you," she said faintly. And in a daze, she headed for her room, *very* glad that she wasn't going to be alone in it.

Peter watched her go, with worry but also with admiration. The girl was holding up under the revelation of horror that would have sent virtually anyone he knew, male or female, screaming or fainting. Or both.

He sighed. Oh, he liked that girl. Brave, amusing, self-reliant . . .

. . . quite pretty, though not in the exotic way of his divas and dancers.

And eminently more sensible than all the society girls his mother kept throwing at him. *Good Lord, put one of those in this situation, and we'd be coping with more hysterics than a cage of monkeys with a snake in it.*

Plucky, that was what she was. Just the sort of girl he wished one of those society wenches was.

For a moment, he was distracted by other thoughts. He was not the sort of fellow to whom an ascetic life appealed, but thus far, he had never found the sort of woman he could see spending the rest of his life with. There were not many unattached female Elemental mages about, and none of them had given him that spark he required, that kinship . . . and he was never going to do what his father had, and marry someone without any magic in her. What a disaster that would be!

Good thing I'm not the heir, only the spare. My dear old brother can take care of the family line. But still . . . no, this was all futile, even if he could get past the expectations of his mother.

Bah. You'd have to be blind not to see how infatuated she is with Charles, poor thing. And the fact is, she can't stay here any longer. We have to get her out of the country.

He shook off his distraction. The main thing was going to be making sure Susanne was not just safe, but able to defend herself. Because she was going to insist on just that, once she got over her shock. Lord, yes! He knew her well enough to know that. There was another thing about her—not just sensible but brave.

Oh, Susanne had plenty of faults. Working with her these past few weeks had shown him that. The chief of those faults was that she was not just stubborn, she was *damned* stubborn, and once she had an idea in her head, right or wrong, it took a steam engine and a chain to haul it away.

And she was . . . well . . . just a simple country girl with a wretched education. Fortunately that wouldn't matter as long as she stayed out in the country among people she knew, but she'd be miserably unhappy anywhere else. She was intelligent enough to recognize just how . . . simple . . . she was, and take it to heart, and feel out of place and slighted. He had the shrewd notion that had been happening even when her father elevated her to the position of daughter and heir, and that had only been within the confines of the house she'd grown up in and the people she'd always known. It would be far, far worse if she went into the great world and people who were technically her equals snubbed her and made fun of her because of that.

And it would happen, even among the Elemental mages, who should know better. Just because someone had power, it didn't follow that they were going to be shining examples of all the virtues the padres preached about.

Well, let's get her safe and get that madman of a father safely rid of, or tucked away where he can't do any more harm. Then we'll worry about what's to become of her.

Yes, indeed, first things first. And the first of the first things—

Get back to Alderscroft. Both by conventional means and arcane. In this situation it was just not possible to be too careful. Magical messages and physical ones could miscarry, but do both, and you should get through. The village post office had a telegraph, so did the Exeter Club, and among his many accomplishments, Garrick knew how to operate one. Time to rouse the postmaster, gain access, and have Garrick do the sending.

This was one message he didn't want anyone else to see.

Garrick and a ten-pound note were able to get the telegraph off to Alderscroft at the Club. Peter had called up his undines and had already spoken to his "twin," Peter Scott, who lived in London. Alderscoft was a Fire Master, and there was not a chance that Peter's Water Spirits would speak with his salamanders, but Scott was a fellow Water Master, and getting hold of him was almost as simple a matter as picking up one of those new telephones and calling him up. He'd gotten Scott in his scrying bowl within moments of setting up the magic. Scott had promised that he would go straight to the Exeter Club and speak with the Old Lion directly. The Kerridges had already started on strengthening their defenses, and the next step in that would be to let everyone on the estate know—quietly— that there might be trouble.

"I'd like to keep Susanne's name out of this," Michael said, as they conferred around the table just before midnight. "Just let everyone know that we've discovered who the necromancer is and that there might be trouble with him."

Peter grimaced. "I'm not sure that is a good idea, but . . . it's your land and your right."

"I don't want anyone blaming her or suggesting we toss her out," Michael replied. "After all, she's the stranger here, and it would be only natural to do so."

Peter was not at all sure that Michael was right; it seemed to him that Michael was underestimating his servants' capacity for compassion.

Then again . . . they were *his* people. And Susanne was a stranger. When it came to a choice between a stranger and your own . . . you couldn't blame people for choosing their own.

"Well, the best thing to do is get her out of England

altogether," he said, feeling a headache coming on. "The farther we get her, the less likely it is that her father will have any way of finding her."

"Scotland?" said Charles.

He shook his head. "I'm thinking right across the Channel. I have some family connections in France. Jean-Paul Delacroix, a distant cousin, another Elemental mage. He's got a little gentleman's farm, probably not unlike Whitestone Hall, in the Ardennes. He'll be pleased to play host to a pretty young woman, and all that water between her and her father will kill the connection dead."

"Whitestone never went any farther away from the Hall than London, and then with extreme reluctance," Michael said with a nod of agreement. "I know for a fact that he doesn't know a soul outside the county, other than other Masters, much less the country."

"Yes, well, Alderscroft will make damned sure he won't be able to use the Lodge connections," Peter replied grimly. Scott had been appalled. Even more appalled when Peter had told him just what Whitestone had planned for his own daughter. Alderscroft was going to get an earful. Peter Scott was *not* a "gentleman." He was a tradesman, and he had been a merchant sea captain. As such, he was not handicapped by the reticence that one member of the gentry often displayed when confronted with the misbehavior of another member of the same. He wasn't going to mince words with the Old Lion.

And he would make certain that Alderscroft got the word out before the night was over.

"Are you sure France will be safe?" Elizabeth worried. "Oh, not *magically.* But with all that nastiness brewing up over there . . ."

"It's just the Balkans, my love," Michael said dismissively. "The farthest it will get is Germany."

Peter was not at *all* sure of that, but there was no point in saying anything. "Believe me, if I could send her to India, I would, and I am thinking strongly of Australia or New

Zealand," he replied grimly. "But I don't have connections there, I don't at the moment have anyone I could send with her, and we'd be sending her over blind. France is the best I can do right now."

"How long will it take, do you think?" Charles asked worriedly.

He shook his head. "A week or two, at least. I have to contact my uncle first, then I'll have to persuade her that this is the safest thing, then I'll have to make arrangements. We can't exactly bundle her into a basket and ship her off. She'll need . . . good gad, almost everything. Wardrobe, since she can't go haring off with nothing to wear but her uniforms, money, tickets . . . I'll need to make sure Uncle Delacroix is available to fetch her right off the ship, because she hasn't a word of French, so he will need to make arrangements at his end."

"Beastly complicated." Charles shook his head. "Is she going to be all right traveling alone?"

"She won't be traveling alone," Peter said firmly. "Garrick and I will take her as far as London. Peter Scott and Maya will see her onto the boat, and Scott will go with her on it. He'll put her in my uncle's hands. I don't think you realize what a treasure she is. *The Puck* taught her the business of being a Land Ward."

Michael gave a low whistle. "Then she is, or will be, damned powerful."

"Is," Peter replied firmly. "I say, who's been teaching her? She just needs to know how to do things other than landmagic. Once she knows, it's no odds, she gets them done. I wish I'd had more time with her. But uncle knows his business, and he speaks fluent English; he can take up where I left off." Peter was very fond of his great-uncle, who would flirt outrageously with the English girl while at the same time making sure she knew she was absolutely safe with him. If she stayed with him for any length of time, she'd even get a certain amount of education outside of magic, and a bit of French polish. He hoped she would like it there.

Would she get enough polish to fit into society at some level?

Mind on your business, Peter.

"Then once we've taken her father into custody . . ." Charles hesitated. "Then what?"

"Then it's in Alderscroft's hands. He'll have to find some way of confining the man, then faking his death." *Assuming we don't kill him, taking him.* He could see that thought in all of their faces, but they nodded. "One way or other, it will take some time before the estate gets settled on Susanne. Then she can come back here. At least then, she'll have a means to support herself."

Mentally he sighed. He had no doubt that she was capable of running the small estate with the help of whoever her father's legal man was and the servants. After all, Whitestone himself hadn't exactly been managing his own property all these years, and she could hardly do worse with her land-sense.

But even with French polish she wouldn't fit into country "society." London, yes, London society had room for all sorts of odd ducks if they had the blood and the money, but Earth Masters could not abide London. She'd probably confine herself to Whitestone Hall and the village and turn into a kind of lone eccentric, as so many Earth mages did, really being friendly only with animals and the Elementals. What a waste . . .

He shook off his melancholy thoughts. No time for that sort of speculation. "Right," he said. "Now, about the defenses. You have me here now, too. What can I do?"

14

JUNE was half spent, and all of Richard's plans for bringing Rebecca back on Midsummer Night had long since
fallen by the wayside. His best hope at this point was for
Hallowmass Night. Now . . . on the one hand that was a better time for the ceremony. The barriers between the Spirit
World and the Material World were thinner. Spirits tradi-
tionally crossed over then. It would be easier to force the
girl's soul out and easier to bring Rebecca across.

But he didn't want to wait. He'd been delayed long
enough. He wanted his property back.

And, at length, the fellow that the housekeeper had
hired came back with the word he had long been waiting
for.

Word that only brought more complications with it.

Richard brooded over the report. The man was surprisingly literate. He had expected some sort of thug, but the
fellow could actually write a coherent sentence. The problem lay in what those sentences said.

Unlike Richard, the man had not supposed that Susanne

had stayed on the roads. He had assumed she would trudge off like a man who was running away and didn't want to be followed. He wrote that he had been sure she would move in a straight line, going across the moors. And he had been right.

She was currently employed (as he had suspected) as a dairymaid.

At Branwell Hall. By the Kerridges. Who were, if not Earth Masters, certainly Earth mages. Of course, the detective had not known that; he had only known that she had been taken on at the dairy, she was doing satisfactory work, and had fitted in. He had concluded his report with the words, "If I may be so bold, sir, if the goal is to be assured that the girl in question is well set up and taken care of, she seems to have as secure a position as any serving girl in England. The Kerridge family is well thought of hereabouts, and places with them are greatly coveted. Now that you know her whereabouts, I should leave her in place, and consider my duty by her to be done."

Well, yes. That would have been true, had the situation been as he described.

The Kerridges . . . this put a different complexion on the situation entirely. Most of the tenants and servants on the estate had at least a touch of magic about them. They had many friends and allies. They were part of Alderscroft's White Lodge and the network of informants associated with the Lodge.

And he didn't know what, if anything, Susanne had told them. It certainly would have sounded utterly absurd for her to complain of being treated too well! If she had fled only because she was uncomfortable in the position as gentry, it was unlikely she would say anything at all.

But if she had noticed anything amiss . . .

Well, that could make things difficult.

She *seemed* to be there in the capacity of a servant, which suggested that she hadn't told anyone anything. It would be his word against hers; he could say she was actually a runaway servant, he could repeat the story he had given the detective, or he could tell the truth, that she was his daughter and he didn't know *why* she had run away, but she obviously was not thinking clearly.

Except . . .

Except that these were the Kerridges. And they were magicians. They knew him, or at least, Michael did. They knew how he had acted, these past twenty years. And they were, almost certainly, going to detect the "scent" of necromancy on him. If they didn't, their Elemental allies *would,* and would tell the human mages instantly.

He dared not set foot in person anywhere near Branwell Hall.

Nor could he send an agent after her. Since it was the Kerridges, they would not accept an agent's word that she was a runaway servant, and they would probably put up a fight over letting her go, and at that point she *would* tell them who she really was. Then of course, there would be questions he could not answer—such as, why was he claiming she was just a servant? And why hadn't he come in person?

If he sent an agent after her as his daughter, who would he send? Again, the question would be, why had he not come in person? He could plead that he never left the house anymore, but Michael Kerridge knew him and would insist. With cursed good intentions they would want to interfere, insist that it would be good for him, insist on playing intermediary between him and Susanne, and of course . . . he would be found out.

And once they uncovered that Susanne was his daughter, however it happened, they would immediately see her powerful resemblance to Rebecca.

Once they added that resemblance to the signs of necromancy, they would know exactly what he had planned. No, this was an impossible situation.

He couldn't have a troll quietly kidnap the wench, Branwell Hall was too well-defended. He very much doubted that a single troll could even get on the grounds.

And he wasn't going to give up.

That left only one solution. An all-out assault.

They wouldn't know it was *him*. He could make sure his flunkies took as many of the servant girls as they could snatch once they got Susanne. The extras could serve as their reward. The Kerridges would have no idea who was behind the attack, and he could keep Susanne safely hidden until he could make the spirit transfer. And once that was done, he could take Rebecca out of the country before the attack could be traced back to him.

It wasn't the best plan, but right now, it looked like the only plan.

There was only one bright spot. He could finally make those wretched servants of his into something less interfering and more useful. After all, when this was done, he would need the kind of cooperation from them he wasn't going to get from those with minds of their own.

It had been several days since that meeting in Charles' office. Peter was still trying to convince Susanne that she needed to go to France. He hadn't managed yet, and the honest reason was she was more afraid of being in a foreign country than she was of her father. He could understand that, actually, but the truth of the matter was they couldn't exactly, as he had said, bundle her into a basket and ship her off. She had to consent to it. It frustrated him no end, but he could understand it.

Alderscroft had responded immediately, via telegram and Peter Scott, then via a longer letter detailing what he was doing. He was not taking this lightly, as well he should not. He had alerted the rest of the White Lodge, who were spreading the word to magicians who were not Masters. He promised reinforcements, so that a Hunting Party could be mounted in force, but he warned that they could not come sooner than a fortnight. That was understandable; the situation with Germany probably meant that many of the Masters were engaged with what was happening on the Continent.

Nevertheless, Peter was worried. He had heard a rumor that he couldn't trace that someone had been showing her picture about down in the village. Of course, it wouldn't have been *her* picture, it would have been her mother's, but if the resemblance was as strong as Michael Kerridge said, that would have been enough for her to be identified.

Now, no one in the village had ever seen her, but enough of the Branwell servants came down to the pub for a drink now and then that one of them, in all innocence, could have identified her.

So he was not relaxing his vigilance. Not until they got her safely accross the Channel and into France.

Which, as it turned out, was just as well.

He and Garrick were still staying at the gamekeeper's cottage. He liked it, and there seemed no reason to move out at this stage. He and Garrick could still go down to the pub in their guise as the gamekeeper and his brother and collect little tidbits of information.

And it didn't hurt at all that they were well outside the bounds of the Hall proper. His Elementals were always close at hand, and it was much easier to tell what was going on at the borders of Branwell lands. So he was the first to know that something was wrong.

It was just after dusk, and he was on the path from the cottage to the Hall, when he got an unsettled, queasy feeling in his stomach. He would have put it down to something he had eaten, except that a moment later, a dozen fauns, all with expressions of panic on their faces, came leaping out of the forest, heading for the Hall.

And right behind them were other Elemental creatures, all running as if for their lives.

The cottage wasn't that far; he doubled back to it, to find Garrick already outside, with the special guns, a pair of shotguns with shells loaded with blessed salt. He took one, Garrick took the other, and they started off in the direction that the Elementals had been fleeing from.

They had not gotten more than a hundred yards when

they were joined by Charles and Michael, both on horse-back with similar weapons slung over their shoulders and gamebags of shells slung over their backs. The two Kerridge men dismounted when they spotted Peter and Garrick and sent their mounts back to the stables with slaps on their haunches. An Earth mage could always command an animal to do what he wanted; Peter wished he had a power that convenient.

"Elizabeth has Susanne," Michael told them. "She's organizing the second line of defense at the Hall."

Peter nodded. There seemed nothing more to say at that point. They continued to move in the direction from which things were running. It wasn't just Elementals now, it was ordinary animals and birds, too.

"I suppose we should count our blessings that he didn't wait until full dark," Peter said, squinting, as he tried to make out anything in the twilight gloom under the trees.

"He'll have to come at us over the boundary," Michael replied. "Charles and several of the stronger servants and I revived all the old protections out there. It won't be enough to stop him, but it will prevent him from conjuring anything up inside our boundary."

"That's—"

They were near the wall now, and suddenly they were hit by a wave of ghastly stench born on an icy wind.

Garrick retched. Charles and Michael clasped a hand over their mouths.

"Dear God in heaven—" Michael said, muffled by his hand. He didn't have to ask "What is that?" because he knew, as did Peter. They had both dealt with necromancers. and they knew exactly what it was.

There was a clear stretch between the wall and the forest, and there was just enough light for them to see vague figures clambering over it and dropping down on their side. Peter was quite glad that the figures were vague. He didn't really want to see them, given the stink. It wasn't just his stomach that was in revolt; his whole body shuddered with revulsion. The magic that animated these things was utterly and completely *wrong* on the bone-deep level. It was anti-life in every possible way, and instinct cried out against it.

With a single mind, they stopped where they were, put their guns to their shoulders, and fired on the things moving toward them.

Normally a shotgun blast at this distance would do little or nothing to a reanimated corpse—which was, of course, what these things were. But their loads were made of blessed salt, and all it took was a grain of that to penetrate the flesh of one of these things in order to drop them in their tracks. The blessed salt dissolved the binding, freeing the trapped spirit from the flesh.

The front line of the things dropped, but more kept coming from behind. They didn't move fast—they couldn't—but they were inexorable. As the Zulu wars had proved, you didn't have to have superior weapons to overwhelm those who did; you just had to have enough soldiers to engulf them.

They opened up with the second chambers.

The next line dropped.

"Stagger the loads!" Peter shouted as he slipped new shells into the chambers. "Kerridges, then us!"

The Kerridges' guns roared while he was still reloading. He had counted on that. The Kerridges hunted far more than he and Garrick did, and they would be able to load faster. Two firing while two reloaded meant they would minimize their vulnerability.

But there were more things behind the walking dead that were not as vulnerable to the blessed salt.

Over the top of the wall tumbled three enormous, blobby things that Peter was just as glad he couldn't see, as well as a swarm of things that were little more than motion in the growing darkness. Then came more of the reanimated dead, some skeletal, some substantial. The stench had become a force all its own.

Trolls and hobgoblins and boggarts . . .

Then the last part of the attacking force rose over the top of the wall. Transparent, glowing in a sickly green or pallid blue, there was no mistaking them for anything living. They wore the tattered shreds of the clothing of varied eras, and they weren't all whole. Plenty of them were missing pieces of themselves—arms, heads, legs. The oldest were dressed in quite antique costumes indeed, the youngest in the usual smock of a country farmer or the suit of a town dweller. These were revenants, those spirits that actually tried to manifest enough to be actual haunts. Strangely, there were few women among them. Or perhaps not so strangely; these were, after all, the creatures bound by Richard Whitestone, who had already proven himself a misogynist.

They seethed and surged against an invisible barrier above the wall; being pure spirit, they couldn't force themselves through the protections around Branwell the way that the physical creatures could. But their mere presence was more than enough to inspire a healthy dose of terror. And Peter knew that if they *did* force their way across, they were perfectly capable of tearing the flesh of a human to shreds.

Revenants.

Revenants were a necromancer's stock-in-trade. Many were little more than unthinking rage, and it was easy for a necromancer to turn that rage against any target he chose. Even one could sicken and injure, and they could certainly weaken and terrify the living enough to allow the walking dead to overwhelm them. A swarm like this could be as deadly as gunfire.

Michael and Charles had changed to another set of loads, this lot made of lead from a church roof. Peter remembered how Michael had gotten it—by the simple expedient of replacing an entire roof on the excuse of "charity" and claiming the salvaged roof slabs as they were replaced. The lead shot was taking care of the boggarts, and making the trolls howl with pain. But this was an army, and no mistake, and without an army of their own, they couldn't hold out for much longer.

"Water Master! Water Master!"

He dared to glance in the direction the call was coming from. He saw undines waving frantically at him—from where? He called up a mental map of this part of the estate—

There was a brook there! And anyplace there was water, Water Elementals could go! *There're my allies!* Water could be an antagonist of Earth as well as an ally, and it was quite clear from where he stood that the undines were prepared to fight for him and for Branwell.

"Retreat toward the brook to my left!" he shouted over the roar of the guns; he sensed Michael nodding rather than saw it, and they began the step by step retreat toward the water.

The boggarts took this as a sign of victory and shrieked their happiness. They surged forward ahead of the walking dead, which were still being decimated by the blessed salt rounds Peter and Garrick were shooting.

The boggarts got closer, darting about like insects, moving too fast to get a good shot at, either with a shell or magic. They were horrid little things. They had mouths full of nasty, yellowed, pointed teeth, tiny eyes like black beads, and they drooled. No two of them were alike, but they all looked misshapen, and all were colors that just seemed unhealthy.

The kobolds were bigger, tougher, and uniformly clay-colored. They moved just as fast, though, and as the group continued to retreat, they began using slings to pelt the humans with sharp-edged rocks.

Peter took a hit to the forehead that cut a gash there that started to bleed. He yelled with the unexpected pain, and the kobolds howled with glee. He blasted them with the salt; they skittered out of the way and resumed their barrage.

And then—then his left foot splashed into the brook.

And a sheet of water sprang up around all of them, deflecting the incoming stones.

A troll lumbered forward and was set upon by undines. They tore at him with long fingers and swirled around him like a swarm of angry bees. To Peter's shock, the creature began to melt, dissolve, howling the entire time.

And that was when their own army arrived. The Earth Elementals of the land of Branwell Hall had rallied, and they were not going to concede without a fight.

Slung stones whizzed over the humans' heads from behind. The fauns had gotten their hands on their weapons. and now they were angry and on the offensive. And they weren't afoot where they would be vulnerable. They were riding the backs of some of the most magnificent stags Peter had ever seen. He hadn't even known that there *were* deer on the grounds of Branwell, in fact.

The deer bounded toward the mass of kobolds; the kobolds tried to swarm them, but the deer fought like the horses of mounted knights, lashing out with their wicked little hooves and slashing with their antlers.

The undines pulled down another troll, now joined by dryads; the fauns and deer had fully occupied the kobolds and boggarts. That just left the walking dead.

There didn't seem to be an end to them. Where had Whitestone found all the bodies? And the power! It took a tremendous amount of power to raise that many dead! Where was he getting that?

Michael and Charles switched back to the salt loads, and still they kept pouring over the wall. The stench was a horrific wave, drowning them, weakening them as they tried to keep their concentration.

And they were running out of ammunition.

"That was my last shell, my lord," Garrick said calmly, as he reversed his grip on his shotgun to hold it by the barrel, the better to use it as a club.

Peter felt in his bag and came up with only two more. He rammed them home, brought the gun up, and fired, point-blank, into the three that were advancing on Garrick. Now he flipped his own weapon around to follow Garrick's example. "Have I ever mentioned how much I hate shootin'?" he asked, taking a swing at a mostly-naked skull and knocking it off the shoulders it sat on.

"From time to time, m'lord," Garrick replied, breaking the arms off a liche that tried to grab Charles.

"Well, I take it all back." He bashed in another skull. Unfortunately, losing their heads didn't seem to affect these horrors. Only being shot with the salt or reduced to broken fragments kept them from continuing to attack. "I'd be damned happy to be shootin' right now." He spared a moment to glance at the revenants pushing against the arcane boundary above the wall. "Michael, if your shield gives way, we're going to be in a bit of a bother."

"Then we'd better hope it doesn't!" Michael Kerridge shouted back.

Another pair of trolls and a wave of goblins came over the top of the wall. Peter's arms burned with fatigue. The walking dead pushed the four of them back a little farther, until they were standing in the middle of the brook. Michael and Charles had reversed their guns as well, and they all stood back-to-back, with the water rushing against their legs. The undines and fauns were doing their best, but they were virtually helpless against the walking dead.

"Now would be a very good time for Alderscroft to materialize," Peter said, hopefully.

And just as the words were out of his mouth, the necromantic army suddenly froze.

Abruptly, what was left of the trolls tore themselves loose from their undine captors and lumbered away. The boggarts and kobolds dove down into the turf as if they were diving into a pool of water, and vanished.

The revenants scattered, flying off too fast for the eye to follow.

And most importantly of all, the walking dead suddenly stiffened and collapsed.

Silence descended.

For a very long moment they all just stood there, back to back, waiting for some new, worse horror to rise up and descend on them. Their allies milled restlessly, looking for the next wave. But it never came. Finally, they relaxed the slightest bit; Peter was finally able to concentrate on something other than staying alive to create a ball of magical light. It illuminated faces haggard with exhaustion. "What just happened?" Charles wondered aloud.

Peter shrugged. He ached with fatigue and bruises. "I haven't the foggiest. I doubt invokin' the Old Lion's name did it."

"Unless the necromancer was within earshot, recognized the name, and thought that you were seriously expecting the Lodge, Peter," Michael pointed out. "He knows Alderscroft. He knows how the Old Lion will regard this."

"He'd better know a place where the Old Lion can't find him," Peter said grimly, and coughed. "Because this was a direct attack, and Alderscroft will rightly read that as a declaration of war. The kid gloves are going to come off, and when the Hunting Lodge gets hold of him, if he lives, he is never going to be out of magical bonds for the remainder of his life. Let's get out of this stench before I disgrace m'self. Good gad, I want a bath and a brandy!"

One of the dryads glided over to Michael. "We will see this is cleansed, if you wish," she whispered.

Michael hesitated a moment. "The bodies came from somewhere—shouldn't we see they are returned to their proper graves?"

"Most of 'em are in bits," Peter pointed out. "Besides that, how would you explain how they all got here?"

"You have a point." Michael turned toward the dryad. "You can do this?"

"Willingly. It is our forest too, we would rather not endure . . . this." She waved her hand at the remains of the carnage. "In the morn, it will be as if none of this had happened."

"Then if you would be so kind, please take care of it,"

Michael said gratefully. The dryad nodded, and faded into her tree. The four of them turned to go back up to the Hall.

But before they moved out of sight, Peter looked back a moment. The turf was heaving and churning, and the no-longer-walking dead were slowly being pulled under it, as if the grass were water and they were sinking into it, never to be seen again.

He hoped.

Back at the Hall, all four of the men, including Garrick, were enveloped in a different sort of swarm—a bevy of servants descended on them and carried them off separately. In no time at all, Peter found himself with that brandy in his hand, soaking his injuries in a hot bath.

There were rather a lot of them. Bruises mostly, and some big ones he didn't remember getting. He had a couple of scalp lacerations and that one cut above his right eye from the kobolds' slung stones. An experimental deep breath proved that the huge bruise across his chest that was already turning black was only that, just a bruise, and not broken ribs. *For small blessings, we are grateful.* He waved off further assistance and dressed himself in the clothing that had been brought up from the cottage. He wanted to find out what had happened at the Hall.

So, it seemed, did the others. Garrick popped out of the suite across the hallway when Peter opened his door, and they followed the sound of voices down to the cozy "little" (in a house this size, "little" was relative) sitting room Elizabeth preferred to use. There he found Michael and Charles, both with sticking-plaster over facial cuts, eating prodigious quantities of Welsh rarebit, and with them, Susanne and Elizabeth. Susanne was not in a uniform; it looked as if Elizabeth had supplied her with a spare gown in the form of a loose Artistic Reform dress. She was drinking tea, looking exhausted and a little pale.

"Join us, there's plenty," Charles said around a mouthful of bread and melted cheese. Nothing loath, Peter helped himself at the sideboard and brought his plate to sit with the others while one of the servants poured him a cup of black tea so dark it looked lethal. He sat down with the rest and looked attentively at Elizabeth.

"Michael already told us what happened to you," Elizabeth said, passing him sugar and cream. "We've just been waiting to tell you what happened up here."

"What did happen?" Peter asked. "I can't imagine from the fire in your eye that you were left in peace."

"Redcaps," Elizabeth said grimly. "They jumped straight out of the dungpile at the stables. And they came straight for Susanne."

"It was a good thing I had a pocket full of horseshoe nails," Susanne said. "And a fireplace poker."

"And she knows how to use it," Elizabeth chuckled, then sobered. "She scattered the nails around her so they couldn't get near enough to grab her, then broke the arm of anything that reached for her across the boundary of the nails. That was brilliantly done, Susanne. I would never have thought of that myself. I think that the attack down at the walls was a ruse so that Richard Whitestone could get inside the grounds elsewhere and conjure his redcaps to come after Susanne. Once he was inside the boundaries—"

"—he could do anything he liked," Michael finished for her. "Damnation! I should have thought of that."

"We did—well, we planned for something to get by you," Elizabeth pointed out. "Even if he hadn't turned into a foul necromancer, I would be exceedingly vexed with Richard Whitestone right now. I know I should be grateful that he so completely underestimated the ability of us womenfolk to defend ourselves, but I feel positively offended by the pathetic force he sent against us."

"Well, I'll be grateful for you," Peter said, and frowned. "You know, there is not a single chance that he is going to allow himself to be caught. He abandoned every one of his walking dead, and he has to know that we know who he is now. He'll go into hiding, and he used to *be* the one who tracked necromancers down. We'll never find him unless he makes a mistake."

"Unfortunate but true," Michael replied, looking worried. "And he won't try another frontal assault; he can't afford to, with Alderscroft watching for him. We're not as powerful as he is; like it or not, he was an Earth *Master,* and his power holds no matter that he's taken the shadow-path." He turned awkwardly to Susanne. "My dear young lady—"

"Na, tha' needn't say it," she replied with resignation. "Tha' canna keep me safe. I'd already reckoned that. I won't be the cause of any more people getting hurt. Next time might be worse than just hurt." She sighed and turned toward Peter. "I'll be takin' tha' boat t'France, my lord."

"Well done," Peter said warmly. "Hang the other plans, those were made before we were attacked in force. Garrick and I will go with you the whole way, and Peter Scott if he can be spared. If your father can track you to the Ardennes, then there's no place safe but the other side of the world."

"Let's hope it doesn't come to that," said Charles.

❦

Richard Whitestone was in something very like a panic.

He had never expected that he would fail. But he had, and now it was a dead certainty that Lord Alderscroft would have the entire White Lodge howling for his blood.

He abandoned his entire army, leaving the reanimated corpses to drop where they stood. He had come here in the farm cart, assuming he would have Susanne to bring back with him; he went over the wall and sprinted to the place where he'd hidden it. He whipped the horse into as fast a pace as he dared set on a night-shrouded road and tried to think of what he could do next.

He couldn't go home; that would be the first place they would look. He had not yet established any bolt-holes on the moor as he had planned to do. The only good thing was that Alderscroft could not possibly set the conventional police on him.

He knew he sounded like a madman as he alternately cursed Michael Kerridge for an interfering busybody and thought out loud about where he should go.

Then it struck him: The one place where no one would look for an Earth Master was London.

Furthermore, he had money there, money from Rebecca's side of the family, money that Alderscroft didn't know about. He could take a flat or even an entire house, the sorts of creatures he could use flocked there in droves, living off the poison, the misery, the filth. His own tainted magic would be utterly lost in the midden that was London.

And no one would ever look for him there. They thought he was just some country cousin who couldn't abide the city and was not familiar with how to conduct himself. Well, he had not been able to abide the place before; but that certainly wasn't the case now. As for not knowing how to conduct himself there—well, he was no country cousin. He had gone to Cambridge. He knew how to move about a big city.

He heard the distant sound of a train whistle above the sound of his horse's hooves. It was the last train of the evening to London; the very opposite of a "flyer," it made stops at every town along the way. Yes . . . yes, he could certainly beat that train to Whitby. He could get a ticket there, get on, and vanish. There was nothing to connect the horse and cart with him; he could just abandon them and leave a mystery for the constables in Whitby to never solve.

And once in London it would be trivial to keep track of Charles and Michael Kerridge . . . because besides wanting his property, he wanted revenge.

Curse them. Charles most of all. Charles was the one who had taken Susanne in. Charles was most likely the one who had organized the defense of Branwell against him.

Well, he wasn't going to give up. He *would* get Susanne back. He *would* complete his transformation.

He *would* have Rebecca back. Nothing and no one was going to stand in his way.

15

IT was nearly the end of June, but it felt to Susanne as though it had been years since May Day. Peter had left her with his great-uncle, but then he had been forced to hurry off because of some pother about anarchists and the assassination of a duke or count or some sort of titled German who had been killed in some place she had never even heard of. He had been tense and distressed, but no one here seemed to be.

"Eh," his great-uncle had said, shrugging his shoulders eloquently. "There will be another to take his place. They breed most efficiently, those Germans."

Nevertheless, Peter and Garrick went back on the same ferry, and Peter Scott went with them. Fortunately, she had not been entirely alone.

She picked the last of the ripe peas from the vines in the kitchen garden and straightened, laden basket in her arms. She smiled to see "Uncle Paul's" other guest still hard at work, frowning at whatever it was she had on her easel and occasionally lunging forward to stab at it with a brush.

Mary Shackleford was a very aggressive artist. She said she was an Impressionist. Well, if she stabbed any harder on that canvas she was definitely going to make an impression on it!

Mary was English, too, and fortunately spoke fluent French *and* Flemish, which was useful this close to the Belgian border. Uncle Paul was a fine fellow, but his English was heavily accented and—creative. Between Susanne's Yorkshire accent and Uncle Paul's eccentric English, half the time they'd never have understood each other if it hadn't been for Mary.

Susanne took the peas to the kitchen, pausing on the stone threshold in hopes that this time she would be allowed inside the sacred precincts to help. She very much wanted to learn some of the cook's culinary secrets; she had a way with vegetables that was sublime, and as for the sauces! But the cook took the peas from her and gave her a wordless *look* that told Susanne that she was not welcome in that kitchen. Uncle Paul's cook had very firm notions of what gentry were and were not to be doing. They might choose to putter about in the gardens; that was respectable. Helping in the kitchen was definitely one of those forbidden things that gentry should never be allowed to try. Susanne turned back to the garden to watch Mary paint a bit more.

Mary had been an addition to the traveling party halfway across the Channel, evidently an old, old friend of Peter's and a fellow Elemental mage. Peter had recognized her in the first class dining cabin and brought her over to meet Susanne. On discovering that Mary was headed to the Ardennes to paint landscapes and was in dire need of a place to stay, Peter issued an invitation on Uncle Paul's behalf.

It seemed that Uncle Paul had no trouble with Peter high-handedly inviting not one but two young ladies to stay with him. Perhaps that was the way of things with Elemental magicians. Susanne made a note to ask him about it.

It was true that he had plenty of room. This stone farm-house was almost as big as Whitestone Hall, though it boasted no grander name than "Paul Delacroix's house." It was a beautiful building, two stories plus an attic with bed-rooms, constructed of gray fieldstone with floors of terra-cotta. Paul, his housekeeper, his three maids, his cook, three boys who idled a great deal and occasionally did some use-ful work, and his farm manager all rattled around in the place, which had bedrooms for eight, not counting the ones for the maids and the farm boys in the attic.

To call this a farm was something of a misnomer, since the land around here was not very suitable for farming. Paul had a vineyard and a great many cattle, which roamed the forested hills of his property at will. Susanne had offered to help in the dairy, but these were not dairy cattle; they were being raised strictly for meat. They had three more cow boys who tended them but didn't sleep at the house. Paul was a "gentleman farmer" in the truest sense: He was indif-ferent to whether or not he made a profit, though his man-ager was adamant about doing so.

Susanne wandered back down into the gardens to see what Mary was painting.

Mary, a tiny doll of a woman whose blonde hair and pink cheeks made her look even more doll-like, was in heaven, and, at the moment, in a trance of creativity. Evi-dently this part of the world provided endless scope for a painter—or, at least, for her. She was out all day and came back to the supper table with a look of intense satisfaction on her face. Right now, as Susanne discovered, she had found a particularly pleasing view of the farmhouse and was painting it. Susanne could see that two or three Ele-mentals were interested in that painting as well, so she tried not to disturb them. They were a pair of sylphs, hardly more than vaguely human-shaped shimmers in the air. The sylphs flocked around Mary; they thrived on anything cre-ative, according to Peter's books. They'd appeared the first time she'd stepped outside with her painting rig.

It had not taken the local Earth Elementals long to find Susanne, either. They were a bit more shy than the ones around Whitestone, but that didn't stop them from spying on her from what they fondly thought was cover. There were some different ones here, but that was to be expected. There were the *fee,* who were very much a mixed bag. Some were like Robin Goodfellow, only not as powerful; some were "white ladies," who were malicious and harmful. There were the *lutins,* who were like goblins and shunned her presence. The *farfadet* was a species of benign or mischievous gnome that looked a bit like a redcap and, as a consequence, gave her quite a shock when she first saw one. There were probably others she hadn't encountered yet. She knew there were undines; this was the part of the world where that name came from, after all, but she never saw them.

There was nothing about this life that bore any resemblance to her old one. Even the lessons in magic that old Paul Delacroix taught her were different from the ones that Peter had taught her. And that was what she spent most of her day doing—either learning from Paul or practicing on her own.

And as for the evening—well, that was where Mary came into her own. Mary was everything that Susanne should have been; now Mary, without being obvious about it, was coaching her in the skills and manners of a girl of her proper class. Susanne was an apt pupil, and she knew very well that when this was all over, her father would no longer be the Master of Whitestone. *She* would have to be "squire." She didn't want to be a laughingstock, and—

And somewhere in the back of her mind, a little voice kept insisting that once she was landed gentry, once her father had been dealt with, then she would have a chance at Charles Kerridge. But not if she had the speech and the manners of a servant.

Paul Delacroix helped with this as well; he seemed to understand what she wanted to learn without her ever hav-

ing to say anything. Gradually the number and variety of
pieces of silverware at dinner increased, and the courses
appropriate to them appeared—though not until she had
mastered the previous lot. Little comments about her deportment, her dress and hair—never unkind ones, mind, but
useful ones—were slowly helping her with her appearance,
and Mary, when she wasn't in an artistic trance, was excep-
tionally useful about fashion. *She* could see a difference
already. And if she could, surely Charles would.

Last of all, together, Mary and Paul were invaluable as
examples of what to *say* in a social setting. Susanne had
been vaguely aware that the gentry did a lot of talking, but
she hadn't quite grasped how you went about making polite
conversation. In the kitchen, talk generally revolved around
farm matters, food, and village gossip. Mary and Paul spoke
about the politics of France and the British Empire, art,
books and—village gossip. Except that their village was
spread across two countries.

So. Not so different after all.

The more she learned, the more confident she became
that yes, when all this was over and she could go home,
Charles Kerridge was going to be so surprised by how she
had changed that he would not be able to take his eyes off
her.

❧

The wheels of justice grind slowly, Peter thought to himself
as he bounded up the stairs of Exeter House. *Let us hope
they also grind exceedingly small.*

With Susanne safely out of the way, Peter was free to
concentrate on her father. He had sent a preliminary report
to Alderscroft, then a detailed one, and now at last had
come the summons he had been waiting for.

Clive was on duty tonight; Peter nodded to him as he
held the door open. The summons was for the War Room,
which meant that the Old Lion was about to organize a
Hunting Party.

Through the Club rooms to the private stairs—he wouldn't take the lift, it wasn't fair to the old codgers who actually *had* to use it—then down the hall to Alderscroft's private suite, he wondered the whole time if they'd left it too late. Richard Whitestone could have easily fled by now.

The question is, does he know we know he's the necromancer? Peter thought, as a club servant standing quiet guard over the door to the War Room nodded and opened it for him. *If he does, he's long gone. Then the question is—*

"—and can we track him to whatever hole on the moor he's carved out for himself," Alderscroft was rumbling, as Peter paused to take in the room and its occupants. Normally the War Room was used for actual magical ceremonies; tonight, however, the meeting table had been brought in, and everyone was sitting around it, *sans* their arcane paraphernalia.

Alderscroft sat at the head, of course. Down the right side were Peter and Maya Scott, Lord Dumbarton, Lord Owlswick. Down the left were Doctor O'Reilly, a fellow in a working-class coat that Peter didn't recognize, and an empty seat, clearly meant for him.

"I'm just here to organize transportation, old man," Owlswick said as Peter's eyes lit on him. "I'm no bloody good at combative magic, and that's a fact, but I have a shielded private railway carriage that can be put on the express at any time, and I can have shielded carriages waiting for you at the nearest station to—" He paused and gave Peter an interrogative look.

"Whitestone Hall," Peter said. "Might as well start the hunt where the scent is strongest."

"Good-oh." Owlswick scribbled a note and handed it to the footman behind him, who handed it out to the attendant at the door.

"I'm sorry it took this long, Almsley," Alderscroft said apologetically, "But we're a bit shorthanded. I sent a number of our people across the Channel just before this blew up, and, to be frank, the count of those who have ever put down necromancers is pretty low."

"Yes, well," Peter said, taking his seat, "Whitestone himself used to be chief of that number, so we're already under a handicap."

He couldn't help but feel a certain satisfaction as he looked around the table. The inclusion of the working-class fellow in the group would have been cause for a revolution a few years ago, and never mind the presence of a female at the War Room table. Yet here they were: a female who was, oh horrors, so unnatural a creature as to also be a physician, and a fellow who clearly worked with his hands, and, lastly, Maya's husband, Peter Scott, a tradesman.

If the founders of the Lodge aren't spinning in their graves, I would be very much surprised.

Then again, they were monstrously shorthanded. The assassination of Archduke Ferdinand had turned the Balkans into a pot about to boil over, and Peter had no idea what was going to get splashed when it did. England would almost certainly get involved. The king had far too many relatives among the Germans and Austrians. And alliances on the Continent were far too tangled.

Alderscroft himself interrupted Peter's ruminations. "Ah, I'm remiss. Peter, this gentleman is Andrew Kent. He is our newest member, a Fire Master from the East End. Andrew, Lord Peter Almsley." Alderscroft made the introduction without even a hint of condescension or distaste. "I found Andrew myself quite recently. He came here from Newcastle in search of work and brought with him a letter of introduction. He's been employed as my agent under the guise of being a common-hauler ever since. *His* mentor was the late Farnsworth Benning-Tate."

"You're old Bunny's apprentice?" Peter said, with astonishment. "I didn't even know he had one! Jolly good thing he did, though; we're shorthanded in the Fire department. Most of 'em went over to the Continent, along with the Airs."

"So Lord Farnsworth told me, m'lord," Andrew replied with a nod of respect. "I hope to be a credit to his teachin'."

"I can't imagine Bunny turnin' out a squib," Peter replied. "And it's just Peter. This is the War Room. We don't stand on ceremony here."

He turned to Alderscroft. "So, other than Owlswick, this is the Huntin' Party? Two Fire, two Water, one Earth, and one Air?"

"Air to feed the Fire, mostly," Dumbarton said. "Given your report of the attack, we are going to have to assume he will have another army of walking dead, and Fire is the best method of dealing with them."

"I'll be reading the ground and talking to the Elementals to track him, and standing by as a physician," Maya Scott said serenely. "I rather expect that Doctor O'Reilly will be too busy incinerating things to attend to injuries."

Alderscroft gave Peter a deferential nod. "You'll be in charge, Almsley. You are the most experienced, and you weathered his first overt attack," the Old Lion said. "The Hunting Party is in your hands."

Over the course of the next several hours, they planned in exhaustive detail. Owlswick scribbled several notes and handed them out, and Peter's estimation of the man crept very much higher when he realized what the apparently ineffectual Owlswick was doing and why he was here. It seemed Owlswick had a knack for organization . . .

And that guess was borne out when they emerged to find a carriage waiting to take them to the station; at the station were Garrick and a heap of luggage being put into a private car. From the feel of the beautifully crafted, wooden-sided passenger car, it had been shielded to a fare-thee-well. Richard Whitestone would definitely not know they were coming.

They were no sooner settled—and advised by Garrick to remain seated for a few moments—when there was a bit of a *bang* and a lurch. They all knew what that meant; they were being added to the Express. A moment more, and they were on their way. Now there was nothing more that they could do but prepare themselves. At the worst, they were about to go tramping across the moor in an exhausting wild-goose chase. At the best —

"I've investigated the car, m'lord, gentlemen, lady," said Garrick diffidently as he offered drinks. "There is a chamber with beds on the other side of the front wall of this one. If you would care to take advantage of those beds, I shall be pleased to turn them down for you."

"I will meditate out here, thank you, Garrick," Maya Scott said, with a smile for her husband. "But the rest of you should sleep while you can."

Peter was only too happy to do just that, and when the others saw how quickly he got up and headed for the chamber in question, they followed.

Sleep while you can. No matter what happens, we're going to be drained by the end of the day.

Thanks to Maya Scott, who had the wisdom of the Indian subcontinent at her fingertips, he had a number of useful techniques at his disposal that would make it possible to sleep no matter how keyed up he was. So while the others were still muttering and tossing restlessly, he employed those techniques and drifted off into slumber.

There had been no one on guard at the gates to Whitestone Hall, which had made them all suspicious. After a hasty conference, they had decided to proceed as if they were unaware of the attack on the Kerridge estate; after all, Richard Whitestone had no way of telling who was in the carriage or even how many of them were in there until they all got out.

But when their driver pulled up to the front entrance, there was no one to greet them. Nor was there anyone in the public rooms of the Hall. But Peter had thought he heard faint noises from the kitchen, so that was where they had headed — only to be stopped dead by what they found there.

"Good God," Peter choked out.

Whitestone Hall was indeed deserted by anything living—but that was not what was making Peter swear and Maya run out to the garden to be sick.

It was the servants, here in the kitchen.

Patiently, dumbly, they were working at their ordinary household tasks, without seeming to notice the presence of the Elemental Masters. There was only one small problem.

They were all dead.

From the look of things, they were mechanically doing the last task they'd been set to when Richard Whitestone left.

They were all very bluish, with bulging eyes and a ghastly rictus.

O'Reilly was extremely pale but otherwise controlled. "Poison," he said. "Looks like the bloody bastard poisoned 'em all. Convenient for him—I assume he could do some sort of wholesale bindin' on the lot."

Richard Whitestone had evidently left them without regard to their condition, which was awful and getting worse by the moment. Necromantic revival did not halt decomposition, and nothing had been done to preserve these poor murdered creatures.

The air was alive with flies.

Oh, this was worse than bad, because O'Reilly was right, there were spirits imprisoned in their bodies; Whitestone had murdered them all and then immediately caught the souls and bound them to the dead carcasses before they could escape to whatever afterlife they anticipated. Peter could feel their torment.

The stench that assailed their nostrils, pent as it was in the kitchen and accented with those clouds of fat flies, was worse than appalling.

Dumbarton was the next to lose control. He clapped both hands over his mouth and nose and followed Maya. Doctor O'Reilly and Andrew looked at one another, and then at Peter.

"Do ye reckon the colleen'll be carin' about th' furnishin'

of this place?" O'Reilly asked Peter. "D'ye think she'd mind havin' t'rebuild the kitchen?"

Peter shook his head. "Do you have something in mind? We are going to have to give the locals some sort of story about how and why these people died."

"Tragic kitchen fire," Andrew grunted around clenched teeth. "Paraffin explosion, terrible accident—we'll let the constables work out what happened. Right, Doctor?"

"Terrible thing," O'Reilly replied. "Clear out, you Peters. We'll need salamanders for this."

Peter was not at all averse to following their orders, nor was his "twin." As they explained to Maya and Dumbarton what the two Fire Masters had in mind, there was a sound like a dull explosion, and when he looked back over his shoulder, the windows of the kitchen were incandescent with flame.

When the Fire Masters called them all back, it was over. Anything in the kitchen that could burn, had; the walking dead were reduced to charred bones, which O'Reilly and Andrew were salting. It looked as if this wasn't the first round of saltings, either.

"Do you remember how many servants the girl said her father had?" asked Maya.

"Six, not including her." Peter counted, and came up even. "We got them all."

"Thanks to the gods," Maya replied fervently.

Just to be certain, they all prowled every inch of the Hall, but they found nothing. When they gathered again in the withered garden, Maya frowned. "I am going to seek a better place to call and question the earth creatures," she said. They won't come near—this."

"And rightly," Dumbarton replied.

"Scott, go with her; I don't want anyone out here alone," Peter ordered. He went back to the shielded carriage that had brought them all and returned with a shotgun and blessed-salt loads. He handed that to Peter Scott, who took it with a grim nod.

Dumbarton was standing very still, his eyes closed, head tilted in a "listening" posture. If Peter concentrated very hard, he could *almost* make out a wavering in the air, like heat-shimmers, but in the form of a human. It was whispering in Dumbarton's ear.

"Sylphs say Whitestone hasn't been back," Dumbarton said, finally. "Not here and not on the moor. And they've been watching for him. All this—" he waved his hand "—it's an affront to every Elemental."

Peter went to look at the stable and see if there was anything to be learned. There was: there had been a horse and a cart kept here until recently. Now they were gone.

So Whitestone had fled by a faster means than afoot and less traceable than by rail. That was useful to know, but not all that useful. He could be anywhere by now.

The others gathered with pretty much the same information. Whitestone had taken out the cart and horse, leading a group of walking dead. He had, at least according to the sylphs, then "resurrected" more for his army from every deserted churchyard or potter's field he passed—which explained how he had gotten so many, though not where he got the power to raise them. And then he had crossed the moor and attacked and—

And then passed out of the knowledge of any of the Elementals here or at Branwell. Which meant he had either created some powerful shields, or he had escaped via human contrivance.

"Do you think he left Branwell by train?" Peter Scott asked, finally.

"It seems logical. It would take only some money to escape undetected by train," Dumbarton pointed out. "It would take a great deal of power and effort to do so anywhere that Elementals might spy on him if he kept to his cart." The man shrugged, but Peter could see he was angry and frustrated. "He could be anywhere. We won't know until he acts again."

"And if the situation on the Continent explodes, we

won't have the leisure to hunt for him anyway," Peter said sourly. "Damn and blast!"

"He won't escape, Peter," O'Reilly said soothingly. "Everyone is alerted now. The least whiff of necromantic goings-on, and we'll have him. All we can do is wait and watch."

"I hate waitin' and watchin'," Peter grumbled. Peter Scott chuckled, despite the gravity of the situation.

Dumbarton shrugged again. "Right, then. Do we report the tragic fire as folks who came to visit and found the place deserted, or do we slip away and let the locals discover it?"

Peter felt sick at the idea of having to deal with strangers who were frantic about the loss of their relatives here. There had been at least two young girls there, who presumably had families. "Call me a coward, but—"

"No, I agree," Maya put in unexpectedly. "We can do nothing to help the relatives, we have done our best by the victims, and we certainly cannot afford to be pent up here when we are sorely needed in London." She looked earnestly at all of them and got nods—mostly relieved—from her fellow Huntsmen. "If we report it, there will be many questions—why we were coming, when Whitestone is a known recluse who never sees anyone, for instance. But other than the fire—and these people know nothing of magic—there is nothing to show that we have been here. No one in the village knew where we were going. Let us get in the carriages and move on to the next village, where there is a telegraph. We can arrange to rendezvous with the private car from there, and send Alderscroft a brief missive. Once on the car, you gents with the salamanders can contact Alderscroft for a more detailed explanation."

Peter gave her an appreciative look. "You have a knack for sifting through chaff, Doctor," he told her.

She shrugged. "When one works at a charity clinic, one becomes accustomed to knowing when one should confront the unpleasant and deal with it directly, and when avoidance is the best course of action. Shall we?"

The drive to the next village was conducted in silence and gloom.

Peter hated losing. And this was losing.

The next village was in the middle of its Market Day, which was a very good thing, as their carriage did not draw nearly as much notice as it would have otherwise. Peter was able to get off the telegraph with no trouble, told the postmaster that if there was any answer where he would be, and joined the others at the village inn rather than the pub. None of them were in much of a mood to eat, but the inn had a private parlor, and while Maya comforted her stomach with tea, the rest of them opted for something a bit stronger.

"He'll have a bolt-hole somewhere on the moors," Dumbarton said gloomily. "Probably several. Shielded, of course."

"Or if he is really clever, he has an entirely harmless second identity somewhere," Peter Scott pointed out. "That would be what I would do. Pass myself off as an invalid in the country for my health. Nerves. Anything can be attributed to nerves. Good excuse for not seeing anyone."

Anything else that might have been said at that point was summarily interrupted by a knock on the door of their private parlor heralding the arrival of the boy from the Post Office with a yellow telegraph envelope in his hand.

He handed the envelope over to Peter without a word. Peter tipped him absently and tore it open.

But the contents were nothing like what he had expected, and the temperature in the room seemed to drop thirty degrees.

Germany declares war on France. Stop. Return at once you are all needed. Stop. Alderscroft.

16

SUSANNE felt distinctly odd, and distinctly uncomfortable, sitting in a Roman Catholic church. The High Altar, with all of its furniture, was entirely foreign to someone familiar with the plain Table. And to have all those statues peering down at one, not only from the area of the altar, but from other niches built into the walls—it was a little unnerving. Not that she believed all that nonsense that some spouted about Catholics being wicked; they weren't any more wicked than anyone else. But . . . Papists . . . the cruel Papists who had conspired to kill Queen Elizabeth, the Papists who had turned English seamen into galley slaves, the Catholic Conspiracies, real and imagined, over the last several centuries . . . there was a long heritage of rhetoric and preaching designed to make anyone raised in England very wary of Roman Catholics.

Don't be ridiculous, she scolded herself. *Nobody wants to burn anybody at the stake, or otherwise. There is no Inquisition anymore. Sir Thomas Moore is not going to rise from behind the altar and point accusatory fingers at the heretic in the sanctuary.*

It was otherwise a very pleasant building to be in. Her Earth-senses approved of the light stone and white plaster of the walls and the clear windows instead of stained glass. Small and narrow, it nevertheless managed to accommodate what must have been almost two hundred people. The parish priest and the — well, she supposed he was the equivalent of the mayor of the village — had tried to bring in just about everyone in the neighborhood, and it looked as though they had succeeded. The sanctuary was packed solid.

The Germans had already come over the Belgian border and were besieging Liège. Young men were streaming toward Paris to join the army, for it was no secret that the Germans were crossing Belgium to outflank the French. But already there was a trickle of people coming the other way, fleeing, with everything they could pack piled precariously on their farm carts. And that was just here, in France. In Belgium, where the fighting was, the roads must be clogged with desperate folk trying to escape.

The Belgians were disputing every inch, now . . . but how long could tiny Belgium hold back the great Germanic tide?

Here in France there was a great deal of rhetoric and some inspiring speeches in the papers. The Army could not process their recruits as fast as they signed up. The general public had been fired with patriotic enthusiasm. The prevailing sentiment was that even if Belgium could not hold out, France would crush the enemy, and it would all be over by Christmas.

The Elementals, however, were terrified.

The local Earth Elementals were handicapped by her unfamiliarity with them, but they conveyed as best they could that something horrifying was coming along with the German advance. It was *not,* as nearly as the three magicians could make out, that the Germans themselves were using the nastier forms of magic. In fact, they didn't seem to be using any magic at all, at least with the Army. The horrors that they were bringing were entirely man-made and solidly physical.

"The boche have never been good magicians," Uncle Paul murmured to her, as if reading her thoughts. "They've never cared for magic. Not scientific enough. And they have not imagination enough."

Susanne only shrugged; she didn't know any Germans, so how would she know? From what Père François was saying, however, she didn't *want* to know any Germans!

The stories the priest had collected, and now recited, were appalling, and so utterly at odds with the tranquility and peace that these walls should have held. At least some of the tales had been passed along from priests and nuns who had either witnessed these things or been told them by the survivors. Entire villages set afire because of resistance in the neighborhood. Aged and infirm priests shoved to the ground and beaten and kicked unconscious. Unarmed and unresisting young men—boys, really—shot dead in front of their mothers. Fathers killed before their children, who were then, in turn fired upon and killed or wounded. Girls and the elderly tied to the doorposts of their cottages and burned to death as their homes burned down. Men going into a cottage, devouring the dinner that had been prepared, then, for sport, burning down the cottage and shooting indiscriminately at the family, killing a baby in his mother's arms, two of the daughters, and leaving the rest wounded and bleeding on the ground.

There were more such stories coming with those refugees, and they were so very terrible as to seem incredible, like the barbarities of the Thirty Years' War. Surely no modern soldier would inflict these atrocities on civilians!

"Clausewitz," Uncle Paul murmured, shaking his head sadly. But he didn't explain what he meant by the name.

Susanne shivered with a sudden chill, and the light in the little church seemed to dim. Mary looked ill. Uncle Paul patted her on the shoulder. "You should pack up and go home while you still can, chérie," he told her. "Your nation has declared war as well. This will be no place for an English, when the boche come." She nodded, then hesitated. Père François had finished his stories; the mayor was trying to make himself heard over people erupting into little knots of talk, furious or fearful.

"What about you?" she asked.

Uncle Paul sighed. "I will sell my cattle and horses to the army at a bargain. For one, I am a patriot, for another, it is better to sell now than wait and see them taken. That is the first thing. But the second, now—"

He turned troubled eyes on Susanne. "I promised to protect you. You dare not return to England, but there is no safety here for you, either. I would say to take shelter in a convent, but from these terrible tales, the boche will not respect convents, either—"

He pondered this a moment. "Well, then. I have my savings, and I will have the money from the sale of my cattle. I know the region about Mons; we will go there and find a cottage to lease. Perhaps the boche will not come so far. Even if they do, perhaps by that time we will be able to find a safe place for you to go." He raised his head a little as the buzz of conversation changed in tenor from fearful to defiant. "They cannot prevail, the boche. No matter what they bring with them. They have sealed their defeat with their atrocities."

Susanne could only hope he was right—but the Puck's warning, back in the spring, made her terribly afraid that he was wrong.

🍁

It was trivially easy to practice the darker side of magic in London undetected—so long as Richard Whitestone kept things relatively small.

"Relative," of course, to all the grime and poison and misery of most of London. He sent his goblins to steal, his trolls to rob, and he no longer needed to visit a bank. He had a small flat in the East End; he needed only one room, really, but the last thing he wanted was a nosy landlord investigating "smells" or "noises." His flat, most conveniently for conjurations, was in the basement.

Two of the walking dead served as his servants. He didn't need a cook as there were dozens of cookshops within walking distance. Eventually these two would get too noisome to keep around; he'd dissolve their soul-binding and have the trolls bring him two new replacements. For now they would do, and the amusing thing was, they were probably behaving with *more* intelligence than they had when gin-soaked and prowling the gutters.

And as for information? He was living in the greatest city on the planet. London boasted dozens of papers, and a good percentage of them were under the impression that *anything* a member of the peerage did was noteworthy and should be reported.

Pathetic, it was. But even more useful to him than Elemental spies.

Unfortunately, Susanne was not a member of the peerage, so he had no idea what had become of her. She wasn't in Britain; that much he was certain of. All of his Elemental creatures had her scent now, and none of them could find her. It was long odds in favor of them sending her away somewhere. If it was across water, he could never find her, and since they would have identified him by now, sending her across the water was a logical maneuver.

The paper he was reading shook with his fury. Charles Kerridge—that was who was to blame!

He was going to get revenge on Kerridge, but first, he was going to get his hands on the man, then he was going to find out exactly where Susanne had been sent. And then he was going to make Kerridge pay. It would be particularly pleasant to have his enemy resurrected as one of his servants.

Richard's sojourn in London was made even easier by

the chaos that erupted within the city when Germany marched into Belgium. Oh, not that most ordinary folk really understood what it meant, and as for the slum dwellers, they didn't even notice. But Alderscroft's wretched Lodge — now, *they* boiled about like a kicked-over hive. He went from being vitally important to find and dispose of to being the last thing anyone was thinking about.

Marvelous, that.

He bought and read six papers a day; he wasn't altogether certain what the Kerridges were going to do about the war situation, but he knew they would react to it somehow, and when they did, it would create a window of opportunity for him.

But it was purely by accident — more because he was reading *anything* that had to do with the movements and plans of their set than because he actually had expected it — that he found, halfway down a list of members of the peerage who had volunteered to serve in the newly formed British Expeditionary Force, Charles Kerridge's name.

He had to read it three times to be sure. And when he understood that, yes, Charles Kerridge was going to France, and, yes, he was going to be in the army, on the battlefield, effectively putting him in ideal circumstances for Richard to enact his revenge —

He very nearly overset his tea in his glee. Kerridge would be fighting for his life, because everything pointed to a very messy engagement at the least. The Germans were superb soldiers, well trained and well equipped, utterly ruthless and armed with weapons the British had not dreamed of. The British were overconfident. This was going to be a bloodbath.

And in such a monumental mess as a war of the sort the British were not prepared for, Charles Kerridge would forget all about Richard Whitestone.

And that was when Richard would strike.

But first, he had to get to France, and now would be the time, before all civilian travel was forbidden.

He rolled back the carpet and exposed the diagram he

had painted on the floor. He was going to need a great deal of ready money.

And there was nothing like a troll for "finding" money.

🍂

"Incroyable," Uncle Paul kept muttering as he leafed through the paper. They sat side by side on a bench in front of the tiny cottage they had leased, a flood of golden sunshine pouring over them and a breeze heavy with the scent of drying hay moving over the fields.

The bucolic scene was rather spoiled by the columns of uniformed men marching up the road to the border.

Susanne didn't blame Uncle Paul for his reaction. The headlines seemed a bad joke. The Belgians had not stopped the Germans, even a little. Oh, Antwerp was holding out under a heavy siege, but it could not do so for much longer, and the Germans had just swept around them anyway. The Germans were approaching the French border.

You could not get passage across the Channel now for any amount of money. Their last three letters and a precious telegram to Peter had gone unanswered.

The press of heavily armed men had made calling on the Earth Elementals absolutely impossible. All that iron and steel repelled them as effectively as a fence. Neither Susanne nor Paul had been able to call in so much as a brownie since the troops started moving through here.

The last of the men in this column marched past, leaving behind an enormous dust-cloud hanging in the air over the road.

At least Susanne had managed to get a magically assisted course in French from one of the little house spirits when they first took over the cottage. She could understand most of what was being said around her now, even if she couldn't read anything. Unfortunately, the house spirits were illiterate.

Just as unfortunately, that had been the last she had seen of any Elemental at all.

"Do you think we should try calling them again, Uncle Paul?" she asked dubiously, as the clatter of hooves in the distance, and an even larger dust-cloud, heralded the arrival of a troupe of cavalry.

"No," Uncle Paul replied. "They are frightened. Such will only frighten them more." He put the paper aside and stared morosely down at his feet.

It all was so hideously *wrong*. It was a wonderful summer day with scarcely a cloud in the sky. When the sounds of nature weren't totally drowned out by the advancing army, birds sang softly in the eaves of the cottage.

There was nothing to indicate the slaughter going on to the north and west.

Finally Uncle Paul sighed. "It is of no use. We are trapped here, chérie. And I do not know what to do."

Susanne smiled wanly. "In that case, Uncle Paul, we will do what we can. And I will try to find a little creature that is braver than the rest."

The elegant little room with its spindly Baroque furniture looked far too dainty for the man sitting at the writing desk. To be fair, Peter's commanding officer really would not look at home anywhere but a campaign tent or the Exeter Club.

"Permission to hunt for my relatives, General," Peter Almsley said, with a crisp salute for General Smythe-Hastings. He and four other Elemental Masters under the general comprised a very special force indeed, and one whose existence was extremely hush-hush, for all sorts of reasons. Most people—well, those that were even aware of them at all—were convinced they were assigned to MI1 or SIS and supposed they were some sort of code-breaking wizards, and not of the magical bent.

In fact, they were their own arm of Military Intelligence, the never-mentioned MI13, the department that officially did not exist. They were, in fact a sort of scaled-down version of Alderscroft's Hunting Lodge, and right now Peter desperately wished he had some of the folks from that larger organization right here. From all that he and the others could tell, the Germans and Austrians were not using magic in combat. He wasn't sure why, nor was he sure if this meant because they were using it for espionage.

That was probably the Old Lion's thinking as well. When Peter had last spoken to him, he was actively recruiting. People who would never have been considered for the Lodge were getting invitations. Alderscroft's plan was to cover all of the British Isles with members or allies of the London Lodge so if the Germans *did* get up to any chicanery, it could be detected and snuffed out quickly. There was also some thought of trying to get the selkies to guard the coastline . . . if they could be persuaded. That, Peter wished to stay out of. It would take a much better diplomat than he.

And would require your definition of "diplomat" to be "Someone who can tell you to go to hell in such a manner that you look forward to the trip."

The British Expeditionary Force had arrived in France three days ago, and MI13 with them. France had officially declared war on Austria-Hungary today, and Britain would probably do so in the next couple of days just as a kind of ironic final flourish to the mess. Both, of course, had already declared war on Germany. The Germans had declared war on just about everyone but Austria-Hungary and were making hash of Belgium, and there hadn't been any time at all for Peter to look for Susanne and his great-uncle. Affairs were rapidly avalanching out of control.

"Scout or scry?" the general rumbled, without looking up from his paperwork.

"Scout, sir," Peter replied politely. Meaning that he would send his Elementals out to look for the pair, rather than look for them directly himself.

Mary had gotten safely across the Channel, and the first thing she had done was to let Peter know that in the event of the Germans getting too close, Uncle Paul and Susanne were leaving his farm and planning to settle in near Mons in anticipation of a quick victory. He hoped that was where they were. Things were not looking very sanguine for the Ardennes region.

"Good. We can't take the chance that the Germans will detect scrying and follow it back to us. Permission granted." The general nodded. "I'll have a word with my opposite number in the French army. He might have some conventional means of finding a stray. I shan't need you for an hour or two, Almsley. Dismissed."

Peter saluted, and—while he actually had a few moments' breathing room—took to his room in the borrowed chateau that Military Intelligence was using as headquarters. It was one of the guest chambers, and the furnishings looked a bit sturdier than the mannered stuff in the public rooms. Locking the door, he cast his protections and called up the local undines in his water bowl. The bowl filled with a mist that then cleared away to reveal four lovely—if rather green and entirely nude—women, who appeared to be miniatures, swimming languidly in the bowl. All illusion of course. Undines were as tall as humans.

"Bonjour," they chorused musically.

Fortunately, he spoke excellent French. Just as fortunately, he had been in this part of the country before and knew what to expect of them.

These undines were . . . very French.

Despite the gravity of the situation, and the real horrors being perpetrated by the invaders, the undines seemed to feel it their bounden duty to flirt outrageously with him before taking his request and going off to hunt. "Ah, M'sieur Master," purred one, batting long green lashes at him. "What a pity you have no time to visit our spring! We would give you a welcome of delight."

"I remember the welcome of delight you gave me the last time I was in these parts, Ma'mselle," he replied. "It was not an experience I will ever forget." *Nor will I ever forget the locals are sisters to the legendary Melusine.* "However, needs must. I have two requests for you, and I hope you will be kind enough to fill them."

"We hope the first is not that we spy on the foul boche army." The undine actually spit the word "boche." All four of them looked sour. "They have taken countermeasures against magic. It would be very dangerous, probably fatal, for us to attempt such a thing."

Peter nodded. A disappointment, but not unexpected; if the Germans weren't *using* magic, they weren't stupid. They knew to protect themselves. "Well, if you can locate those countermeasures, we might be able to do something about them. The other favor is that you hunt for my Uncle. He seems to have packed up and gone missing."

"Paul Delacroix has left the Ardennes? Then he would not be aware that you are here, now. It would be a pleasure," the undine replied, and the others in the bowl nodded, undulating in and out of his vision. "If he is to be found, we will find him."

"Bless you. Anythin' more you can tell me about the boche?" he asked, because although the undines couldn't get near, they still might have observed something from a distance, and if you didn't ask, they likely would forget all about it.

The undine who seemed to have appointed herself as spokes-creature frowned. "There are . . . rumors," she said, finally. "You understand we have not been able to speak with our German or Austrian sisters."

I'm not sure I'd want you to, Peter thought soberly, knowing very well that their "sisters" were the deadly Lorelei. Oh, they wouldn't be a hazard to another Water Elemental, but—well, if any Elemental were to be working with the Germans it would be the Lorelei. "The second favor is if you could somehow tell Paul Delacroix where I am. There is a young lady, an Earth Master, with him."

"You are sure they have left the Ardennes?" The undines began swimming in rapid circles in agitation. "It is beyond dangerous there! The boche spare no one, not the old, not children, not women—"

"They've fled," Peter assured them, making little calming motions with his hands. "It's all right. That's why I need your help. I need to find them."

"They have?" The undines went back to drifting. "That is good. We will look for them. We will tell them where to find you."

"*Merci.* That is a great relief," Peter said sincerely, just as he heard someone in the hallway bellowing his name. His free hour must be over. "I hate to summon and run," he said uncomfortably, "but—"

"Go, you are needed," the chief undine said, and all four of them vanished, leaving only the bowl of clear water.

He cleaned everything up just as the general's orderly reached the door.

He checked his watch as he trotted back to the office. Already eight. It was going to be another long night.

Everyone was saying that now that the British were here, things would be wrapped up before Christmas. Everyone was certain that the Germans would retreat even from Belgium. Even the Water Elementals did not seem *terribly* worried; yes, it was true that the Germans were indulging in horrific behavior in Belgium, but . . . well, the Elementals were not human, and very few had much sympathy for humans. Humans were ruining their Element, humans inflicted atrocities on each other, and even the most kindly inclined Elementals probably felt that fewer humans in the world would mean a better world.

Besides, if they were not killed outright, they lived virtually forever. They'd seen plenty of atrocities in the Thirty Years War. This probably wasn't even a ripple in their pools.

So everyone, or nearly, seemed to be convinced it would all be over soon. Everyone except General Smythe-Hastings.

And, if Susanne was to be believed, the Puck.

If it had only been the general, Peter might have concluded the old man was worrying too much. But combine General Smythe-Hastings' military acumen with Robin Goodfellow's kind regard for humanity *and* his way of knowing what was likely to happen in the world of men ...

Peter was planning for the absolute worst. If one could plan for the absolute worst when one simply did not know how bad the "worst" could be. He'd sent detailed instructions back, not only to his grandmother but also to his older brother, about setting up the estate to be run without men, citing the general's grim predictions. Thank heaven, for once his brother had listened to him. *Plan for doing without men, without horses, without fuel for farm equipment. You have time to geld some cattle and turn them into oxen to work in the fields. You have time to mobilize the unmarried girls, and the children, by appealing to their patriotism. Think about alternate sources of meat, if the army takes the beef and mutton. You have time for all of this before things truly become bad.*

Fortunately, his brother was, at heart, a pessimist. This doom-saying had actually made him—well, not *happy,* precisely, but feeling effective. Not only was he too old to enlist, at least at this point, he was also too nearsighted. Literally. The poor fellow could not see without thick spectacles. He would die in seconds on a battlefield. His reply had cheered Peter as much as Peter could be cheered at this point.

Patriotism can mean beef as well as chucking bullets about. Contacting proper channels for Army contracts at fair prices, preparing estate for the worst. Thanks for the warning, old man.

Peter had done what he could for his own people at home. Now he had to do what he could for the people here.

One solitary little gnomelike creature had finally put his nose out into the kitchen as Susanne was making breakfast. This was definitely a cottage, and not the sort of "cottage" that Uncle Paul owned. Given what they had been hearing, she was glad now that they had abandoned it. His people had orders to strip the place to the stone, hide or cart away everything portable, and generally make it look abandoned before they sought safety for themselves. Somehow—she suspected bribery—an entire railcar full of his belongings had ended up in Calais. Then again, how much bribery would it have taken? Things were being shipped *to* the Front, not away from it. Well, the furniture, the paintings, the household goods were all in storage now. If they were not safe in Calais, she had confidence that Peter would manage shipment to England.

This was a tiny little cottage, much like the one that Peter and Garrett had shared. That was not so bad—it was less for her to clean, even if the kitchen, which consisted of a heavy wooden table, some cupboards, and a fireplace, was less than what she was used to for cooking. She did what cottagers did at home. She bought breads from the baker—and oh! French breads were a revelation! She left dishes that needed a long roasting or baking with the baker in the morning and got them again in time for dinner. She made soups and stews in a pot on a moveable hook over the fireplace and learned to fry on a griddle on the coals. Uncle Paul had actually begun complimenting her. Just yesterday he had said that she was beginning to cook like a good French housewife, which she took for a compliment.

She had smiled at the little Elemental reassuringly; this was obviously some sort of house Elemental, and they were notoriously shy of being seen by anyone but an Elemental mage.

It whispered something to her in French, too soft to understand. She shook her head and cupped her ear to indicate she couldn't hear it. It tried again—

"Little fellow is trying to tell you there is another Earth magician approaching," said Uncle Paul, coming in from his morning wash under the pump in the yard. "Probably with the English troops. They landed a few days ago and are finally heading to the Ardennes. Or so the paper says."

"I don't suppose there is a chance we would know him," Susanne said, slowly, as her heart began to beat irregularly. Surely it wouldn't be Charles! He was the only son, he wouldn't be mad enough to volunteer.

Would he?

It was a ridiculous idea, but she couldn't help herself; once breakfast was eaten and everything tidied, she positioned herself just beside the door, shelling peas for dinner, with one eye on the road. Just in case.

And when she spotted the familiar figure in the unfamiliar uniform, her heart nearly burst out of her chest. "Charles!" she exclaimed, jumping to her feet, and scattering the peas regardless. "Charles!"

At the sound of someone calling his name in a familiar accent, Charles Kerridge's head snapped around, and his eyes locked on her. A wry smile greeted her, and he halted his men.

"May we use your pump, miss?" he asked politely. Clearly this was an excuse so he could talk to her. She nodded, and he ordered his men to fall out and replenish their canteens. Covered by this, he turned his attention back to her.

"Peter's artist friend swore you were getting out of the Ardennes," he said, and as Uncle Paul poked his head out of the doorway at the commotion, he nodded genially in that direction. "Paul Delacroix? I'm Charles Kerridge, Peter's friend. I'll have someone send a message back to him that you're here. We need to keep in touch so we are able to get you and the young lady out of here."

"Surely the boche cannot prevail against—" Uncle Paul began, indignantly, his patriotism aroused.

Charles held up a hand. "I don't think they will get this far; we should stop them at the Ardennes. But it's always wise to have a plan just in case. Don't you agree?"

Uncle Paul muttered, but he finally agreed.

"Good. As soon as I am someplace with a radio or a courier making a trip back to Command, I'll make sure he knows exactly where you are." Just then, the last of his men finished filling his canteens at the pump. "And now I must go. Be careful, Susanne."

"I am not the one marching into a battle!" Susanne objected—and at that very moment, she had a brilliant idea, which she was *not* going to tell Charles. Peter, though— Peter would understand. Robin had said that things were going to be very bad. She did not think that all the optimistic predictions of a two-week war were accurate. The Puck had said that things would be bad for a very long time, and she had no reason to doubt him. Which meant that Charles would be here for a very long time. She was *not* going to allow herself to be shipped off to the colonies where she would never see him again, especially not if he was going to be here, on the Front.

This would be a way in which she could be close to Charles and protected at the same time. Although she wouldn't put it as being "close to Charles" to Peter; she would put it as "doing her part."

Rather than reply to her, Charles just looked to Uncle Paul, who shrugged.

Then there was no more time; Charles got his men formed up into their column, and off they marched.

"You are thinking of a thing," Uncle Paul observed. "And of that young man, so I think the thing you are thinking of will give you a way to be near to him."

She almost denied it, but what was the point of doing that? She shrugged. "I am an Earth Master. We are healers. It would be irresponsible of me not to volunteer as a nursing sister."

Uncle Paul stared at her for a very, very long time. "That is true," he said, slowly. "And it is also true that doing so would send you back to the Ardennes in the wake of the troops."

Again, she shrugged. "And I can save lives. We both know this."

"War . . . is a terrible thing," Paul replied, as if to himself.

"And this one will be the worst mankind has ever seen, I think. Are you prepared for that?"

She was shocked. She had thought that Uncle Paul had been as certain as anyone else that this would be a short war. She looked at him askance. Again, he shrugged.

"There is something in the air of doom," he told her. "I cannot say more than that. This is why I ordered my house to be stripped. I would not be surprised if it was soon a ruin."

Now that shocked her, and she blinked at him. "The— one of the Elemental Princes warned me that a long, bad time was coming."

Uncle Paul nodded again, as if this did not at all surprise him. "You are powerful; they would do that. I say again, are you prepared for more horror than you have ever seen before?"

"How can I be?" She sat down again and began shelling more peas, mechanically. "But if it is going to be *that* bad, how can I hold back and still be able to look at myself in the mirror?"

Uncle Paul sighed. "I just hope that for your sake, your spirit is very strong. Come with me."

He motioned for her to get up, and she looked at him quizzically. "Why?"

"Because you might as well go to the nursing sisters here and persuade them to take you on now," he said, as if this were quite the worst plan he had ever heard of in his life. "They have not enough in their ranks. They will test what you can do and give you some training. When they know you can nurse, they will send you to the Front."

"They will?" she blurted. He sighed again.

"And, of course, since I promised Peter I would guard you, I must come too," he said in a resigned voice. "At my age! Ah, well, I do not need two good legs to drive an ambulance. Come along."

17

"IT will all be over before Christmas," Charles Kerridge muttered, huddled in his soggy Army greatcoat, an equally soggy woolen scarf wrapped around his head and his ears, looking out of his bunker at the shattered remains of what had once been a village. It was behind their lines—for now. That could change if the Germans made a push. Then they would fall back to trenches they had left a few weeks ago, and the Germans would take these. Or maybe they would make a push, and it would be successful, and they would have the German trenches. It would be very good if that happened; the Germans were better builders. They had built their trenches assuming they would be in them for a long time; the British and French trenches had been dug assuming it would all be very temporary.

Mid-December was no time to be living virtually out in the open in this part of the country, but that was exactly what Charles and his men were doing. They were not far from a town called La Basse, but they might just as well have been on the surface of the Moon for all the good it did them. Rain poured out of the sky without any let-up; changes in the weather only seemed to amount to "more rain" or "less rain." Both sides had dug in after the "race to the sea," and "dug in" was literal. The two sides had built an elaborate series of trenches facing each other, across a stretch of shattered countryside that had been dubbed No-man's Land that went from the coast north of Calais to the Swiss border. What the generals who had ordered this had failed to take into account was that in relatively flat land like this, trenches rapidly filled with water, and the water had nowhere to go. The men lived, ate, and slept in anything from ankle-deep mud to waist-deep water. The sides of the trenches and the dugouts that provided the only shelter were inclined to collapse, and there were nothing like enough sandbags or boards to shore them up.

Death was as common a visitor as the ubiquitous rats. Snipers on both sides ensured that anyone who poked his head above the parapet was killed instantly. Artillery bombardment . . . well, that was as impersonal a form of death as the sniper was personal. A soldier could be doing anything— eating, sleeping, waiting for the enemy to decide to come over the top and charge across the empty space between the trenches. Then there would come that ominous whistling . . .

Those who knew what it meant would feel their hearts hammering as their bodies scrambled in a futile attempt to find shelter. Those who didn't would look up dumbly.

Then would come the bursting shell, which might hit a patch of empty ground, or might hit a dugout, burying who-ever was in it, or might hit the trench, obliterating everyone there. The veteran on hearing that whistle would often try to find a shell hole, thinking that, like lightning, shells would never hit the same place twice.

Right now, no one was shelling this part of the lines. Charles was not grateful; this only meant that everyone was waiting for the shelling to start again. Shelling was like the rain—more or less, but never absent. And no shelling meant that the rats were out in force.

The damned things were the size of cats and utterly fearless. They ran over your face at night; put down food for a moment, and there'd be a dozen on it when you turned back. The brown ones were the worst, gorging themselves on the dead, starting with their eyes.

Oh, yes. The dead. They were supposed to be removed and shipped home. Reality meant that unless you were an officer, that was unlikely to happen. You got shoved into a shell hole, and if you were *lucky*, you got dirt shoveled on top. Or if you'd been blown to bits, the bits just got shoveled any old where. At least three times Charles had had an arm or a leg fall out on him when he had been helping the men dig a new trench.

All that water meant that the men, unable to keep their feet dry or even *get* them dry for a little while, once a day, were contracting something everyone called trench foot. At its best, it was disgusting and painful. At its worst, it turned into gangrene, and the foot had to come off.

And the stench . . . there was no way to get away from it. Over everything, the bitter fug of rotting flesh. Layered on that, the different fug of men who had not washed in weeks, and who had been sleeping, eating, fighting in the same clothing for all that time. Layered on that, the smell of sickness—trench foot, trench fever, infection. You were supposed to report to the field hospital when you were wounded, but the reality was that no one could be spared unless they couldn't shoot anymore, and untended wounds festered quickly. Grace notes of urine and feces from the latrine trenches, rat piss, rotting sandbags, stagnant mud, filthy water, creosol, chloride of lime, cordite, cigarette smoke, woodsmoke, coal smoke, cooking food.

Sometimes Charles thought that the smell alone would drive him mad. The men said they got used to it. He didn't believe them. No one could get used to this.

If the smell didn't drive him mad, the lice might, first.

Lice were everywhere. You could strip down (in the freezing rain,) delouse yourself, delouse your clothing, put it back on, and the eggs hidden in the seams would hatch and infest you all over again.

Around him, the men were repairing and draining the trenches—the draining being an exercise in futility, since the water pumped out wasn't pumped out very far, and it would find its way back into the trench again. Unless there was an attack, that was the daytime routine: fix the trench, fill sandbags, hope that night had brought a supply of duck-boards to put a floor in with, and maybe some tin. Keep your head down. Listen for artillery. Read or write letters. Read a book, if you had one. Snatch a few minutes of sleep. And remember to keep your head down.

This was no place for an Earth mage. The pervading aura of *wrongness* was so intense it clogged Charles' throat, and made it hard to choke down food.

Oh, yes. The food . . .

There were supposed to be field kitchens supplying everyone with hot meals three times a day. Well, that might be happening off the front, but no one was willing to get shot just to bring food to the soldiers in the trenches. There might be one hot meal in the morning, brought before first light. Often there wasn't that. They weren't going hungry—but—

At first light, Charles would give the order to "Stand to!" and all along the zigzag trenches, as the men were roused from their little rathole dugouts, they got up onto the fire step to prepare for a morning raid. If there was no raid forthcoming, the little exchange known as the "morning hate" ensued, with both sides letting off tension by firing at each other. Once feelings had been relieved and the gunfire died away, the morning rum was issued. Charles had been appalled by this at first. Now he drank down his ration as quickly as anyone else. It was the only way to dull the constant headache and feel a little warmer.

Then, inspection, which consisted these days of making sure each man had cleaned his rifle and no one's feet were falling off, followed by breakfast. Which, unless an unofficial "breakfast truce" was in effect, was not always the hot food from the field kitchens, but rather bacon cooked over little trench fires, tea, bully beef, bread, and plum and apple jam. Sometimes there was cheese. They were supposed to get vegetables, dried or fresh, but Charles hadn't seen any in weeks. They were *supposed* to get a great many things that never materialized. Two things never seemed to be in short supply: rum, and plum and apple jam. The same food turned up for dinner and supper, unless there was a lull and the field kitchens could send real meals. Or unless things were so bad that nothing got through, and they had to fall back on ration-biscuits, concoctions that were literally hard enough to drive nails with. Charles' orderly generally boiled water and soaked them in it to make him a kind of mush, with plum and apple jam atop it. At least it was hot.

Charles was an officer; he had better conditions than his men. He had a bunker with a floor of duckboards, walls of sandbags, and a tin roof with more sandbags on top of it. He had an orderly to cook his bacon, make his tea, and—resourceful fellow!—round up whatever variations to the menu he could manage. In the early days, he'd been able to set snares and catch rabbits; now all the snares caught were rats.

They were supposed to spend only eight days in the trenches, four in the support trenches behind the front, and twelve days in reserve, followed by eight days of rest. That never happened, not here. This rotation had been the longest they had been stuck out here. Charles and his men had been here for two weeks, and he had been praying daily for word that they would finally fall back to support.

His orderly ran up, in the hunched-over position the prudent man always took when running along a trench, a muddy scrap of paper in his hand. Charles took it, and could have sobbed with relief.

He passed the order down the line: Gather up your kit. Be ready to move out at dark. Being relieved at last, and not to the support trenches, but all the way to the reserve.

Reserve! Hot meals, a bath, a delousing—sleep in a bed, clean uniforms, dry feet at last. Visit the hospital tents and get the "little things" attended to . . .

The hours until dark passed with interminable slowness, and then, finally, the relieving troops arrived, crawling up the trenches, loaded down with their own guns, equipment, supplies. The officer relieving Charles looked like an angel . . .

Of course, this was an angel wearing the expression of one assigned to hell.

He cheered up a little at the sight of Charles' bunker; this had been Charles' work, and that of his orderly, during the two weeks they had been there. When he had arrived, there had only been a little rathole of a dugout, like everyone else's.

Four hours later, he and the men were crawling back toward the rear, past the support troops, and then, finally, far enough away that they could stand safely, stand and march like men, back to the reserves, behind the lines.

They reached the relief tents at last. Real tents, waterproof canvas, with stoves in them keeping them warm. There was *fresh* hot food waiting for them, really hot—hot enough to burn your mouth, the first they'd had in two weeks. The men fell on it like starving wolves. He took his time, eating slowly, feeling a fog of fatigue coming over his brain. At the start of his time at the Front, when he and his men got to the support or the relief barracks, the first thing he did was to make straight for whatever passed for a bathing facility— rarely an actual bath, but at least there would be hot water, soap, something to kill the damned lice. Now . . . now he was worn down by six days more at the Front than he had reckoned on, and all he wanted was to lie down someplace warm and relatively soft. Someplace where rats wouldn't run over him.

But no; he'd clean up first. Exhausted he might be, but he *would* clean up first. Wash the stink off, then sleep without dreaming of wandering aimlessly through a city of the dead. Finally, finally get that stink out of the back of his throat, out of his nose.

He finished his stew, got his directions, and stumbled through the rain to his assigned quarters, where someone had left buckets of steaming water, soap, a sponge, and creosol to kill the lice. He dropped his filthy, stinking uniform, stiff with mud and crawling with lice into one of the empty buckets; it would have to be fumigated. Smelling like a tar factory of creosol, he pulled on gloriously clean pajamas and fell into the bed at last, lulled to sleep by the steady roar of artillery, which sounded, in his dreams, like thunder.

Some of the girls said they dreamed of home, of dancing, of handsome, unwounded men. Susanne dreamed of bandages.

In her dream, she would open a huge crate and find it packed to bursting with beautiful pure white gauze and white cotton bandages, clean and new. In her dream, these bandages were miraculous; she rushed into the ward and began putting new dressings on all the boys, who began to heal as soon as the clean fabric touched them. She woke from that dream with silent tears pouring down her face, sobbing into her pillow.

The little old lady with whom she lodged always met her reddened eyes over the breakfast table and nodded knowingly. Then fed her a bowl of boiled milk, an egg, and that marvelous French delicacy, a croissant. With butter. The nursing sisters got generous rations; food was one thing there was no shortage of here at the field hospital. It wasn't always the sort of food she would have preferred for her patients, but between them, she and Madame Lebois could turn it into something that actually *was* suitable.

"You had that dream again," Madame said, handing her the jam. "Did you say good-bye to another last night?"

That was Madame's polite way of asking if one of her patients had died. She nodded. "I couldn't do anything," she said, helplessly. "I—"

"Earth Master you may be, but you cannot mend everything," Madame said wisely. "Eat your egg."

When Suzanne had so blithely told Uncle Paul that she would be a nursing sister, she'd had no idea what the job would be, exactly. She assumed it would be mostly waiting on the patients. With ample opportunity to slip in some magic now and again.

She was too determined to be horrified when she learned that she, and not a doctor, would be expected to clean out wounds and irrigate them with Dakin's solution or alcohol. That she, not the doctor, was expected to put in drains and keep them clear. She, not a doctor, would change the dressings on even the worst wounds.

She'd also discovered it was a good thing she had the uneasy patronage of someone rich, for she had been expected to supply virtually everything for herself. The list that the Red Cross had presented to her was astonishing:

Coat with unbuttonable collar or turndown cloth 1
Hat, bonnet, or headcloth 1
Cap Vest, Cloth or knitted scarf 1
Washcloths 2
Wool dress 1
Collar or neckcloth 6
Aprons, white 3
Aprons, colored 4
Night jackets or nightshirts 3
Shirts 5
Wool undershirts 2
Corset or Reform-corset 2
Petticoat 2
Dust-skirt 2
Bloomers 3
Trousers 4
Stockings 6
Leather laced boots, high 1
Leather shoes, half-height, with double heels, pair 1
Shoes, warm, pair 1
Galoshes, pair 1

Handkerchiefs 9
Gloves, pair 2
Umbrella 1
Toilette kit, incl. toothbrush, nail brush, comb 1
Hand-towel 1
Mirror, small 1
Clothes brush 1
Shoe cleaning kit 1
Sewing kit 1
Mending bag 1
Knife, fork, spoon; in a case 1
Drinking cup 1
Canteen 1
Pocket knife 1
Pouch with writing implements 1
Change purse 1
Travel inkwell 1
Lantern 1
Lighter 1
Stearine candle for lantern 1 pack—1
(Collapsible) Rubber basin 1
Neutrality insignia 3
Identity card 1
Expenditure book
Bandages 75
Bandage packets 2
Identity disk 1
Iron Ration 1

Fortunately, Uncle Paul had taken care of the list, with the help of the estimable Garrick, who was serving as Peter's orderly. Garrick had also helpfully added other things: a spray bottle for antiseptic solution, two thermometers, and her own syringe kit with extra needles and a sharpening stone. She hadn't needed to use the ward's syringe, which kept getting "borrowed."

It was raining again; she and Madame finished breakfast

in silence that had the constant rumble of artillery fire beneath it. She pulled on the boiled-wool cape—selected by Garrick and infinitely superior to the plain woven capes the other nurses had—slung her kit over her shoulder, and stepped out into the muck.

She wondered, often, if the other nurses noticed that she took a little longer beside each patient than they did. But then, "her" doctor, the one who was in charge of her ward, was a fanatic for antiseptic irrigation, and she was the one that had to change the complicated dressings, tubes, and drips. Some of the other nurses thought he was mad, obsessed, or both; she thought he was a genius. His system, even without her help, was saving twice as many wounded as anyone else, and was saving men other doctors thought doomed. With her help? While she did lose the ones who really were too badly torn up to survive, the ones with ruptured spleens, perforated intestines, livers that looked as if Zeus's eagle had been pecking at them, or multiple amputations, most of the men who came into her ward left it healing.

What happened to them afterward, when they were evacuated to recovery hospitals? She couldn't say. She did her best for them, and that was all anyone could do. At least they were going to places where the sheets were changed daily, where rats didn't scamper among the beds at night, where they weren't in danger of being killed by shells or bombs in their beds.

There was one small problem, of course. If anyone ever found out that she was *not* a real nurse, nor French, she would probably get shipped summarily back to England. And now that she had found Charles, that was the last place she wanted to go. So far, Peter had held his peace, but if something happened and she was in danger—he might just reveal it all.

I just have to make sure that nothing does, she told herself, then amended the thought. *Or, at least, nothing that he finds out about.*

As she neared the hospital, which had been set up in a donated farm building of the sort that Uncle Paul owned (or *had* owned), she saw ambulances discharging their cargo and speeding away, Uncle Paul's among them. She broke into a run.

"What happened?" she asked the orderly at the door, breathlessly, as she paused long enough to shed her cloak and hang it on the hanger.

By now she was conversant enough in French that she could pass as a provincial native from the north. It was funny, there were as many dialects of French as there were of English, and those from the Ardennes found it as hard to understand the Parisians as a London Cockney did broad Yorkshire.

"Cursed boche got their artillery fixed on a company coming off the lines for relief," the man spat. "There must have been a spy or a spotter behind the lines, or maybe a nighttime balloonist. We're only now getting them in, as no one dared get to them before dawn."

Susanne nodded, ran to the scrubroom, and doused herself in Lister Solution. It was going to be a long day, and she would need to be at her best for every man still alive.

When she stumbled out of the ward, it was dark, and she ran right into an officer just coming in the door. "Scuse moi, mam's—" said a familiar voice, *"Susanne?* What are you doing here?"

Charles caught her elbows and held her upright as she swayed with fatigue. She looked up at him and smiled wryly. "Just doing my part," she said. "I can't exactly go back to England, after all."

He looked at her sternly. "No, but you can go somewhere else. New Zealand. Australia. Canada. Even America!"

She bristled a little. "So it is perfectly all right for you to risk your life, and not all right for me to be safely behind the lines doing what I can?"

"But it's not safe behind the lines!" Charles objected. "Hospitals have been shelled!"

"And I could be run over by a cart, or a flock of sheep, or a—a—kangaroo!" she retorted. "Meanwhile, you *know* I am an Earth Master, and you must know how many I have helped and *will* help!" Then she stopped, set her jaw, and let her broad Yorkshire come through. "And tha' knows that short of bodily restraining me and puttin' me on a boat in chains, tha'art not going to keep me from doing what I wish, so tha' might as well give over."

He stared at her. And then, ruefully, began to chuckle. "Cursed stubborn woman, you are true Yorkshire stock. But I'll persuade you, see if I don't!"

She sniffed. "Tha' can try."

"What if I knew where you can get a hot bath?" he countered. "A real bath."

She stared at him in disbelief.

"A mile down that road—" he pointed "—is a lunatic asylum. It has a men's side and a women's side. Part of their treatment is hydrotherapy, and they have opened the bathing facilities to us. You can have a real hot bath there, provided you don't mind the company of people who wear dead bats on their heads."

Her skin itched at the mere thought of a hot bath. Her landlady was a lovely old dear, but the only tub was an ancient thing you had to fill from water heated on the stove, and was hardly big enough to sit upright in, with your knees to your chest.

"This is *not* going to make me go to New Zealand," she told him.

"And if I were to take you to dinner?" He smiled.

"It still won't," she temporized. "But I will listen to your arguments."

"Taking her to dinner," of course, meant either bringing her to the Officer's Mess or getting what could be scrounged up at the local bistro. She wondered which he would choose and was pleasantly surprised when it was the bistro. There were no actual regulations forbidding officers from consorting with nursing sisters, but she had no wish to attract any more attention than she had from the English military. She wasn't a religious sister, she wasn't a trained nurse, and she wasn't French, even though she was serving with the French nurses. And she certainly didn't have official or parental permission to be here.

She really didn't notice what dinner was. Horse, probably; when it came to anything that you might cook and eat, the French were inclined to put a sauce on. And it didn't matter. It could have been boot soles for all she cared. She had Charles all to herself, for the first time ever, and she set out to make a good impression on him.

It must have worked. He invited her to dinner the next day as well.

The six days—only six—of being in reserve passed far too quickly. The men in reserve got a chance to eat decently, sleep in beds, clean up, get rid of lice, have minor injuries and problems like trench foot cleared up. They got light drill daily, but mostly, they were supposed to rest and recover. Charles would be the first to admit that a great deal of his pleasure during those six days was in the dinners he had with Susanne. Finally he could talk to someone else about magic, about the bone-shaking distress he felt in the land because of the horrors of this war, the fear that the Elementals of this part of the world were being destroyed or driven off. You could say things to a woman you couldn't admit to a man. She was a good old thing, was Susanne; she listened patiently and carefully, and if she couldn't reassure him, at least she didn't shower him with platitudes.

They even managed to round up Almsley and his man Garrick for two of these dinners, making for a lively discussion over the table. Peter tried briefly to persuade the girl that it was in her best interest to emigrate, but his heart didn't seem to be in it.

He felt as though he was living like a human being again for the first time in months. Six days was not enough. His men clearly felt the same, and to be honest, they didn't *look* recovered when their six days were up.

So it was with decidedly gloomy feelings that he and his troopers made their way back to the Front—to a different series of trenches this time. Besides having to work really hard to convince himself that his country needed him out there, he was laboring under a sense of failure for another self-imposed task. He hadn't been able to talk Susanne around to evacuating to the colonies, and now it would be at least two weeks before he could see her again. She was so damned stubborn; if only she would see reason!

Once they got into the relief trenches, it became a matter of going silently and with no lights. The relief trenches were within reach of the guns, and any light would give the spotters something to sight in on. This was a night of no moon, which was good for keeping undercover, and it was good because the boche artillery had to fire blind; but it was bad because he couldn't see anything, and he was rearmost man.

Perhaps that was how he got separated from his own troop. Because he went around a corner—and suddenly, he was alone.

As in, *completely alone*. There was no warning, it was as if he had suddenly been transported to a place that had been abandoned. The sense he always had, of knowing where his men were—well, he couldn't sense them. He strained his ears, but he could hear nothing but the ever-present rumble of artillery and, nearby, the soughing of the wind. No footfalls, no murmurs of voices, nothing.

Something was wrong. Something was very, very wrong. His stomach felt queasy, and if he'd had hackles to raise, they'd have been up.

And just as a chill crept down his spine, he felt with a shock of recognition that he wasn't alone anymore.

He sensed it first: a draught of icy cold wind, colder than the winter wind he was used to, and carrying the scent of corruption with it. Then he heard it—a faint, but menacing moaning.

Then a starshell burst overhead, and he *saw* it. Saw, as the shell dropped lower and lower, the limbs clawing their way up out of the muck on either side of the trench. Saw the half-rotten corpses dragging themselves to their feet. Watched in horror as they turned their eyeless heads toward him.

With a yell, half fear, half panic, he opened up on them with his service revolver.

It had no effect, of course. They were already dead. Worse, he *knew* some of them; the decomposing features weren't so far gone that he couldn't recognize some faces, and some of them had been his own men. With horrible sucking sounds they pulled themselves out of the mud and to their feet. As they piled into the trench, hands grasping for him, the paralysis of terror suddenly wore off, and he turned and ran—

Only to stumble to a halt when a second starshell burst and showed him that he was blocked on both sides by an army of walking dead piled into the trench and spilling over the top.

He pressed himself against the wall of the trench. *Maybe they won't find me....*

But within moments, he knew that was a false hope. They all turned their eyeless faces in his direction and started forward at a shambling walk.

He scrambled up the side of the trench, frantically clawing at the boards shoring up the dirt. He made it out just ahead of the horrible groping hands and stumbled away.

The damned things followed, piling up against the side he had just scaled and using the bodies of those who had gotten there first as a staircase.

Sheer, total terror engulfed him. He shook like a leaf in a high wind, and his mind spun in circles. He appeared to be the only truly living thing in this entire landscape of death.

The dead glowed with their own phosphorescence as they surged after him, moving much faster than they had any right to.

He screamed and ran.

But more of them were pulling themselves up out of the earth in front of him, and he dodged frantically out of their way. This wasn't like the fight back at Branwell Hall; then, there had been four of them, they had the proper weapons, and Peter had fought these things before. Now he was utterly alone, without the right weapons, on alien ground—and the things that were after him wore the faces of his dead companions. He would never see Rose again. She might not even learn what had happened to him.

So he did the only thing he could. He ran, spurred on by fear that ran hot through his veins and galvanized him

Only to fall headlong into a shell crater.

He turned his fall into a tumble, managing not to break his neck or anything else, until he fetched up in the muddy bottom of the crater. He scrambled up the other side, or tried to, but the silent dead ringed the rim, cutting him off from escape.

He had no blessed salt, no blessed iron, no—anything. As he put his back to the wreck of a cart down in the bottom of the crater with him and fumbled his rifle with its fixed bayonet off his back, he could only send out a single, magical, despairing cry for help and pray that someone, anyone, was near enough to "hear" it.

He did not expect the answer that he got.

From the earth at his feet, a dozen or more little brownie-like creatures erupted. In their hands were tiny flint blades. He heard a shrill whinnying sound and the pounding of hooves, and a moment later, a shining white equine form plunged through the mob of walking dead, slashing from left to right with the single horn in the middle of its forehead.

A second white creature, this time a stag with a magnificent spread of antlers, appeared on the opposite side of the

crater; it bugled a challenge and charged the dead with lowered horns.

Its challenge was answered by the little manikins at his
feet and by a long, drawn out howl. Three white wolves appeared between the stag and the unicorn to attack, as the
brownies charged from below with those wicked little
blades.

Every time the unicorn's horn touched one of the dead,
it dropped to the ground, lifeless again. The stag merely
broke them in pieces. The wolves did likewise, and the
brownies set upon the broken and cut them to pieces.

For a moment his heart leaped. But another starshell
showed him the truth: Charles' rescuers were themselves
wounded and weary—and sick. They were inextricably
linked to the land, and the land was sickening, dying. The
stag missed as often as he hit, and he stumbled a little when
he tried to charge. The unicorn looked to be on his last legs;
the light of its horn was dim, and its coat was harsh and
dingy. The brownies only had their little flint knives, and the
wolves were emaciated. They had come to his rescue, but
they themselves were falling.

One of the wolves went first, then three of the brownies,
pulled down and buried beneath piles of walking dead.
Then the stag went down with a despairing squeal.

And that was when the shelling began.

He heard the telltale whistling first and instinctively
flinched to one side. A moment later, the shell exploded
not far off, sending a rain of dirt and body parts down on
him. Another shell followed the first, and another, while
the Elementals and the dead tore and fought at each other
in unnerving silence. Charles too fought on, in a haze of
exhaustion and terror.

A third shell—a fourth—bracketed them. The Elementals had descended into the shell crater with him; they were
all standing together now, facing the horde of walking dead
that stumbled and tripped down the sides of the crater
toward them.

Another pair of shells landed even closer, this time, throwing half-corpses down the side of their crater. These things writhed and snapped and grabbed until the brownies cut them to bits, bits that, horribly, still moved. An unattached hand clamped itself around Charles' boot until he bayoneted it into the ground.

Two more shells fell even closer. The remaining wolves whimpered, and the unicorn pressed into his side.

Where were his men? Hadn't they figured out he was missing by now?

Despair clawed at his soul. He was going to die, and it would not be a clean death.

Five more shells, one after the other, whistled through the sky and sent gouts of debris up to rain down on them. The walking dead paid no heed at all.

What were the wretched Germans trying to shoot at? Had they actually spotted the white hides of his Elementals? Were they using *those* to sight in on?

It didn't matter. None of this mattered.

Belatedly, he remembered that he had hand grenades in the rucksack on his back. As more and more of the walking dead poured down to meet the combined weapons of his allies, he slipped out of the straps and fumbled one out, armed it, and tossed it.

The resulting explosion wasn't as impressive as the shell, but it cleared a path partway up the crater wall.

He urged the Elementals to follow him, and scrambled toward that gap in the enemy lines. If he could get there, he could clear more of a path out with another grenade. If he could do that, they might be able to—

He heard the shell whistling overhead.

Overhead.

No! he thought, and then the world erupted in light and sound and then plunged into darkness.

18

THE little bistro was very good about giving Peter and Susanne a relatively quiet table, and even better about turning the provisions Peter supplied into quite decent meals. They even managed to turn that wretched plum-and-apple jam into a rather delightful sauce. "You're being rather foolish, old girl," Peter said, as he refilled Susanne's glass with the decent pinot noir that Garrick had managed to find, somewhere. "Think about this: You could do just as much good, if not more, doing your nursing back in Australia. The lads that make it back will need someone who knows what they've been through."

She shook her head, her mouth set in a stubborn line. He sighed. He knew that look. "There aren't enough nurses *here*," she countered. "You know that, you've seen the wards when a rush comes in."

"But the magic—" he protested. "Think of what you could do with Earth magic for them!"

"I'm using it all the time here, every day, or half of those fellows wouldn't live through the first night." She raised her chin and defiantly challenged him to counter that, and he knew that he couldn't. She could do what no doctor—other than Maya—could do. She was right, she was keeping men alive who by rights should have died.

Peter sighed anyway, because he also knew that the real reason she was not going to leave had nothing to do with the nursing. He knew what was going on; it was as plain as could be every time she looked at Charles. She was utterly smitten and probably had been from the moment she first set eyes on him. For a moment he was silent, caught up in an internal debate.

Should I tell her about Rose? That was the question. The poor thing had no idea that she had a rival, because the rival had only materialized after she'd been sent across the Channel.

In the weeks following the invasion of Belgium, when *everyone* knew that it was only a matter of time before Britain declared an official war, lives had suddenly accelerated. Men tidied their affairs, sold horses and yachts and motorcars. Some who had put off engagements proposed and wed within days, while others broke off engagements on the grounds that they didn't know if they were going to come back alive. Thankfully, there were a lot fewer of those. There were so many applications for civil marriages and special licenses, in fact, that clerks could hardly keep up with them. Churches and registry offices were booked solid with weddings religious and civil. And when that started, Peter had had no doubt that there was going to follow a veritable rain of babies around about April.

He would have bet that cool, calm Charles would not have been affected by that frenzy, that primitive urge to make sure you produced at least one child before you went off to an uncertain conflict. Charles, unlike most Britons, had been sure that it would *not* all be over by Christmas, but he hadn't rushed into anything. Peter would have wagered any amount of money that Charles would never let his instincts overcome him.

He would have been wrong.

It all happened over a garden party. The magicians of England all knew, by now, that this was going to be a long and hideous war. They knew that many would be called up, and many would not return. Elizabeth Kerridge had known, had been certain, that this gathering of both sexes of magicians was going to be fevered, and she had figured that at least one, if not several, engagements were going to come out of this gathering. She had said as much to Peter, half in jest and perhaps half in warning. Had Charles known that? He might have; he might have simply decided that his mother was going to pitch girls at him until he decided on one. It might have been that, the moment he saw one he had known as a boy and been friends with, he figured he had better just give in and take someone he could get along with. Branwell was going to need another generation. He was the only child, the heir. It was his duty.

Or perhaps they really *were* meant for each other.

Peter had not seen the actual meeting, but he'd had it described to him. The two had looked equally surprised to see the other. There had been a moment when the eyes of Charles Kerridge met the young woman's, followed immediately by Charles leaving the reception line and going straight to the side of young Rose Mainwright, and not moving away from her for the rest of the night. The next morning, it was official. They were engaged. Charles told Peter later that Rose was an old friend he had long ago lost track of, someone he'd played with as a child until her parents moved to Blackpool. She was an Elemental mage too, a Water mage, like Peter.

Peter liked her; she and Charles were obviously comfortable together.

Susanne didn't know about Rose. Not that Charles was hiding anything; he just never would think to tell her. So far as Charles was concerned, Susanne was just someone he was helping, certainly a friend, but nothing like as close a friend as, say, Peter. They weren't of the same social class, as

Charles had pointed out before this. Why should she care if he was engaged or not?

He was completely oblivious to the fact that Susanne was infatuated with him; Charles could be desperately thick about emotional matters sometimes.

So should I tell her about Rose? Peter pondered this while Susanne ate hungrily and talked about her work on the wards. He finally shrugged to himself and decided that it wouldn't matter what he told her, she wouldn't believe it unless she saw it with her own eyes.

Which, if he finally got his way, was simply not going to happen. She would be in Australia, where there was a shortage of women. She'd have dozens of hearty young fellows vying for her, and in no time at all, she would forget about Charles.

He was about to change the subject to how she thought the Elementals here were faring, when he felt it.

She did too.

Cold, and dark, and death. And they recognized the signature of that black pall of magic.

Richard Whitestone.

They both clutched the sides of the table as if the earth itself had moved, and fought free of the clinging tentacles of that horrible power. Susanne was the first to speak.

"Father—" she said, looking terror-struck and nauseated at the same time. He didn't blame her. *How* had Richard Whitestone managed to find them across the Channel? And how had he gotten here in the first place? Was an attack imminent? How much time did they have before a horde of walking dead broke down the door to the little bistro?

She looked stunned. Peter had already gotten the inadequate little knife in one hand and the fork in the other and was looking around for liches. Richard was obviously working necromantic magic, and very powerful stuff—

He couldn't possibly be using it against the Germans, could he?

When no walking dead appeared, he shoved away from the table. "I'm here, and you're here, and there's no army of dead coming at us—so who is he attacking?" he wondered aloud.

And both of them got the answer at the same moment. "Charles!" they chorused. "He knows Charles helped me," she said, anguish in her voice. "And your trick worked; he can't possibly know that I am here, so he's going after Charles!"

"Revenge," Peter agreed grimly.

"We have to get to him!" she cried, and flung herself out of her seat and dashed out the door.

"Wait!" Peter called out. "Wait!"

She was already gone, the door slamming shut behind her. He ran to follow, hoping he could catch her before she ran off into the night to do something brave but stupid.

But she had not, as it proved, gone very far.

He had barely gotten out of the door himself when the clatter of horse hooves and the rumble of wheels on cobbles to his right warned of a cart approaching at high speed.

But as it whipped around the corner, he saw it wasn't a cart, it was an ambulance, driven by his own Uncle, whose grim face told that he too had sensed the dark perversion of Earth magic out there somewhere between the village and the Front. Susanne was already up beside him; Uncle Paul pulled his horses to a stop just long enough for Peter to fling himself in the back, and they were off again.

He clung to the side of the ambulance, being thrown all over the vehicle as Paul directed it regardless of the presence or absence of roads. It was a terrible ride, not only because of the nausea he felt from that foul magic out there, but because as they neared the first line of trenches, it was clear that there was a bombardment going on. Shells pounded into the earth ahead of them—occasionally, one exploded far too close to them for any sort of comfort. Evidently Paul didn't care; the horses were not allowed to slack or swerve, and when an Earth magician determines that an animal *will* do something, that animal has very little choice in the matter.

He fought sickness, fought despair, fought the crushing demand that he simply lie down and give in. He couldn't imagine how Susanne and Paul were feeling; he only got the reflection of the necromantic magic because it was not of his Element, but they were getting it right in the teeth.

They were heading directly into the thick of the bombardment. Shells were falling all around them, and still the ambulance plunged through a night made hideous with explosions and the stench and bitter chill that accompanied necromancy. Inside the wagon, Peter could only cling and ready his own magic.

Then, suddenly, the chill vanished, and the stench, though it remained, went back to the normal stink of the trenches, if such a thing could be considered normal.

A moment later, the ambulance slewed sideways as Uncle Paul skidded it to a halt.

Peter plunged out, over the now-vacant driver's seat and invoked mage-sight so he wouldn't have to strike a light. Susanne and Paul were ahead of him, descending into a crater with entrenching shovels in their hands. They too must have invoked mage-sight, since they were moving as surely as if it were broad daylight.

Susanne glanced up as he displaced a shower of dirt onto her. "Down here!" she shouted, and at first he wondered why she was shouting at him, but then he saw the faces of three men looking over the rim of the crater on the opposite side. "Charles Kerridge is down here! He's buried, help us get him out!"

They jumped as if they'd been stung and tumbled down into the crater, that being the fastest way to get to the bottom. They joined Uncle Paul and Susanne in pitching aside rotting body parts and digging. Just as Peter got there, one of the men threw a torso aside and exposed a still-living person. Charles!

Quickly, Susanne put two fingers under his jaw to get a

pulse. "He's alive!" she shouted. "Hurry! We have to get him out of here before the shelling starts again!"

Now all six of them worked feverishly to free the unconscious man from his noisome burden. Within moments, they had him out, and they carefully rolled him onto his back. He was still unconscious.

Paul scrambled up to the ambulance for a canvas stretcher; they rolled Charles into it, then, as Susanne took temporary charge of the horses, all five men manhandled the thing and its burden up the slope of the crater and into the ambulance.

"Field hospital," grunted Uncle Paul. "Closest one is English."

"Go!" Peter shouted, waving them to go on. "I'll find my way back; I need to look for someone."

"All the other men are accounted for, sir," said one of the soldiers who had helped them get the stretcher out.

Paul nodded, but Susanne would know what he meant. He was going to try to hunt down Richard, who surely could not have gotten far!

"Go," she told Uncle Paul, just now climbing onto the driver's bench and taking the reins from her. He nodded as she dove into the back of the vehicle to be with the patient. He slapped the reins on the backs of his horses, and they shot off again.

Peter watched them go. Charles Kerridge would live or die by the combined skills of Susanne and whatever doctor he got. There was nothing that *he* could do about that.

But he had a necromancer to hunt, and when he found the man . . .

. . . things were not going to go well for him.

🌺

Uncle Paul pulled up his lathered horses at the tent marked with the red cross, shouting in French—which, of course, the English staff didn't understand. Susanne decided it was safe enough to leave Charles for a moment and stuck her head through the flaps at the front. "English officer!" she shouted, motioning Uncle Paul to be silent. "Buried by shelling!"

A dozen men swarmed over the ambulance then, extracting Charles and the stretcher he was still tied down to, and running him to the tent, while Susanne kept alongside, her medical bag bouncing off her hip with each step. Someone pulled the tent flaps aside ahead of them, and they were inside the heat and glare of the field hospital.

Someone grabbed her elbow before she could follow Charles to the surgeons. "You speak English?" asked a man with orderly badges.

"I *am* English," she replied. "I'm working with the nursing sisters of St. Claire down the line."

"Good!" The man pulled her away. "We've got a full ward, more coming in, and only two nurses—"

He didn't have to say anything more. He pointed her at a line of men bedded down wherever there was space, and she went to work.

It was the job of the nurse, not the doctor, to remove small pieces of shrapnel and the odd bullet and to clean and bandage the wounds. The doctor only diagnosed, operated, set bones, or sometimes set up an irrigation station to keep a particularly bad wound clean. The nurse took care of everything else.

So all the smaller wounds on these men had been left for the nurses to tend.

As gently as she could, she did her job, adding a dose of healing magic with every bandage she tied in place, every suture she set. The orderly hadn't lied; the tent was inundated, so much so that the ones it was not possible to save had been shuttled to one side and were being seen to by a French priest and a chaplain.

Susanne felt a lump rising in her throat, and her eyes stung with tears, to see so many. All those lives, all those boys—so many of them *were* boys, barely eighteen, who should have been enjoying life right now, not dying on the cold ground in a foreign land.

She dashed the back of her hand across her eyes and went back to work.

It seemed like an eternity laboring in a hell of blood, shattered limbs, moans and screams. Finally, she finished working on a boy who cried for his mother as she pulled bits of shell casing out of his thigh and mercifully had passed out before she was half done. She looked up.

There were no more patients.

The ward was quiet. The orderlies were going from patient to patient administering sedatives, but the doctor in charge was watching her with bemusement, his arms folded over himself.

"I know what you're doing," he said bluntly. "Did you follow a lover over? Are you even a nursing sister?"

Caught off-guard, she avoided the first question, and answered the second. "Not . . . exactly. What I could do convinced the Mother Superior that I was a nursing sister."

"Oh, you're good," the doctor acknowledged. "And you can be using those skills on the men on the ship on the way back across the channel. But since you aren't a trained nurse, and you shouldn't be here in the first place, I'm going to make sure you go back. When you get permission from your father and the proper training, you can come back."

"But—" she protested. Or tried to.

"No buts," the doctor said, frowning ferociously. "You are going back. You aren't a nursing sister, and you aren't French. Don't argue. There's a spare cot behind that partition. Feel free to get some sleep on it. I'll be needing your skills until the hour that the ship leaves. Oh! Where are you staying?"

Too tired to resist him, she told him. "I'll send someone for your things," he promised. But at that point, she didn't care. She found the cots for the staff, with two already occupied, and fell into the nearest. She was vaguely aware of someone draping a blanket over her as she was bludgeoned by sleep.

She woke to someone shaking her shoulder. That same

someone pressed a cup of hot liquid—coffee—into one hand and a plate of beans and bread into the other, then moved on to the next sleeper.

Then it was all to do over. She still was unable to get to Charles. She did hear from Peter, however, in the form of a note delivered along with her things. *Did not find RW. Trying to get you assigned here. So far, no luck. Looks like you're being shipped back no matter what. P*

Well, there it was.

She returned to the cot to find all of her things neatly packed beside it. It was a relief to at least be able to change her clothing but a shock to find a very official-looking document inside, ordering her to a transport ship. The document informed her that if she did not comply, she would be assumed to be a spy, and would be arrested and charged.

She could scarcely sleep that night, despite exhaustion; she kept having nightmares—in some, she was back in England, at Whitestone Hall, being pursued by trolls. In others, she was here in France, in a gaol cell, with walking dead trying to reach her through the bars. None of her magic would work, and she was utterly alone. No one answered her screams for help.

The next morning, she was awakened the same way—except that the meal this time was bread and bully beef—and went about the ward doing what she was ordered to in a fog. She rapidly lost count of the days she had been there, and while her diligent work finally made the doctor stop frowning every time he looked at her, she eventually had to make up some nonsense about being an art student to get the others to stop treating her as if she were a camp follower. At least she had listened diligently to all the art talk and was able to pretend to some expertise, though she feared what would happen if somehow, someone got hold of some art supplies and pressed her to paint.

That would be a total disaster.

Perhaps a week after she and Charles had arrived at the field hospital, she woke to someone shaking her roughly, without the usual coffee and food. "Get yer gear, miss," said a strange voice. "Yer bein' shipped out with the invalids."

Only half awake, she huddled herself into her clothing, got her bags, and—

And stopped a moment, to leave the medical kit with the precious syringe and needles on the bed of one of the other nurses. She wouldn't need it where she was going, and they would.

Then she picked up her gear and followed the sound of voices out into the gray dawn.

Stretchers were being loaded into more ambulances, all motorized ones. Without so much as a word, a soldier looked at her, looked at a paper in his hand, and took her by the elbow. She was summarily boosted up into the back of a crowded ambulance.

"Take care of' em," the man said brusquely, and banged on the side of the vehicle. It took off with a lurch.

She checked all the drugged and semiconscious passengers in her care; none was Charles. From the records left with each, all were common soldiers.

She was beginning to get an idea of why she was being kept from Charles. Not because anyone suspected anything—because he was an officer. Suspect, with no clear idea of what, if any, training she had had, she would not be allowed near an officer. But she was a pair of hands, and that was better than nothing for the Tommys.

She set her chin stubbornly. If that was how it was—well, these men were going to get better care from *her* than the officers got from their "real" nurses. She tended them assiduously, trickling healing into them as soon as she could concentrate. As the light grew and the ever-present pounding of guns faded slightly into the distance, traffic on the road increased. Abruptly, the ambulance lurched, and the sound of the tires on the road changed to the rattle of tires on cobblestones.

We must be at the port.

But the rattling woke several of the boys, who, confused

by their surroundings, thirsty, anxious, began making plaintive requests of her. That kept her occupied right up to the point where the ambulance stopped again.

The canvas doors were pulled open; the same soldier with the papers was there, waiting, along with several stretcher bearers. He didn't so much "help" her out of the back of the ambulance as pull her out, and dump out her bags at her feet. Clearly she was expected to deal with them herself.

He gave her just enough time to pick them up before taking her by the elbow again and marching her up the gangplank, following and preceding men with invalids on stretchers. At the top, there was another soldier, and with obvious relief, her escort surrendered her, and her papers, to this fellow.

He passed her off to a sailor, who, with a bit more courtesy, escorted her to a tiny bunk in a room with six of the same in the bowels of the ship, showed her where to stow her things, and then took her to a giant ward in what must have been a ballroom. Clearly this had been a passenger ship, now pressed into service as a hospital ship for the journey across the Channel, and a troopship back to France.

This time she found herself in service not as a nurse, but as a lowly aide. It was with a profound sense of relief that she felt the ship begin to move. At least the trip across the Channel would only take a few hours.

And then what?

She considered this as she emptied basins, scrubbed the floors after accidents, took away filthy, bloody bandages and dressings. Right now, she had nowhere to go but Whitestone Hall, and that, she would never do. Richard was clearly in France now, but there was no guarantee that he would stay there.

And she wanted to be near Charles, no matter what.

Peter had managed to get her quite a nice sum of money when he understood that she was being sent back. It was more than enough to set her up anywhere.

All right, then. She would stay in London. It would be hard for Richard to find her there. He would never expect that she would be working in a hospital. She could get another job as an aide—and since she didn't drink, didn't steal, didn't purloin the patients' drugs for herself, she could probably get transferred to Charles' ward fairly quickly, assuming that it just didn't happen as soon as they found out that she was several cuts above the usual sorts of aides.

She smiled to herself. That was the answer. She'd be there, even when she wasn't officially on duty. She'd be there whenever he needed something, and when he *did* need something, she would make sure that she was the one to give it to him, by hook or by crook. Men fell in love with their nurses all the time. Why not this time?

Indeed. Why not?

19

IT wasn't hard to get a job at Bethnal Green Hospital. She was clean, young, and not drunk. She also used an assumed name, figuring that Susanne Whitestone was on some sort of list; she became Constance Weatherby, which was the real name of one of Prudence's sisters. Prudence would never know, and it was unlikely that anyone would ever travel out to the wilds of Yorkshire just to verify the story of a nursing aide. Nor was anyone going to find Richard Whitestone to verify the reference letters that Susanne forged.

Peter's money paid for a clean little room in a boarding house; all of the other boarders were actual nurses. The room was scarcely bigger than a closet, but after the Front, it seemed like the height of luxury.

As she expected, the fact that she was sober, honest, hardworking and uncomplaining swiftly elevated her to the officers' ward, a floor of private and semiprivate rooms, so the work wasn't as hard, though it was just as back-breaking and unpleasant. Within hours of getting the assignment, she had found Charles' room and knew what was wrong with him.

He had lain unconscious or semiconscious all of the time in France and for the better part of a week after he had arrived here. They had no means of caring for a man in what amounted to a coma in France, hence the haste in shipping him back to England.

As soon as she determined which room was his, she spent as much time as she could in it or near it, pouring healing into him, willing him to come out of his blank state while she scrubbed floors. His physical wounds were all broken bones, relatively easy to repair. It was clearly his mind that had gotten the worst of it.

November passed, and December arrived, bringing with it more cold rain. She couldn't help but think of Peter and the others still over there, and what this meant to the ones in those stinking trenches. The papers no longer spoke of it all being over by Christmas, but they kept up the fiction that the men on the Front were living in decent conditions, making life in the trenches sound like a stint of rough camping. When she read that, she wanted to *hurt* someone. The only comfort was that as men trickled back to Britain on leave, people were actually learning the truth. Or at least, as much truth as their loved ones would give them, or let slip.

She channeled all her fury at the idiot generals, the lying politicians, and the hateful Germans into an outpouring of healing for Charles. And it must have worked.

On Friday of the first week in December, he woke up.

She wasn't in his room when he did, but she heard the nurse's exclamation and the familiar sound of his voice, weak, raspy, and querulously asking where he was. Her heart leaped and started pounding; she wanted to jump up and run into his room, but she knew that if she did that, she would find herself reprimanded at best and dismissed at worst. So she restrained herself and slowly scrubbed her way closer to his door.

She listened while the nurse carefully explained where

he was, how he had gotten there, and how long he had been unconscious.

"Wait," she heard him say. "What war? Where am I? And who am I?"

There was a long pause. Then the nurse said, "I need to go find the doctor."

As she lurked outside the door, listening to the doctor talk to Charles, it quickly became obvious that Charles had lost his memory completely. He seemed completely bemused by it all, quite cheerful, in fact—but clearly, he had no idea who he was, what had been happening, or that he was an Elemental magician. On the one hand, that just might protect him; if he didn't know how to use magic, he wouldn't be revealing himself.

On the other hand, he wouldn't know how to shield or defend himself, either.

This was bad. This was very bad.

Her mind raced while she scrubbed. She considered putting her own shields on him, but if Richard saw them, he would *know* who they were sheltering, just because there could not be that many mages in a military hospital.

She had to keep reminding herself to move at intervals, otherwise she was likely to wear a hole in the floor.

Peter will have told the man in charge of the White Lodge—what was his name? She couldn't remember. But then, it hadn't seemed important at the time, just one more Peer of the Realm who wouldn't be bothered to deal with the daughter of a renegade Master. *He will have told Lord Whoever-he-is all about the attack by now. And Peter will have told His Lordship where they were sending Charles. So why hasn't one of* them *come to shield him?*

Well, the obvious answer was, *because there isn't anyone about London who can.* That might be oversimplifying things, however. The simple answer could be *because he doesn't need shielding.* Richard surely thought Charles was dead, and Richard was in France. Unless he was planning on joining the other side—which was possible—getting back was going to be a great deal more difficult than getting over was. Virtually all the traffic was being watched. Most of the large vessels had been commandeered for military transport. Susanne had no idea how hard it would be to stow away on one, but she didn't think it was anything that Richard would care to attempt. It would be even harder to disguise himself as a leave-bound soldier; he was too old to be a regular Tommy, and he didn't know enough to pass himself off as one of the highly visible officers. She was very certain that every available transport ship was being watched for spies trying to get into England.

As for, say, fishing boats? It was going to be very difficult to persuade a fisherman or the like to take him over, and they would probably report the attempt.

And after the attempt to murder Charles, every mage in the White Lodge would want Richard's head.

So . . . no. There probably was no need to shield Charles. Richard probably would not be able to get back for some time, and when he did, it would be to find that the hunter had become the quarry.

But then, just as she felt great relief in that realization, she was struck with another shock.

He wouldn't know her. He wouldn't know *anyone,* of course, but in particular, he wouldn't know *her.* And he didn't remember anything about magic, so as far as he was concerned, she was just another menial with nothing special about her.

She hadn't been allowed to approach him before, and that wouldn't change now—unless, or until she could somehow restore his memory.

But how?

Peter was thanking his lucky stars that Alderscroft and his own commanding officer were in constant contact, and that his report about the attack on Charles Kerridge would be able to get through without any censors laying eyes on it. It had taken him hours to write, and he was pretty sure that if any censors *had* read it, he would be heading straight for a transport ship, trussed up like a Christmas goose. After all—walking dead? Magic? Anyone reporting such a thing must be mad as the proverbial hatter.

General Smythe-Hastings had given him *carte blanche* to try to track down Richard Whitestone. In fact, at the moment, that was his sole assignment. Which would have been very good, if Richard Whitestone had been holed up somewhere in the middle of nowhere without a war going on.

Unfortunately . . .

Everything he tried either gave him no results at all or lit up all over the map, because, *quelle surprise,* nasty things like goblins and trolls and *svart alfen* were crawling all over the battlefields, wallowing in the death and pain and misery. Richard Whitestone could not possibly have chosen a better place to hide.

Which, sadly, was what he had to report to the general. He felt a little like an errant schoolboy, reporting on his failure to finish his sums.

". . . and that is all I have to tell you, sir," he concluded. "If I were an Earth Master, I probably would get better results. Even my uncle hasn't gotten anywhere."

"And those damned fools sent the only Earth Master we had packing back to London," the general growled. He shook his head impatiently. "Between those daft fools thinking they can fight this war like the last ones, and the daft fools who won't let me override their edicts when I was willing to personally vouch for the girl . . ." He sighed heavily, and Peter felt a sense of guilty relief that Smythe-Hastings wasn't going to take *him* to task. "I tell you, Peter, the only reason we are going to win this thing is because at some point the German bastards are going to perform some outrage against the Yanks, and the Yanks will *have* to come in. Then we'll have a flood of supplies and allies. I just hope that every man between the age of sixteen and forty isn't dead on the battlefield before that happens."

Peter had *never* heard the general express himself so . . . openly. Or so at odds with the official line. He kept his mouth from falling open in surprise and wisely said nothing.

The general ran his hand over his head, wearily. "Forgive me, young Peter. I do not suffer fools gladly, and when they are going to cost the lives of good men, I do not suffer them at all."

"Is it that bad, then?" Peter asked, troubled.

"I fear it is even worse," Smythe-Hastings said, glumly. "All we can do is follow our orders in such a way as to prevent the lives of good men from being thrown away for nothing. Meanwhile— " He paused and extracted a sheet of paper from his dispatch case. "—the Old Lion wants you back in London for a briefing, and to hear what you have to say about the Whitestone case. Oh, and also track down the Whitestone girl; she seems to have done a bunk."

"Oh, I know where she is," Peter said, with relief that there finally was *some* question he could answer. "She's kept in correspondence with me; she's volunteered as an aide at Bethnal Green hospital."

"Isn't that where Charles Kerridge was sent?" the general asked, a bit sharply. At Peter's nod, he frowned. "Under other circumstances, I would be relatively pleased about that, but . . ."

"Exactly so. I'm not sure what her reaction will be when she and the affianced come face to face. I only hope she doesn't do a *real* bunk."

"Then it's your job to get back there and make sure she doesn't!" the general snapped. "Off with you! First boat back you can get on!"

Peter saluted crisply and went to collect Garrick. The weather stations were all saying there was a storm coming over the Channel. This was not going to be pleasant.

Susanne slipped into Charles' room when the last of the visitors had cleared out. She was officially off-duty, so she doubly was not supposed to be here. The visitors, predictably enough, had been Charles' parents—

—and another young woman. Susanne had immediately sensed she was a Water magician, not a Master, but definitely a magician. She had not been able to linger close enough to determine just who she was. She *hoped* that the young lady was a relative, perhaps a cousin. But she feared—

Well, there was no reason for the young woman to be allowed here unless she was engaged to Charles, or Elizabeth and Michael *said* she was.

Now, there were a great many reasons why they would do so, even though—or even because—Charles had lost his memory. He was the only son, the heir, and since he hadn't managed to get married before he left, they'd want him to do so now. Especially since it was now clear that the war was going to go on a lot longer than the optimistic projections of August. Even if he never got his memory back, Susanne was not sure that the Army would particularly care. He could still be retrained and sent to the Front again as long as he was able-bodied and perfectly capable of thinking.

And for his parents' purposes, well . . . not getting his memory back might be preferable to having it. If he had been resisting marriage, they could tell him now that he had been engaged and very much in love with this woman. And he, being basically good-hearted, would go along with it. They could get him married and have the next generation safely on the way again before he was sent back to the Front.

And although Elizabeth and Michael had treated her well enough before . . . the fact that their son had very nearly been killed because of her was not likely to make her particularly attractive to them.

And that is a very good reason to stay out of sight for now.

Charles looked up as she came in. He smiled pleasantly at her. She smiled shyly back. "Is there aught I can be getting' tha'?" she asked in her broadest Yorkshire accent, hoping that would trigger some memories.

He didn't seem to notice. "No, nothing, I am doing well, thank you," he replied politely, then laughed. "Or at least, as well as someone who can't even remember his own name can be said to be doing."

Well, speaking to him in the accent of his home hadn't worked. She wondered if she could get a bit of heather somewhere—hadn't someone told her, once, that scent was the most likely thing to trigger memory? Or—cheese! Some of the cheeses that she herself had made! She moved around his room, tidying and cleaning—just in case someone came in or spotted her from the hall—while talking to him, and pummeling her mind for anything she might use to bring those memories back.

Scrumpy? Parkin? Yorkshire pud' and onion gravy? Where on earth would she get what she needed to make those things? And where would she be able to make them in the first place? Well, she couldn't make scrumpy, and she rather doubted that the aristocratic Kerridges drank it anyway, but everyone had parkin on Bonfire Night. And Curd Tart . . .

She continued to chatter about the things that he should find familiar, and he continued to be pleasant but . . . absent. Clearly he had no idea what she was talking about, and he was . . . well there was no other way to put it. He was humoring her.

Finally she gave up. She finished putting his room to rights and excused herself. It was going to be dark soon, and this was the East End. It didn't do for a woman to be out on the street alone after dark.

As she hurried through the cold streets, she continued to try to think of ways she could wake up his memory. The most obvious was also the most dangerous: use magic. If Richard was back in England, he would certainly be looking for signs of Earth Magic, and he would associate it with Charles. She might just as well mail him an invitation if she used magic.

Well . . . if *she* used magic. There was someone else who might and who was too powerful for Richard to trifle with.

She also had the impression that he wouldn't care a fig about all the barriers other Elementals found to being within an urban center like London.

The main question was, could she prove to him this was something he really should do?

"Food shortages," mused Alderscroft, swirling the brandy around in his glass.

They were sitting in two of Alderscroft's leather wing chairs in front of a nice coal fire in his sitting room at the club. Outside, December made itself known. Inside, all was warm and comfortable. They had just finished one of the Exeter Club's excellent dinners.

Peter had been thinking about the poor bastards in the trenches with a great deal of guilt.

"Eh?" said Peter, startled. "Not that I had noticed."

The Old Lion snorted. "Ask your watery little friends about the German submarines. It's only a matter of time before they start torpedoing merchant ships. They'll wear us down by starvation—or at least, they'll think they can."

"Good gad." Peter blinked. "I never thought of that. I'm just not used to thinking in war terms. Especially not this modern warfare with all the—" he waved his hands vaguely, trying to signify *terrible scientific weapons.* "How soon, do you reckon?"

"End of next year, I expect there will be rationing." Alderscroft shrugged eloquently. "Your brother should be told; all the country dwellers should be told, if they'll listen, which most of them won't. But your brother will. You know what best to advise your people to do. There are plenty of things that can be grown that won't be taken for the war effort. Country folk will be all right, if they start planning for it now; it will be the city dwellers that will feel the pinch." He shook his head. "Back to the subject at hand. Now please remember, young Peter, that I don't want the Whitestone girl harmed. I also don't want Charles Kerridge harmed. On the other hand, they make excellent bait to draw out Richard Whitestone."

"I'd need informed consent for that," Peter warned him. "I won't do that any other way."

Alderscroft gave him a level look. "You'll get it from the girl, I expect. She doesn't strike me as the shrinking kind, from what you've said. But Charles—"

"Still doesn't remember a thing," Peter confirmed. "And it's not malingering. Maya's been to see him, and she says its genuine."

Alderscroft cursed quietly for a moment. "Well, in that case, we have to treat him as we would a child. Ruddy well can't use him as bait. That only leaves the girl. I wouldn't mind it if it were the two of them together, or Charles alone, but the girl alone? I don't like it."

"Nor more do I," Peter replied, feeling his blood run cold at the very notion. "He keeps getting stronger and more clever. I've no notion how he managed to separate Charles from his men, but he did it. And then he attacked Charles on *his* ground, and he used the barrage to his advantage. That's getting devilishly clever, and deuced if I know how he's controlling that many liches. Then there are the ambushers to consider. I might be a Master, but Water isn't the most effective power against Earth, unless we can get him somewhere that my Elementals can get at him."

"Neither is Fire," Alderscroft pointed out. "His Elementals can smother most of mine. It should be Earth and Air against Earth, with Fire and Water as support—or in a pinch, Fire and Air together and Water as support. And I'm damned shorthanded right now. Maya can't be spared, nor can her husband. I need her in the hospital and him on coast watch. The rest of the Lodge are scattered from Scotland to Wales, and some are serving under the general. But we can't leave Richard Whitestone free a moment longer than we have to. You saw the results of what he could do with a battlefield of corpses and six months of war to draw from. Imagine what he'll be like as it goes on!"

"Thank you, I'd rather not," Peter replied frankly. He drank the last of his brandy, and put the glass aside. "I'll just toddle along and let the girl know I am here. We'll put our heads together. She's clever, that one."

"I just hope she's clever enough," Alderscroft replied, glumly.

It was growing dark by the time he stepped out of the door of the club; he decided that he wouldn't stop at his flat to change out of his uniform. Even in Bethnal Green it would go a long way toward keeping him from being interfered with, and an officer's uniform would guarantee respect at the boarding house where Susanne was living.

He knew how to pick his taxi drivers; he found one in relatively short order that had no qualms about taking a fare into Bethnal Green, and they were on their way.

"I'd like you to wait for me," he said, as they neared the address.

"Long as yer payin' guv'ner," the cabby replied. "Got me a cosh in the front seat. Nobody'll trifle wit' me while yer in there."

"I rather thought so," Peter said with satisfaction. "If there's trouble, give a toot on the horn, and we'll settle them."

The driver laughed. "Shouldn't be surprised, guv'ner. Ye don't look loik much, but in my 'sperience, it's the skinny ones as fights the nastiest."

Despite his anxieties, Peter laughed aloud. "True, o' wolves! I should be right out."

He ran up the door to the boarding house and rang the bell. A suspicious-looking woman in a maid's dress answered it, and her eyes went round when she saw what was clearly an officer on the doorstep. "I should like to speak to Constance Weatherby, if you please," he said, with a little tip of his hat. "I know it's late, but we are old friends, and I need to speak to her about her father in France."

The maid's hand flew to her mouth. "Oh, cor!" she breathed. "He's not—"

"No, not yet anyway," Peter said truthfully. "But I do need to speak with her about him. Tell her Peter is here to talk to her about her father."

"Come in, sir," the maid told him, and showed him into a tiny parlor, empty at the moment. "I'll go fetch her down."

Peter chose the least uncomfortable-looking of the chairs and perched on it, grateful for the little fire. After a moment, two sets of footsteps on the stairs coming down told him that "Constance" was coming.

"Constance Weatherby, sir," the little maid said, as if she was a herald announcing the queen's arrival. Then she gave a little curtsy and left.

"Have you got a key?" Peter quietly asked Susanne. "Can you let yourself back in after the landlady locks up? There are things I would rather not talk about here, and I'm likely to keep you out late."

"I have a key, and my cloak is still down here in the hall," she replied, and went to fetch it. "We're likely to be on at all shifts, here. The landlady is used to us coming and going at all hours." Peter helped her on with it, and the two of them went out into the blustering night to the waiting cab.

"You don't mind being taken to my flat, do you?" he asked, as he helped her in and got in next to her. "I promise, I will have Garrick there as a chaperone. He's as fierce as a dragon."

"I haven't a reputation to ruin," she said with a shrug. "I think I would like to see your flat. It's probably stuffed full of naughty Hogarth etchings."

He looked at her curiously, gave the cabby the address, and settled back. "You're a little chameleon, did you notice? You've got no trace of Yorkshire in your speech, and I would reckon that in a few months you'll sound London-born if you stay here."

"Thank you, I'd rather not. This is a *wretched* place for an Earth Magician." She shuddered.

"Well, it's no joy for Water, either, let me tell you," he said feelingly.

"But yes, I know, I mean, I know *now,* that I take on the accent of a place. I bartered a favor from one of the Elementals in the Ardennes, a bit of magic to make me 'speak and understand like a native' wherever I go—though it takes me a couple weeks to become comfortable with a foreign language." She chuckled a little. "I suppose this is another case of 'be careful what you wish for,' though in my case it doesn't seem to have done any harm."

"No, and it can be quite useful." He hesitated a moment longer, then shrugged. "It certainly will serve to mask your presence. Unfortunately, Alderscroft and I would like to ask you to do the very opposite. I'll explain when we get to my flat."

It was no more than a few minutes to reach the flat in any event. Peter paid the cabby and handed her out, and he soon had her settled in a much more comfortable chair with Garrick pouring her a good, strong cup of tea. She sipped it and smiled. "I feel so guilty being in a place like this, when I think of all the men—" she nodded her head eastward.

"And women, too," Peter pointed out. "There are some nursing sisters at the field hospitals, and their conditions are not much better than the men in the trenches, except that they get canvas tents to keep the rain off. But I know what you mean. I was just enjoying my own slice of guilt with my dinner." He paused and let her get a little more comfortable.

"If Charles has his memory back . . ." She paused. "I don't know what will happen. I don't know what will happen if he does not. But . . ."

He could almost hear her thoughts. And again, he was tempted to tell her just exactly how close Rose and Charles were—it was the kind of closeness that didn't require constant affirmation, because they both understood, at the level below thought, that they were the completion of each other. Like Maya and his "twin."

And as Peter sat there and watched those thoughts move behind her eyes, he knew that would be the wrong thing to tell her. It was something she needed to see for herself in order to understand how impossible her infatuation was.

But this is a woman I would fight my entire family and all the world for, if she would have me.

The realization hit him like a body blow, and he almost gasped. But he was an Elemental Master, and disciplined above all; he kept himself steady, and he knew that nothing of what he was thinking or feeling showed on his face.

"If I find myself otherwise at loose ends," she said slowly. "Once Father is ... disposed of, of course. Well, I will get properly certified and go back. I cannot in good conscience sit in England in comfort while fine men are suffering so on the Front."

Oh, well done, he thought. He was still trying to come to terms with what his heart had just told him, but her words were just a reinforcement that this was *right*. This young woman would never be content to sit and watch—and he could never care for one who would be.

But there were more important things than what he wanted right now. "Well, that rather brings us around to what I wanted to discuss with you."

He explained to her what he and Alderscroft had in mind, and she listened intently. "We have ways of letting it get about, among the Elementals, that you'd flitted back to England," he continued. "After what happened to Charles, the last thing we want to do is confront Richard on what he's made his own ground there in France, where he's so incredibly strong. We want to bring him here. Ideally, we want to bring him where he would have the least access to—well—bodies and revenants."

She pursed her lips thoughtfully. "To be honest, that would probably be back on the moors," she replied. "He had to have exhausted everything he could muster in the attack on the Kerridge's estate. If we make sure to confront him before he has time to entrench himself again—"

"Don't count on that," Peter warned. "He's gotten impossibly powerful."

She paused, then nodded. "You would know better than I. You do have my consent to act as bait. Go ahead and lay your trail of crumbs, and it might as well end here in London as anywhere. Then—"

"A wise general once said that no plan survives first contact with the enemy," he said wryly. "We'll do what we do best." He refused to think about what would happen if they lost.

"And one of those things is that I will see what I can do as well." She licked her lips nervously. "I might be able to persuade Robin to help me."

That startled him. "If you can—that would make all the difference!" he exclaimed. "I was going to warn you that we are few, not even half a Hunting Party, and this was likely to be very dangerous. But if you can get the Puck—"

"If. We'll see. I have a half-holiday tomorrow, so before you start anything, let's see if he'll 'come when I do call him.'" She smiled shyly. "I don't want you to plan based on something that I can't manage."

"True words, dear lady, true words." He smiled at her, and then he thought of an excellent excuse to stay in close contact with her. "Well, before I whisk you back to your solitary chamber, I'd like you to finish partaking of Garrick's most excellent tea and cakes, and then, as I understand you are a reader, I offer you the run of my shelves." He waved his hand around the room, which was, indeed, wall-to-wall bookshelves. "*Much* more temptin' than a lot of old etchings."

20

"I CAN call spirits from the vasty deep," said Glendower.
And Hotspur replied, *"Why, so can I, or so can any man;
But will they come when you do call for them?"*

Susanne had taken the train out as far as Hampton
Court Palace. There were few visitors on such a bleak day,
and none seemed interested in the maze. The palace and
grounds were quiet and a little forbidding as the start of a
winter fog began to wisp around the buildings. This was as
close to forest as she could get, and the Puck and the Tudors
seemed to have a special relationship anyway, so it seemed
a good plan all around.

The hedge-maze was very popular on warm days, but the
visitors today were hurrying to get inside the buildings for
their tours, and there was no "helper" on his platform above
the maze. So she worked her way to the center of the maze
unassisted—no great feat for an Earth Master—and stood
for a moment beneath the leafless tree planted there, listening for voices. Just in case. People who got into a maze generally did so in groups of two or more, and they couldn't

resist talking and calling to one another, and laughing when they got lost.

Silence. The only voices were distant, up near the Tudor part of the palace.

So, here was the sticking point. As Hotspur had said in Shakespeare, anyone could *call* spirits; the question was, would they answer? Robin seemed to think that he and she had a special kinship, but would that be enough for him to come to her now?

He had made it clear that he felt controlling her father was strictly human business, her business in particular. But that had been before France. Richard had learned something in the interim or, perhaps, bargained with something; it was hard to tell what her father might do. There were very powerful Elemental creatures out there, much too powerful to even think of controlling. Robin had warned her about even bargaining with such beings. *"If they're bad, they'll cheat you. If they're good, they'll help you regardless if they take an interest in you. But best just not attract the attention of either side."* Had Richard sought one of these things out? Had it sought him? He was strong enough that Peter was afraid of him, strong enough to have nearly killed Charles. Was he now so strong that the Puck could be persuaded to help?

Well, she wasn't finding out by standing under a tree in the thickening fog and doing nothing.

She slipped a twig of yew out of her pocket and carefully drew the open-sided circle that she used to summon Earth creatures with. It was nothing coercive, more in the way of an invitation. The creatures themselves could close the circle if they wanted to feel protected; that was the point, offer them a safe space. She put the right signs at the four cardinal points, then drew up a trickle of power and sent it into the circle. Now it was a beacon for any Earth Elemental, and it said as plain as plain, "Please come, I would like to talk."

"O Fairest Maiden, you needn't have gone to all that

trouble," said a voice behind her, and giggled as she turned. A pair of mischievous eyes peered out at her from inside the hedge. They glinted at her as the voice continued. "An Earth Master on Queen Bess's ground? We've been watching since you entered the gates."

"And glad I am of it, then," she replied. "I need to speak to your Master, the Oldest Old One, if he would spare me a moment."

Before she could add that she had bread and honey, the little faun in the hedge giggled again and said, "Then you should turn yourself around again."

Half expecting a trick, she turned again, and there was Robin, arms crossed over his chest and a grin on his face, laughing silently at her. She was tempted to hurl one of the Bath buns she had brought with her at him, but instead she held out the brown paper parcel they were in. Without a word, he took it from her, opened it, and began tossing buns over her head to whatever was now behind her. The faun, and several other Elementals by the sound of the giggling.

He was not in the guise of the Yorkshire gamekeeper now, nor the careless young fellow who had played with her as a child, nor even the relatively sober magician who had taught her. This was a Prince of the Fair Folk, silver circlet around his head, green velvet tunic, silver silk shirt and trim trousers tucked into silver-embroidered green boots, silver-lined half-cape in green velvet, massive silver chain around his neck and a silver belt at his waist. He didn't have a weapon, but he didn't *need* a weapon. Unlike most of his kind, Cold Iron bothered him not at all, nor salt. His hair, dark as the feathers of a raven, was in a single long braid down his back.

"Off with you," Robin ordered them, with obvious amusement. "None of your gossiping and goggling."

There was the sound of feet and hooves, and the whir of wings, and still more giggling that receded into the distance, muffled by fog. The fog was definitely growing thicker, but curiously, it seemed warmer in the maze now, almost as if it were spring and not the dead of winter. Susanne looked to Robin with a quizzical expression.

"Yes, my doing," he said, and made an odd little gesture. The fog shaped itself into a kind of couch, or perhaps a giant cushion, and he indicated it with a wave of his hand.

She sat. It felt exactly the way, in a child's mind, a couch made of fog ought to feel. Soft as swansdown, warm and comforting as a featherbed. Robin sat down beside her.

"I am not sure where to begin," Susanne said, hesitantly. "I know you told me to deal with my father myself, and I do agree that this *should* be merely mortal business. And it would be—except for this terrible war."

Quickly she described what had happened to Charles in France, as Robin studied her with an unusually sober expression. "So my father has gotten much, much more powerful," she continued. "Meanwhile, the White Lodge members are scattered across France and all over Britain. The ones who are here will help me as much as they can, but I am not sure just how they can ever hope to best someone as powerful as my father is now."

Robin shook his head. "You plead a powerful case, my young friend," he replied, and a flash of something in his eyes reminded her of just how old the Puck really was. "Nevertheless, nothing you have told me makes this *my* business."

"I know that," she replied. "And if he were the same man that lived the life of a recluse, I would agree with you. But what he is doing is an offense against the very Earth itself. He can't be going about it the way other necromancers have, at least not as I understand it from what Peter has told me. He's poisoning the Earth, or else making use of those lands poisoned and ravaged by other mortals. Please, Robin—" she held out both hands in entreaty. "I don't think he'll stop once he has me. Peter says his idea is to ritually kill me and force my mother's soul into my body." She rubbed her temple, a headache coming on. "He may think he'll stop with that, but I don't think he can. I don't think he's sane anymore, if he ever was. He's had a taste of great power, though, and even for sane people, a taste like that is never enough; I don't think he'll stop until vast amounts of England are as dying or dead as those battlefields in France and Belgium." Her voice faltered. "I think to have a kingdom of corpses to rule over, he will bring the war here."

Robin's eyes flashed at that, and she was glad she wasn't the one making him angry, because what she saw there made her shrink into herself. But he confronted her sternly. "And what would you do if your dream of that mortal boy is thwarted and you lose him as your father lost your mother?"

She firmed her chin and looked straight back at him. No point in asking how he knew what she had never told anyone. This was the Puck. "Let him go. Then—I told Lord Peter that I was going to become a real nursing sister and go back to France. I can use my magic there in truly useful ways."

Some of that icy heat went out of his eyes. "Good. Then let us make a plan. I can arrange for your father to learn that you are here easily enough—"

"Lord Peter said the same." She pondered that. "Perhaps you should speak with him."

"Perhaps I will." Robin unbent a little. "Perhaps *you* should reveal your presence to the young mortal's family."

She swallowed. That was one thing she really didn't want to do, actually. But on the other hand . . .

"I suspect, given how few mortals there are to aid, we will require at least that they have knowledge of what we are doing," Robin continued, but he patted her hand comfortingly. "It would be best that way."

She nodded in agreement.

"And it would be best to include them in your plans," he continued. "After all, your father attacked *him* in France. Leave all that to Lord Peter. He is, I have observed, very good at diplomacy."

She blushed, but she had to agree that Lord Peter was much better at it than she was. She was Yorkshire blunt, which . . . was not diplomatic at all.

"Time for you to go, else it will be dark and dangerous by the time you return to your dwelling." Robin stood up, offered her his hand, and when she was standing, put something into it. "When you need me, cast this on the ground, and I will come to you."

She looked at it, curiously. It was a tiny oak leaf, made of silver. "Thank you, Robin," she said, looking back up.

But he was already gone.

Susanne decided that for once, she was going to be a coward. She sent a note in the morning mail to Lord Peter, begging him to reveal her presence to Charles' family. When she returned to the boarding house from her shift at the hospital, there was a note waiting for her by afternoon post.

Don't trouble your heart about it. It isn't your *fault that Richard Whitestone is a lunatic. I'll handle Michael and Elizabeth. But expect to be summoned some time tomorrow afternoon.*

She winced a bit. All right, no one could prove she had been talking to Charles. And no one could accuse her of shirking her other duties to hang about his room. So it wasn't likely she would be dismissed over the fact that she knew him. No one in the hospital knew how well, and Michael and Elizabeth certainly were not going to reveal why she knew him.

So she was not going to find herself cashiered—probably not even assigned to another ward.

Still, there was no doubt that they could make things very uncomfortable for her. She just hoped that Lord Peter was good at talking people around.

The little parlor of the boarding house was unusually full. The young women were putting up holly and evergreen boughs, red bows and little tin ornaments, and their landlady contributed a few precious glass trinkets for the little

Christmas tree. Susanne found herself with a little lump in her throat, remembering all the celebrations that she and the others at Whitestone had made together—with their own little Yule log and tree, the parlor opened up as it only was once a year, and special treats from Cook. Were they doing all that now? She hoped so.

They hadn't even noticed she was standing there, but that was hardly unusual, since she went out of her way to remain unnoticed. One of them started singing "Good King Wenceslas," and the others joined in; the air was full of the scent of pine boughs and cinnamon, and the tiny parlor had never looked so warm and welcoming. She recalled with a sense of shock that Christmas was only a week away. And she hadn't gotten anyone here anything! There would be some sort of exchange of gifts, and even if all the others gave her were little bags of nuts and sweets, she should get them something.

Hastily she turned around and caught a bus for the shops. At least she knew exactly what she was going to get for each of the others in the boarding house—something that would be more than just a gift for each of them. And Peter's generosity made it possible for her to do so.

The apothecaries in question gave her quite the strange looks at what she was buying, until she explained that she was shopping for nurses who were being sent to the Front.

They still looked a bit uneasy, however, so she alleviated their worries by asking for each of the hypodermic kits to be gift-wrapped. That was when they all relaxed; surely no dope fiend would ask for a gift-wrapped syringe for a Christmas present!

She bought only one conventional gift. For their land-lady, she got a box of chocolates. She was tempted to put in a note "Save these, there will probably be rationing soon," but decided not to.

When she returned, they were nearly done decorating the parlor. She wove her way through them and installed eight identical small packages and one large one under the tree, to the bemusement of the others, who were putting the last little adjustments on the greenery.

"Presents? But Constance, you really shouldn't—" protested one, and that was when she decided to simply tell them what the presents were and why she had gotten them.

She stood beside the tree, twisting her hands nervously, with nine pairs of eyes on her. "I—haven't said anything before this, but I was caught in the Ardennes when the war started," she said hesitantly. "I was working with French nursing sisters until I found a way back. That's why I am here now." Truth, just not all of it. "I know many of you are going to go to the Front, if not soon, then at some point, and there was one thing more precious to the nursing sisters than gold—because there was generally only *one* for two to three wards. That was a hypodermic kit. So I got you all your own to take with you." Tears welled up in her eyes, real tears, astonishing her. But when she thought of how precious her kit had been, it almost undid her. "It is as much a present to all those brave boys you will be serving as it is to you—"

For the first time since she had returned, she found herself breaking down and crying, crying for the men she had not been able to save, crying for the men who had lain in their beds, suffering, waiting for the medicine a nurse could not give them because the syringe was elsewhere. Crying, because there were not enough dressings and they had to risk infection using old ones, crying, because fresh-faced boys lay for hours in agony because the doctor was up to his elbows in some other poor boy's insides and could not tend to them. It all cascaded into her, and she could scarcely bear it. She had known all these things at the time, of course, but until now she had not allowed herself to feel them.

She was not sure why she had now. Maybe because she was here, with young women who daily tended the aftermath of that death machine that was the Front and who understood—but were not yet themselves eaten up by the machine.

And the young women here in the parlor, who had known her only as "Constance, the aide," or maybe "Constance, the aide that isn't a drunk," must have suddenly seen her as something other than a pair of hands that did the filthiest work. They knew better than to believe the cheery newspaper stories. They listened to their patients' nightmares, to the stories, however sanitized, that they told. They might not have seen the worst of the worst on the Front as Susanne had, but they *were* tending the horrific consequences in the ones that lived to make it to the Bethnal Green Hospital. So they had some inkling of what she had seen, lived through.

They stopped what they were doing and gathered around her, more than one lending her a handkerchief as she soaked through the practical squares of linen, two putting their arms around her, another bringing her tea from the kitchen. It was an amazing feeling. She had never had this—girls her own age, intelligent and clever girls, girls who were her equal that she could befriend and be friends with. Patience or Prudence? If she had broken down like this in front of them, they'd have wrung their hands under their aprons, then fled. If she had told them what she'd seen, they'd have clapped their hands over their ears and run away. And although she was weeping herself sick, until her eyes burned and her cheeks were raw, it felt like—

Like a great relief. She had let go of something she didn't even know she was holding on to, in her fear and dread of her father and what he might do. Right now, that was irrelevant, as all the faces of the men who had died in her care passed through her memory, and she mourned each and every one.

The girls readily, willingly, crowded close about her to offer comfort. No few of the others cried too, and that was somehow as comforting as the arms around her shoulders.

"It's not—fair!" she sobbed, "This war is *beastly!*" And they nodded and hugged her and cried.

This was not something she could have said to Peter, who would never have understood. Men thought war was somehow noble, glorious.

Or they did until they found themselves legless, armless, so terrified by what they had been through that they hid under the bed like little children when something startled them.

Women—women knew better. War might be necessary sometimes, she couldn't judge that, but it was never, ever glorious. It was a terrible monster, that took men and chewed them up and spit out the dead, the dying, and the maimed. War was a beast that murdered as many innocent people who were just in the way as it did soldiers. And she wept for them, too, for the fresh graves in the villages, for the terrible stories she had heard out of Belgium.

Finally, when she was cried out, she looked up through swollen eyes to see that every girl in the house was crowded around her in the parlor, each of them holding her little package to her chest as if Susanne had given them the Crown Jewels.

One of them dropped gracefully to her knees beside Susanne. "I don't think I've even said hello to you, yet," said the plain little brunette, holding out her hand. Automatically, Susanne took it. "For that, I am very sorry. I'm Mabel, Mabel Duncan. I can't even begin to thank you enough for this. You see, I'm going to the Front in a week, and—well, they've given me a list of things I need, and I got them, of course, but I had no idea about—" She stopped, her face transfixed with guilt and curiosity mingled. "I know it's dreadful of me to ask, but I think they are not being honest with us. I don't know what I'll be facing when I get to the field hospital. I know the injuries will be terrible, but I didn't know that there was such a shortage of the basic needs!" She looked distressed and rueful, all at the same time. "Can—can you possibly tell me what I should bring besides what's on the list? Would it be unbearably hard for you to tell me what I can expect? Some of the boys have told me a little, but I am afraid they are trying to spare my feelings. I want to hear the worst of it . . . if you can? If you would?"

Susanne stared at the girl in astonishment, and then around at the rest of the faces, some sympathetic, some still weeping, all finally looking *at* her, seeing her as a person for the first time. As she was seeing *them* as people for the first time. Not just the people she had to work around.

"It wouldn't matter if it was unbearably hard," she said, finally, giving Mabel's hand a squeeze. "It's for the Tommys, isn't it? I'll tell you all I can. Have you got something to write with?"

"I do," their landlady said, and stepped forward with a pencil and some paper braced on a book in her hands. "Please, tell us. Tell us everything. Mabel is going in a week, but there are more girls here who are going next month, and I am sure there will be still more that come through these rooms. If I can help send them out better prepared, it will be a blessing to all of us."

Susanne took a deep breath. "Well, Mabel is right. They are *not* being honest with you. They don't tell you half of what you'll really need, and they tell you nothing of how you will be living, especially if you are assigned to a field hospital. This is what it's like—and this is what you should bring, if you possibly can."

She was grateful, terribly grateful, that all these young women were sensible, and had been listening to their patients, because none of what she had to say was a terrible shock—although she was fairly sure that the young soldiers in their hospital beds had not been telling their nurses the worst of it, except by accident. She, however, was honest with them—Yorkshire honesty—and although there was some dismay, there were more nods, and more than the landlady began to make notes. Lists of things they would need for themselves. Lists of things they would need for their patients. Lists of things to beware of, things a little forethought could prevent, things to avoid. What it was like when being bombarded with artillery. What it was like to ride with an ambulance. How to find a friendly and reasonably clean French family to rent a room from, since often there were no accommodations for the nurses. How to get a bath. How to get rid of the ever-present lice. How to manage food. She talked until she was hoarse, and finally she got to the end of it.

Mabel looked at the list she had written down and shook her head in dismay. "This is horrid! There's—so much here—I'm so used to having all the supplies we need right there in the hospital!"

"But we can get it all together for you before you leave!" exclaimed another of the lot.

"Yes, and you can send boxes to her when she is there," Susanne urged. "Stay in touch! I had someone to ask, but he was at the Front too, so he couldn't get things as often as I needed, but you, you are all here, where there *are* bandages and socks, and cotton for packing wounds—and chemists where you can buy things."

"I'll have my mother speak to the vicar at home," said another, with a nod. "I know that she has at least one sewing circle, maybe more. Making bandages would make far better sense for the Ladies' Society than sitting about crocheting doilies as they've done in the past."

"And they could be knitting socks—if the men are so short of dry socks—" said another. "Well! So could we! I can knit."

And soon they were full of plans, chattering excitedly to each other as new schemes were hatched. Susanne listened to them, feeling her sense of relief unfolding even further. When she had thought about conditions out there, it had all seemed so hopeless, but now—now it didn't seem quite so impossible.

She finished her tea and slipped away. Some of the enthusiasm would without a doubt vanish over the course of the next few weeks or months. And some of these plans would fail, or never get set in motion.

But some, they would carry out. And every bit of help to the men at the Front would be a little more that would keep them alive.

And that, in itself, was a kind of magic.

21

THERE was just one problem with this plan.

It depended entirely on waiting for Richard Whitestone to decide what *he* was going to do.

This was, of course, the first thing that Michael Kerridge pointed out.

The five of them—Peter, Susanne, the Kerridges, and Charles' fiancée—were in Peter's sitting room in his London flat, having just been served an excellent tea by Garrick. Susanne was being very quiet, but it was not a passive quiet. Peter suspected that if anyone actually made any overt accusations, she would not wait to be defended but would come to her own defense.

"We're completely dependent on Richard Whitestone's whims, Lord Peter," Michael said, with a bit of frost in his voice. "I don't see how you letting him know where to find the girl is going to help us any."

"It doesn't *hurt* us any either," Peter snapped. "If I might venture to point out that it was only a matter of time before he discovered that Charles lived through the attack and had been sent back to England? At least now we control *when* he learns that, and at the same time, he will learn that Susanne is again within his reach. He missed Halloween for his plans for Susanne, and he'll miss Winter Solstice as well. I'll wait until we have all our Water Elementals alerted and watching for him to cross, and we'll know when he comes back. He cannot go undetected, not when he is on the water; the selkies can detect corruption a hundred miles away. Once he's across, it won't be long before he attacks. He might be able to vanish from the sight of our Elementals once he reaches land, but once he reaches land he will know where Susanne is, because we'll allow his damned kobolds to find her. And once he knows where Susanne is, Charles becomes much less interesting for him. I very much doubt that he'll make even a token effort to go after Charles. We'll want you to guard him, of course, but frankly, the man wants Susanne for his mad scheme. In my opinion, the only reason he pursued Charles was for revenge, thinking Susanne was out of reach, as we had intended her to be."

"Tha'd be worse off, if I'd gone to Colonies," Susanne said, her accent back. "I can be bait in tha' trap now. And this bait has teeth." She raised her chin and looked defiantly at both Elizabeth and Michael, who were taken aback by the fierce anger in her eyes.

"Well . . ." Michael began.

Rose Mainwright interrupted him. "I think it's only fair for her to lure the wretch in. You and Elizabeth and Charles defended her once, now she can pay that back." Rose spoke with cool and calm that gave no sign of animosity, but Peter was momentarily amused, because it was quite clear that Rose knew very well about Susanne's attachment, and she was having none of it.

Susanne couldn't very well retort at this point, since she had already volunteered, but Peter guessed by the flash of her eyes that she was no more impressed by her rival than Rose was impressed with her.

"All right," Michael agreed. "But what if he gets the chance to come after both of them?"

"I already thought of that," Susanne replied. "Peter made arrangements for me."

"Susanne is being transferred to a teaching hospital for nurse training," Peter explained. "In four days, in fact, after Christmas, on Boxing Day. Once she's settled there and we've done what we can to secure the ground, she will stop concealing herself from Earth powers, and I will make use of some neutral Elementals who will think they are bartering valuable information to Richard Whitestone." He made a crooked smile. "It's sometimes as useful to know who cannot be trusted as it is to know who can."

"I see." Although Rose didn't lose a bit of her cool hostility, Elizabeth and Michael both relaxed, and their attitude shifted subtly. "It seems you've thought of everything."

"Everything except how to get a full Hunting Party together," Peter replied, a bit grimly. "The war, and the season both, are conspiring against us. It will be me, Maya and her husband, Garrick, Alderscroft, and possibly one or two others."

One or two others, old, frail, and the only reason they would even take part is because the attack will come here, in London, and they needn't travel far.

He didn't mention Robin Goodfellow. There was no telling what kind of help they'd be getting from the Fair Folk, nor how strong it would be. Robin might not have any trouble with Cold Iron or church bells, but that didn't mean the other Fair Folk could be as cavalier about such things. The most logical place for Richard to attack would be in London and its suburbs; like the battlefield in France, in places here the ground was literally soaked in centuries of blood. The water was polluted, the air poisoned, and the ground dead. Perfect for his purposes. Then add in the many, many graveyards, marked and unmarked, that he could rob for his armies ... well, their best case would be that he would get impatient and attack before he actually had a large force of revenants and liches. The longer he delayed to build that force, the worse it would be for them.

And London itself would likely weaken any Fair Folk that ventured within it.

Michael and Elizabeth nodded, but neither volunteered, nor offered anyone else's name who might be willing to be part of the Hunting Party.

Peter cursed his ability to see both sides. He should be angry at them, but he could also understand their point of view. They had taken in a stranger, arranged for her magical education, and become targets of something far more powerful than they could face. They weren't going to throw that stranger to the wolves, but they also had their own son, and their own people, to protect. In that hierarchy, Susanne came a very distant third. No, it wasn't Susanne's fault that her father had decided to take revenge on Charles. But if they had never sheltered her, they would even now be blissfully unaware that the necromancer even existed. And Charles would not have come so close to death.

"That, however, is not your problem," he continued smoothly, betraying neither his irritation nor his sympathy. "Your problem is to defend and protect Charles when Richard Whitestone strikes. And I need to think of a way to alert you instantly when he does."

"It's a pity there aren't telephones everywhere," Michael replied, rubbing his temple a little. "Much as I loathe them, they're damned useful. Once you're out of the countryside, Earth Elementals are bloody well useless as messengers."

"Michael, language," Elizabeth chided gently.

"I'll contrive something," Peter said, vaguely. He wasn't sure what . . . maybe he could rig some kind of signal. Make a vial of water burst? Something, anyway. Anything that would get their attention.

"Well," said Rose, crisply. "I think we have covered everything. Don't you, Elizabeth?"

Charles' mother nodded. "It's probably better not to lay out too detailed a plan. Plans never last long anyway, when you are dealing with someone as unpredictable as Richard Whitestone."

"Ah, but that's where tha'rt wrong," interjected Susanne. "He may be mad, but he's right predictable. He'll go through anything to get his hands on *me.*"

With that uncomfortable thought hanging in the air, the Kerridge party made some awkward good-byes, leaving Peter, Garrick, and Susanne alone.

Peter cleared his throat. "Please say you'll come here for Christmas Day," he said plaintively. "Otherwise I'll be forced to listen to Garrick murder carols alone."

Susanne hesitated, then nodded. "There's Christmas breakfast at the boarding house instead of Christmas dinner. I'll come after that."

She was probably thinking that she wished she could spend the day at Charles' side, but Rose would certainly make sure that didn't happen. Peter was very happy with Mistress Rose at the moment. "Capital. Is there anything you would particularly like or loathe for dinner?"

"Ah . . . I don't know, really," she said, startled. "The only Christmases I've ever had were 'downstairs' sorts, and to be honest, there often wasn't anyone there but me and the housekeeper for dinner. Everyone who had family went to them after church."

"Well, then. Nothing traditional at all but Christmas crackers. After, we'll go to the panto." He grinned. "I'll lay odds you've never been, and it will take your mind off everything."

"I—I think I would like that," she faltered. "Very much."

"Capital!" *And so I lay siege to the castle.* "Shall I see you home? It's no trouble, I need to tootle round to the club and plot with Alderscroft."

She managed a ghost of a smile. "I'd be very grateful."

He kept up a steady stream of conversation the entire way to her boarding house—some just prattle, some recollections of past conflicts with rogue magicians or the nastier sorts of Elementals, and just a bit about Maya and *her* Peter.

She listened to it all attentively, and he found that encouraging.

They said goodnight in his auto, rather than on the steps of the boarding house. She ran up to the door, and when she got there, looked briefly over her shoulder and gave him a little wave. He saluted her with two fingers, and once she was inside, he drove off.

He spent the rest of the evening researching his notes and everything in his library concerning necromancers—and wished devoutly that the Old Lion had managed to find the way into that secret room at Whitestone Hall to get whatever books Richard had been studying. Richard was more powerful than any necromancer he had ever encountered before.

Then again, when that happened, the Old Lion would probably burn them all on the spot, and Peter wasn't sure he could blame him. The last thing anyone would want would be to recreate what Richard Whitestone had done. Mind, it might take a war to do so ... Peter was beginning to think that what was happening on the battlefields of France was causing the equivalent of a veritable flood of energy to anything that was practicing magic on the Dark side of the Path. For a moment, as he thought about that hell-on-earth that was the Front, his cozy study became unreal to him. He felt, for a moment, that he must still be there, and this place was nothing but a dream of a time that would never come again, that all the world would become the vast, gray slaughterhouse, mired in mud, giving life only to rats, lice, and frogs.

Eventually he went to bed, but his dreams were full of horrors, and he was glad of morning when it came.

The sitting room was warm and aromatic with cinnamon and clove. An evergreen garland draped the mantle, adding to the fragrance, and a holly wreath hung in one window. Peter had overruled the idea of a Christmas tree, however small, but other festive touches in the form of more holly, a big bowl of apples, and a few enormous red velvet bows made it clear that there was no lack of Christmas spirit here. "Garrick, you have outdone yourself," Peter said gratefully. "And thank you, Mary. Susanne likes you, and having you here will make things—"

"—look less like you're trying to seduce the girl?" Mary Shackleford said with a laugh. Her blue eyes glistened with amusement, as she leaned back into the comfort of the big wing chair and held her feet toward the fire on the grate. "Oh, don't bother to deny it. If you didn't care about her, you wouldn't be trying so hard to make everything proper."

Peter lifted an eyebrow at her. The Mary *he* knew had never cared a jot about what people said or did. When had she gotten so shrewd? Or interested enough in people to pay attention to them? "I knew you were discernin' with paint, but I never suspected you were that observant about real people."

"Pish!" she waved a hand at him from the depths of his wing chair—the other hand being occupied with a glass of sherry. "There's a lot you don't know about me. One of these days I'll carry you off to one of my Socialist meetings. You'd probably enjoy it, because they'll be yapping at your heels because you're a peer, because you're rich, *and* you're an army officer. They won't give you a minute's rest. You have a good chance of meeting Shaw there. Or Wells. Or both."

"You terrify me. I'd rather face a necromancer than Shaw. The necromancer can only have his liches tear me to bits; Shaw can eviscerate me with his tongue, then use me as a comic figure in a play." The doorbell sounded at that moment, and Garrick went to answer it. "I believe our guest has arrived."

Garrick ushered Susanne into the room, and her face lit up when she saw Mary. There was a flurry of happy greetings, then Garrick cleared his throat and announced dinner, and all of them retreated to the tiny dining room of the flat.

Like the sitting room, the dining room had been decked

out festively. Since Peter often had guests for dinner—he really preferred not to dine at one of his clubs—this was a practical room, well suited to leisurely dining and lingering over coffee or brandy. More evergreen and holly garlanded the mantel, surrounded the candlesticks on the table—Peter preferred candles on the table, even though the flat had electrics *and* gas laid on. Though once again, Peter had a pang of guilt, looking at the feast spread out over the white linen cloth and thinking about the men in the trenches, who might or might not have packets from home, who probably would be eating bully beef and that ever present plum-and-apple jam, and who certainly would be cold, wet, and weary.

Peter insisted that Garrick—who had done all of the work, bringing the feast up from the cookshop, setting the table, and so forth—sit down and eat with them. "Not standing on ceremony today, old man," he said firmly, so Garrick (a little reluctantly) took his place in the fourth chair at the table, and with great merriment, Peter insisted that Garrick play the part of the "father" at the table.

With evident amusement now, Garrick did just that, carving the beef and sending around the various courses so they could all help themselves, as if they were a real family. Peter had opted for a fine roast, Yorkshire pudding for Susanne, and all the trimmings of a fine Christmas dinner. Mary kept up most of the conversation, telling them all what she had done since her escape from France, peppering the narrative with anecdotes about her Socialist and Bohemian friends, and drawing Susanne out to describe what her fellows were like at her boarding house. There were no allusions to the war, to the hospital, to the Kerridges, or to Susanne's father.

Peter was intensely grateful to her.

There were Christmas crackers of course. It would hardly be Christmas without them. They all put on the paper hats from the crackers, and read the silly mottos. Peter's was *"What runs but never walks? Water!"* which was uncannily apt considering his Element. Susanne's was *"Why can't a bicycle stand up by itself? Because it's two-tyred!"* which elicited a groan. Mary's was *"What's the best thing to eat in the bath? Sponge cake!"* which triggered what turned out to be a truly funny story about a mishap she had involving a sponge cake and the Bishop of Bath and Wells. And Garrick's was *"On which side do chickens have the most feathers? The outside!"* Bad jokes and puns were the tradition of Christmas crackers, but Peter wondered if Garrick had managed to suss out just which ones did *not* contain sentimental love notes before he purchased them. If so, well done to him.

Then again, Peter had never actually ever purchased Christmas crackers himself. *For all I know, they come in "joke assortment" and "love note assortment."*

There were no presents; Peter knew that Mary wouldn't have thought to bring anything, and Susanne had had much more pressing matters on her mind. But everyone had fun with the trinkets in the crackers, Mary (much to her amusement) got the wedding ring in her slice of plum pudding, and then it was time to bundle up in the coats and go to the panto.

Garrick drove the auto; he firmly told Peter that he had seen quite enough panto as a youngster, and he would much prefer to wait with the chauffeurs at the pub nearby. So they tumbled out of the auto and made their way inside the Hammersmith Odeon, ready for the delights of childhood.

Panto—short for "pantomime," even though there was precious little miming involved—was a tradition at Christmas all across the length and breadth of England. It was ostensibly a children's play, although the "play" was buried in layers and layers of ballet dancers and music-hall acts, and indeed, many music-hall troupes and individual artists changed up their usual performances to do panto at this time of year. London panto was—well—spectacle. The Hippodrome boasted camels and an elephant this year. And every panto, no matter what the story, always had the same things that never failed, much to the delight of the children. There was always a charming little actress playing the Principle Boy. The hero's mother was played by a man in a dress. The Principle Girl was always some sort of fairy or princess or both. There was always a clown, in this case, Aladdin's brother, Wishee-Washee, who made mischief, ate prodigious quantities of sausage, beat all and sundry with a slapstick club, and generally wreaked havoc. There was an amazing amount of double entendre, presumably for the entertainment of the adults in the audience. And the audience was not only encouraged to participate, it was practically required.

The panto they were coming to see was *Aladdin*, set, as according to tradition, in an entirely fanciful China that bore no resemblance to the real thing, and they all acted like the children that surrounded them. The children were rambunctiously pleased to see the three adults acting just like them. "My favorite panto is *Aladdin*," the little girl sitting next to Susanne said, before the curtain came up. "Which is yours?"

"I don't have one," Susanne confessed in a stage whisper. "I've never been before."

Never been before? The children on that side of the row were all astonished, and took it upon themselves to coach Susanne as to what was expected. She watched them for her cues, and when the villain was sneaking up on Aladdin, she was able to shout *"Look behind you!"* with the same gusto as any of them. She laughed at the clown eating a neverending string of sausages, chuckled at the antics of the dancing pantomime horse, watched entranced at the ballet of the jewels and the dance of the Slave of the Ring and the Genie of the Lamp, gasped when Aladdin fought a dozen of his evil uncle's guards at once, all of them popping up and down on the stage by means of trap doors, sighed over the grace of the pretty singer playing the princess, and applauded wildly when Aladdin finally married her.

Of course, that was only the middle of the panto, because there was all the excitement of the wicked uncle stealing princess and palace and all and Aladdin having to rescue her.

But there was one moment when she went suddenly silent. This version of Aladdin featured a stunning pair of twin girls as the principal boys—plural—and the producer used that to his advantage. Not only did that make appearing and vanishing stage-magic much easier, but Aladdin was able to dupe his evil uncle into fighting his shadow while Aladdin himself escaped with the princess, newly freed from her chains, and ran off with the lamp.

And that was the moment that Susanne went silent and very thoughtful.

She's thought of something! Peter realized. And from the look on her face, it was something very important.

She went back to simply enjoying herself after that, but it was with a gusto that was quite unrestrained, and that made him itch to question her.

He didn't get a chance, though.

Garrick brought the auto around, and they all got into it. "Oh, and to think all my friends wanted me to go to a ballet with them!" Mary laughed, as she deposited herself in the middle of the back seat.

"Wasn't that a ballet? It said 'ballet' in the program," Susanne asked innocently.

That kept Mary busy explaining the difference between a 'real' ballet and a panto ballet, which did indeed have *some* ballet dancers in it, which then required more explanation. And before Peter could ask what had aroused Susanne's attention, they were at the boarding house. He hadn't had the heart to interrupt. Mary was unusually jolly, keeping them all laughing with a steady stream of stories and very comic explanation, right up until Garrick pulled up to Susanne's door.

"Are you sure you won't come back for cake and some tea?" Peter asked, putting on his most entreating expression.

"Oh, do," Mary urged, with a sly glance at Peter. "We likely won't get a bang-up evening like this again, and we should make it last!"

"I'll be moving closer to the new hospital tomorrow," she said with a look of apology. "I need to make sure I haven't forgotten anything. Thank you, Lord Peter! I don't think I have ever had a better time, or laughed more."

And then she was gone, and he knew that however impatient he might feel, she was not going to tell him anything until she was ready to.

"Well, I tried," Mary said, settling back into the seat.

"So you did," Peter replied. "And for that, you shall have cake."

🍃

The moment Susanne saw the double Aladdins, she knew how she was going to handle her father—at least, in part. But first, she had to make certain she still possessed the key element. She ran up the stairs to her room and reopened the first box she had packed, certain she would never need anything in it. She hoped, fervently, that she hadn't lost the thing in her race from Whitestone to Branwell, from Branwell to the Ardennes, from the Ardennes to the Front, and then to London again. Granted, she could make another, but it would be time-consuming, and more to the point, it would not hold that "essence of blissful ignorance" that she'd had when she made the first one—

As she reached into the box, she *felt* the object she wanted "reaching" for her, and she fished the little bundle out with a smile of triumph.

It was wrapped in her old apron—tucked into the front pocket for extra safety, in fact. If there was one thing that Robin had driven home to her, over and over again, it was that a magician should never, ever allow something this personal to fall into the hands of anyone else. She'd not had the time nor the opportunity to properly unmake it—you couldn't simply burn something as personal as this little packet was. You had to unmake it, destroy any tie that it had to you, and only then could you set fire to it as the final act of dissolution.

Such a tiny thing to hold such potential—both potential to aid her and potential to destroy her.

She cradled the small packet, now gray and dirty, but even more potent for having been with her all this time. So innocuous; a clean, white handkerchief, a scrap of the dress she had been wearing, snipped from an inside seam, a little earth moistened with her own blood, a single hair, an appleseed.

And now . . . it could be a weapon.

22

RICHARD Whitestone crossed the Channel on January fifteenth.

He had been something less than careful, which told Peter that he was either very desperate or very confident. He had not taken passage on the sort of vessel where he might, possibly, have been able to conceal his movements—one of the great commercial steamers of riveted iron and steel. No, he had paid a very great deal of money (where had he *gotten* it? Peter was afraid to speculate at this point) to a small fishing boat to take him back over. He had actually put one foot in the water while getting into the vessel.

The selkies had his scent at that instant, and they trailed him all the way to the English coast, despite the fact that his shielding was very, very good. They'd linked the scent of corruption, which would never leave him, to the scent of the boat. They had, of course, alerted the other Water Elementals, who had come straight to Peter as soon as they had him and knew in general where he was going.

Peter had, by contrast, been extremely careful *and* clever.

It had occurred to him that although Richard Whitestone was diabolically clever when it came to magic, he was not nearly so clever when it came to living with the modern world.

Peter had placed a private detective near the likeliest docks, in an office with a telephone; it helped to be a Peer of the Realm in this case, as Customs was reasonably willing to help him in this as long as Ben didn't get in the way. Ben Landers was armed with a description and a sketch of Richard Whitestone and the knowledge that there would be a substantial bonus for keeping track of the man. As soon as Peter knew which port the fishing vessel was bound to — Gravesend — he had rung up Landers, and told him where to go and what to look for. Then he settled back and waited.

As he had expected, as soon as the boat docked, the Water Elementals lost all trace of Whitestone. It was very clear that on land, the man could vanish from the ken of anyone and anything he cared to, magically speaking. The only question was, could he vanish from the sight of someone who was as good at following as Whitestone was at vanishing?

Around about midnight, Landers called again. "Your man has taken a room in the Granby Hotel in Gravesend," he said. "Shall I stay with him?"

"Don't let him out of your sight," Peter replied immediately. "Bring in another man or two to watch round the clock."

Well. He went straight for the bait. Susanne was assigned as a nursing student at Gravesend Hospital.

"Garrick," he called. "Rouse up, old man, the Hunt is up."

Again, by Peter's planning, Susanne had resources that Richard would not have expected. She was not in a modest boarding house anymore. She was in the best hotel in Gravesend, and fine hotels had telephones, desk clerks, and concierges who were employed to take messages to the guests, among other things. Peter put in a call to the front desk.

"This is Lord Peter Almsley. I'd like a message taken to Susanne Whitestone, please," he said, when the call went through. "Yes, immediately, she is expecting this message, and it is worth disturbing her. Please tell her that her relative has arrived and is at the Granby. Yes, please call me back if there is an answer."

Poor old Garrick. He must not have gone to sleep either. "M'lord?" he said, coming into the room still completely dressed.

Peter hung up the phone. "Whitestone landed. He's taken a room at the Granby in Gravesend. My man is watching him."

"Very good, m'lord. We'll be moving to the Royal Dartford then, will we, sir? I have your bags all packed." Once again, Peter thanked his stars for Garrick; Garrick had taken care of every tiny detail.

"Indeed we shall. Get the auto, would you?"

"Very good, m'lord." Garrick vanished briefly, then returned, bundled in his overcoat and headed out, his bag and Peter's in hand.

The phone rang. Peter answered it. *"Miss Whitestone's compliments and thanks, my lord. She asks if you would join her here for breakfast."*

"I shall indeed, after spending what remains of the night in one of your excellent suites," Peter replied. "I trust you have one available?"

After the call, Susanne couldn't sleep. She got dressed, bundled up in a coat, and made her way downstairs. She nodded at the clerk at the front desk, then thought better of her plan and approached him. "I just cannot sleep, I am afraid," she said, with a little grimace of apology. "I thought a little walk might help."

"The gardens are still lighted at night, miss," the clerk, a remarkably dignified old gent, replied. "I don't know how long we'll be allowed to do that—some say that the Huns have flying machines that can cross the Channel, and we'll have to stop all outside illumination. So you'd better make use of it while you can." He nodded at a little glass door she had never yet made use of; she smiled at him.

"Thank you very much," she said with warmth. "Lord Peter's message has me rather excited." Now there was an understatement.

"I'll have a nice pot of hot cocoa sent up to your room, miss," the clerk called softly after her. "That will be just the thing to send you off."

She was both amused and bemused. Living here at a fine hotel could not have presented a greater contrast to her life as a servant or that at the Front. Lord Peter had represented her as a cousin, and although there had been some initial eyebrow raising, and probably speculation about her morals (or lack of them), the fact that although he *was* paying the bill, he had not shown so much as the tip of his aristocratic nose, had laid those rumors to rest. She in her turn had been careful to dress modestly when she was not in her nursing uniform, had always spoken of him respectfully and as "Lord Peter," and had made sure never to make any demands on the staff. One of the maids ventured a few mild questions; Susanne had answered them by saying that her cousin did not really trust the safety of the boarding houses near the hospital (correctly, as it turned out) and had insisted on putting her here, himself, until she should be granted the title of "nurse" and sent off to France. The nursing uniform and her destination won her respect, her attitude won her acceptance. Whatever they were telling each other now, it was not tales of Lord Peter's mistress.

Once in the gardens, she found that they were, indeed, nicely illuminated by gaslights, which reflected off the unmarked snow on either side of the carefully shoveled paths. She walked until she could no longer see the door, or be seen through it, and stood in the dark between the lights, breath steaming out in the bitter air. "Robin?" she called, softly.

She'd had the feeling he had been waiting for her to call.

He materialized out of the shadows of some topiary, walking over the snow without leaving a mark on it. "So, Daughter of Eve. He is come, I marked his passage by the blankness on the Earth."

"You did?" she blinked. "How clever, I never would have thought of that, nor did Peter. He hired a detective."

There was a moment of silence, then Robin burst out with laughter. "Oh, that was well done. It is the last thing your father would have considered." Then Robin sobered. "He has been hard at work; he is full of dark power, and the Dark Court and fell Elementals gather about him, bringing him what he needs."

"And your Fae?" she asked.

He paused. "I fear . . . he has chosen his ground, and it is not a good one for us." His tone had turned somber, even — even a little apprehensive.

"But the Fae, can they spin illusion?" she persisted. "Or rather, can you choose those who can?"

His eyes gleamed in the gaslight. "You have a clever plan?"

Hers glinted back. "And do you remember exactly what my mother looked like?"

"As if it were yesterday," he replied, and he showed a ghost of a smile. "You *do* have a clever plan!"

"I certainly hope so," she said. And she told him what she wanted him, and his Fae, to do.

⁂

Lord Peter put down his fork and stared at Susanne, allowing the truly excellent omelet to lie neglected on his plate. Every time he thought that he had seen the best of her, she surprised him yet again. He refused to think of the possible dire consequences; his own imagination was going to supply all of the worst possibilities when he was alone. Instead, he allowed his admiration to show plain in his expression.

"My dear Susanne," he said fervently. "If this works, you will be the stuff of legend."

"And if it doesn't—" she shivered. "Well, Robin has promised that one way or another, I won't be in my father's hands for long."

Her words stopped the enthusiastic reply in his throat, as his imagination supplied exactly what that meant. She was right, of course, on many counts. Right, that she was the only magician they had that could do this, and right that it was incredibly risky. She would have no one there to battle her father but Robin Goodfellow, and depending on just how much Richard understood about the Puck, even Robin could be forced to retreat.

Especially if Richard had somehow bargained for aid from the Dark Fae. Even the Puck couldn't hold out against something like the Winter Queen, and this was her season. Peter felt his heart growing cold with fear inside him.

He wanted to tell her that she couldn't do this—but he knew that if he did, he would lose her. Not that he actually *had* her at the moment, but he would certainly lose any hope he had of winning her over. Perhaps when she had first been driven to Branwell Hall, he might have been able to say something like that to her. Not now. She had been through too much, seen too much, grown too much. She was no longer the isolated, naïve young Yorkshire country lass she had once been.

"Please be careful," he said instead. "If things look grim, run. We can't replace you, you know."

He thought for a moment that she might retort, but she didn't. At least not at once. She ate a few bites of her grilled kidneys, then looked up and said, wryly, "Better a live dog than a dead lion?"

"The dead lion won't get a second chance; the dog will certainly learn from his defeat and come back with a pack," Peter pointed out. Then, despite his best intentions, his emotions got the better of him. He put down his fork and captured her free hand. "Please, *please* be careful and be wise," he said, with an intensity that made her eyes widen. "I . . . care for you, you know."

He quickly took his hand away, before she could pull back, and attempted to pull a mask over his raw emotions. He was rather good at that. He had had a lot of practice. "I did have a notion that we might be able to lure Richard out, make the bait so tempting that he can't resist it, even though he might not be ready. I think that matches with your own plan. If we do that, we can make him come to us."

"How would we do that?" she asked, though he thought she looked and sounded affected by what he had revealed.

"You'll apparently go to the last place he would think that you would, making regular visits every night. A graveyard." Peter took a map of Gravesend out of his breast pocket, and spread it out between them. "This one, here," he said, pointing to it. "He doesn't have to know *why* you would do such a thing, but if you appear to be there two or three nights in a row and stay there for about an hour, I don't think he'll be able to withstand the temptation to call up another of his armies of the dead before he's quite ready. He'll think he can simply raise up everything in the graveyard. As strong as he is—a lot of those things that attacked Charles in France weren't his usual slaves. They were just animated bodies, without spirits bound into them. It's harder to do things that way, if I understand this foul magic correctly, but it means he can put together a large force quickly!"

She looked from the map into his eyes and back again. "And you have something to stop him from doing so?"

"Sow as much of the graveyard as we can with blessed salt," he replied instantly. "The sort used at christenings. I know a padre, you see. Even if he manages to get hold of ... bits ... to do his usual binding, the dead can't rise in the presence of blessed salt. Even if we only manage a patch, that patch will be a protected spot."

She nodded, slowly. "All right. Shall we start tonight?"

He wanted, so badly, to say no. He wanted, once again, to whisk her up, carry her off to a ship, and take her far away, where she would be safe. But there was too much at stake. "Yes," he said. "I think we should."

*   *   *

For the third night in a row, Susanne sat on a stone bench beside the new graves of several of the Tommys from the hospital where she now was a nursing student. Every day four of the five guarding her now had managed to sow a bit more of the graveyard with the blessed salt—starting with those very graves. Only Alderscroft had not participated in the salting since his time was at a premium, and he had the magical side of the war effort to conduct. They had covered less ground than anyone liked; it was a bit difficult to go strewing salt about by day, in a graveyard that was surprisingly busy, and by night they were either guarding Susanne or trying to thaw out and get some sleep afterward.

Well, they were guarding something that *looked* like Susanne and, to all magical senses, was identical with Susanne. But it was, in fact, an illusion, built on a tiny packet of grimy linen sitting right in the middle of that stone bench. The illusion breathed, moved slightly, and in general would fool just about anyone, even from quite close. And since it incorporated blood and hair from the living girl herself, it *felt* like her to anyone looking for her magically. Especially since, once she placed that packet on the bench, the living, breathing Susanne immediately hid herself behind intricate layers of shielding.

The first two nights had been uneventful, but tonight there was something in the air that felt portentous, ominous. The atmosphere felt heavy, and an aura of despair hung about the graveyard. It only got worse as the hour progressed. Peter was nearly on fire with the feeling that he had to leave, and leave *now.* He couldn't tell if it was the same for the others in their various places of concealment, and maybe this was only his nerves, but—

He came instantly and completely alert as a freezing chill closed down over the place, and with the chill came a stench he knew only too well.

He's taken the bait!

He paused just a moment to remove a vial of water from

his pocket and smash it on the ground. An identical vial in Michael Kerridge's possession would have shattered at the same instant, alerting the family that the attack had begun. Then all five of them burst out of whatever cover they had chosen and raced for the bench. And not a moment too soon.

From all over the graveyard, everywhere they hadn't spread their preventive salt, the earth heaved under the snow and burst upward, and the graves disgorged their unquiet dead.

"We really need to stop meeting like this, Peter," said Doctor Maya Scott, as she and her husband Peter Scott went back-to-back with Lord Alderscroft and Garrick. "I'd much prefer the theater, or even a nice little tea shop. I'd even put up with that wretched excuse for a club of yours."

It was much too cold for most of her familiars; granted, they were occasionally the Avatars of Hindu gods, but when they weren't briefly filled with demidivinity, the frigid cold would likely have killed the delicate parrot and Hanuman ape, and it would not have done the Asian owl and falcon any favors either. The peacock was too large to bring out to the graveyard from London. But the two mongooses were quite habituated to London winters, and they swarmed out of her coat and down into the snow at her feet to dance their angry little hackles-raised mongoose dance.

"Perhaps I should see to having the Visiting Ladies parlor brought up to date. Almsley wouldn't be caught dead in a tea shop. And why would you prefer the theater to excitement like this?" the Old Lion rumbled, bringing his walking-stick up into a guard position and throwing a ring of fire around all of them. The flames danced on the snow without needing conventional fuel. Peter suspected they might actually be salamanders.

The liches paused for a moment, as if waiting for orders. *They probably are,* Peter thought. As he had suspected, these were not bound to unwilling spirits; they could only follow orders. The stench was horrific, almost as horrific as the sight of the long-dead cadavers ringing them. Alderscroft's fires showed them only too plainly.

Then the "generals" of the army appeared—at least six enormous trolls, their ugly faces transfixed with grins, and a swarm of goblins, the latter weaving in and around the legs of the cadavers too quickly to be able to count them.

"Well, it is warmer for one thing," Maya replied—and then there was no time for more words, for the horde of walking dead, led by the wave of massive trolls and goblins descended on them.

🍂

As soon as Susanne, hidden in the doorway of a crypt, smelled the stench of corruption, she knew her father had not been able to withstand the temptation she had presented and had finally struck. She did not wait to see the horror that was coming; instead she retreated, swiftly but stealthily, out of the graveyard proper. A stretch of waste ground—part of the graveyard that had not been used as yet—provided a clean, uncontaminated space she could use. There, she cast down Robin's token, and waited.

She didn't have to wait long. Robin appeared, with at least a dozen lesser Fae.

She started when she saw them and stifled a cry with her hands; to be honest, they almost looked like liches themselves, clothed in tattered gray gowns and shrouded with cobwebby veils.

But she didn't have time to say a word; Robin's head came up, and he sniffed the air like a dog, then seized her wrist and pulled her along after him as he went off at a fast trot.

Behind him, the other Fae faded away. She knew why; they had only appeared to reassure her that they had come in the first place. It was all they could do to maintain their forms in the middle of a mortal town like this, and they would have to save their strength for the action to come.

She almost resisted him, almost went back to try to help

the others. But that was not part of the plan, *her* plan, and if it was to have any chance of succeeding, she had to follow it exactly.

They moved quickly along the street that led to the graveyard. The street was utterly deserted, the buildings on both sides dark and locked up for the night, and an ice-fog descended out of nowhere, laden with sorrow, despair, and a hint of fear.

She couldn't help it; she shivered uncontrollably, with fear as much as with cold. They didn't go far. Robin stopped, suddenly, as the stench of corruption welled up all around them. By now the fog had closed in so thickly that the only thing she could make out was the vague form of a building in front of them.

She knew, then; she could feel it too, feel the Earth itself rejecting this *thing* that walked upon it, this bringer of un-life.

Richard was here, in or near that building, directing his army of the dead against her friends.

Robin held up his hand, and a faint glow came from it, illuminating both their faces in the fog. "Time to go," he whispered, his eyes, too, glowing, with an unearthly, cold rage.

She nodded.

Steeling herself, she felt her way to the building; ran her hands along it until she came to a door, and opened it.

And the darkness inside billowed up and swallowed her.

"I thought blessed salt would hold them at bay!" Lord Alderscroft didn't have to shout to be heard; the dead fought in unnerving silence, with only the occasional snap of jaws as one got close enough to the party to try for a bite. And the trolls and goblins weren't making any noises either. The only sounds were those of weapons on bodies, or the shattering of brittle old bones.

"It does—" said Peter, dodging a troll's immense club,

and countering with a vicious blast of ice-shards at the creature's face. Alderscroft made the fire encircling them flare up, buying them a little breathing space, but the goblins were not deterred, sending sharp flints at their heads from their slings.

"But we had to sow it on snow," Peter continued, "Except right around this bench—" A flint gashed his forehead before Maya could deflect it, and he cursed at the pain. "I think some of it blew or was brushed away—"

The mongooses were too fast even for the goblins to catch; they dashed in and out of the horde, severing what was left of the tendons of ankles and knees and getting in bites on the goblins when they could; the liches collapsed but kept coming. Peter knew from past experience that nothing would stop them but having their heads and hands severed from the rest of the body. Alderscroft was doing just that to any of them that got within reach of the sword that had been in his cane, and Garrick was doing likewise, wielding a pole-arm that had decorated the mirror above the bar of the "Owl and Mirror" pub until three days ago. Garrick and Peter Scott each had pole-arms; Scott had been a ship's captain and was using a boathook with deadly accuracy in grim silence.

"This isn't going well," Alderscroft growled, as the simulacrum of Susanne cowered on the bench in their midst. "We're going to have to break for it in a moment."

Despite the sweat pouring out of every pore, Peter went cold. The moment they retreated from the bench, the ruse would be exposed. The illusion had only two modes—contemplation and cowering. The illusion would break as soon as they touched the spell-bundle; they couldn't retreat "with" Susanne, and they did not dare leave the spell bundle, so intimately connected to Susanne, behind.

So one of them would snatch up the bundle, the illusion would break, and Richard Whitestone would know at that moment that Susanne was elsewhere. And only the Good Lord—or perhaps the Devil himself—knew what he would do when that happened.

"Just hold on," Peter begged them all, and deflected a shower of flints from Maya with a thin sheet of frozen fog. "Give her a little more time."

But time was precisely what they were rapidly running out of.

The building was cavernous. A barn? A warehouse? It had an air of neglect about it, and was full of dust and the sickly smell of rotting flesh.

There was a dim light in the very middle; "corpse-light" was the name that Susanne would have put to it, the phosphorescence of decay. Her father stood in the middle of this patch of sickly blue-green light, utterly still, utterly alone, eyes closed. Directing his terrible army, she suspected. Perhaps seeing through the dead eyes of his slaves.

But as she ventured into the enormous room, her footfalls alerted him, and his eyes flew open. "Who's there?" he demanded, his voice harsh, as if he had not used it much for weeks or even months.

It sent chills down her back, and she wanted nothing more than to turn and run. This was insane. Even with the help of Robin's Fae. But she put one foot in front of the other and slowly made her way toward him.

"It's me," she croaked. "Susanne." *Your daughter,* she had meant to add, but she couldn't force herself to speak the words. "You have to stop this. You have to stop it now. It's wrong! How can you, an Earth Master, possibly *do* something like this? Can't you feel how the very Earth revolts against what you are doing?"

She had to give Robin the chance to get his Fae into place. He needed time; they needed her distraction to come close, and they needed time to put on their illusions. It was just a good thing that this was a wooden building, so there was no iron frame to cause them pain, but there were still thousands of Cold Iron nails holding it together, weakening them.

She felt him really *looking* at her for the first time. "So . . . you did inherit some of the magic."

She felt tears, unfeigned tears, running down her face as she approached him. What had he done to Charles? Doctor Maya was of the opinion now that he had something to do with Charles' loss of memory. How many unwilling spirits had he bound back into their festering corpses? "You have to stop this. Please, this is wrong. You're hurting people, good people. I can't let you do that."

"And what do you intend to do about it, girl?" His voice was strange, harsh, as if he hadn't actually used it in a very long time. "Fight me?" His lips curled back in a sneer. "Just because you know *about* magic, you aren't a Huntsman, girl. You aren't even trained—who was there to train you? You are no match for *me*!"

"No!" she interrupted him desperately, as out of the corner of her eye she sensed movement. "No! I'm not going to let innocent people suffer when—I'm going to come back to you, Father." Oh, how the words tasted like spoiled meat on her tongue. Yet she had no choice. She had to tell him what he wanted most to hear. "I'll come with you now, I'll do whatever you like! Just promise me that you'll stop all this, that you'll leave the Kerridges alone!"

He stared at her, dumbfounded. He certainly had not expected to hear her say *that*. But he recovered quickly. Knowing how he thought, now, she was pretty sure she could guess what was running through his mind. *I'm a simple-minded, simple girl, no more clever than the kitchen maids. I don't know what he is, not really. I have a little magic, perhaps, but not enough to threaten him.*

She spoke quickly, playing into that. "I was afeared, Father," she said, putting on her thickest accent. "I was afeared tha'd send me t'school, and all the girls there 'ould make mock of me." She was so terrified now that it was no effort at all to let her eyes overflow with tears and her limbs tremble. "I never could be like them! The clothes tha' got for me, they was like to strangle me . . . the lessons tha' set me, they made my head spin! I jest wanted everything t' be same again! So I run. And when tha' sent tha' monsters, I run again! Kerridges, they couldna see the back of me fast enough, an' put me on boat. But I couldna stay, I hated it, it were all strange and foreignlike, I couldna understand anyone, the food wasna right, the soldiers sent me home an' I was glad to go, an' all I want is for everything to go back to how it was!"

The last words ended in a sob. She buried her face in her hands, but she kept her fingers spread a little so she could see his face. His expression was changing, from anger, through surprise, to a smug satisfaction. She had done it. She had convinced him. And now—

"My dear child," he said, wheedlingly. "I thought the Kerridges had managed to turn you against me. That was why I attacked them! I thought they were keeping you, my own daughter, my own flesh and blood, from me! I'm not like them; I don't have an army of servants. I tried to get you back using the only army I could—and what did it matter? The dead are dead and don't care what happens to them anymore."

Hurry, Robin, hurry! she thought, as he edged forward, one hand crooked and twitching, ready to seize her the moment he got within reach. Crying into her hands, she backed up a step for every one that he took forward. She had to get him out of that circle—she knew it was there, it was invisible, but she could *feel* it. She had to get him out of his protections, or the Fae could do nothing.

At any moment she expected him to realize what she was doing and stop moving. But he didn't. He kept his eyes fixed on her, and his expression of avid glee made her blood run cold.

And then he stepped over the circle. Then got three feet past it.

"Richard!" The voice that came out of the darkness behind him made him start. And a woman dressed in the remains of what looked like a wedding dress appeared in

midair, glowing faintly with her own light. Susanne knew who she was, of course, but it was still startling to see her own face reflected in those pale features.

"Richard, what are you doing? How could you do this to our daughter, to my baby?" She had told Robin what she wanted them to say, and Richard Whitestone reacted exactly as she had thought he would.

"I'm doing this for *you,* Rebecca!" he shouted, his face pale and his brow beading with sweat, eyes wide and wild. "I'm doing this for *us!* I'm going to bring you back, we can be together again! It will only take one little ritual and—"

"Murderer!" the Fae shrilled in horror. *"You would murder my child! How could you? Don't lie, Richard, this is murder! You would slay her just as you slaughtered the servants, our servants, to fulfill your foul needs!"*

Susanne was suddenly struck dumb. This wasn't anything she had told the Fae to say—

But the guilty expression on Richard Whitestone's face told her that it was nothing less than the truth. He *had* murdered the others, her friends, her protectors—the only real family she had ever had.

Agatha. Old Mary. Nigel and Mathew. Prudence and Patience. People who had never done her, never done her *father,* anything but good. People who had comforted her, taught her, cared for her.

Gone. All gone. She felt as if a bomb had dropped beside her, and she had lost a limb but hadn't quite realized it yet.

Another Fae appeared, this time from the side, wearing a yellow summer dress. *"Don't try to deny it! You never cared for me, for myself, you only loved the reflection of yourself in my eyes. I loved you, Richard, but I cannot love this monster you have become!"*

A third Fae appeared, on the left, this one in a winter cape. *"You are reeking with the stench of death! You would house my soul in a rotting, walking corpse! You say you love me, but you would murder the child I loved, the child I gave up my life for, and force me into endless pain and living death! You are not even a beast, Richard Whitestone! You are worse than the evil things you used to hunt!"*

Now more and more Fae crowded around him, hissing, weeping, fiercely accusing him of all the horrors he had tried to hide. And Susanne stood there, locked in the paralysis of shock.

All she wanted to do was collapse on the ground and scream, weep, howl for the deaths of her *real* family.

With a supreme effort of will, she wrenched herself out of her shock. She could not afford to mourn, not now—now she had to stop her father, as only she could.

As the Fae encircled him, he backed up, step by step, eyes darting from one to another of them. She forced herself to move, forced herself to edge around him, to get to that circle he had built to protect himself. Armed with the knowledge that Peter had given her, she took a deep breath, forced herself to be calm and steady and then—

Then it all sprang into focus. She could see the circle, but she also saw, clearly, just *how* he had built it. And he had been careless. Anyone of his bloodline could alter it.

While he was occupied, she redrew the glyphs, repurposed the energies, and called on the living rock beneath the dirt floor of the warehouse to answer her. Just as he broke free of the Fae, shouting incoherently, she felt the rock respond to her.

He dashed into his circle, running past her without really seeing her.

And she closed the trap.

He stopped, quite literally, in his tracks, his feet suddenly unable to move, held in place by the power of the earth itself. He tried to wrench them free and found he could not, and before he could see her, the Fae pounced, interposing themselves between him and Susanne, resuming their accusations and recriminations.

Suddenly, he made a terrible sound, a cross between a wail and a scream, and collapsed into a fetal curl on the ground.

Then, without warning, the Front came to England.

All those months had honed her instincts, and when she heard the faint, familiar whistle above her, she instinctively flung herself to the side onto the floor and covered her head.

And the world blew apart around her.

❦

The walking dead all, suddenly and without warning, froze in place.

Susanne! Peter thought exultantly, but neither he nor the others stopped to congratulate themselves. At any moment, the liches might start to move again.

Peter and Aldercroft stepped forward, side by side, their hands glowing—and in Alderscroft's case, on fire—with the respective Elemental powers. Peter fixed his gaze on what appeared to be the leader of the trolls—a huge, ugly creature with greenish, warty skin, its primitive clothing encrusted with dirt and stains.

"Flee," he said, sternly. "Go now, and you will not be pur—

There had been an odd sound approaching for some time; it sounded like an aeroplane, but it was moving very slowly. Some part of Peter was wondering just what an aeroplane was doing up at night, when he heard a far too familiar whistling sound.

"Get down!" he shouted, flinging himself sideways and taking Maya and Peter Scott down with him.

And the graveyard exploded around them.

He'd never been that close to a bomb bursting before, and he never wanted to be again. There was a moment of blankness, then he came to himself and shook his head, hard. His ears were ringing. He looked around; the others were covered in bits of corpse and dirt and snow, but they seemed to be all right.

He couldn't hear, at least not well. He thought he heard Maya shouting something, but it was all muffled.

Zeppelins. They must have been bombed by zeppelins. Nothing else had the range to get across the Channel. *Aldurscroft's circle of fire,* he realized. *It might just as well have been a target.*

Five hundred yards away, there was the flash of another explosion—all his damaged ears heard was a muffled *thud.* But this one had hit something more substantial than a graveyard; it must have hit a building, because there were flames shooting up into the sky.

Susanne couldn't hear, and she felt muzzy-headed, but she knew she had to get out of there. That mutated into something a great deal more urgent when a burning beam fell between her and her father, who was still in his fetal curl on the floor. Robin and the Fae were nowhere to be seen— they must have vanished as soon as the bomb hit.

Perhaps she might have tried to get to him and get him out as well before that chunk of flaming wood landed close enough to make the hem of her skirt smolder, but there was no way she could get to him now.

Incendiaries. They're dropping incendiaries. She'd seen the men, hideously burned by the hellish bombs and shells, but she had never seen one herself. She never wanted to again. Already the roof of the building was fully engulfed, and bits of flaming debris raining down on her. In another moment, she wouldn't be able to get out herself.

Fear galvanized her. She scrambled to her feet, hauled up her skirts, and sprinted for the door. She managed to wrench it open, even though the incredible heat had started to warp the frame, and paused for a quick glance back.

Richard Whitestone was still curled on the floor. And as she darted out into the cold air and freedom and safety, the roof above him gave way and buried him beneath a pile of burning wood and shingles.

She staggered out the door just in time to see the flash of another explosion, farther away. It couldn't be aeroplanes—

It must be zeppelins.

She strained her eyes toward the sky; the clouds were incredibly low, but she thought she could make out three dark shapes, too regular to be cloud formations. There were three more explosions just beneath them, confirming her guess.

Peter! Peter and the others! Thank goodness Peter and Garrick had been on the Front, and they knew what bombs sounded like—

But she ran for the cemetery where she had left them, more fear flooding through her. Had they managed to hold off her father's creatures? Had any of the bombs struck near them?

She met them staggering out of the cemetery, Garrick and Peter supporting Lord Alderscroft between them.

By now, the town was roused—and her hearing was coming back. She heard the bells and sirens of the fire brigade, heard people screaming, and heard the distant explosions of still more bombs, turning the night into horror for everyone in Gravesend.

When Peter saw her, he dropped Alderscroft's arm and ran toward her, catching her in a frantic embrace that she was in no mood to shake off. He took her face in both his hands after a moment. "Are you all right? Richard—"

"Dead," she said, and all her energy ran out. "A bomb dropped on the building we were in." Her knees wobbled and threatened to give way. She kept herself standing by holding onto him.

"Dear Lord." He held her up.

"Almsley, the best thing we can do right now is get away from here," Lord Alderscroft rumbled as he pulled away from Garrick. "There is nothing we can do to help, and there are too many questions we cannot answer."

"The hotel is close," Peter replied. "And my automobile is closer. You're right. There is nothing we can do here."

The six of them staggered to where Peter had left the auto, and crammed into it, Susanne between Peter and Garrick in the front, the others in the back, as they had on the journey to the cemetery. Garrick took the wheel, and Peter did not object. Instead, he put his head against the doorpost, and closed his eyes.

Garrick drove in silence for a while. The bombardment seemed to have stopped, but the night was alive with alarms and Black Marias and fire engines racing to the rescue. Finally, just as they pulled up to the hotel, Peter spoke.

"You're wrong, Old Lion," he said, his eyes still closed. "That bomb is going to explain quite well why there is a carpet of cadaver parts strewn all over that part of the graveyard."

"So it is," Alderscroft replied after a moment.

When Susanne tried to get out of the auto, she nearly fell. Her legs, inexplicably, would not hold her up. Peter solved the problem by picking her up and carrying her in himself, and she was getting so muzzy-headed that she was not inclined to argue with him. She recognized the symptoms though—

"Con-cussion," she said thickly. "I'm con-cussed."

"Without a doubt," he replied, and then they were in the door, into the light and warmth of the lobby, and the hotel staff fell upon them with cries of concern.

Peter would not allow anyone to carry her but himself; he asked for the hotel physician, and brought her to her room, only leaving her there and allowing others to take him off to be tended when a maid and the doctor were in the room.

After that, things were blurred together in a vague dreamlike way. The maid undressed her and put her properly into bed, bathing her face and hands and combing bits of debris out of her hair. The doctor examined her and ordered monitoring and rest. They all left—and that was all she remembered until she woke, and her windows streamed with winter sunlight.

Epilogue

SUSANNE stood just outside Charles' room and watched as his fiancé Rose comforted him. There was no doubt that her father had had something to do with his memory loss—perhaps trying to make him an easy victim that could not defend himself against a second attack. His memory came back to him all at once about the same time that Richard Whitestone had died.

Including what must have been the horror of the attack. He had recognized some of the faces of the dead that had come at him—and had been forced to "kill" them a second time. He had been buried under a pile of bodies and body parts to the point where he'd had to be dug out. Small wonder he needed to be comforted.

But not by her. He had barely greeted her—and had instead turned to Rose to weep unashamedly in her arms. To her credit, Rose had not lorded it over her defeated rival; she had been too concerned with Charles.

The elder Kerridges had been civil to her and even thanked her, but it was clear that they wanted to see the last of her. They had already arranged for Charles' transfer to a hospital Maya recommended in Yorkshire. It was very clear that his nerves were utterly shattered, and he would be a very long time recovering. Military doctors were not very sympathetic to men with these symptoms; the Kerridges were going to find someone who would be.

There was nothing for her here.

With a sigh, she turned away from the door and nearly ran into Peter.

"Steady on, old girl," he said, taking her shoulders to keep her from falling. He looked into the room and released her with a little pat. "Cup of tea?" he suggested.

"I —" she was going to say "no," then thought better of it. "I just have time," she said instead.

The little hospital tea shop was deserted. They took the farthest table and waited until the serving girl was gone, leaving their orders. Then they both spoke at once.

"What are you —"

"Why did you —"

They looked at each other, and Peter laughed. "Ladies first," he suggested.

She compressed her lips into a hard, angry line. "Why didn't you tell me he'd — he'd — everyone I knew at home! That they were —"

Dead. Murdered. She still couldn't bring herself to say it.

He sighed. "I tried. But you were fretting so over Charles, over the men you were caring for — there never seemed to be the right time — never seemed to be a moment when telling you wouldn't utterly shatter you."

She thought about that and finally, reluctantly, nodded.

"It's all yours, you know," he continued. "Richard's body was identified today. You inherit the lot."

She thought about that and shuddered. "I don't want it," she protested. "I don't want any of it." *Especially not the house . . .*

"If you want, my solicitor can take care of it for you. Once you tell me how to get into that secret room so we can burn those foul books. He can sell it, lease it . . . you can certainly live modestly, but well, on the income." One of his hands slipped across the table and rested on hers. "You won't need anything for a while. If you're serious, that is, about going back to the Front."

She looked at his hand. Looked up at his face. Some might have called it rabbity, but that would be wrong. His face was often a mask—the mask of the silly lord, the mask of a fool, the mask that hid all his feelings. Just now, it wasn't. His face was that of a kind man, a man of great intelligence, with a longing in his eyes that made her breath catch in her throat.

I care for you, he'd said.

"I am serious," she replied. "I—I'd really like to find somewhere that I can use the Earth magic as well as nursing skills."

"Do you really mean that?" he asked. At her nod, he continued. "MI13 could certainly use someone like you. I've looked over some of your father's papers. It seems he had help." Peter's expression hardened. "From Hun magicians. Hun necromancers."

Her breath caught in her throat. "So that's where—"

"Where and how he got so powerful." If she were to put a name to the expression in his eyes, it was rage. Then the anger faded. "That is why I think we can use you and your talents. It's obvious this won't be the last such attack on those of us who are magicians. It's obvious, to me at least, we will need someone whom magicians can trust to care for the victims of such attacks. We have Maya, but she obviously cannot leave England."

"And I can." She thought about that, but not for long. "I would like that. I would like that very much." She made a face. "The Kerridges aren't making any secret of the fact that they intend to get Charles invalided out." Her resentment overflowed. "Given what you just told me, can't they see how he'll be needed even more, once he's better? I would have expected more out of them, considering how they go on about taking care of their people!"

"Don't be angry with them," he said softly. "Their ... they take very good care of the people they know, but they can't extend that to anything much beyond the boundaries of Branwell. Many people are like that. The world calls to them in need, but they can't extend themselves to see it. They can't see past their own walls."

Charles couldn't see past his own walls. And one of those walls was class. She realized now that she would never have been someone he would look at as—

—as Peter was looking at her now.

Idiot, she thought, suddenly. *I was like a silly thing with a pash for a theater actor. He was kind because it cost him nothing to be kind to me. But Peter is kind, and cares, when it costs him everything.*

"Tell your people I would like that position very much," she told him, and managed a smile. "After all, I still have a lot to learn. I'd like to stay near my teacher."

"Well, you could study with Doctor Scott," he began, then blinked. "You're not entirely talking about magic, are you?"

She turned her hand over so that it was clasping his. "No," she agreed. "Not entirely."

His smile lit up the room.

MERCEDES LACKEY

The Elemental Masters Series

"Her characteristic carefulness, narrative gifts, and attention to detail shape into an altogether superior fantasy." —*Booklist*

"It's not lighthearted fluff, but rather a dark tale full of the pain and devastation of war, the growing class struggle, and changing sex roles, and a couple of wounded protagonists worth rooting for." —*Locus*

"Putting a fresh face to a well-loved fairytale is not an easy task, but it is one that seems effortless to the prolific Lackey. Beautiful phrasing and a thorough grounding in the dress, mannerisms and history of the period help move the story along gracefully. This is a wonderful example of a new look at an old theme." —*Publishers Weekly*

"Richly detailed historic backgrounds add flavor and richness to an already strong series that belongs in most fantasy collections. Highly recommended." —*Library Journal*

To Order Call: 1-800-788-6262

www.dawbooks.com

MERCEDES LACKEY

Gwenhwyfar
The White Spirit

A classic tale of King Arthur's legendary queen. Gwenhwyfar moves in a world where gods walk among their pagan worshipers, where nebulous visions warn of future perils, and where there are two paths for a woman: the path of the Blessing, or the rarer path of the Warrior. Gwenhwyfar chosses the latter, giving up the power she is born to. But the daughter of a king is never truly free to follow her own calling...

978-0-7564-0585-4
Hardcover
978-0-7564-0629-5
Paperback

To Order Call: 1-800-788-6262
www.dawbooks.com

DAW 135

MERCEDES LACKEY
The Novels of Valdemar

To Order Call: 1-800-788-6262
www.dawbooks.com

MERCEDES LACKEY
The Valdemar Anthologies

"This high-quality anthology mixes pieces by experienced author and enthusiastic fans of editor Lackey's Valdemar. Valdemar fandom, especially, will revel in this sterling example of what such a mixture of fans' and pros' work can be. Engrossing even for newcomers to Valdemar."
—*Booklist*

SWORD OF ICE
978-0-88677-720-3

SUN IN GLORY
978-0-7564-0166-5

CROSSROADS
978-0-7564-0325-6

MOVING TARGETS
978-0-7564-0528-1

CHANGING THE WORLD
978-0-7564-0580-9

FINDING THE WAY
978-0-7564-0633-2

UNDER THE VALE
978-0-7564-0696-7

To Order Call: 1-800-788-6262
www.dawbooks.com